Cobb Island

Blayne Cooper

Quest Books

Nederland, Texas

ISBN 978-1-932300-67-3
(Formerly 1-930928-39-4)

Second Edition

Revised, Re-edited, Reformatted in 2006

First Printing 2006

9 8 7 6 5 4 3 2 1

Cover design by Donna Pawlowski

Published by:

Regal Crest Enterprises, LLC
4700 Highway 365, Suite A
PMB 210
Port Arthur, Texas 77642

Find us on the World Wide Web at
http://www.regalcrest.biz

Printed in the United States of America

This book is dedicated to my treasured spouse. If I had more than my heart to give, it would already be yours. I love you.

Chapter
One

And We Begin Again

HONK, HONK. A tousled blonde head poked itself out of the window of a black pickup truck and shoulder-length tresses were picked up and swirled by the morning breeze. "Where is that fool little brother of mine?" Olivia Hazelwood resisted the urge to lay on her horn for the third time. Abruptly, a mop-topped teenager flew out of the front door, letting the screen slam loudly and dragging an olive drab army duffel bag behind him.

"Thanks, Liv," he panted as he climbed into the cab. "I didn't think Aunt Ruth was ever going to let me outta there."

Two identical sets of sea-green eyes rolled.

Liv revved the engine but left the car in park, drawing out her younger brother's anticipation. "All set then, Dougie?" she taunted with a grin.

"You know it. Let's rock and roll!" he yelled eagerly.

Liv chuckled, allowing some of the teenager's exuberance to rub off on her; it was her vacation, too, after all. Aunt Ruth's was the only house around for miles, so she didn't bother to look behind her as she pulled out of the driveway and onto the lonely country road. After several quiet moments, Liv turned back to her brother, studying him in detail as he fiddled with the radio station, desperately looking for anything that wasn't a country station. *Why does he bother? He already knows exactly what he'll find,* she silently mused.

Her gaze drifted over his face and down to his white, high-top sneakers. She felt a pang of guilt when she noticed how much he'd grown since the last time she'd seen him. His jaw was starting to square, and his wobbly looking Adam's apple didn't seem nearly as prominent as she remembered. *God, he's growing up.* Distracted by Doug's face, she forgot about the empty road and carefully focused on his chin, reaching over and unceremoniously yanking out a lonely hair amid what appeared to be fair fuzz.

"Ouch! What did ya do that for?" Doug scowled as his hand

flew to his chin and he rubbed the tender spot.

"You're starting to get a beard, aren't you?" she asked, hoping her voice didn't sound as surprised to her brother's ears as it did to her own.

"Well, Jesus, I'm almost seventeen years old. What did you expect?"

Liv already knew what was coming and winced in anticipation.

"If you visited more often—"

"I know it's been six months," the blonde interrupted. "I didn't mean for time to get away from me like this." She reached over and patted the teenager's denim covered thigh. "I'm sorry, Dougie. Forgiven?" she asked hopefully.

"It's Doug now." The teenager made a show of sighing before smiling brightly. "And aren't you always?"

Liv shot him a sharply raised eyebrow at the comment, but silently agreed. Doug always forgave her anything. Just like she did him. She couldn't help herself.

"So how did you get Aunt Ruth to agree to this?" Liv wondered aloud, changing the subject. She figured the high school junior had probably had to beg, borrow, and steal to get this little vacation approved.

"Ha." Doug snorted. "I brought ass-kissing to a new level of excellence for this one."

The siblings shared a brief, if somewhat rueful laugh. Aunt Ruth was strict, far stricter than their parents had been. The older woman and Liv had gone around more than once over the proper way to raise Doug. Liv knew he must have pulled out all the stops to wrangle a week alone with her, away from Ruth's supervision.

"So, Romeo, this girlfriend must be pretty special for you to go to all this trouble."

"She is," Doug said seriously, making Liv instantly feel mean for the teasing.

"I'm sure she is, Dougie. I mean *Doug*." She corrected herself with a slight roll of her eyes, laughing as her brother's heated retort was shot down before he could utter a sound.

The slim teenager shifted in his seat and ran a nervous hand through his messy curls.

Dad used to do that to his hair all the time, Liv thought. I do it, too.

Oblivious to his sister's musings, Doug began to whine. "I really miss her, Liv. I haven't seen her since spring break, although we do chat every night on the computer. If Aunt Ruth knew we were going to meet Marcy, she'd never have agreed to this visit."

Liv sighed, mentally editing the long string of curse words that sprang to her tongue at the mention of Ruth's name. "Aunt Ruth loves you, Dougie," *just not as much as she should*, "but she wouldn't know romantic love if it jumped up and bit her on the ass. I can't wait to meet your girlfriend. I'm already certain she's something special."

Doug beamed. His sister's approval meant more than he ever intended to let anyone know. Well, maybe anyone except Marcy.

Liv swerved the car to avoid a particularly deep pothole. "So, how does a no-account pissant like you manage a girlfriend who still adores you even a full year after her family moves away, while I can't even get a date on Saturday nights? Hmm?"

"Well," he drawled smugly, "maybe you're past your prime, Sis."

"I'm twenty-nine years old! I'm right in the middle of my prime, for Christ's sake!"

"That's almost thirty."

"So?" Pale eyebrows rose as Liv sneered, but there was no heat behind it.

Doug shrugged as if his last statement spoke for itself. "Don't worry. In another couple years you'll be in that really desperate age group. Your biological clock will be about ready to explode, and you won't be so picky anymore." Doug's gestures became more animated as he threw himself into the teasing. "I'm sure you'll get a date, then," he added cheekily.

"Shut up, butt-munch. As if I need kids when I've already got you." Liv smacked the laughing young man in the belly, causing him to exhale loudly. "Any more cracks like that, and I'll tell Marcy about the time you got sick on the merry-go-round at Wal-Mart."

"Liv," the teen whined, "that was forever ago."

"Ten years is not forever. Just your bad luck that my memory is still sharp as a tack, sonny," she cackled in her best old-lady voice, trying not to look her brother in the eye and dissolve into laughter. Then she abruptly sobered. "Dougie, please tell me that Marcy's parents know she's meeting us at this island. I'll deal with Aunt Ruth if I have to, but I won't go against your girlfriend's parents."

Doug's expression turned petulant. He'd already gone over this a hundred times. "I'm telling you, Liv, they know everything."

"You swear?" Liv eyed him speculatively, looking for the slightest trace of deception. Doug could lie through his teeth if he had to, and she knew it.

"I swear. And don't be such a granny. Marcy's sister is coming along too, so we'll be *fully* chaperoned," he pouted, wondering if he'd get any time at all alone with his girlfriend.

"Okay then. Jeez, Dougie, put your sad lip away." Liv poked at the body part in question. Mostly convinced that her brother was telling the truth," she smiled wickedly. "Has Aunt Ruth talked to you about safe sex yet?"

"Oh, God!" Doug groaned, as he buried his face in his hands. Maybe this wasn't such a great idea. They pulled off the gravel country road and onto the highway, leaving nothing but a dissolving cloud of dust in their wake.

"HOW LONG Y'ALL gonna wanna leave it fer?"

"A week."

A meaty hand scratched a bearded cheek as the man's eyes swept over the lanky woman in front of his counter, lingering inappropriately on two of her more striking attributes. With a quick turn of his head, he loudly spat his remaining tobacco into a bucket on the floor. Some women, after all, were funny about chew. Though, he couldn't imagine why.

She was a beauty all right, even dressed in a plain blue tank top and faded blue jeans. Her impassive, tanned face was cut with classic chiseled features. Her thick dark hair was the color of rich red wine and braided in a single heavy rope that flowed between broad shoulders and down to the middle of her back. It was tied off with a simple leather strap.

The man wondered if she was alone or willing, and looked out the shop window, hoping he wouldn't see a husband or boyfriend. What he did see was a younger girl with short hair the same shade of dark red, waiting with arms crossed, tapping her foot impatiently at one of the gas pumps. *Mother and daughter? Nah.* The woman in front of him appeared to be only in her early or mid-twenties.

"Well?" she drawled impatiently, her accent not nearly as pronounced as the clerk's, but resolutely Southern nonetheless. Kayla briefly wondered if this goober had ever been in the company of a woman who wasn't dead drunk or on his payroll for the evening.

"And yer wantin' a boat fer that entire time, too?"

Bright blue eyes narrowed behind dark sunglasses. Was she going to have to explain this *again*? She took a calming breath. "I want a place to stow my car, and I want to rent a boat for a week. This is a boat rental store, isn't it?" Her impatience began to peek through as she pointed a long, slender finger at a large red sign that proudly proclaimed "Ernie's Boat Rental and Storage. Enjoy the Best Virginia has to Offer."

"Yes, ma'am, sho' nuff is." He thought for a second more and considered the nice car parked at the gas pump. "Three hundred fer the boat, and I'll store yer car in my garage outta the August heat for another fifty. I'll even throw in the first tank of gas fer the boat fer nothin'."

The tall redhead bristled, but handed over her VISA card anyway. She feared Marcy would simply expire if they didn't have the boat ready to go when her boyfriend arrived.

After running her card through a rickety carbon press, the clerk handed it back, rubbing the dark-purple ink off his fingers and onto the mostly white T-shirt that barely covered his flabby, protruding belly. "You ladies ain't goin' out ta Cobb Island all alone, are ya?"

And you care because? "We won't be alone."

"Yes, ma'am, ya sho' nuff will. There's only three houses out there ta begin with. The Redding place has been empty since ol' man Redding died two years ago, and the renters of the other two done already left fer the season. Too damn hot this time a year, I reckon," he added, squashing a buzzing mosquito with a quick smack of his sweaty hand.

"We'll be fine," the tall woman answered tersely as she opened the shop door and was greeted with a blast of humid summer air that still managed to be cooler than the sweltering heat inside the boat rental shop. The clerk trailed eagerly along behind her.

"Did you get it, Kayla?" Marcy asked nervously as she approached her sister. Kayla had been in the shop way too long, and judging by the way the clerk was drooling over her, it wouldn't be long before he ended up getting a free tour of the emergency room.

"I got it, darlin'. Relax. We'll be all ready for Mr. Wonderful." Kayla was happy for her baby sister, though she didn't quite understand all the fuss. The concept was foreign to Kayla. While she accepted her own need for privacy and the slightly awkward feeling she usually felt in the company of others, a tiny part of her was sad, mourning the loss of something that appeared to lie just beyond her grasp. She might not understand it, but she was happy for her sister.

"Marcy, you go watch for Doug," *as if I could stop you,* "and I'll load our bags and my equipment into the boat. Come on, Ernie," she glanced over her shoulder, not caring whether that was the clerk's name or not, "time to start earning that three hundred."

"TURN LEFT HERE."

Liv pulled the car into a small, dusty parking lot beside the boat rental shop. Before she could say a word, or even shut off the ignition, Doug was out the door, running towards a dark-haired teenaged girl. *The fabulous Marcy, I presume.*

Liv's attention turned to the dock, where she watched a greasy looking man set a large metal box into a boat before wiping his hands on his T-shirt and moving back into the shop. Exiting her pickup truck, she strode over to her brother just as a striking woman, who looked to be an older version of the one Doug was fiercely hugging, joined them.

The young couple eased their death grip on one another just enough to share a desperately passionate kiss. Arms wrapped tightly around each other, both teenagers let out throaty moans as they moved closer together in an enthusiastic fury.

Kayla simply stared, shifting uncomfortably, too amazed to even blink. Out of the corner of her eye, Liv's presence was warring for her attention, tugging insistently at her focus. The Virginia sun itself didn't come close to emitting the heat Doug and Marcy were producing. The tall woman's own body temperature began to rise, and a scarlet blush erupted across her face and neck. Several unwelcome feelings, whose erotic origins were very clearly the entwined couple, entered her mind quite without permission and began to make her squirm. *Jesus, Marcy! You little pervert. Kids aren't supposed to think stuff like that,* she squeaked inwardly.

Kayla fought the urge to withdraw, step away from her sister, and pull the plug on the sixth sense that was so much a part of her...a part of her whole family. But thankfully, the feelings and vague images from Marcy began to fade. Kayla slowly focused on her surroundings, easing her urge to retreat and allowing her to suppress and control the invasive ramblings of her sister's mind.

The tall redhead eyed the young couple dourly as Marcy's thoughts subsided. Her sister seemed *very* attached to the kid. Too bad she was going to have to murder Doug on the spot. Marcy would miss him...for the three seconds of life she had left before Kayla strangled her, too.

Finally, when she began to wonder if Doug would ever get his tongue back, Liv interrupted the lip-locked teens. "Ahem, Dougie...I mean, Doug. Would you like to introduce me to your friend?" Liv resisted the urge to fan her flaming cheeks.

Doug reluctantly pulled away and smiled sheepishly at Liv, intentionally not looking over to Kayla, whose intense stare he could feel boring into him at that very moment. The grumpy looking woman was obviously not pleased by the teenagers' admittedly extreme display of affection.

"Sorry," Doug muttered. "Marcy, this is my sister Olivia...Liv." Then he surprised everyone by adding, "Actually, she's sort of like my mom." The boy turned to his sister, hoping he hadn't said anything wrong.

Unbidden, tears pricked Liv's eyes as her jaw worked silently, a sudden tightness closing her throat. Temporarily ignoring Marcy, she pulled Doug into a tight hug. "Pretty sneaky there, Dougie." Liv swallowed hard as she regained her composure. "Lucky I love you to death, or that crap wouldn't work," she whispered in his ear, feeling her brother's smile against her cheek. "We'll talk about that kiss later." Pulling away, she addressed the pretty girl invading every inch of Doug's personal space.

"It's a pleasure to meet you, Marcy." Liv extended a hand, which Marcy shook warmly. Then the girl, who was much taller than Liv and an inch or so taller than Dougie, bent down and stole a quick kiss on the cheek.

"I know all about you, Olivia," the girl said excitedly, wiping a smudge of lipstick away from Liv's cheek. "Doug talks about you all the time." They weren't strangers after all; Liv just didn't know it yet.

The sweet words managed to make Liv feel even guiltier for her lack of participation in Doug's life over the past couple of years. She vowed on the spot that she would never again let so much time pass between visits with her baby brother. Aunt Ruth could go to hell. Maybe when he started college in another year, she could talk him into attending George Washington University. It wasn't unreasonably far away from her Washington D.C. apartment. Liv focused on Marcy, who was staring at Doug like he was a walking, breathing god. *Then again, maybe I should be talking to her. I have a feeling Dougie's going to be following this girl around like a puppy on a string.*

The foursome stood awkwardly for a long moment before Marcy suddenly remembered her manners. "Oh, I'm so sorry. Doug, Olivia, this is my big sister, Kayla Redding."

Kayla gave Liv a tentative smile. She couldn't help but be just the tiniest bit distracted by the blonde woman's smiling face, but she simply glared at Doug. "I'll go and make sure everything is ready for the boat ride to the island. If you'll excuse me," she offered curtly, before turning on her heel and striding purposefully across the parking lot.

"Oh, shit," Doug mumbled, as Marcy shot him a helpless glance then quickly followed after her sister, a slightly panicked look on her face.

Liv let out a long sigh. "Oh, shit is right. What were you thinking of with that little display, Dougie?" She threw her hands in the air to forestall his answer. "Never mind, you don't need to say a word. I know exactly what you were thinking, you little shit." Her eyes twinkled, but Liv managed to keep her chuckles to herself. "She's gorgeous." *Nearly as gorgeous as her taller, darker, and far more pissed off sister.*

"Her sister hates me already, doesn't she?" Doug stuffed his hands in his pockets in an adolescent gesture that reminded Liv of the boy who had lived with her until two years ago.

"Looks that way." She clasped Doug's shoulder, giving it a sympathetic squeeze. "I wouldn't worry too much about it right now. We've got a whole week to get to know each other; she'll come around." Liv tugged her sunglasses down to the tip of her nose and gave her brother a disapproving look over the tortoiseshell frames. "*Assuming* you can control yourself long enough for her to stop glaring at you like she's about to rip your head off, that is."

The boy flashed his sister a toothy grin. "But you'd save me, right, Liv?"

"If that was my little sister you just kissed that way..." She let the words trail off meaningfully.

"Hey. More than one set of lips were involved, you know."

"Dougie." It was a warning.

"Okay, okay, I got it." The corners of Doug's mouth pulled into a slightly sheepish grin. "More charming, less alarming."

"Exactly, little brother." Liv wrapped her arm around Doug's shoulder, noticing how small her five-foot, four-inch frame felt next to the still rapidly growing teenager. She took a deep breath of the salty air, glad that the light ocean breeze had made a dent in the stifling heat.

The Hazelwood siblings began moving toward the rental office as one. "C'mon, Sis, let's hurry, so I can go see what grunt work I can offer in a pathetic attempt to redeem myself."

"Dougie, my boy," Liv laughed, "it appears I've been remiss in your education when it comes to women. First, grunt work is good; but, trust me, it's already expected of you so you won't score too many brownie points there. I recommend chocolate. Lots and lots of chocolate."

"Really?" the young man asked interestedly.

"Absolutely, why one time..."

Chapter
Two

Welcome Home

THE THIRTY-HP MOTOR buzzed loudly as the sixteen-foot aluminum boat slowly made its way through the choppy, dark waters of the Atlantic. Cobb Island was about two miles off the Virginia coast and, on clear days, was easily visible from the dirty, tree-strewn beach alongside the boat rental shop.

After the first few moments at sea, the wind had picked up and the temperature had dropped. Kayla seemed to know what she was doing, so no one questioned her when she piloted the boat closer and closer to what appeared to be nothing more than a dark blob rising from the shore. As the boat approached the island, even Doug and Marcy's excited chatter quieted, and the foursome simply stared in awe.

There was almost no beach. In fact, the lush vegetation stretched beyond the boundaries of the island itself, as massive overhanging branches extended a remarkable distance out over the water. Several trees appeared to be growing directly out of the ocean floor. The woods were incredibly thick, almost cruel looking, as the gnarled black tree trunks and limbs fought for space and light above the dense undergrowth. Prickly brown vines intertwined with ivy and covered nearly every possible surface, including the jagged rocks that occasionally poked out of the inky soil only to disappear into the salty water below. Leaves and stray branches formed what appeared to be a nearly impenetrable wall around the island's edge.

Kayla finally reduced the power to the engine, and the loud buzz faded to a constant hum. They were now about thirty yards from the shoreline, and despite the constant breeze, the insects had appeared in dramatic fashion, their steady drone blending with the sound of the motor. "You're sure there are houses on this island?" Liv asked, as she swatted a mosquito.

"Papaw's house, yes, although we've never visited it," Marcy answered on a slightly shaky exhalation, her gaze fixed on the terrain before her.

Doug's eyes widened as Kayla turned the boat eastward and drew it right along the shoreline, following the curve of the island's edge and passing into the long shadows created by the forest and late afternoon sun. "Wow."

Liv could only nod, completely agreeing with her brother's sentiment. Despite the shy fawn whose ebony, liquid eyes peeked out at her through the thorny bushes then vanished silently, the island *felt* harsh and unforgiving...dead even. *Well, except for the bugs,* Liv mused, as she swatted away a dragonfly that seemed to want to nest in her hair. *What kind of people would have their summer home here?*

"It's not just a vacation home," Kayla offered quietly, breaking into Liv's thoughts. "Papaw lived here his entire life." She suddenly winced, realizing what she'd done and grateful that Liv was looking toward the island. *I've got to be more careful. I've already done that too much.* But she'd never been around someone whose thoughts she registered so strongly within her. It was as unsettling as it was intriguing.

"Bu...but what would a person do on an island this size for an entire lifetime?"

Kayla tugged off her sunglasses and tossed them onto her soft bag resting underneath the boat's steering wheel. She turned her head to face Liv, causing her eyes to glint and pick up the rays of sun. "That's an interesting question," she finally answered awkwardly, fully aware she hadn't satisfied Liv's curiosity.

To say more would only encourage the conversation, and it was heading in a direction she simply was not willing to go yet. Besides, either they wouldn't believe her and would call her a liar outright, or it would send the Hazelwood siblings screaming into the night. And somehow she didn't think Marcy would appreciate that.

Kayla had her own agenda on this trip. One that she prayed would give Marcy a shot at a normal life. And her plans didn't include a nosy blonde—she smiled inwardly—no matter how cute she was.

Liv suddenly stood up, tilting dangerously as the boat listed to one side. She was angry at Kayla's intentional reticence. It was one thing for Marcy's sister to be upset with Doug and Marcy for making a spectacle of themselves with that kiss, but it was quite another to be closed-mouthed to the point of rudeness with her. They didn't even know each other. This was more than quiet or introverted; this was socially inept. Since they'd left the mainland, Kayla had refused to answer most of her questions with more than a "yes," "no," or "That's an interesting question."

Doug reached over and tugged Liv's arm, hoping to stop her from saying something combative to Marcy's sister. He failed. "Is there a reason that you won't answer my questions, or are you just plain rude?" The anger and mounting frustration were apparent in Liv's voice. *God, what the hell is wrong with me? It must be this sweltering heat.* She felt an unpleasant nervousness building in her belly as the boat drew closer to the island. "Liv!" Doug hissed. "What are you doing?"

"Be quiet, Dougie. I have the feeling there's something Marcy's sister is not telling us about our vacation destination." Liv pointed an accusing finger at Kayla. "Well?"

Kayla shot Marcy a meaningful look, but the teenager shook her head, her jaw clenched tightly. "You didn't say anything to them?" the tall woman whispered harshly.

"No," Marcy answered, embarrassed. "There isn't really anything to tell."

"You *know* that's not true."

Marcy began to get irritated. She'd never believed those stupid old tales — at least not the more wild ones. Why should she frighten Doug and his sister for nothing? "You'll have to excuse Kayla." She pointedly addressed the Hazelwoods. "My sister has a rather vivid imagination for someone who usually can't manage to pry herself away from her sizemahickies, photo lab, and tape recorders for more than a few hours a day. I swear, even when she was a child, Mama claims she enjoyed ripping up floorboards and checking the dark attic for secrets." Marcy turned to her sister and glared. "It's like Stephen King crawled up her butt and took up residence."

A slender, dark-red eyebrow arched sharply but was quickly followed by a small smile that seemed to tug at Kayla's lips for only the briefest of seconds before disappearing. "Skeptic," the older woman shot back at her sister playfully, astounding Liv and Doug who were watching the exchange in confusion.

The small boat made its way around a blind corner, and the landscape seemed to open up before them. A huge wooden home stood proudly on the island's rocky edge. It was three stories high, with a large wrap-around porch that overlooked the water below. An overgrown trail led from the front door, down a steep hill, to a rickety wooden dock.

"Is that it?" Marcy breathlessly asked her sister.

"I think so. The guy who rented us the boat said it was the first house I'd hit if I continued around to the east. And this fits that description."

"Holy sh—"

Liv elbowed her brother in the ribs. Hard.

"Cow," he finished lamely, shooting Liv a hateful look.

This time Kayla did smile, albeit discreetly, and Liv did her best not to stare. That simple act took years off her face, and Liv realized for the first time that Kayla was probably younger than she was. Torn between azure eyes and the magnificent, but somewhat dilapidated house in front of her, Liv's trance was broken by Marcy's voice.

"It's just like Daddy said it was."

Kayla nodded as she pulled the boat up to a rickety wooden dock. She studied the house with evident distaste. "I'm sure it was a fabulous looking place...once," she added wryly. "Damn." Kayla frowned. "You'd think Papaw could have sprung for a couple buckets of paint."

Doug quickly jumped up and onto the dock, where he immediately shed the hot, itchy life jacket that his sister had insisted he wear. Kayla tossed him a frayed yellow rope, and he tied the stern of the boat to two wooden poles that disappeared below the dock.

"Will this hold me?" Liv asked doubtfully. She reached for her brother's outstretched hand, while he bounced playfully on the unstable wooden structure.

Doug grinned cheekily. "Lucky for us, you haven't eaten dinner yet."

"Ha ha. Dougie, what are—"

"I called ahead last week and had some food and other supplies delivered," Kayla interrupted. *Shit. I did it again.* "We should be all set," she finished weakly. Kayla groaned internally, deciding Liv didn't need to know just how much effort and money it had taken to get one of the mainland locals to deliver groceries and gasoline, put fresh linens on the beds, dust the bedrooms, and check on the well.

Liv cocked her head to the side and wrinkled her nose as she studied Kayla. "Are you psychic or something? I never seem to get a sentence out before you break in and answer my question." *And that answer was a complete sentence. She can talk.*

Kayla studied her shoes. "I didn't mean to interrupt," she apologized quietly. *Stupid! Stupid! Keep your damn mouth shut! But it's so strong around her, and different than it usually is. She can feel it, too. I'm sure of it.*

Liv laid a hand on Kayla's forearm, feeling the tension running through the other woman—who suddenly looked angry or frightened, she wasn't sure which. "I wasn't trying to get an apology out of you. It just seems like—"

"Liv, could you give me a hand with these?" Marcy interrupted quickly as she pointed at several large bags in the bottom of the boat. She recognized Kayla's stressed frown.

Liv didn't turn away from Kayla as she spoke to Marcy. "Just a second. I—"

"Please...they're really heavy."

Reluctantly, Liv let go of Kayla's arm and moved to the end of the dock, but not before glancing back at the woman, who suddenly found something terribly interesting about the boat's steering wheel. With a puzzled shake of her head, Liv began helping the dark teenager unload the bags. *Something's going on here, and I won't be distracted forever.*

Liv's eyes drifted to her brother, who was gazing adoringly at Marcy, his mouth literally hanging open. She smirked. *Oh, brother. He wouldn't notice if his own head caught fire.*

When Liv appeared to be fully occupied with the luggage, Kayla shot her sister a pathetically grateful look that was anxiously returned. They would talk about this later.

LIV STEPPED THROUGH the front door of the house...and back in time. Oak paneling stretched from ceiling to floor. Although the wooden floors were in desperate need of refinishing, they looked freshly swept. The sparsely scattered furnishings were covered with yellowing sheets, and from what little she could see, Liv recognized the style as colonial. "My God." Her voice dropped to a reverent whisper as her eyes scanned the intricate but decaying wooden moldings that lined the top and bottom of the large entryway. "How old *is* this place?"

Kayla set down one of two large metal boxes that she refused to let anyone else carry. "It was built sometime in the late 1600's, I think. By a very distant relative."

Liv nodded, pleased with Kayla's obvious, if sudden, effort at making idle conversation, and feeling a little guilty about her earlier outburst. The smaller woman squinted a bit as her eyes adjusted to the dim light. The house looked that damn old. "How has it managed to survived all these years, especially with all the storms and hurricanes?" Without waiting for an answer, the blonde impulsively stepped into what appeared to be a library, and gazed out of the dirty picture window facing the Atlantic Ocean. She wrapped her arms around herself, feeling a sudden chill despite the stagnant, humid heat of the day. Then, just as quickly as the chill had come, it disappeared.

Doug moved to join his sister, watching the darkening sea for a moment before breaking the silence. The young man gathered his courage and decided to try addressing Kayla, who had stepped away from the room's doorway for the first time and joined him and Liv at the window. "You said something about food?"

Kayla nodded as she wiped a bead of sweat from her brow with the back of her hand. "You wanna help me find the kitchen and get something started?"

Doug smiled, relieved she was actually talking to him. He made a mental note to ask Marcy what he could do to get on her good side, being pretty sure there weren't any places to buy chocolate on the island.

On the way out of the room, Doug ran into Marcy. He gave her hand a quick squeeze. They'd get some time alone together soon; he just might have to beg Liv to distract Kayla, who was already evoking images of a guard dog. Doug silently chuckled. Okay, so this guard dog had an ass to die for...just like her kid sister. Things could be worse.

When Doug and Kayla left the room, Marcy shifted nervously from one foot to the other. It was so important that she make a good impression on Liv. As far as Doug was concerned, Liv was his mother; it didn't matter that she wasn't really old enough for the part. "You want to sit down and just...um...talk I guess?" She tilted her head towards a small sofa covered in a dingy yellow sheet.

Sensing the girl's nervousness, Liv smiled what she hoped was a reassuring smile. "Sure, but let's go outside where it's cooler." Her gaze traveled to the side door where Doug and Kayla had exited. "Will he be okay with her? She seems sort of...well, sort of..."

"Intense?"

Liv nodded, relieved that she wasn't forced to come up with a word to describe Kayla.

"She is." Marcy shrugged. "I mean she always has been. I know it seems like she's off thinking in her own little world most of the time." *'Cause she is.* "But she's really great once you get to know her."

Liv didn't look convinced, so the teenager pressed on. "She's a genius, you know. A real one."

Two pale brows lifted. "I never doubted her intelligence." They exited the house and Liv leaned forward, resting her elbows on the porch railing. *Beauty, brains, and no personality; what a waste.*

Marcy sighed. This wasn't going as she had planned. Both she and Doug had hoped their sisters would hit it off. "Listen, Liv, the only way to really know Kayla is to experience her for yourself."

Liv straightened and kicked a pebble off the porch, watching it tumble to the rough ground. "Okay, then," she said brightly, determined to make her best effort for Doug. "Let's go help with supper, and then we can all get to know each other better. Besides, you're here to see Doug, not me."

The girl opened her mouth to protest, but Liv held up a

forestalling hand. "'S'okay. Believe it or not, I do understand. You're dying for some time alone with Dougie, right?" Marcy blushed, causing Liv to laugh out loud as she spoke. "I think...no, I know, I'm totally jealous." She smiled warmly.

"You're not seeing anyone, are you?" Marcy inquired, trying not to sound overly eager. Doug had said Liv almost never dated, and she had caught her sister and Liv checking out each other when they thought no one was watching. She could have sworn she saw sparks of interest dancing behind their eyes, confirming what she and Doug suspected about their preferences in lovers: *breasts, good; body hair, bad.*

Liv wrinkled her forehead and picked idly at the wooden railing with her finger. "Nope. I guess you could say I'm in the 'love free' zone and have been for quite some time."

A happy smile creased Marcy's face. "Oh, that's too bad."

Liv's eyebrows shot skyward. *Man, she's a little weird, isn't she? She's so perfect for Dougie.*

"Oh, I mean that's too bad," Marcy said, her tone more serious. *Shit.* Now she knew why she was the understudy's understudy and costume designer in her high school play.

Liv stared at the girl for a moment, then shook her head slightly, not quite sure what was going on with Marcy. But it didn't matter. What did matter was that Marcy was important to Doug. "C'mon." With a tug on Marcy's wrist, Liv led her back to the door. "I'm starving."

"Me, too." Marcy laid her hand on her stomach as they made their way across the porch.

"Too nervous to eat much earlier?" Liv guessed.

The teenager nodded sheepishly. "It's just...I mean you're —"

Liv pulled open the door and motioned Marcy through. "You needn't worry about me, Marcy."

The dark-haired girl stopped and regarded Liv seriously. "I don't, do I?" Her words were hopeful and relieved. "I mean, Doug said I wouldn't; but I still was," she shrugged, "you know, a little worried."

Liv smiled sympathetically, her attention split between Marcy and the enormous foyer. "I know. But I'm an easy person to know and get along with. You'll see." She waited for Marcy to offer the same words of reassurance about Kayla.

But they didn't come.

Chapter
Three

Midnight Wanderings

IT WAS NEARLY midnight when one by one the house's occupants began claiming rooms to sleep in. Marcy appeared a little apprehensive at the idea of sleeping too far away from the others, and shrewdly suggested that they all sleep on the same floor. That way, if anyone needed to go down to the kitchen or bathrooms, which were all on the main floor, they could easily enlist a buddy. After all, the house was a labyrinth of odd-sized rooms and twisting, adjoining hallways. It would be easy to get lost, particularly at night.

Recognizing the girl's fear, Liv immediately pronounced it an excellent idea and claimed the room nearest the stairs and directly across from Marcy. It was mainly intended to ease Marcy's mind. But Liv wasn't above admitting that she liked the idea of having Marcy and Kayla, who selected the room next to her, close by.

Truth be told, Liv thought the house was a little unsettling. Creepy, really. Especially at night. *Disneyland's Haunted Mansion has nothing on this place.* The blonde half-expected a ghoul to be residing under the bed, a butler named Igor to show up in the parlor, and bats in the belfry, or whatever the hell lived in a three hundred year old garret.

Liv bent down to unzip her suitcase and the floor creaked beneath her feet, instantly causing her to jump. "Jesus," she gasped, taking a large step backwards, her eyes riveted on the dark-wood floors. Then she burst into laughter. "Crap, I scared myself."

She exhaled explosively and looked around the empty room. "And I'm talking to myself, too. Maybe I should ask Dougie if he wants a roommate before I go completely bonkers." Her eyes traveled in the direction Kayla and Doug had headed after tucking Marcy in for the night. "Nah...I'd never live it down." Liv smiled wryly, her white teeth glinting in the soft light of a solitary candle. "How old am I, again?"

The house had lights that ran off a gas generator, which also ran the refrigerator and stove. But this convenience only extended to the first floor. There were three floors in total, not including the cellar and attic, both of which Liv silently swore she'd never see anyway. To her dismay, there were no beds on the first or second floors, so they were forced into the pitch-blackness of the third floor.

Liv pushed away a surge of uneasiness, cursing the numerous horror films she'd indulged in throughout her childhood. They'd always struck her as humorous. Right now, however, she wasn't laughing. *Enough.* "Okay..." The blonde began rummaging through her bag. "Something to sleep in..."

"THIS IS GOING to be your room," Kayla said as she pushed open the door to the bedroom that was as far away from Marcy's room as was physically possible while still being in the same house. She only hoped it would be habitable.

"Thanks." Doug mumbled. *For nothing.* He walked past Kayla through the doorway, pulling his T-shirt away from his sweaty mid-section.

This room was slightly smaller than the others, and warmer because it overlooked the forest rather than the sea. But it was clean, and far closer to Marcy than he'd been yesterday. Right now, that was all that mattered to Doug. Tomorrow he'd work on winning Kayla over.

"Well then, good night, Doug," Kayla offered awkwardly, regretting her rigid stance with the boy, but believing it was the wisest course of conduct, nonetheless. *A little healthy fear never hurt anyone, did it?* "Listen, Doug—"

"Don't worry." The young man let out a long-suffering sigh that made Kayla wince. Was she really that harsh? "Liv already told me that I'd better not come anywhere near Marcy's room...or else I'm fish food. I'll behave."

Kayla smiled. Liv was so right. Although she thought her sister was too young to be in such a serious relationship, she actually did like Doug.

While fussing with the candle she was lighting, Kayla took a long moment to covertly examine the boy who had so thoroughly captured her sister's heart. While Liv didn't share in Doug's naturally curly locks, Kayla couldn't help but notice that the siblings did share impish, fair features, and energetic, friendly personalities that could be downright charming when they extended themselves.

Liv had made a special effort to get to know Marcy over the course of the evening. And the older Redding sister was more than a little embarrassed that Liv had drawn out several facts about Marcy that she herself didn't know. Kayla was certain that by the time Marcy had gone to bed, the teenager had a crush on both Hazelwoods.

She and Doug weren't hitting it off nearly so well, and she accepted that that was at least partially her fault. For Marcy, she would try harder.

"I'll see you in the morning, Doug." Kayla took a step down the hall before turning back and poking her head around the corner of the doorframe. The boy had just started pulling some shorts out of his duffel bag. Kayla cleared her throat to get Doug's attention. "Marcy is really glad you're here." Blue eyes dropped to the floor, their expression unreadable in the flickering candlelight. "I...um...I do appreciate that." They didn't have to be supervised every minute, did they? "Maybe tomorrow you guys can go swimming or something."

"That would be great. Thanks, Kayla." *Score one for the home team!*

AT THE OTHER end of the hall, Liv had just slipped into a T-shirt and shorts, glad she'd packed such cool clothing, even if she was likely to be eaten alive by mosquitoes. When Doug had discussed spending the week at the Redding family's summer home, she had pictured something with air-conditioning. Hell, something with lights, television, and a phone. It wasn't like she had to have all those things, but a girl could hope.

Liv laid a hand flat against her drenched forehead. The stifling heat made the thought of going to bed unbearable, and even though the house was huge, Liv was starting to feel sluggish and trapped by the stagnant air within its walls. *God, why didn't I open the window earlier?*

She quickly moved over to the window; curling her hands around a tarnished brass handle at the bottom, she gave a mighty tug. Nothing. Liv tried again. Still nothing.

Suddenly a warm breath tickled the back of Liv's neck, and strong hands covered her own. She opened her mouth to scream just as the grip on her hands tightened and the window flew open, extinguishing the single candle and bathing the room in total darkness.

"Are you settling in all right?" a quiet voice burred.

Liv wrenched her hands away and stumbled backwards, right into Kayla. "What? What? Kayla?" she finally asked, not even hearing the words over her thundering heart as the voice's likely owner began to register.

An eyebrow rose, unseen in the darkness. "You were expecting someone else?"

"That's not funny!" Liv balled her fists. "Haven't you ever heard of knocking?" Her voice was rising along with her temper.

"Hey, calm down." Kayla held her hands up in surrender, trying not to laugh. "I didn't mean to scare you."

Liv opened her mouth, but Kayla beat her to the punch. "Your door was wide open, and I saw you having trouble with the window. I was just trying to help."

Liv relaxed her hands and forced her breathing to slow. *She didn't mean it. It's not her fault you're a big chicken. Take it easy.* "It's okay." Liv moved over to the window, relishing the cool breeze that was pouring into the room. "Do the kids—"

"Yup, both of them have their windows wide open. It'll cool the rooms down considerably. I don't think you have to worry." *She is like a mother to him.*

Liv closed her eyes briefly as a sudden gust blew back the thick curtains and dried the perspiration from her neck. "Kayla..." She turned back to face the taller woman. "Would you like to go sit on the porch with me? I think I need to cool down before I even try to go to sleep."

Kayla simply nodded and stepped towards the door.

"Wait." Liv motioned to the nightstand alongside the window. "Shouldn't we bring the candle?"

Kayla smiled and shook her head no. Reached into her jeans pocket, she pulled out a silver lighter, clicking it on.

Liv stared into the dancing eyes, gone violet in the faint light.

"Why, you're not afraid of the dark, are you, Miss Hazelwood?" Kayla drawled ominously, her breath causing the small flame to flicker.

Liv's immediate instinct was to shout, no. Even though the opposite appeared to be quite true. Instead, she seriously pondered the question, all the while studying the intense face in front of her. "Should I be?" she finally answered, causing Kayla's cheeks to crease into a brilliant smile.

"Nah." Kayla motioned Liv toward the door and began leading the way down the steep staircase, the sound of the creaking steps magnified by the silent house. "Mostly good things happen in the dark."

Liv blushed. Deeply.

"YOU'RE KIDDING." KAYLA laughed.

"Nope," Liv said proudly, lifting her feet just a bit and allowing the porch swing to sway backwards.

"I guess it really pays to be a linguist sometimes, huh?"

"Well, maybe not monetarily, at least not with the Peace Corps. But it did keep me from accidentally eating monkey brains. That alone is worth my monthly student loan payment."

Kayla shifted on the swing and looked up into the cloud-covered sky. Liv was nice. Really nice. If Doug was half this nice, then Marcy was a lucky girl. She leaned forward, elbows on knees, and asked interestedly, "So, how long have you been back from Africa?"

"About three weeks." It was easy to talk to Kayla, Liv discovered. The woman was an excellent listener, remaining active in the conversation in a quiet, non-intrusive but encouraging way.

"When I left two years ago, I only intended to be gone for four months, then I was coming home to train other Peace Corps workers in our Washington D.C. office. I didn't take Dougie with me because I was convinced it was too dangerous, and, of course, he was still in school." Regret colored her voice, and jade eyes, long since adjusted to the night, turned to the lapping water and jagged rocks just beyond the porch. "Then things got out of hand; and four months stretched into six, and six months into a year, and one day I woke up and realized I'd been gone for two years, with only a few isolated visits back to the States." Liv was silent for several moments, wondering just how much she felt comfortable in telling Kayla. "I could have stayed longer. The work was...is...important. But it was time for me to come home."

"Doug?" Kayla guessed. The bond between the two went beyond brother and sister. That much was obvious, and Kayla found herself wondering why.

Liv nodded. "He needs more than Aunt Ruth can give. And I guess...I mean...I guess we need each other."

"What about your folks?"

Liv blinked. "Marcy never mentioned the car accident?" It had taken years for her to be able to say the words without her throat closing around them.

Kayla shrugged sheepishly. "I haven't lived at home since I graduated from high school. Marcy was only seven then, and we didn't have a lot in common. Marcy and I don't see all that much of each other. I travel a lot. And I think this," Kayla motioned, indicating everything, "was her way for us to get to spend a bit of time together. But mostly it's an opportunity for her to see Doug without our parents being underfoot." *And I have my own reasons, too. I don't think I'll be getting too much sleep tonight.*

"Why here?" Liv couldn't help but shiver at the thought of where "here" was. Some people's idea of a vacation spot was just twisted.

Kayla swallowed. She had known this would come up, but she still didn't like talking about it. "Papaw's estate finally cleared probate, and I'm..." She paused and glanced over to find Liv staring interestedly back at her. She'd done her best to steer the conversation toward Liv all night, but somehow the other woman had gotten Kayla talking about herself. "I mean...I'm..."

"Here to check on the property?" Liv offered, unnerved by Kayla's obvious reluctance to answer.

"Something like that. Yes." *Shit.*

Pale brows furrowed. Conversation was a two way street, and while Kayla was a good listener, it was her turn to do a little talking. "What does that mean, 'something like that'?"

Kayla's back stiffened.

"Something weird is going on, isn't it?" Liv accused. *Jesus! She's doing it again. Being evasive just like on the boat.*

"You've seen one too many spooky movies, and I'm going to bed." The darker woman's voice was flat as she rose to her feet. She had neither the time nor inclination to subject herself to ridicule from someone who could never understand anyway. Kayla had been down that road before, and she wasn't anxious for a repeat trip.

Kayla crossed her arms and looked down at Liv, consciously softening her voice. "Are you coming in?"

"You're really not going to answer my question, are you?" Liv asked incredulously. What was going on with Kayla? One moment they were having a pleasant conversation...then BAM. Nothing.

"No." Kayla shook her head defiantly. "I'm really not. Good night, Liv." Kayla dropped the lighter in Liv's lap, then disappeared into the dark house.

"GREAT," LIV GRUMBLED. "Now I get to try and find my room...alone."

"It has *got* to be here somewhere," Liv softly uttered to herself as she turned yet another corner. "Damn! I can't believe this. Why didn't I just go inside with Kayla when I had the chance?"

The linguist had been wandering around the old house for nearly an hour, and still hadn't found her way back to her bedroom. She'd gone back and forth from the main to the second floor several times, each time starting up what she knew to be the right set of stairs. That staircase ended on the second floor, forcing her to meander through a maze of rooms and hallways in order to find the next set of stairs ascending to the third floor and her bedroom.

The blonde chastised herself for not paying closer attention to

her surroundings when she'd gone up to the third floor the first
time, or when she'd come back down again with Kayla. That time,
however, her eyes had been too preoccupied with the muscular
thighs shifting with each step on the stairs ahead of her, to notice
much else. *More proof that I'm related to Dougie. We're both as easily
distracted as a dog with a bone, and unwittingly attracted to weird
redheads. It must be a genetic defect.*

The tiny flame managed to cast long, broken shadows down
the winding hallways, illuminating the numerous alcoves and
rooms she traveled through. Liv had reduced the flame of the
lighter to its lowest setting in order to conserve fuel, and was
frankly surprised it had lasted this long. Straining her eyes, she
paused, hoping to recognize the intricately carved oak door in front
of her.

Yes, this was it. She'd stopped at this door several times
before, but never opened it. Now she stood outside it again, feeling
the same sense of vague foreboding that she'd felt the other times.
The flame from the lighter began to hiss and sputter, and she knew
that in a few seconds she'd be thrown into total darkness.

Liv reached for the doorknob and noticed her hand was
shaking. *What's wrong with me?* she questioned herself desperately,
as her anxiety level rose another notch. What had been a fine sheen
of perspiration, transformed into a nervous sweat, causing Liv to
wipe her hand on her T-shirt. Suddenly, she had to see what was
behind the heavy wooden door. She *had* to know. The linguist
wasn't sure if it was irrational fear, curiosity, or anxiety that
propelled her forward. But where she'd turned back before, this
time she forged ahead.

The knob turned silently in her hand, and unlike the other
doors, this one opened with a barely audible click.

Liv pushed through the doorway, the scent of sandalwood and
clean, salty air flooding her senses. The window was wide open,
and the gauzy curtains were fluttering wildly in the damp night
breeze. The lighter's golden flame died in her hands, and she
tucked the metal rectangle into her pocket, wincing at the heat that
briefly stung the tender skin of her upper thigh. Wide, green eyes
surveyed the dark room.

It was a simple room, nothing even close to sinister. Both relief
and embarrassment welled up within Liv, as her energy level
plummeted and her heart rate slowed. When the nerve-wracking
tension fled her body, she found herself fighting to stay awake, to
even stand up. Liv was simply too tired to be frightened by her
confusing surroundings any more tonight. She could always freak
out another night, she reasoned; they would be here a week.
Besides, things never looked as bad in the daylight. She just had to

make it until then.

The backs of her thighs brushed against a smooth surface that she immediately recognized as soft linens. *A bed? I never even made it to the third floor. There must be other bedrooms on the second floor we didn't find this afternoon. God, how long ago was that?*

She kicked off her sneakers and removed her shorts and bra before settling into the soft bed. It didn't matter where she was. What did matter was that she could finally close her eyes and let the day's tension melt away.

Liv absently noted that the sheets had been turned down, as if someone was awaiting a guest. She drew a gentle breath and recognized the linens as the source of the faint sandalwood scent. A pale head sunk into the fluffy goose-feather pillow as the relatively cool breeze washed over her, and her eyes slid shut. She could hear the crashing of waves against the rocks beyond her window, and somewhere in the back of her mind, she wondered if a storm was moving in.

A FAINT PRESSURE circled the tender skin on Liv's wrists. It wasn't unpleasant, and it wasn't nearly enough to rouse drowsy, impossibly heavy eyelids. A handful of heartbeats later, the pressure on her wrists disappeared, only to begin again a little higher. The touch was cool and soothing against her warm flesh, as it slowly moved in a path along sensitive forearms and past her elbows.

Liv began to stir as the delicate fingertips trailed over her neck and cheeks, finally settling in honey-blonde tresses. An easy sigh escaped her lips when the touch reversed its course, and the pressure shifted from a delicate tracing, to firm massaging. "Mmm...feels so good," she mumbled, enjoying her phantom masseur's caresses, as well as the first twinges of arousal the touch evoked.

Long fingers carefully circled slender wrists, and with a gentle tug, spread Liv's arms wide open. Unexpectedly, the fingers that were wrapped around her wrists disappeared. But before Liv could grumble her displeasure at the loss of sensation, a firm body settled solidly atop her, causing her legs to involuntarily spread to accommodate the warm, naked thighs that were now pressing against her own.

Liv groaned her approval as lips attached themselves to her neck, and she wrapped her arms around the lanky, but decidedly female, form. Soft, clean smelling hair spilled across the sides of her cheeks and jaw, and hands that were already becoming familiar by their touch pushed up her T-shirt and gently cupped aching breasts. Thumbs grazed painfully hard nipples and the smaller woman gasped, arching into the sensual touch but never opening her eyes.

A loud bang caused Liv to awake abruptly and jerk upright in the bed. Her breathing was labored, her face flushed a rosy pink. "Bu...but?" She swallowed hastily as she tried to rein in her wildly coursing libido so she could actually form something like coherent speech. "What in—" The words died on confused lips.

The gray light of morning was pouring in the window, illuminating the room in an almost foggy, dull haze. Doug was giving the window latch a final tug. The nervous boy actually wrung his hands as he addressed his sister. "It's past eight a.m. I was trying to let you sleep in, but I noticed that your window was open and the floor was getting all wet from the rain," he explained, desperately trying to avoid direct eye contact.

The teenager had been on his way downstairs to scrounge some breakfast when Liv's moans drew him to her room to investigate. When he pushed open the slightly ajar door, she was groaning in a way he found beyond unsettling. There were a great many things a teenage boy didn't want or need to know about his sister. What she looks like in the throes of an obviously erotic dream had just shot up to the very top of that list.

"How did you find me?" Liv sprang out of bed and began to spin in circles. As her gaze flicked wildly around the room, she saw her suitcase exactly where she'd left it yesterday evening. This was *her* room. Not the room she'd wandered into in the middle of the night, but the room she'd picked out the day before. *What the hell?* "What do you mean, 'find you'? This is right where I left you before Kayla exiled me to the opposite end of the house."

Liv ran a frantic hand through her hair, sending the shoulder length shaggy locks into further disarray. "No! No! No! I was lost!" She looked over at Doug, who was plainly confused. "Kayla and I spent half the night talking on the porch." Liv spun around once more, unable to believe she'd been in her room all along and simply hadn't recognized it in the dark. "When I tried to find my room again, I got lost somewhere on the second floor."

"Okay," Doug drew out. "If you say so, Sis."

"You don't believe me, do you?"

"Well, you're here now. How do you explain that?"

A frown. "I can't."

Doug nodded, pleased with his rational argument. He really didn't want to think about what Liv was implying. The house was spooky enough without wondering whether you were going to fall asleep in one spot and wake up in another. This vacation was supposed to be about spending time with Marcy and making out in the moonlight, not worrying about a bunch of overgrown bushes and a rickety old house.

"I must have...well, I—" Liv blew out an exasperated breath. "I...I don't know what happened last night," she admitted as she noticed her shorts on the floor and bent over to retrieve them. Tentatively, she reached in her pocket and pulled out a shiny, silver lighter. The blonde let out a relieved breath. She had been starting to wonder whether the entire evening with Kayla had been a dream. But she wasn't about to complain about the last part of the dream. *That* she liked.

Doug eyed the lighter appreciatively. "Very nice."

"Here." The older Hazelwood handed the boy the slender device, covered with intricate etchings. "Kayla lent it to me last night."

With a quick flick of his thumb, Doug clicked on the lighter and gazed into its strong, blue-gold flame.

"Hey. It stopped working last night." Liv snatched back the lighter and shook it. It was nearly empty, but she could hear a small amount of fuel sloshing back and forth. The crease in her brow intensified. *I could have sworn it was empty last night. I even remember the hissing sound when it went out.*

"Are you going to wear those downstairs, or do you just want Marcy and Kayla to know you still sleep in froggy underpants?" Doug pointed at Liv's white panties peeking out below the hem of her T-shirt. They were covered with hundreds of tiny green jumping frogs.

Liv wriggled her eyebrows wickedly, but slipped on her shorts. "C'mon, let's go." She motioned to the door, and Doug eagerly bounded out of the room towards a hearty breakfast. When Liv reached the top of the stairs, she stopped and glanced over her shoulder into her quiet bedroom. Something strange was niggling at her senses. Something wasn't right.

"Dougie," she called after the rapidly disappearing teen. "I'll be down in a few minutes. I'm going to change into some clean clothes first."

"Okay, but if I eat all the donuts, no whining from you," he yelled as he jumped off the last step and onto the second floor.

Liv smiled warmly. She was glad to be back with her brother. Until she'd seen him again, she hadn't realized how much she had missed his cocky grin and easy laugh. Maybe Dougie wouldn't have to wait for college to live with her again. With her background, a decent job wouldn't be hard to find. Then she could afford a bigger apartment.

When Doug's footsteps faded away, Liv turned on her heel and padded back into her room, shutting the door tightly behind her.

Her face had lost its warmth, and anger darkened jade eyes. She grabbed her purse off the dresser and clutched it tightly as she moved to the bed and perched warily on its edge. Her lips shaped into a snarl as she reached into the small leather bag and removed a slender canister. Then, without warning, she propelled her purse at the closet door. A loud bang rang out in the room, and the door shook in its frame.

"Get your ass out here, right now!" she said.

There was no sound from the closet and Liv clenched her fists, trying to control her anger as she gripped the canister with malicious intent. "Come out, *now!*"

After several more tense seconds, the door silently opened.

Liv's eyes widened, and then narrowed dangerously. "What the hell are you doing here?"

Chapter
Four

Revelations

"YOU'RE GOING TO attack me with a travel-sized can of hairspray?"

What in the hell makes you think it's hairspray? Liv's fingers tightened around the can in a white-knuckled grip, and she lifted her chin. "It could be pepper spray."

"It could be, but it's not." Kayla turned her back to Liv and shut the closet door, hoping the action would give her heart a second or two to resume its normal rhythm. *I must be losing my touch. I was barely breathing in that closet. She couldn't have heard me. God, she has to feel it, too, doesn't she? It's more than me just wanting her to. It has to be.*

Liv slammed the worthless canister of hairspray down on the dresser. "Why were you hiding in my closet?" Then the blonde froze. A tortured groan escaped her throat as visions from her vivid dream came flooding back to her. *Oh, God.* Her eyes raked over Kayla, her mind flashing to a scene of warm bodies pressed tightly together, of roaming hands and tongues. "Last night, or this morning really, it was you, wasn't it?" Liv's eyes widened at the prospect. "In my bed? It was real."

A blush shot up Kayla's neck, turning even the tips of her ears a bright crimson. "No. Well, sort of...but not the way you think...I...I...I..." the darker woman babbled as she took a backward step away from Liv, who had begun stalking her like a lion after its prey.

A mixture of fear and anger, and an unexpected surge of pure desire, left Liv wondering which she wanted more, to smack Kayla, or take her right there against the bedroom wall. "Was it your hands and mouth all over me, or not?" she ground out, already knowing the answer.

Her eyes telegraphed guilt, embarrassment, and something else; yet still Kayla remained silent.

Finally, the younger woman's reticence caused Liv's temper to flare once again. "You think it's appropriate to climb in bed with a total stranger while they're sleeping, and then touch them?"

Kayla winced internally, but outwardly she remained totally impassive as Liv's rant continued.

"Explain! Give me one reason why I shouldn't think you're some weirdo pervert!"

Kayla felt that last statement as though it were a physical blow, the shouted words sending a jagged crack through her rapidly crumbling veneer. As a child, the neighborhood kids had taunted and teased her, calling her different, strange, a weirdo. *Liv feels the same way,* she thought disgustedly. Kayla pushed off the wall and stared directly in burning green eyes. "I am *not* a pervert. And I was never in your room last night," she hissed.

Liv could feel Kayla closing herself off, once again unilaterally ending their conversation, but still she pushed forward. "That can't be true," she challenged, even as her anger was derailed by the almost imperceptible look of soul deep pain that swept over Kayla's chiseled features before vanishing completely. *I hurt her feelings? No. I don't care if I did.* "I felt you. You were here with me. When Dougie came in, he must have sent you scurrying for cover like a rat trying to find its hole."

Liv's anger hit Kayla squarely in the chest, and she cursed herself again for letting it bother her. The redhead squared her shoulders, then simply walked past Liv to the bedroom door. But before slender fingers could tighten around the doorknob, Liv grabbed her by the arm and roughly spun her around, pushing her back against the hard wooden surface. The unexpected physical contact combined with the high emotions of the moment sent a jolt of sensation through both women, momentarily confusing them.

But it was Liv who recovered first, her anger focusing her on her need for an explanation. "I want some answers, Kayla! You're not just waltzing out on me like you did last night. You're not leaving this room until you explain yourself!" she shouted, having lost any semblance of control.

In the blink of an eye, the women's positions were reversed, and it was Liv who was pinned by strong hands. They were both breathing raggedly, and Kayla could see Liv's pulse pounding wildly in her neck. Kayla leaned into the wide-eyed blonde until they were touching all along the length of their bodies, then spoke in a rough voice tinged with fury and rising passion. "Don't manhandle me, Liv," she growled, inches from the shorter woman's face. "I don't like it."

Liv closed her eyes as she was bombarded with the memory of strong but tender hands roaming beneath her shirt and hot breath tickling her throat. Kayla smelled like sandalwood, and Liv's mind quickly discarded the obvious reason — that all the linens had been washed with sandalwood soap. Instead, her body refused to believe anything other than that *this* woman had been in her bed.

"I won't push you again," Liv whispered, her voice remarkably calm, considering it took nearly all her effort not to melt into the firm body holding her against the wall. She could hear the sound of her own blood rushing in her ears, and if she listened carefully enough, she swore she could hear Kayla's as well. *Impossible.* She took a deep breath to collect her thoughts. "I'm sorry."

Kayla swallowed convulsively, suddenly finding herself with the inexplicable urge to cry. "I'm *not* some *weirdo.*" Her tone was achingly painful, and Liv felt a pang deep in her chest at the sound.

"I know," Liv assured fervently, a bit unnerved by the intensity of her own voice, not to mention the intensity of this entire exchange. But, even though Kayla hadn't explained herself yet, at that very moment, Liv simply decided to trust Kayla. It was an unexpected leap of faith, and Liv wasn't sure which surprised her more — that she made it or that it felt so good.

"You don't have to be afraid of me, Liv." *Please don't be afraid of me.*

Their eyes locked as the sound of the constant rain outside the window filled the silent room, until Liv spoke again. "I'm not." It was a simple truth whose origins she didn't understand. But that didn't stop it from resonating within both women's hearts.

Kayla turned her head toward the bed as she exhaled shakily. "You were going to spray me with your hairspray," she finally chuckled weakly. Her eyes rolled. "Excuse me, your pepper spray."

Liv felt a grin tugging at her lips despite herself. This was definitely the most disturbingly uncomfortable beginning of — she wasn't sure what the hell it was the beginning of — that she'd ever experienced. "I didn't know it was you in the closet."

"Sure you did."

A blonde head shook. "I didn't. I—"

Kayla released Liv's arms, stepping away from the other woman even though she was loath to break the physical connection. "If you thought a dangerous stranger was in the closet, would you really have shut yourself in the room alone with them, demanding they come out so you could spray them with Aquanet?"

"I guess it would depend on their hair, now wouldn't it?" Liv deadpanned. Then her face took on a horrified expression. "I would never use Aquanet."

Kayla laughed and the tension between them plummeted.

As she truly considered Kayla's question, pale brows furrowed. *That was an incredibly stupid thing to do.* "God, I'm as dumbassed as those spook movie victims that go into a basement to search out a strange noise. I guess I would do that, 'cause I did."

Kayla frowned. "You're wrong, you know," she said quietly. "You *knew* it was me...you just didn't know it."

"What?" Liv threw her hands in the air, frustration filtering into her voice. "How is it that I can be fluent in five languages and still not understand a word you say? And, not to belabor the point, but you *still* haven't explained why you were hiding in my room." *We'll get to the touching and kissing part later. I hope.*

You know you want to show her. Just do it. Stop being afraid. "Okay, since I've done such a rotten job of explaining myself, why don't I just show you?" Kayla padded over to the closet and opened the door. A dark eyebrow rose in question. "Coming?"

"No, thanks. I've already been in the closet; I didn't like it."

A second brow joined its twin, and Kayla's lips shaped a lopsided grin. "Do you want to see why I was in there, or not?"

Liv nodded reluctantly. "I've mentioned before that I really don't like the dark, haven't I?"

Kayla glanced over her shoulder and down at Liv. "And do you remember how I replied?"

The older woman swallowed. Oh, yeah. She remembered. Liv and Kayla stepped into the long, narrow closet, and Kayla pulled the door shut behind them.

"WHERE IN THE heck are they?" Doug swallowed the last bit of his donut. "Liv said she just wanted to slip into some clean clothes." The young man leaned heavily against the kitchen cabinet as he drained a large glass of milk.

Marcy stood to join him, laying her hand on his still broadening shoulder. "Have you seen Kayla yet this morning?"

"Nope." Not that he minded. He was enjoying this time alone with Marcy. But wondering when Kayla might suddenly walk in on them was making him nervous. And, he wasn't even doing anything wrong.

"Maybe they're together," Marcy speculated hopefully.

Doug frowned. "Why would they be together? I told you, Liv's getting dressed." Doug picked up another donut. "Besides, I don't think they're really hitting it off. Yesterday, every time Liv said something to your sister, all Kayla did was grunt in her direction. And whenever Kayla does say something, Liv practically bites her head off." Doug shook his head. "It's going to be a long week for those two."

Marcy's shoulders slumped. "Maybe you were wrong about Liv?"

"Wrong about what?"

"You know...about that." Marcy emphasized the last word with a seductive purr.

Doug laughed and began choking on his pastry, causing his curly dishwater locks to bounce wildly. "Maybe you were wrong about Kayla, but I know Liv prefers women," he coughed out through a smile.

"How do you know? Did she just come out and tell you?"

Doug bent over the sink and filled his cup with cool water. Taking a long swallow, he wiped his mouth with the back of his hand while Marcy gave his chest a small pat, acknowledging that his choking must have been painful. "Yep. Before she left for Africa, I heard Liv and Aunt Ruth fighting about some friend of Liv's named Cindy. Aunt Ruth was not only loud but...um..." Doug tried to rub the blush from his face with a nervous hand, "quite explicit." Finally he gave up and dropped his hands. "There was no chance of me misunderstanding. So I just asked Liv if what Aunt Ruth accused her of was true, and she said yes."

"You didn't know before? Jesus, Doug, you'd been living with Liv since you were six years old."

"She never went out more than a few times a year. And when she did, a neighbor would baby-sit me. How was I supposed to know exactly who she was going with?" the teen added defensively. "Besides, thinking about Liv doing *it* with anyone makes me gag."

"What?" Marcy exclaimed indignantly. "That is so narrow-minded."

"Marcy," Doug interrupted his girlfriend, "picture your parents having sex."

"Ewwwww!"

He made a face, echoing her sentiment. "See what I mean?"

"But she *is* still your sister."

Doug shrugged one shoulder. "She's the only mother I remember."

Marcy pulled Doug into a strong hug, sorry she'd brought up the subject.

"So where is this Cindy person now?" Marcy remembered Liv's comment about the love free zone and wanted to change the subject.

"I think she's still in Africa. Liv stopped mentioning her months ago."

The darker teen nodded. "Good."

"Marcy." Doug meant it as a warning.

"What?" the girl replied innocently, batting long lashes.

"Maybe it's your sister who—"

"Oh, puuhleezz." The tall girl rolled gray, laughing eyes. "I may not be as close to Kayla as you are to Liv, but I'm not totally blind, either."

Doug's gaze drifted to the window. "The rain's stopped. Do you think Kayla will let us take the boat to the mainland so we can go out this afternoon? Maybe we could go to the movies or something?"

Just then, the house let out a settling groan that caused both teenagers to jump and huddle together.

"Nothing scary, though, okay?" Marcy pleaded.

"I was just thinking the same thing." Doug chuckled nervously as he suppressed the immediate urge to find his sister so she could tell him to quit being such a big baby.

"DON'T BE SUCH a big baby," Kayla whispered when Liv nearly jumped out of her skin at the sound of the closet door closing. "I'm not," Liv whispered back, straining her eyes to see the other woman. "Why are we whispering?"

Kayla blinked. "Umm...I don't know," she offered grumpily, in her normal tone of voice.

For the next few seconds, the small closet was silent. "Well, here we are in a dark closet together," Liv reminded, tapping her foot several times for emphasis.

"Do you still have..."

With a quick flick of Liv's thumb, a tiny flame illuminated the cramped room. "I was going to give it back today. We don't have much time; it's almost out of fuel." Her gaze darted around the closet, then settled on Kayla. "What exactly am I supposed to be looking at?"

"Turn around."

Liv obeyed immediately, spinning to face the back of the closet.

"Push."

"Push what, Kayla? I'm up against the wall, as it is." Liv was beginning to feel uncomfortable in the tiny, enclosed space, her breaths coming more and more rapidly. Before she could utter a word of protest, Kayla placed a comforting hand on her shoulder, then reached around Liv with her other hand and gave the wall a strong push.

Nothing happened.

Liv exhaled loudly. "If this is your idea of a joke, Kayla, it is so *not* funny."

Letting go of Liv's shoulder, Kayla added her other hand to the effort and leaned forward, putting her body weight into the second shove.

A sudden blast of cool, musty air tickled Liv's face, blowing her hair over her shoulders as the back of the wall swung away, revealing a pitch-black corridor. "Holy shit!" Liv sucked in a breath of stale, dank air. With a slight nudge from Kayla, the blonde took a tentative step into the inky passageway, turning up the lighter's flame to its highest setting and peering out as far as the dim light cut into the darkness. "Where does this lead?"

Kayla shrugged. "I dunno. Our rooms are right next to each other. I discovered a hidden door in my own closet, and ended up in your closet. I had just found this door..." Kayla patted the wall, which was really a hidden door to the secret passageway, "when you yelled for me to get out...*now*." *It's mostly the truth.* "I haven't gone exploring yet." Excitement threaded her voice as she inched closer to Liv.

The flame flickered out, and the closet and passageway went black. Liv's unhappy moan was interrupted by Kayla's not so subtle push forward. But the Liv's feet were firmly rooted to the ground.

"What are you waiting for?" Kayla asked anxiously. "Don't you want to see what's down the passageway?"

"Hell no, I don't. At least not in the dark." Liv was a little embarrassed by her obvious fear. But even in the midst of her own apprehension, she found herself strangely enticed, wanting to know what lay in the darkness beyond. "I...would..." She paused, firming her resolve. "I'll go with you, but we need a flashlight." *You were exploring this alone, in the dark? You're nuts.*

The sound of tiny paws scurrying in the distance sent Liv stumbling backwards, reaching for Kayla. Off balance, the smaller woman ended up pushing them both completely back into the closet.

"Umfphhh..."

"Oh, there you are." Liv smiled awkwardly as she untangled herself from Kayla, who was pinned against the back of the closet door. "Sorry."

Kayla flexed her trampled foot. "Where else would I be?" she shot back more roughly than she intended, unable to completely let go of the anger and hurt from their earlier argument, and frustrated by Liv's desire to wait to explore the hallway. *Of course she wants to wait, assuming she'll go at all. Can I blame her for being afraid of me?*

Her words were greeted with total silence.

Liv sighed to herself, feeling a pang of regret over the way she'd behaved earlier. *Since when do I jump to conclusions and call people names? I've been so edgy since we got here. I hurt her feelings, and she's angry. I'm sorry,* she anguished silently.

"No, I'm the one who's sorry," Kayla said softly, knowing full well what she'd just done and praying it wasn't a horrendous mistake. It always was. But this time might be different. *I need it to be different.*

Her eyes widened as Liv felt her stomach drop. "Oh, my God! You just read my mind." This time, it wasn't a question.

THE LATE SUMMER rain had brought an abrupt end to Virginia's staggering heat wave; the air was finally on this side of tolerable. Seemingly overnight, the island's tangled, dense vegetation had added a rich shade of green to its muddy russet and ebony hues. The wind had tapered to a light breeze, and several hours of continuous rain and heavy winds caused waves of dark, murky water to break vigorously against the salt-stained wooden dock.

"Doug, this is not a good idea," Marcy said, even as she was stepping into the rocking aluminum boat and tightening the straps on her life jacket.

"The rain's stopped. We can't find Kayla or Liv. And we want to go into town." Doug shrugged, trying not to look as guilty as he was already feeling. Other than a cursory peek into their rooms, they hadn't made much of an effort to find their sisters. "We'll have a great time and be back on the island before dark."

"And," Marcy drew out the word, "don't forget the part where Kayla tears out your liver and uses it as bait."

Doug flashed a smile filled with the indestructibility and arrogance of youth. "Oh, I know they're both gonna have a cow." *I am not afraid of Kayla and Liv. Okay, I am. But Kayla already hates me, and I'll make it up to Liv, assuming I'm still alive, that is.* "But we don't have to worry about that until tonight." Doug patted his bulging back pocket. "I took Liv's cell phone. Kayla has one of these, right?"

Marcy nodded.

"We can call them from the mainland so they won't worry."

Marcy's apprehensive, slightly guilty look faded. "Why don't we just call them now?"

"Huh?"

"Kayla always carries her phone with her."

"Excellent." Doug reached out and grasped Marcy's hand, pulling her out of the boat and onto the wet dock, her sneakers splashing in the long shallow puddles that dotted the rickety structure. He was already relieved that he could ask before taking out the boat without looking chicken in front of Marcy. "What's the number?"

The tall teen winced, biting her lower lip. "That would really help, wouldn't it?"

"LET'S TALK," KAYLA suggested, drawing a disbelieving snort from the shorter woman.

Liv couldn't help but smile when she heard a faintly accented "Smartass" mumbled in the darkness.

Kayla maneuvered around the linguist. "We might as well take the short cut to my room." Instead of opening the closet door at her back, Kayla pushed on a side wall, that gave way easily. Kayla's closet door stood open, and the dull light from the window beyond caused both women to squint and shield their eyes as they entered the room.

"Here." Kayla smoothed the already immaculately made bed and motioned for Liv to sit at the foot. The redhead nervously licked dry lips as Liv sat down. *Okay. I can do this.* Kayla opened her mouth to speak, but left it hanging open when the words failed to come. After several uncomfortable seconds, she turned away from Liv and began pacing, desperately thinking of some way to tell Liv so that Liv would both believe and understand.

Liv waited, the gnawing deep in her own guts building until she feared she would upchuck from pure stress. With effort, she tore her eyes from Kayla and looked around the room that was the mirror image of her own.

A medium sized bag sat in the corner of the room alongside the two large metal boxes Kayla seemed so protective of. On one box, a map was neatly spread out, its edges being held down by a compass and a brass candlestick. In the center of the map were several pencils, a ruler, and a pair of dark-framed reading glasses. *I wonder what she looks like in the glasses.*

As she turned to face Liv, Kayla opened her mouth for the second time; and once again, when verdant eyes focused on hers, the words died on her lips. *Shit! I'm a moron.*

Finally, when Liv couldn't stand watching the other woman's discomfort for another second, she interrupted Kayla's movements. "Enough," she abruptly announced. "You're making me so nervous, I can hardly stand it. You don't have to tell me anything if you don't want to."

Kayla stopped dead in her tracks. "But—"

"It's okay. Now I know why you were in my closet."

"But—"

"I'm sorry I accused you of hiding in my room. I was...I mean...I was a little disoriented when I woke up this morning and I...um...had an unsettling dream." A pink blush began working its way up Liv's neck.

Unsettling? A faint smirk teased Kayla's lips before she sobered. "You're not going to press me for answers?" she questioned skeptically. Kayla knew Liv was about to go insane from wanting them.

Liv stood and moved to Kayla's window, staring out of the smudged, dirty glass, but not really seeing, unable to believe what she was about to say. She was dying to know more about the beautiful woman. Who she was, what she was thinking when sky-blue eyes snapped or sparkled or laughed. But most of all, she wanted to understand the nearly electric energy that somehow poured off the tall woman; and why, just occasionally, Kayla appeared to be able to meld her mind with Liv's, allowing her to be privy to the linguist's private thoughts. "No. I'm not going to press." *Crap, crap, crap!*

Kayla cocked her head to the side. "Do you hear that?"

Liv was just about to shake her head no when she heard a faint humming. No, more like a buzzing noise. Her gaze drifted downward, and she saw the boat, with her brother and Marcy aboard, pulling away from the dock. "Shit!" Liv whirled around, glaring at Kayla as her hands moved to her hips. "Did you say they could take the boat out alone?"

"Of course not."

The women locked eyes for a split second before they flew out of the room after their wayward siblings. With each step, Liv muttered another angry curse, pausing only when she needed the extra breath to keep up with Kayla's longer strides. She was taking the steps three at a time.

By the time they reached the decrepit dock, the boat had disappeared under the low hanging branches that framed the island's edge.

"Goddammit!" This time it was Kayla's flashing eyes that pinned Liv. "If anything happens to her—"

"It will be her fault as much as Dougie's." Liv interrupted. "She was driving the boat, for Christ's sake! So don't go blaming this all on Dougie."

Kayla's face flushed a bright crimson, and her body shook slightly as she tried to think of a suitable retort. Problem was, she knew Liv was right. *God, I hate it when that happens.*

"Dougie's ass is grass," Liv said, as she turned and slowly made her way back to the house.

Kayla kicked a piece of driftwood out of her path, sending it flying into the bushes alongside Liv. "Trust me. He won't be alone."

The very faint echo of thunder sounded in the distance, causing both women to stop and cock their heads towards the barely audible sound.

Kayla sighed. "Do you think they're smart enough to turn around?"

Liv glanced over her shoulder at Kayla, lifting a pale eyebrow meaningfully.

"I didn't think so." A deep frown creased Kayla's face. "I hope they took enough money for a motel."

Liv stopped so abruptly her feet dug into muddy ground. "What? Are you crazy?"

Kayla's gazed drifted to the open sea, then the horizon. "According to yesterday's weather report, we're supposed to have a nasty storm late this afternoon. That," she pointed in the direction of the thunder, "was just the edge of the front. It should pass to the east of us for now."

Liv moved closer to Kayla, her gaze sweeping over the lightly churning ocean, a dull worrying ache settling in her chest. She looked to Kayla, hoping her next words were wrong. "So if they don't come back in the next few hours, they won't make it back at all?"

A jagged flash of lightning pierced the gray horizon. "At least not today."

Chapter
Five

Stormy Weather

BEFORE MOUNTING THE steps for the house, the two women lingered for a moment at the stairs' base, staring out at the swirling sky and lightly churning water, as the moist, salty air dampened their skin. They both wished they could have made it to the dock faster and stopped their headstrong siblings. Now all they could do was wait and worry.

Liv pounded up several steps before stopping. She turned back to Kayla, very aware of the anger still radiating from her. *Time to get her mind off the million ways she's planning on torturing Doug and Marcy. Nobody tortures Doug but me.* "Are you hungry?"

Kayla's stomach was twisting, and she didn't think she could keep down a single bite. "Sure," came the casual answer.

Liv nodded and smiled softly. *She's trying to be social. Wow.* "Okay, then. I'm going to get cleaned up, and then I'll meet you in the kitchen for an early lunch? I won't be long, okay?" *Say yes, Kayla.*

Kayla heard the uneasiness in Liv's voice and reassured her without hesitation. "I'll be there." *She doesn't want to be left alone for long.* Kayla watched in silence as Liv heaved a sigh of relief and disappeared into the house, her step a little lighter.

Kayla didn't know what she should do now. The storm would keep the kids away, giving her the perfect opportunity to search the secret passageway. She had come to Cobb Island on a mission. A quest to find something. And the moment she inadvertently discovered the hidden space, she knew what she sought had to be there. It was the only thing that made sense. But she shouldn't abandon Liv, either. She wouldn't. Deep inside she wasn't even sure she could. Kayla bit back the urge to scream out her frustration.

"Maybe she'll take a nap after lunch," she mumbled, the prospect of sneaking away for her exploration both tempting and completely unacceptable. She sighed explosively as she glanced back toward the mainland, wishing for the teens' safety but hoping they'd be as worried about getting caught on their little adventure as she and Liv were for their wellbeing. The chaperones shouldn't be the only ones suffering. With that self-acknowledged uncharitable thought, she took a cleansing breath and trotted up the remaining steps to scrape together a decent meal for Liv.

"MY COMPLIMENTS TO the chef," Liv offered around a bite of vegetable soup, as she waved her spoon towards Kayla before pushing the bowl away.

Regally, the statuesque woman bowed deeply at the waist. "It was my pleasure, ma'am," Kayla drawled, trying to maintain her smile even though she couldn't help but notice that most of Liv's food remained untouched. *She should eat more. I know she missed breakfast.*

Kayla sat down heavily in the chair next to Liv's and held out a cookie she had fished from the box of supplies she'd had delivered. With a waggle of her eyebrows and an almost shy smile, she offered it to Liv.

Liv reached out, only to have Kayla pull it away several times before finally presenting it with a flourish. A delighted smile crept its way onto Liv's lips. Kayla was actually playful when she wanted to be. Marcy was right. Kayla had to be experienced. The aloof, powerful personality she presented at first blush was nothing like the interesting, if slightly introverted, woman she became once you scratched the surface.

The last couple of hours had been spent much like the night before, only this time the kitchen table was the meeting place for their quiet conversation. And although Liv could tell Kayla vehemently disliked talking about herself, she had managed to wheedle out a few interesting details about her companion.

She came right out and asked if what Marcy had said was true, that she was a genius, causing the redhead's eyes to drop to the tabletop.

Kayla shrugged self-deprecatingly, then admitted, "Only a little bit."

When Liv responded by saying, wasn't that like being a little bit pregnant, both women burst into laughter.

Liv found out Kayla was twenty-five years old. She was incredibly well traveled for someone her age, having lived in Ireland, Germany and Mexico, all within the past several years. Surprisingly, Kayla had confessed that, despite her extensive travels, her favorite spot was a small town nestled in the Blue Ridge Mountains of West Virginia, where her grandmother had a nonworking ranch that still boarded a few horses. Kayla had moved there last month, having only recently returned from Mexico.

The blonde also found Kayla to be complex and, as Marcy had said the night before, intense. *And it's not just those eyes. It's more.* She was already finding it difficult not to touch Kayla when they spoke. Liv was a touchy kind of person anyway; but for some reason, the urge to make physical contact with Kayla was nearly overwhelming.

As they talked, Kayla was able to resurrect her appetite. Having finished her soup before Liv had made even a small dent in hers, she moved from task to task around the kitchen, giving Liv the opportunity to study the woman's sturdy, but lanky form.

She's like a mystery, all intense and smoldering. The few glimpses of the real woman behind the reticent exterior made Liv determined to see and know more. *I haven't heard even one remotely personal story, at least with any detail. I wonder if she's ever been in love.*

"You didn't eat very much," Kayla pointed out, hoping she didn't sound like too much of a mother hen.

Liv stopped her perusal immediately, hoping her lack of appetite hadn't insulted the cook. "It was really delicious. Honest. I'm just worried about the kids."

Kayla nodded and rejoined Liv at the table again, her restless energy not allowing her to remain in any one position for long. "Why haven't they called? Marcy knows I have a cell phone and that I'll be worried."

Liv smiled knowingly. "'Cause they're not thinking about us. They're thinking about each other."

Slender eyebrows drew together. She wanted to understand. She really did. But her rational mind wouldn't let her. "They're too young." Kayla's voice was unyielding.

"They can't help that."

"But that doesn't change the facts."

"Exactly. They're in love."

Kayla exploded out of her seat. "Dammit! Why are you acting like this is okay, like it's nothing? You *know* what's going to happen when they end up at some motel."

Liv slammed her palms down on the table, rattling the small wooden structure and sending her spoon clattering across its dark-wood surface. She instantly mirrored Kayla's emphatic stance. "I do *not* think it's *okay* or *nothing*. But what the hell do you want me to do about it? Swim to shore and crawl in bed between them?"

Kayla roughly pushed her chair away and stormed out of the kitchen.

Where is she going? Her eyes widened. *She wouldn't. Oh, shit! I'll bet she would.*

Kayla had only meant to have a quick lunch with Liv before she began exploring the passageway. Instead, she'd spent hours talking with Liv and wishing the phone would ring. *God, how could I waste so much time and not even realize it?* She bounded out of the house and onto the porch, where a light drizzle was soaking the gently swaying porch swing. Kayla looked to the darkening sky then dropped her focus to the sea. The height of the waves had increased along with the winds, but the heart of the storm hadn't hit yet. She could normally swim that distance in around fifty minutes. But with the waves...

"Don't even think about it, Kayla," Liv said from behind the agitated woman.

Kayla's gaze remained firmly rooted on the sea. "What are you talking about?" *I don't have to justify myself to you.*

"You are *not* swimming to the mainland with a major storm about to hit. That's not only incredibly reckless, but just plain stupid. You're crazy, aren't you?"

"If I was, it wouldn't be any of your business." Kayla whirled around to face Liv, a small piece of damp hair sticking to her cheek. "Well, would it?" she prodded acidly.

Liv sucked in a breath, shocked at how the simple but true words hurt. "I care if a friend is about to do something dangerous. I guess it was presumptuous of me to think of you that way. Do what you want." Her tone was cool and laced with hurt as she turned on her heel and re-entered the ancient home.

Kayla spun away from the slamming screen door. *I am not reckless. I was taking the weather conditions into account,* she thought petulantly, the sudden desire to find Marcy and wring her neck draining away.

As the rain drizzled down her cheeks, Liv's words reminded her of the fractured arm and ribs she'd gotten outside of Belfast, the pneumonia in Munich, and her personal favorite, the twenty-six stitches while in Mexico City last spring. The redhead sighed. Either she *was* reckless or the biggest klutz on the face of the earth. Kayla admitted to herself that her desire to get to the mainland was as much an attempt to regain control over the situation, as it was to separate two incredibly horny teenagers. She'd never been in charge of Marcy's wellbeing before, and she obviously wasn't handling the stress and responsibility very well.

"Liv, wait up!" Kayla ran inside, catching a flash of movement out of the corner of her eye as she passed the library.

With her back to Kayla, Liv was scanning a tall shelf of leather-bound books, making a rather obvious attempt not to acknowledge the other woman's sudden appearance in the room. But when Kayla cleared her throat loudly, announcing her presence, Liv felt compelled to say something. "Why are you still here? I thought you'd be doing your live-bait imitation by now."

"Ouch." Kayla winced, but still managed to chuckle lightly. "I...um...decided that you were right. It wouldn't be a good idea for me to swim to the mainland." Kayla dug her toe into the rug, trying not to stare at Liv's lightly muscled arms and shoulders as she reached for a book high over her head.

Kayla rushed to her side and tugged loose the dusty hardcover. "Here ya go." She handed it to Liv. "It wasn't one of my better ideas, anyway, seeing as how I have no idea where they went."

Liv exhaled shakily, relieved that she wouldn't have to worry about Kayla, too. *She needs someone to watch out for her and make sure she doesn't take silly chances. She needs someone to watch her back. I could do that.* The odd thought came unbidden and she accepted it without question, instantly warming to the idea.

Blue eyes fluttered shut and a strange look of concentration washed over Kayla's face as she processed the bombarding images and emotions that were enveloping her. *Friendship. Protectiveness. Affection?* A dark eyebrow rose.

Liv stood transfixed, her gaze rooted on Kayla's face.

"Close your eyes, Liv," Kayla whispered, feeling Liv's stare.

Green eyes immediately slid shut, and Liv forgot how to breathe.

"Concentrate."

A sudden sense of quiet strength and security flowed through Liv, filling her completely. Then, like a puff of smoke, it simply disappeared.

"You felt it, didn't you?" Kayla asked nervously. She couldn't be wrong about this. Liv had to be feeling it. It was too strong for her not to.

Liv opened her eyes and was greeted by Kayla's nervous smile. She nodded, not knowing how to put into words what she'd just experienced. "Did —" she swallowed, "did you do that to me?"

Kayla nodded. "Just the same way you did it to me."

"Are...are you magic?" Liv asked, in awe.

"No," Kayla laughed deprecatingly. "It's not magic." She grasped Liv's hand and tugged her toward a low, leather-covered sofa that faced a large picture window overlooking the ocean.

In tandem, they dropped onto the soft cushions. Liv began to pull her hand away but Kayla held fast, giving it a slight tug. Her eyes asked permission for their hands to remain joined.

A small grin shaped Liv's mouth as she relaxed her arm and gently squeezed the palm resting in hers. Permission granted.

The rain increased from drizzle to a light but steady

downpour, as the staccato rhythm of pelting droplets sounded against the window's heavy glass. The flashes of light that had pierced the distant horizon this morning were much closer now, and the storm appeared to be taunting the island with its looming, dangerous presence.

Kayla straightened her shoulders and said a little prayer before she began her tale. "My family, for as far back as anyone can remember, has had unusual gifts." The last word was tinged with a mixture of sarcasm and sadness. "These abilities have been diluted and most certainly diminished over time. The Reddings don't live in small, mediaeval European villages anymore." Full lips quirked, and Kayla let loose her thickest southern drawl. "And contrary to what the rest of the country thinks, we can't count on intermarriages to strengthen these particular traits."

Liv smiled in understanding, having endured many an inbreeding joke when she left rural Virginia for college in Washington, D.C.

"For the past couple of hundred years, only a few people in a century have been blessed...or afflicted," she added wryly, "with these traits. And it seems, as far as the twentieth century is concerned, well, now that Papaw is dead, anyway...that I'm pretty much it." *Well, almost.*

"You're the only one in your family with special..." Liv searched for the right word, still unsure of exactly what Kayla was trying to tell her, "...abilities?"

Kayla shook her head. "We all have a little. Everyone does, really, just to varying degrees. But almost no one has the ability or knowledge to understand and exploit what's naturally theirs. What I have runs stronger than most, and I'm more successful at harnessing it."

"So, you're telling me you're psychic?" Liv shifted so she was fully facing the woman alongside her.

"No. I don't predict the future."

Liv frowned unbecomingly. "I don't...Kayla, I don't understand."

Kayla took a deep breath. "I'm what you would call moderately telepathic." Again, an understatement.

Her eyes went round. "A mind reader?" Liv had mentioned that a couple of times in the past two days. Once in jest, and again when the situation wasn't so funny. But even as she asked it, she didn't really believe it could be true. She let go of Kayla's hand and turned her gaze out over the churning, rolling waves, whose movement seemed to mirror how she felt. Nervously, she ran her hand through golden locks as her mind raced.

Kayla's heart lurched at the implied rejection.

Liv felt the twinge of pain in her own chest and her head snapped back, dark-green eyes locking on glistening blue. "You're upset," Liv stated plainly, but in a gentle voice. "Don't be. I'm just trying to process what you're telling me, okay?" *And what I'm feeling. Whatever the hell it is.*

"Do you want to know more?" Kayla asked hesitantly. She knew Liv was starting to get a little freaked out. Who could blame her?

"Yes. I want to know anything and everything you're willing to tell me." Liv slid her hand back into Kayla's, wrapping her fingers around the longer, slightly trembling ones.

Kayla let out a breath she'd been holding before returning Liv's solid grip. *Her hand is so much smaller than mine, but still strong,* she thought idly before continuing. "Okay, this is the part that's going to sound pretty weird."

A pale brow lifted, causing a bubble of laughter to work its way out of Kayla's throat. "Okay, more weird than what you've already heard."

Kayla felt her chest expand fully with the deep breath she sucked in. "When I'm around you, what I feel is so much stronger than it is with other people, more intense. All my life, I've had flashes or impressions of thoughts that I oftentimes couldn't even put into words. I score very high on those ridiculous blind study tests where I guess the playing card someone has drawn, or whether they're concentrating on circles or squares. But I've met others who score higher. Around you, Liv...around you I not only get glimpses of imagery, I *feel* your emotions. I've never experienced empathic links along with the telepathy before."

Liv looked a little pale. "And this only happens around me?"

Kayla nodded.

Liv bit her lower lip and shook her head. "And somehow you're making me feel things, too?" Kayla had to be doing something to her.

Kayla smiled a little sadly. Communication was never her strong suit. "No, don't you see? You're doing that all on your own."

"Don't you think I would have noticed if I was psychic?" Liv said mildly exasperated.

"Not really. I already said that most people have some paranormal abilities—they just don't know it. If mine are heightened around you, why wouldn't yours be heightened around me?" she asked reasonably. "I felt something from that very first moment when I saw you in the parking lot at the boat rental shop, although Marcy and Doug's three alarm kiss sort of split my attention. Didn't you?"

"You mean other than me thinking you were gorgeous and wanting to jump your bones?" Liv blurted out, immediately blushing a deep scarlet, her pale eyebrows standing out in stark relief.

The room darkened visibly and a loud boom of thunder exploded overhead as the sky opened up over the small island. Liv jumped and Kayla put a comforting hand on her knee, happily replaying Liv's admission in her mind, relieved her attraction wasn't one-sided. "Let me guess, not only do you not like the dark, you don't like storms either."

"It makes sense to me." Liv shrugged. "And do you have to guess?"

"Yes, I have to guess. Paranormal abilities aren't all-or-nothing." Kayla sighed unhappily, thinking of the few times she'd tried to explain this, and the reason she'd finally stopped trying altogether. Kayla's abilities, even with people other than Liv, were an invasion of privacy most people simply couldn't handle. It didn't matter that she wasn't trying to read their thoughts, that sometimes it just happened. And when she couldn't do it on command, or *stop* doing it on command, they became angry or mistrustful.

"So every time I talk to you, you don't automatically know what I'm thinking?" The thought of someone inside her head with her, especially when she didn't know about it, made Liv shiver.

Kayla felt a sinking sensation in the pit of her stomach. "I'm not sitting here reading your mind. It's just that occasionally, and it seems to happen mostly when your emotions are really intense, I get a mental picture of what you're thinking. It's not a word for word kind of thing."

"Oh, right." *That was a stupid question.* "You already said it was more impressions and emotions." Intense eyes studied Kayla's face, plainly seeing her worry and fear, and not knowing what to do about it. Liv's natural urge to comfort Kayla fought with her own uncertainty and doubts. This was a lot to accept, even as just a friend. And there was no denying that Liv wanted more than friendship from Kayla.

A light flashed, quickly followed by a crackling hiss and thundering boom. Liv jumped again, practically crawling onto Kayla's lap.

"It's okay, Liv," she laughed. *Not that I mind your current position.* "We're safe in the house."

"What do you mean safe?" Liv asked incredulously. "That lightning hit the island! I can practically smell the burn. Do you really think half an inch of glass will protect us?" She flinched at the sound of another more distant clap of thunder. "Granted, we're not in a trailer park, but this place is so old I'm surprised the wind alone hasn't sent it into the ocean."

As if Liv's words were prophetic, a powerful gale sent a broken branch flying by the window and slamming into the porch railing. Liv shot up in a near panic, but was stopped, then wrapped in strong arms. "I'm sorry I teased you. I didn't know you were truly afraid." Kayla could feel Liv's heart beating wildly against her own chest.

"Do you...do you really think we're safe in here?" Liv knew she was seeking a ridiculous reassurance that Kayla couldn't possibly give. But she decided to ask for it anyway.

"You're safe. I promise." Kayla tightened her arms around her new friend, daring the storm to break her grip. "The entire house is protected, Liv. The storm can't touch you inside."

"What do you mean, 'protected'?" the blonde asked in confusion, shamefully absorbing Kayla's close, reassuring presence. "I don't give a shit what kind of insurance you have."

"I mean, by a spell."

A loud boom sounded and the house shook as everything went black.

Liv buried her face in the crook of Kayla's shoulder and neck. *A spell?* "You have a lot more to tell me, don't you, Kayla?"

Slightly adjusting Liv's position, Kayla brought her hand up to rest on the soft fabric of the T-shirt between Liv's shoulder blades. Closing her eyes in pleasure, she leaned back into the sofa, taking Liv with her. "Yeah. I sure do."

Chapter
Six

Nature's Wrath

"OH, MY GOD, they're going to kill us. We're dead. Dead. So dead. And it's going to be a looong, slooooow, excruciatingly painful death," Doug worried aloud. The teenager was standing in the lobby of the cheapest motel he and Marcy could find, counting out his cash as the sheets of rain and dark skies made it look as though it were nighttime and not mid-afternoon.

"Yup. We are *totally beyond* dead," Marcy agreed, digging through her purse and adding a few bills to Doug's small pile. "Do we have enough for a room?" She'd convinced Doug it wasn't worth trying to make it back to the island in a storm; though since he wasn't overly anxious to face Liv or Kayla, it hadn't taken too much convincing. They might as well spend one last night together before Kayla and Liv annihilated them both.

Doug frowned and began mentally calculating the sales tax. "I think so. If we spend next to nothing on dinner, we should barely make it." The blond poked his head around the corner and spied a greasy looking man at the reception desk.

Marcy followed his gaze. "Let me get the room, Doug. If he sees us together, without any parents, he'll never rent it to us."

Doug knew that wasn't true. The man looked as though he'd rent them the room in fifteen-minute increments if they asked, but he handed Marcy the bills anyway and watched her turn the corner to the reception desk. There was no use in making her feel dirty about getting a room here. They needed a place to stay, and this was all they could afford.

They were both soaking wet. Worry over their impending deaths was taking its toll. He only wished he'd brought more money or was old enough for a credit card. He hadn't planned on staying the night, and most of his cash was squirreled away in his duffel bag on the island. He sighed inwardly. Marcy deserved to stay someplace nice, not this fleabag.

Doug hadn't even completed his thought when a large

cockroach darted across the floor in front of him. With impressive speed, Doug lunged towards the bug, hearing the satisfying crunch under his shoe. *One down, 999,999,999 to go.*

The middle-aged desk clerk dragged his gaze from the small black-and-white television playing behind him when he heard the annoying ringing of the bell. A scowl was firmly planted on his face. Nothing put a man in a bad mood faster than being interrupted in the middle of watching the stock car races. When he saw his young customer; however, his scowl instantly disappeared. "Hel-lo, baby doll. Mmm...mmm," he hummed. He hadn't seen such a fine looking young thing in quite some time. "You need a room?" He turned and waved his hand towards a rack full of room keys attached to neon pink and green key chains.

"Yes, please. One room." *Jesus Christ. Another one just like at the boat rental shop? Don't they have their own women to drool over in these parts?*

"A single room?" he clarified hopefully, unable to keep his stare from becoming an outright leer. She was a beauty. He generally didn't care for shorthaired women, but his interest lay further south anyway. His eyes eagerly slid down a body that was as firm and young as the day is long.

Before Marcy could answer, the man stepped out from behind the desk, moving alongside her. Then he slowly circled her, as though his actions were part of some bizarre mating ritual. While behind her, he leaned towards her, taking a loud sniff of her scent.

Marcy stepped away, torn between laughing and getting sick. "No. On second thought, I'd like a double room." She'd skip dinner and pay the extra few dollars if it meant he wouldn't think she was by herself.

"Well now, baby, it looks to me like you're all alone. Why would you need a double room? Our beds are real roomy." He moved around in front of Marcy and smiled broadly. Now that he'd gotten a closer look, he could tell she was younger than he'd suspected. Maybe he'd be her first. A man could always hope. Reaching down, he pressed a key into one of her hands, while taking the cash from the other. Not bothering to count it out, he stuffed it all into his shirt pocket alongside his cigarettes.

Touch me and die, asshole, Marcy thought darkly.

"Hi, Sis," Doug said brightly as he stepped between Marcy and the desk clerk just as the man's hands were about to meet Marcy's skin. "Did you get a room yet? You know how Dad gets," he warned.

Marcy stared at Doug for a moment, a little relieved and a lot confused. After a full five seconds, a light bulb clicked on in her head. "Yes. This," she paused, searching for a word with more than four letters, "person was helping me."

The man looked at Doug doubtfully. If this curly headed blond-haired boy was related to the beauty, then he was the goddamned King of France. "Where's your daddy then, boy?" he said crisply, pissed off at the interruption. He was about to make the girl an offer no woman in her right mind would refuse.

"He's still at the bar, sir. He sent us ahead to get a room. He should be here any minute," Doug lied smoothly, looking just a bit pathetic.

Marcy shook her head sadly, following Doug's lead and trying to look broken up over their poor Daddy, praying Doug wouldn't expect her to speak, much less ad lib.

Doug smiled inwardly. Yanking this dimwit's chain was great fun. "Marcy," Doug chastised, "you know how Daddy gets after he's been drinking." Then the teen turned wholesome, painfully honest eyes on the clerk. "We need to get to our room fast, Mister. After a bout with Jack Daniels, Daddy's not the most patient man in the world."

The teenage boy leaned into Marcy and asked in his best stage whisper, "Did you check to see if they have a safe?"

Marcy's eyes went round. *Oh, crap. Why did Doug have to make things so complicated?* "Umm...no?" she hazarded, hoping she'd guessed correctly.

"We don't have no safe," the clerk interrupted, wondering what valuables a drunk might have.

"That's okay, sir," Doug sighed. "We can never get them away from him anyway."

"Get what away, boy?"

"His guns," Doug replied gravely.

Marcy's jaw dropped, and the young man moved to comfort his "sister." "There, there, Sis. We can always hope he'll pass out before anyone can make him angry." Doug focused on the clerk, while gently patting Marcy's back in what he hoped was a brotherly way. But she smelled so good. "Daddy sleeps with his damn 12 gauge. I was just hoping we could manage to keep him away from his Colts for at least one night."

Marcy lifted her head, unable to resist joining in. "But he loves them so. The only way anyone will get those guns away from him is to pry them from his cold, lifeless hands."

"I know." Doug's eyes began to tear. "I never thought he'd actually use them 'til that fool waiter in Atlanta pinched your ass."

The clerk took a large step away from Marcy.

Doug leaned in toward the rapidly paling clerk and whispered conspiratorially, "I hope that waiter already had himself a son, if you know what I mean."

"Damn," the clerk drawled, shaking his head and trying not to look at Marcy. Even a gorgeous young thing like her wasn't worth getting shot for. Thank God it was the boy who came looking for her and not her daddy. "I know exactly what you mean, son." The man's head bobbed up and down rapidly as he reached for the rack of keys, pulling one off the very end. "Here t...take this one. It's for the very end room, outside and around the corner. It has two nice beds." He pointed out the front door. "It's real quiet over there. Nobody will be tempted to bother your sis...I mean daddy. You kids go on now, and wait for your daddy out front."

"Thank you kindly." Doug beamed and grabbed the new key, taking the old one out of Marcy's hand and tossing it on the counter.

"Doug?" Marcy said, as the couple began walking out of the motel.

"Yeah, Sis?" he replied smugly.

Marcy cupped her hands around her face, trying to see through the torrential downpour as long legs picked up the pace to a trot. "Remind me never to believe anything you say...ever again, okay?"

"Okay," Doug yelled, trying to be heard over the wind. He grabbed the girl's hand, leading the way, flinching with every flash in the sky and thinking about his sister's fear of storms. *Shit. Liv must be terrified.* His sister had had a nearly paralyzing fear of lightning ever since a neighbor's house was destroyed in a storm when she was a child. *I really fucked up this time.*

"Don't worry," Marcy said loudly, jumping over a large puddle, "Kayla will take care of her."

Doug glanced over at his girlfriend for a quick second as they reached the door. Wet slippery hands tried to fit the key into the lock. With one hand, he pushed drenched curls out of his eyes. *Did I say that out loud?*

THE WOMEN WERE pressed tightly together, and what should have been an incredibly uncomfortable position for virtual strangers felt surprisingly natural. The first few seconds of awkwardness were swept away by the smell of wet wood, leather, and Liv's shampoo that filled Kayla's nostrils, as the fairer woman seemed to relax into their embrace, despite the storm. They had adjusted to the dim light and the nearly constant claps of thunder that interrupted the low burr of their voices.

Kayla and Liv fell silent, listening to Nature's fury and considering what had just been said. For Kayla, it was a chance she hadn't taken in her adult life. Bad experiences in her youth had left her wary of the reactions of non-family members. She wasn't interested in being viewed as a carnival sideshow or a mental Peeping Tom. The emotional exposure she felt now that Liv knew her secret caused a nervous ache in her belly that her friend's close presence went a long way toward curing.

For Liv, it was a lesson in acceptance. To believe Kayla was to deny the logical and rational, and jump off a cliff into the unknown. That's what it came down to—believing Kayla. She wasn't sure she could do that yet. Not completely. Liv's mind was awhirl with so many questions she barely knew where to begin. Finally, she decided to just start with something...anything...and hope Kayla would take it from there. "So, if this house is protected, then how come we're sitting in the dark?"

Liv's simple, commonsense question surprised the younger woman. It was almost ridiculous in its unimportance, especially when compared to what Kayla had just told her and what she had yet to explain. "Well, as far as I know, the spell only protects the house. The generator is outside. I umm...I think it was struck by lightning."

"I knew it," Liv mumbled into Kayla's shoulder, trying to control her fear. The lightning caused her to huddle even closer, rubbing her cheek along the cool fabric of Kayla's shirt. Liv's obvious distress spurred the arms around her to tighten to an almost painful degree, as Liv greedily soaked up the comfort they offered. She hated storms, and especially lightning. She hated dark and spooky places, and basically disbelieved all things supernatural. But that wasn't possible now, was it?

The linguist didn't want to believe. But how could she not? She herself had felt what Kayla had described, and knew deep in her bones that Kayla was telling her the truth.

"This storm should blow over by tomorrow," Kayla began, feeling the tremors running through her companion. "But the kids may not be able to bring the boat across to the island until fairly late in the day, when the waters have calmed. After that, you can get a motel on the mainland for the rest of the week."

Liv nodded. If Kayla hadn't suggested it, she would have herself. She wanted off this island. Now. But if tomorrow was as good as she could get, she'd take it. Then she backtracked over the woman's words. "What do you mean *you* can go to the mainland? Where will you be?"

"I have to stay on the island for a while."

"What? You're not coming with us?" She pulled away to search Kayla's face in the dim light. "You'd stay here alone?"

"Of course. There's nothing to be afraid of," she commented reasonably.

"But you said this place was haunted."

"I never said haunted. I said it was protected by a spell. There's a big difference."

"But how did I end up in my own room last night, when I know I didn't find my way back there? That's not the kind of thing that happens in a normal house."

"This place is a maze, Liv. I'm sure you only thought you were in a different room, but actually managed to find yours and then fell asleep. It's easy to get confused in the dark." Kayla shrugged one shoulder, not overly concerned with that particular mystery. "Or maybe you dreamed you were wandering around the second floor. Who knows?"

A pale brow lifted. "I know. And it was not a dream."

"All I can do is assure you that this place isn't haunted. It is, however, under a spell."

"And there's a difference, huh? God, I can't believe I'm hearing this." Liv covered her eyes with her palms as she shook her head. "Okay, for argument's sake, let's say they are different. Why would you stay here in either case?"

"I have to find a missing family history, and it's somewhere in this house." Kayla paused to collect her thoughts before launching into another complicated story.

Liv cocked her head to the side and waited for Kayla to elaborate. To her credit, she made it a full ten seconds before going berserk. "*More! More! More!* You need to say more. I have no idea what you're talking about. I don't know what this 'history' is, or how it's connected to you or this house. I—" Liv's words were cut off by the hand that clamped itself firmly over her rapidly moving mouth.

"Okay. Christ, I was just getting to that part." In actuality, Kayla wasn't bothered in the least by her friend's mini-explosion. But somehow she felt the need to at least pretend to be indignant. "Will you let me finish now?"

Liv nodded sheepishly and mumbled her apology into long, smooth fingers.

"All right, then." Kayla gingerly removed her palm from Liv's full lips, their softness imprinting itself on her mind. She carefully watched Liv's face for signs of another outburst.

Liv opened her mouth again. "I'm—"

Kayla's hand flew up but stopped inches from the older woman's lips, waiting to see whether the blonde would utter another word. She tilted her head meaningfully and lifted her eyebrows, reminding Liv to remain quiet.

The linguist grinned. Kayla was playing with her. If she wasn't going to be talking, Liv decided she didn't need to be facing Kayla. The hedonist in her, who was already missing Kayla's warm skin and unique aroma, snuggled back alongside the lanky woman, waiting for her to begin. The prolonged silence caused Liv's mind to sidetrack for a moment, hoping the kids were safe and fed and someplace out of the vicious rain.

Kayla moved slightly, recapturing Liv's attention before she began. "Last month, a manila envelope somehow found me in Mexico. Considering I was residing in a tent at the time, I was fairly shocked."

Liv wanted to ask why Kayla was living in a tent in Mexico, but barely resisted the urge by biting her tongue.

"It was from Papaw's lawyers. Looking at it, I figured the old man had finally passed over — he was a hundred if he was a damn day."

"You weren't close, I take it."

Kayla smirked. She'd have better luck at trying to still the storm than with trying to keep Liv quiet. "No. I never met him. He was my father's grandfather, and Daddy hadn't seen him since the '50s. Anyway, the envelope contained some legal papers concerning his estate that I assumed every direct descendant got. There was also a smaller, handwritten envelope addressed to Kayla Marie Redding."

"That's a pretty name," Liv complimented softly.

Kayla felt the warmth in the sincere words, and grinned broadly. "Thanks," she uttered, a bit flustered. Before she could speak again, she became acutely aware of the steady vibration of Liv's heartbeat pulsing against the hand she had resting on Liv's ribs. She stopped for a moment to absorb its strong, constant rhythm.

Liv prompted her gently with a little poke. "Go on."

Kayla blinked, a little unnerved by how easily just about everything about Liv could distract her from what she was trying to say. "Right, where was I?"

"The personally addressed letter."

Kayla nodded. "The letter contained instructions about the house and the name of the person Papaw had chosen as guardian for the histories."

"What does that mean, 'guardian'? And while you're at it, explain the term, 'histories.'"

"I'm getting there." Kayla reached down and lightly pinched Liv's thigh, eliciting a surprised, but delighted squawk. She felt comfortable with a bit of physicality, especially since Liv was practically plastered to her.

"Sorry," Liv giggled. "Please continue." She could tell Kayla was trying to help keep her mind off the storm, and found it impossibly endearing.

Kayla's face went very serious as she closed her eyes, hearing her grandmother's words and feeling the weight of the past and family ties settle over her like a heavy cloak. "Since ancient times, my family has been persecuted because it was different...because of its abilities. And I'm not just talking about telepathy. A whole host of other paranormal powers runs strongly through my family." She opened her eyes and peered down at Liv. "If you find what I can do startling, can you imagine the powers my ancestors possessed, before time and travels had diluted our bloodline?"

Liv nodded, totally drawn in by the intense low voice and pale eyes that glinted with each flash of lightning. She thought briefly that the stories of sorcerers and wizards must have been based on people with the kind of abilities that ran in Kayla's family.

"Their abilities were seen as evil, a direct extension of whatever demonic power was the flavor of the month during that age. Several times throughout history, my line was nearly wiped from the face of the earth. They were hunted down and murdered, branded as criminals, insane, or followers of Satan." Kayla's words took on an angry edge. "They were seen as an affront to the gods or God, and considered a perversion of man's ordained nature. They were intolerably different and feared by those who knew their secrets."

Liv's chest constricted. Was this how Kayla saw herself? As a perversion? Her words from that morning came crashing back to her. *Oh, God, that's what I called her.* Her mind flashed to the memory of hurt blue eyes, and she felt her stomach twist again.

Kayla stopped speaking and tilted her head down to look at her companion. "Hey, are you okay?" she asked in a low concerned voice, alert eyes widening at the intense, almost angry look on Liv's face. "Liv?"

"There's nothing wrong with you!" Liv said savagely, as she convulsively grasped Kayla's shirt.

Kayla blinked. "Whoa, hey, calm down. You don't need to convince me."

"Kayla, I mean it. I—"

"It's okay, Liv. I know that. But...umm..." Unexpected tears pricked pale eyes. *But it's so good to hear you say it.* Kayla turned away from Liv, focusing on the rain that was pounding relentlessly against the wide picture window, trying to regain some measure of control. Her jaw worked for a moment. "I'm glad you think that," she whispered.

"I do."

Kayla smiled and tried to think of something to say. When she couldn't, she wrapped Liv in a heartfelt hug. This hugging thing was something she could see herself getting used to, very quickly.

Even before long arms had tightened to their full extent, the linguist was struck by the difference in the touch. This hug wasn't meant to comfort. It was one of pure affection, and it caused a light blush to work its way onto Liv's cheeks as her body and soul responded without conscious thought. She heard the clap of thunder that invaded the silence of the cavernous library, but this time it rolled over her. Liv's senses were otherwise engaged.

Soft blonde hair tickled Kayla's nose as she turned her head to the side and let her cheek rest on Liv's shoulder for just a second, before withdrawing with a soft sigh. "Well," Kayla's gaze dropped to their linked hands, which seemed to have a special affinity for finding their way back to each other again, "now that that's settled, I'll umm...keep going, okay?"

"Absolutely."

Kayla crossed her long legs at the ankles and shifted slightly. "At some point in history, we aren't sure exactly when, but it was well before the time of Christ, a sickness swept through the English countryside, killing thousands and decimating entire communities. For some reason, the illness didn't touch a single member of my family. Every one of them was spared, and in that season of sickness, the Reddings were able to work their crops and prosper. The superstitious local peasants saw that as definitive proof that the Reddings, although they didn't use that name in ancient times, were somehow behind the plague."

"You're kidding."

Kayla shrugged. "It was an excuse, I guess. A good reason to slaughter the lot of them. And they were very nearly successful. But somehow, a handful of people managed to survive.

"In the generations before the slaughter, our family embraced storytelling as a way to keep our traditions, and the collective experience of generations of men and women with paranormal abilities, alive. After the slaughter, it was decided that each generation would record its experiences, births, deaths, marriages, and the evolution of our powers in a family history. A diary, if you will. With so few remaining elders, they were worried too much would be lost by relaying the stories only through the spoken word."

"The writings survived?" Liv inquired doubtfully. "All this time?"

"No, not all of them. Around the time of Christ, a fire claimed almost half the existing histories. And more than three hundred years of histories were lost in the early thirteenth century, when the boat carrying them from England to Ireland sank off the coast of Wales. But since then, we've managed to take pretty good care of them. And considering how old some of them are, they're in pretty good condition."

"You've actually seen them?" Liv whispered in surprise.

Kayla smiled. Liv was gonna love this part. What linguist wouldn't? "You've seen them." Kayla spread her arms wide. "Look on the shelves around you."

Her eyes widened to an almost comical degree. "Oh, my God. These books here are the histories you're talking about?" Liv's gaze scoped the tall shelves loaded with dusty, leather-bound books of all colors, shapes, and sizes. At the very top, her eyes strained to recognize what she'd seen only once, during a museum field trip for a college ancient writings course...scroll cases. "You leave them sitting here in this old house?" she asked incredulously.

"No," Kayla laughed. "Well, I guess we do. But it's not as bad as you think. The house is protected, remember? They're perfectly safe here."

Liv scowled. Writings that old should be scientifically preserved, not gathering dust.

A dark eyebrow arched and Kayla leaned in towards her companion. "I don't want to burst your bubble or anything, but, umm...Papaw had them all copied onto CD-ROM before he died. Three thousand years of loving, fighting, and living have now been condensed into something that would fit in your purse and resides in a safety deposit box in downtown Washington, D.C." Kayla chuckled again. "Kind of takes the romance out of the story, don'cha think?"

"Not at all," Liv protested instantly. And it didn't. "This is fabulous." She craned her neck, trying to get a good look at the books on the shelves surrounding her, despite the darkness. "Damn storm," she mumbled, drawing an immediate grin from Kayla.

"Don't worry, you can look at them later. Spend as much time as you like. Although it might be easier with a little light."

"You'd actually let me look through them?"

It was time to show a little faith in her new friend. "Of course." Kayla grinned engagingly. "It's not like they're full of secret recipes for magic potions or anything." *Okay, maybe a few are.*

Liv was stunned. These documents had to be practically sacred to Kayla's family, or there was no way they would have survived wars, weather, and time itself — not for this long. The fact that Kayla had even told her about them indicated a level of trust that wasn't lost on Liv. "I don't know what to say." She let out an excited breath. "Thank you."

Liv's dark eyes continued to flicker around the room. All those lives. All those stories. "Do you know how rare writings from the time period you're describing are?" Liv's scholarly curiosity was brimming. There must be dozens of different dialects in the texts.

The glint of happy eyes caught her attention, and she smiled enthusiastically in response. "I guess you can tell I'm just a bit interested and dying to look at them."

"Just a bit," Kayla laughed, realizing that doing something nice for Liv felt better than she could have ever imagined. The excitement fairly radiated off her and was downright infectious, despite the reason Kayla was here.

"Most people couldn't even read or write then," Liv offered rapidly, caught up in her passion.

Kayla nodded, quietly agreeing. "Not all the histories were written by family members. For different reasons, sometimes people were paid to transcribe them. Exactly how they were prepared was up to the head of the household. There are no guidelines for their compilation. The only rule is that they must survive, and that responsibility rests on the guardian's shoulders. They protect the histories."

"And your Papaw named you as the guardian?" Liv hazarded. Kayla had said her abilities were stronger than the rest of her family. It made sense that she would have the most compelling interest in the lessons the histories undoubtedly contained. "No," Kayla said with a bitterness that surprised Liv. "Papaw didn't choose me. And I'm glad. Being the guardian is not a coveted position, Liv. It comes with certain family responsibilities that can be all-consuming. Papaw's role as guardian kept him on his island for nearly all of his adult life."

Liv's brow furrowed. "Why? If the histories are safe here, did he really need to be physically present to watch over them?" Liv was suddenly relieved Kayla hadn't been chosen as the guardian. The books were diaries of the past, and nothing in them could be worth sacrificing her friend's freedom or future. Family obligation be damned.

A dark head shook as Kayla's mood took another downward turn. "He wasn't here to watch over the histories. He was here to find a missing history, a very important missing history."

"How did he know it was missing?"

Kayla shrugged. "There was a gap between recorded generations."

Pale brows lifted and Liv cocked her head. "He spent a lifetime looking for a missing book? In this house?" She turned disbelieving eyes on her friend.

"As the guardian, it was his duty to maintain and preserve the histories. That's not something my family takes lightly," she shot back, a little defensively.

"Yeah, but a lifetime?"

A flash of blinding light exploded into the storm-darkened

room. Before the women could move, or even blink, there was an earsplitting crack and thunderous boom. A jagged, white bolt pierced the sky and exploded into the old wooden dock in front of the house. It shattered instantly, sending splinters of flaming wood high into the sky, which then plummeted into the crashing black waves.

This time it was Kayla who jumped. She sprang to her feet and stared down at what was left of the flaming dock. "Holy shit!"

Liv scrambled off the sofa and away from the window. A surge of anxiety welling within her, she felt herself begin to panic. Her heart hammered painfully in her chest as a cold sweat broke out across flushed skin.

At the sound of Liv's whimpering, Kayla spun around and found her huddled in the corner of the room. Her breathing hitched at the sight.

The shorter woman's eyes were darting wildly from wall to wall, searching desperately for a way to escape the storm. Her hands clutching ineffectually at the wooden shelves alongside her.

Kayla approached her much the same way she would a frightened animal. "It's okay; we're safe in the house, remember?" she reminded softly, slowly making her way to the hysterical woman.

"No! You can't know that! There are no such things as spells!" Liv's hands flew to ears. She tucked her chin to her chest as another loud clap boomed out.

Kayla had never felt so helpless in her life. Liv looked as though she was ready to bolt from the room, even though there was no place for her to go. She clenched her jaw in frustration and tried to speak in her calmest, most comforting voice. "You need to believe me," Kayla urged patiently. "I know it seems impossible, but it isn't. Trust me." *You can trust me.*

Dilated eyes, full of fear, focused on Kayla's sincere gaze. "Do..." Liv paused, trying to calm down, sounding frantic even to her own ears. "Do you swear?"

"I swear." The reassurance was unwavering, coming without the slightest pause or hesitation, and backed by a wave of confidence sent from one heart to the other.

Kayla's conviction gave Liv no choice but to believe. Slowly, she uncurled from her crouched position, reaching for the strong hand that was offered as Kayla leaned forward. Tears collected in pale lashes, and Liv began to cry helplessly—partly in relief over Kayla's reassurance and partly because of an odd sense of embarrassment. She didn't like looking weak or needy in front of Kayla. And Liv knew that was exactly how she looked, curled up in the corner of the room, hiding from lightning like a frightened child.

Kayla pulled her into her arms without thought. Any self-consciousness about this type of physical contact between them had simply disappeared. Comfort was freely offered and just as freely accepted, as Liv drew from Kayla's strength.

Kayla crooned softly into the pink ear alongside her lips, willing Liv's fear away. Finally, after several moments, Kayla could feel the pounding of Liv's thundering heartbeat against her chest begin to calm, and the linguist's death-grip on the back of her T-shirt relax, even as the storm's fury continued to pound the house.

Kayla gently pried Liv from her, maintaining physical contact but at arm's length, so she could examine her tear-stained face. "Are you okay?" *Duh. Does she look okay, dumbass?*

"Not really," Liv answered honestly, not bothering to hide exactly how she was feeling. "I feel relieved, but stupid and pathetic at the same time."

"Don't." It was a simple request that tugged at Liv's heart.

"Okay." Liv let out a shuddering breath. "I'll try."

With a quick nod, Kayla grasped Liv's hand and led her out of the room and toward the stairs. While she couldn't help Liv escape the storm completely, she didn't need to subject her to a panoramic view of the angry sky. Kayla cursed herself for not thinking of that sooner.

"Where...where are we going?" Liv asked, wiping her eyes with the back of her hand, suddenly feeling very weary.

"We're going to start searching for the lost history. It's the main reason I'm here, to be honest."

Liv sniffed, but didn't object to Kayla's idea. They had nothing but time to kill until the kids could make it back to the island with the boat. "What makes you think we'll find it if your Papaw spent a lifetime searching and was never successful?" Liv flinched as another flash of bright light lit up the stairs in front of her, a crackling hiss right on its heels. She felt the squeeze of Kayla's hand as the sound faded away, replaced by the howl of the wind and unrelenting hammering of the rain.

"Because I'm guessing Papaw never knew about the secret passageway we found this morning. It has to be there. Every other inch of the house has been scoured."

Liv stopped mid-step, causing Kayla, who was leading her by the hand, to jerk backwards and stumble back to the step occupied by Liv.

"Ah...Kayla, I umm, I know what I said earlier. But I, uh..." She fidgeted worriedly. "I don't think I want to go searching around that dark passage." *God, I'm such a chickenshit. Give me a snake-filled jungle any day. Tribal wars — no problem. But one nasty summer storm, and I fall apart like the goddamned 'House of Usher.' Oh, that was a bad,*

bad thought.

"Look," Kayla's face was compassionate but deadly serious, "there won't be any windows, so you won't see the lightning. And these old walls are so thick, I doubt you'll even know there's a storm going on." She smiled mischievously. "C'mon, Liv. Aren't you the least bit curious? Where's your sense of adventure?" she baited.

Liv closed her eyes in frustration. She wanted to help Kayla, and there was no denying that curiosity's teasing tendrils were licking at her soul. But she was still uncertain, her mind reeling from everything she'd been told and what she was learning about herself. Pushing aside her apprehension, she bit the bullet. "The sooner we find these papers, the sooner you can leave the island, right?"

Kayla nodded and answered Liv's unspoken question. "Right. We'll kill Marcy and Doug for making us worry, and then we'll find some peaceful time to get to know each other. I really want to do that." It was a promise.

"And you'll explain more about this spell, and why this missing history is so important?"

"Everything I know," Kayla swore, tilting her head and sending loose tresses cascading over broad shoulders. She lifted her eyebrows in entreaty as she moved to the step in front of Liv. "I could really use your help," she finally added softly, meaning it in a way she didn't understand yet.

And that did it.

Liv ran a determined hand through pale hair as her eyes fixed on a deep, icy blue. She was completely hooked, and she knew it. Her feet unfroze, and she moved alongside Kayla as they ascended the remaining stairs to the second floor. "Just because this is your family's creepy old house..." she teased, consciously allowing her anxiety to begin to drain away, "doesn't mean that you're in charge, or that I'm just a side-kick in this little adventure, ya know?" she informed, surprising herself. She blinked.

Never just a sidekick, Kayla's heart supplied without thought. "Yeah, but I'm much taller. I should be in charge," she bantered back with a grin.

"But I'm older." Liv protested with an answering smile, enjoying the juvenile banter.

"And you're bragging about that? Doug was saying you were pretty decrepit."

She playfully slapped Kayla's belly with the back of her hand, drawing a loud "ufff" from her companion as they rounded the corner and headed up to the third floor.

Chapter
Seven

Confessions

NERVOUS GRAY EYES surveyed the dingy motel room whose burnt orange and avocado color scheme was reminiscent of the decade before Marcy's birth. "Ewww," the girl complained, wrinkling her nose. Stating the obvious, she tugged her soaked cotton shirt away from her stomach, unsure what was rainwater and what was just plain sweat. "This place looks totally gross."

Doug nodded, poking his finger through a cigarette hole in the edge of the rusty-orange bedspread.

Marcy cringed as she moved around Doug toward what she assumed was the bathroom door, ignoring the squishing sounds her sneakers made on the worn carpet. "Don't touch that, Doug," the teen said disgustedly as she stuck her finger down her throat in a gagging motion, adding a few retching sounds just for effect. "God only knows the last time that was washed. Motels wash the sheets between each guest..." *at least I hope so*, "but not the bedspreads. I don't even want to think about what people have done on that recently."

The young man yanked his hand away from the bed as though it had been burned, vigorously wiping the potentially germ-infected finger against his denim shorts. "Good point," he muttered, scanning the room's meager furnishings, his eyes locking on an old black rotary phone on the nightstand between the beds. *We could call Marcy's folks. They'd know Kayla's cell phone number.*

Marcy disappeared into the bathroom as Doug sat heavily on the bed, deciding to ignore the disease risk. He rolled his eyes at the loud "boing" the bedsprings made as he shifted. He could insist they call Marcy's parents. He knew they should. Doug's gaze drifted back to the phone, then dropped to the floor. Knowing what he should do and actually having the nerve to do it, were clearly two *very* separate things.

Truth be known, Doug was far more afraid of what Liv would think, than of what Kayla would do. He'd spent two long, mostly lonely, years waiting for his sister to come home, living for the colorfully stamped letters addressed solely to him, and wondering what kept the person he loved most in the world, except for Marcy, so far away. Liv had only been back in the States a few weeks, and he'd already ruined his own plans. After this, assuming Kayla let him live, his sister wouldn't trust him again for a very long time. Not that he could blame her, but the thought still sucked.

Doug sighed and focused on the steady, rhythmic pounding of the rain. God, he hated disappointing Liv. Sure, he'd made lots of mistakes in the past; and once or twice in the last two years, Aunt Ruth had actually called Liv in Africa so she could talk to him and straighten him out about something. Usually just the sound of Liv's voice and a few gentle reminders mixed in with some good-natured sibling jibes were enough to ground Doug, reminding him that he wouldn't live with Aunt Ruth forever.

To make matters worse, a tiny, petty corner of his heart resented the fact that he cared so much what Liv thought of him, that he needed her to love him unconditionally. The young man frowned, allowing his thoughts to turn dark and his insecurities to enjoy free rein.

Liv always had so much confidence in him, even encouraged him to ask Marcy out on a date after he'd gone on and on about her in several of his letters. She'd supported him when he wanted to try out for the baseball and debate teams, even when Aunt Ruth had complained that he wouldn't stick with them. And he hadn't, of course. But Liv had said that wasn't the point. He should never be afraid to try new things. He didn't have to make a life-long commitment, just a reasonable effort. Liv had backed up her words with money, something Aunt Ruth easily understood and begrudgingly respected. It wasn't much, he knew; but it was enough that Aunt Ruth wasn't about to turn it down.

His aunt wasn't a bad person, just someone who was not cut out to be a parent. She tolerated his presence with a stoic sense of duty, cashing the monthly checks Liv sent for his care as though she were boarding a burdensome family pet. Simply put, it was Liv that supported Doug in every way. He groaned and, during a rare moment of teenage insight, wondered if the price of the airfare home, coupled with the fact that Liv was probably sending home most all of her already meager salary—for him—was what had kept her away for such long periods at a time.

He wanted to ask Liv if he could come and live with her again when he finished school. He only had one year to go. Maybe he could even take his GED or finish high school in Washington, D.C. But how was he going to convince her after this stunt? No, D.C. was farther away from Marcy. He could make it one more year with

Aunt Ruth. Then maybe they could all be together, like families were supposed to.

"Doug," Marcy moaned, interrupting the fair-haired teen's morose thoughts, the thin wooden door barely muffling her voice. "I don't think they cleaned this place since the last guests. I found a pair of tennis shoes in the shower."

"In the shower? Sorry," the boy chuckled miserably.

"It's not your fault," Marcy reminded him simply, already wishing she could take back what sounded like a complaint. Doug's ever increasing guilt over the worry he was undoubtedly causing Liv was eating away at her more than her own. She didn't need to add to it. "I'm just glad we're together, that's all," she reflected out loud as a powerful gust of wind rattled the bathroom window.

"Me, too." Doug reached down and pulled off the bedspread, tossing it into the corner of the room. Tentatively, he bent down and sniffed the sheets. They looked surprisingly fresh and carried with them the clean, if slightly institutional, scent of bleach. Satisfied that he wouldn't catch a dreaded disease from the bedding alone, he slipped off his wet T-shirt and tossed it on the floor alongside the bedspread. Moving to the second bed, he stripped its bedspread as Marcy's voice rang out from the bathroom again.

"I don't suppose there's an air conditioner in here?"

"Stupid question, Marcy."

"A fan, then?"

Doug peered over the edge of the bed. "Yup, there's a small one in the corner."

"Good. Here." Marcy's arm snaked out of the bathroom with a wad of wrinkled, wet, soapy smelling clothes clutched tightly in her hand. "Can you hang these to dry?"

Doug stood frozen, staring at the wet, naked arm, his mouth agape. *She's na...na...naked in there? Yes!* He had heard running water in the bathroom, but with the rain and wind, it hadn't registered to him that she was actually in the shower. Nude. In her birthday suit. Clothingless. Completely and totally without clothes.

"Doug?" Marcy's head popped out of the small bathroom; her wet, dark-red hair was slicked back, accentuating high cheekbones and a slender, long neck. But the rest of her body was hidden safely behind the door. "What's wrong?" Her gaze dropped to Doug's bare chest and a single eyebrow rose in a fair imitation of Kayla. Doug was slim but powerfully built, despite being an inch or so shorter than her 5'9" Marcy couldn't help but notice the young man had added considerable muscle since the last time she'd seen him in a similar state of undress, at the beach the summer before. She mentally praised his decision to take a part time job as a stable boy, the physical labor adding mass and definition to his naturally slender frame.

For a long, quiet moment each of them got lost in their thoughts, which were mostly lascivious. A loud clap of thunder boomed and the lights in the room flickered, snapping Marcy back to the present. She swallowed, suddenly feeling far more nervous than she'd been a moment before. "Do you want me to wash your clothes, too? Then we can dry them in front of the fan."

"Ahh...I uh..." Doug shifted onto his heels, his mind working a mile a minute. Any thoughts of guilt or sorrow were instantly wiped away as he tried to wrap his mind around the simple fact that his girlfriend was a few feet away from him...buck-naked. His mind derailed again.

"Doug, what is with you?" Marcy knew damn well what Doug was thinking, but enjoyed watching him squirm nonetheless. Her eyes fluttered closed as an unfamiliar surge of emotion washed over her. A warm, rich wave of Doug's desire flooded her senses, and she sucked in a surprised breath, trying to push down her panic. In just a few seconds it was over, leaving her so bewildered she wasn't sure whether she'd experienced it at all. She stared at Doug with wide eyes, but when she opened her mouth to say something, Marcy was interrupted by Doug's flustered voice.

"What was the question again?" he asked, recognizing the fiery heat in his own cheeks as a scarlet blush. The young man shook his head to clear it of his decidedly carnal mental wanderings. He was completely oblivious to Marcy's sudden turmoil.

Marcy smiled and allowed herself to be distracted by Doug. Whatever she had felt was over now. And it had been so unsettling, she found herself more than willing to push it out of her mind. "I asked if you'd like me to wash your clothes. I know how sticky and sweaty I was; that shower felt great, and now I'll be able to put on clean clothes."

Doug licked suddenly dry lips; he hadn't heard a word past "sticky and sweaty." "Oh, yeah." He focused on the droplets of water that had collected in the hollow of her throat. "You're sooo hot," he muttered dreamily. Marcy's indulgent chuckle drew his eyes back to her face. "I...um...I mean, I know you were hot," he corrected himself, embarrassed again.

"Marcy, um...what are you going to wear while your clothes are drying?" *Nothing! Nothing! If there is a God in heaven, then please let her say nothing.* So fervent was his mental chanting that he began to feel a little lightheaded and stumbled backwards on unsteady feet until he felt the cool sheets rub against the back of his knees. With a light groan, he flopped down gracelessly on the bed and stared at the textured white ceiling.

Marcy's chuckle became an outright laugh. She couldn't think of anything more flattering than having a boyfriend who thought she walked on water, and literally got weak in the knees just thinking about seeing her naked. She simply adored him. "Doug, I was planning on using towels or the sheets from one of the beds...before getting dressed again," she added firmly, making sure her meaning was crystal clear, even as her libido screamed otherwise.

And with that, Doug's commitment to atheism was restored.

LIV SAT ON Kayla's bed as the younger woman padded quietly over to an empty cloth backpack that was resting alongside a wide maple dresser. She watched with interested eyes as Kayla picked it up and carried it to one of the metal chests that she'd been so secretive about the day before. The redhead dropped to her knees in front of the chest and inserted a small metal key into its lock. With an almost inaudible "clack" the lock released, and sure hands pushed open the lid.

Liv was far enough away that in the dim light she couldn't see into the box. She resisted the urge to get off the bed and join Kayla on the floor. Liv was vaguely surprised that she felt she was sitting altogether too far away from the enigmatic woman, and was already missing the reassuring physical contact she'd received downstairs.

"Aren't you going to ask me what's inside?" Kayla prompted mischievously as she withdrew a black sack and unlaced its top. From the sack, she pulled out two large flashlights. Setting one on the floor next to her knee, she fumbled for a moment to find the other's switch, aided only by the brief flashes of lightning that illuminated the room. Then, with a click, everything was bathed in a soft, golden glow. She picked up the second light and tossed it over to Liv, who let it bounce several times on the bed's springy mattress before reaching for it.

The heavy flashlight was the size of a coffee can, and had several more knobs and gauges than Liv had ever seen on a flashlight before. Its lens was tinted an amber color. She looked at the high tech gadget for a moment before deciding to conserve her batteries. Kayla's provided more than enough light. "Jesus, Kayla, were you planning on spending a lot of time in the dark?" She motioned to the enormous light. Even though Kayla was facing away from her, she easily conjured the image of her friend's smirk as Kayla's head cocked slightly to the side while she continued to sort through the box.

"And, no," Liv continued, "I'm not going to ask what's in those boxes. Again," she emphasized. "The other times I asked, all I got from you was, nothing, nothing important, and my personal favorite, nothing to concern yourself about. If you had added, blondie, to the end of that response, I'd have been forced to smack you."

Liv could tell by the sudden slump of Kayla's shoulders that she didn't like having her own words thrown back at her. But she continued anyway, remembering how she'd felt when Kayla had dismissively brushed off her questions. She wondered why Kayla was offering the information so freely now. Kayla was a bundle of contradictions, at times startlingly open, and at other times infuriatingly closed-mouthed. "I may have been a little slow on the uptake, but eventually I did get the hint."

Kayla felt the sting of Liv's words and winced, not missing the echo of frustration and hurt in her voice. She'd been downright rude when it came to the boxes, and she knew it. It was nothing personal, she just didn't think explaining what was in the boxes, scant moments after meeting someone for the first time, was a good idea.

Once Kayla had gotten a good look at the island and house, she was more certain than ever that she'd made the right decision. Why freak Liv out and possibly ruin her trip? The island was scary enough on its own without encouraging people's imaginations to run wild. Of course, that was before she told Liv about her own abilities and the histories, before she explained what she was feeling, hoping against hope Liv wouldn't simply think she was a nutcase. Things were different now. *She* felt different now.

Kayla girded her mental loins but couldn't bring herself to turn around and face her companion. "I'm sorry for being such a first-class bitch," she flatly told Liv.

Liv's jaw dropped, not expecting the blunt admission or apology. "I never said —"

"I know you didn't. But I was. And I'm sorry. I didn't feel like explaining myself, so for some stupid reason I figured it was just better to avoid your questions." *And feel like shit for doing it.*

Liv leaned forward on the edge of the bed, resting her elbows on her knees as she eyed Kayla's back intently. "You don't have to explain yourself to me. I was just curious." *And interested in you and every little thing about you.*

"They contain the equipment I need for my job," Kayla said, ignoring Liv's previous statement and feeling very much like she needed to explain herself to the woman behind her. That had been another thing Kayla had avoided discussing, her profession. If she had it to do all over again, she'd be completely forthright with Liv. But since she couldn't turn back the clock, she decided full disclosure was the next best thing. Instinctively, she knew if she wanted to pursue a relationship with Liv, those soulful, compelling sea-green eyes would ask questions that she'd be powerless to ignore.

"Your job?" Two pale eyebrows shot skyward. "So you're finally going to tell me, huh?"

Kayla took a deep breath, exhaling slowly as she dug a few more items out of the metal chest and stuffed them into her backpack. "I'm a..." a deep breath, "private consultant, usually hired by individuals but occasionally by universities or corporations, especially real estate companies. I guess you could call me a researcher," she finished in a rush.

Liv smiled knowingly. She'd always figured that "private consultant" was secret code for unemployed. "And you research..." she left the sentence hanging, hoping to prod the other woman along. Verdant eyes were focused on Kayla expectantly, when a bright flash of light suddenly filled the room and Liv bent over, covering her ears, waiting for the boom that would surely follow.

Kayla glanced over her shoulder just as the earsplitting boom exploded over the house. She shot Liv a sympathetic look and tried her best to hurry. She stuffed the items she'd pulled from the metal box into the small backpack and strapped it behind her, cinching the straps with a sharp tug. "I research paranormal phenomena."

Liv scrunched her eyebrows together in thought. "You study psychics?"

"Not exactly." Kayla rose to her feet. "I'm not a parapsychologist. I'm more of a field researcher who focuses on the...spiritual aspect of things. I travel to where the paranormal activity is supposedly taking place, and try to determine if it's a hoax."

"And if it's not?"

"It always is." Kayla smiled weakly. "Almost."

A mischievous grin edged its way onto Liv's lips as Kayla's profession finally became clear. "You're a ghostbuster, aren't you?" she exclaimed delightedly.

Kayla's head sagged. *Shit. Not the song. Anything but that.* "Silly me. And here I thought you'd be afraid," she muttered sarcastically, shaking her head.

"I ain't afraid of no ghosts," Liv immediately shot back, mimicking the song perfectly. Then her smile slid from her face as she considered what she was actually saying. This was no joke or movie. This was real. "Wait. Oh, Christ! You're telling me that ghosts are *real* and in this house?"

Kayla watched helplessly as the color drained from Liv's face. "Liv—"

"Then, hell yes, I'm afraid of ghosts!" Liv suddenly exploded, surprising both herself and Kayla.

A slender eyebrow arched. "Gee, I wonder why I didn't want to tell you sooner?"

"You said this place wasn't haunted!" the blonde roared, ignoring Kayla's sassy remark. "Downstairs: you said a spell was different. Though why *that* comforts me I'll never know." Angry eyes darkened further. "You knew all along that something was wrong with this place, and you still let me bring Dougie here, knowing there might be danger?" Liv's fear had been fully swept away by anger.

"That is not true." Kayla immediately protested. "I would *never* endanger anyone intentionally. You seem to be forgetting that I brought my own sister along, too."

"Then why —"

"Liv," Kayla said in the calmest voice she could muster, "I wasn't sure what we'd encounter here. I only brought my equipment so I could check things out."

Liv covered her face with her hands and spoke between her fingers. "I cannot *believe* I'm asking this, but, are there ghosts here, or not?"

"After I left you on the porch last night, I did a little investigating: checked for pressure and temperature differences in several rooms, set up some photography equipment on the second floor, stuff like that. So far, I haven't found anything out of the ordinary."

Liv sat back down on the bed and wrapped her arms around herself in mute comfort, swaying slightly. "Oh, God. What if my dream last night wasn't a dream? What if some *thing* was touching me?" She shuddered, completely disgusted with herself because she had to admit that whatever it was had felt utterly fantastic.

Kayla was instantly at her side on the bed, grabbing both her hands and gently rubbing her thumbs across the soft skin of Liv's wrists. "No. It was just a dream. Nothing more."

Liv jerked her hands out of Kayla's. "How —" She stopped and swallowed hard. "How can you possibly know that?"

"Well...um..." Kayla was suddenly flustered. "I was in the middle of a very...ahh...arousing dream." Kayla winced at her babbling voice and the understatement of her own words, hoping the dim lighting would hide her blush, "before something woke me up. At the time, I thought it was something in my closet; but now I think it was just Doug in the hallway. I went to check out where I thought the noise was coming from and somehow I ended up in your closet. I...I guess you know the rest."

Liv closed her eyes for a moment, cursing her temper. She

reached out to retake Kayla's hands, which were nervously twisting the bedspread. "Kayla, what does that have to do with my dream?" she whispered softly, her fear and anger melting away as she began to focus on the uneasy woman next to her. She lightly gripped the larger hands in hers. "Were you dreaming about me?" Liv asked hopefully, unable to think of why else Kayla would look so mortally embarrassed. Her eyes, gone gray in the glow of the flashlight, dropped from Liv's. But the older woman gently grasped Kayla's chin and lifted her head, demanding eye contact once again.

"I'm not sure," Kayla admitted. "Were you dreaming about me?"

Now it was Liv's turn to be a bit embarrassed. "I'm not sure, either; but I think so," she offered bravely, voicing what Kayla was too afraid to say. "Were you feeling my dream? Or was it the same dream, and somehow we were both sharing it? Is that even possible?" Liv hadn't thought so. But obviously the simple truths she believed before coming to Cobb Island didn't seem to apply here.

"It's not an unheard of phenomenon," Kayla answered clinically, even as she remembered the overwhelming rush of desire and wellbeing that coursed through her during the dream. Unable to stop herself, she pulled Liv onto her lap and wrapped long arms around the linguist's back, tugging her tightly against her, until they were sitting nose-to-nose.

If Liv was surprised by the intimate contact, she didn't show it. Kayla's sudden movement had forced her to straddle her thighs or fall off the edge of the bed. And the resulting position was overtly sexual, sending a bolt of desire tearing through both women. Liv tilted her head forward until her lips were barely pressing against the tender skin on Kayla's throat. She took a deep breath of skin and clean perspiration and sandalwood, closing her eyes in pleasure. "That's the smell from my dream," she finally whispered dazedly, her words barely carrying over the sound of the howling wind.

Kayla's heart began to pump furiously when Liv's warm breath tickled her throat, causing goose bumps to chase up and down her spine. She nodded at the other woman's soft words, then fell backwards, taking Liv with her and twisting until Liv's shoulders met the soft bedspread and she was lying fully atop her. At that moment it didn't matter to Kayla if she'd shared Liv's dream or vice versa. She licked suddenly dry lips and sank into Liv, overwhelmed with the certainty that Liv was *meant* to be in her arms.

Liv moaned at the exquisite contact, keeping her eyes firmly closed and eagerly soaking in the sensation of Kayla's weight rooting her firmly to the bed. *This* was the feeling she remembered.

Kayla leaned forward until her lips were pressed softly against the tip of Liv's ear. "Tell me if this is what you remember, Liv," Kayla said huskily as she began whispering in hushed tones, describing the dream from the night before.

Liv let out a soft groan, a slow burn igniting between her legs as she heard the dream recounted in vivid detail, but from the perspective of the person whose tongue had bathed her in kisses and whose tender caresses had set her on fire.

When Kayla finished speaking, she placed a soft kiss on Liv's ear and started to pull away, knowing she'd gone further than she'd intended, and afraid if she stayed in her current position for another second, she wouldn't be able to stop herself from physically recreating the words she'd just spoken.

"Don't even *think* about moving yet," Liv said softly, threading her fingers through thick, dark-red locks and tugging Kayla's ear to her own lips. Liv wrapped her legs around Kayla's thighs, pulling Kayla's center to her own and feeling a tremor run through her before Kayla leaned into the intimate touch, giving up any pretense that this was something other than a mutual seduction.

By the time Liv finished her side of the story, both women were flushed and breathing raggedly. Reluctantly, Kayla began to pull back from Liv, and this time the other woman let her go. She wasn't sure whether she was disappointed or not.

"Yup," Kayla said taking in an enormous gulp of air. "I think we...er...experienced the same thing. I'm sorry," she apologized sheepishly, feeling a trickle of sweat drip down her belly. "That...I mean, I got sort of out of hand."

Kayla's hands were shaking under the weight of her own arousal, but she recognized that neither of them was ready for things to go any further. Kayla wanted more than bed sports with Liv, and that would take time. But she also knew that if Liv so much as crooked her little finger, it would take a crowbar to pry them apart.

Liv could only nod, turning her head away from Kayla. One deep look into dilated eyes, and she knew she'd be tearing Kayla's clothes off. She couldn't remember the last time she'd been this aroused. "It's okay," she finally breathed roughly. "I um...I sort of held you down while I was talking. I'm sorry, too."

Kayla sat up and put a respectable distance between herself and Liv, trying to remember why it was a bad idea to sleep with people you'd just met. "Did you hear me complaining?" she snorted.

Liv moved to the edge of the bed and threw her feet over the side as she sat up. "No." She smiled and ran an unsteady hand through her hair with one hand, and fanned herself with the other.

Kayla grinned broadly, inordinately pleased by the gesture.

Liv stuck her tongue out in response to Kayla's smug smile. "I guess I didn't." Kayla's hand found its way to her knee and Liv grasped it tightly, lifting her eyebrows in question. "Let's continue this...conversation after we know each other a little better, okay?"

Kayla's head bobbed vigorously. "Soon."

Liv let out a frustrated breath as she pushed herself up onto unsteady feet. "Verrry soon."

Chapter
Eight

Secret Places

"HOW COULD ALL this be here with nobody knowing about it?" Liv asked, shining her flashlight into an empty room — investigating every corner and crevice, the floor, and even the ceiling — before stepping back into the hallway and shaking her head at Kayla, who was right on her heels. Silently they resumed their trek forward.

Liv and Kayla had been in the passageway for hours, exploring room after room — each one an oddity of architecture. Some were no larger than a walk-in closet and perfectly square, while others were long and narrow with sloping ceilings, curved walls, and multiple entrances which only led to more rooms and corridors. The only thing the unique spaces appeared to have in common was that they were all hidden between, below, and behind the regular living areas of the home.

As Kayla had suspected, other than the occasional, distant scampering of rats' paws against the hardwood floors, it was deathly quiet in these secret spots. The storm outside had been easily forgotten once the women began their exploration into the inky blackness.

By unspoken mutual consent, they remained together in the same room, or very near to it, at all times, searching the cobweb covered shelves, tables, and bureaus that filled the sometimes-furnished, windowless rooms and nooks.

"It's a house within a house," Liv whispered reverently, continually astonished at what she found around every corner and up or down each staircase.

The air was stagnant, heavy with dust and the scent of damp, rotting wood; the sweltering heat was oppressive as they ventured deeper into the maze. Liv sneezed for the hundredth time, and Kayla wordlessly passed her a large bottle of lukewarm water that she retrieved from her backpack. The blonde took a deep, satisfying drink, wiping an errant drop from her chin with her fingers and shaking off the droplets with a flick of her wrist. "Thanks," she muttered gratefully as she handed the bottle back, allowing her damp fingertips to linger against Kayla's for a timeless second before her gaze dropped bashfully.

Utterly charmed by the shy gesture, Kayla grinned, her white teeth glittering even in the dull glow of the flashlight. She ran the tip of her tongue along the roof of her mouth. Absently deciding it felt like lamb's wool, she followed Liv's example and took a healthy swig from the bottle before sliding it back into her pack. "My pleasure," she replied as her mind shifted away from the attractive woman at her side to business. Family business.

As they reached the end of the hallway, Kayla stopped unexpectedly, sending Liv crashing into her back. "You'll do anything to touch me, won't you, Liv?" Kayla bantered. She pushed open a heavy door, and its creaky hinges protested loudly as it swung open.

Duh. Yes. "Umm..." Liv laughed, unable to think of a lie to cover the truth. After a few flustered seconds, she just gave up. "No comment."

Kayla shone her light through a curtain of tangled spider webs and onto a small four-poster bed, whose dust-laden, pale canopy hung in tattered ruins around the tall, dark-wooden posts.

"Pffftt. Pffftt." Liv spat dryly, trying to dislodge a gauzy mass of web that had managed to stick to her lips as she entered the room alongside Kayla. "God, that's gross."

Kayla's gaze flickered from wall to wall. "It looks like a regular bedroom."

"In Norman Bates' house, maybe," Liv said as her fingers frantically brushed her mouth, her disgust reflected on her face.

Liv spun in a circle, quickly scanning the room to make sure it didn't contain something unexpected and otherworldly, or something expected, but with beady black eyes and a slender long tail. "Kayla, why would anyone do this?"

The tall woman sighed as she tried to tug open a drawer in a short oak dresser next to the head of the bed. "Sometimes members of my family can be a little...umm..." she searched for the exact word she wanted.

"Eccentric?"

"I was actually thinking wacko." She gritted her teeth while doing her best to try to slide the drawer out gently. "But your word will work, too." Kayla ran her fingertips around the edge of the drawer. "Dammit, the wood must be swollen." She placed her flashlight on the dresser's top. "Shit!" Kayla cursed, a furious tug sending the flashlight tumbling off the dresser top as the drawer handle broke off in her hand.

Kayla blinked at Liv, who had caught the flashlight with a lunging grab. "You've got quite some reflexes." *And a lot more than that. I'll bet you're one of those people who is good at everything.*

The blonde shrugged self-deprecatingly, but smiled anyway. "Not really. I figured that was going to happen. I was just waiting for you to get angry enough," she teased.

Dark brows drew together in a mock scowl. "It seems you already think you know me, Ms. Hazelwood."

Do I? Liv's smile broadened. *Maybe.*

"Why don't you look around the rest of the room, while I keep fiddling with this?"

"Kayla, why are *you* here at all?" It was the one question that Kayla still hadn't answered. Even after explaining all she knew about the spell, which wasn't much. Liv began to wonder what was fact and what was simply local or family lore. "You said your Papaw appointed someone else as guardian of the histories." Liv sneezed violently. "Shouldn't that poor bastard be here going through these rooms instead of you?"

Kayla's eyes flashed as her ire rose. "That poor bastard is Marcy, and I won't let her waste her life looking for the details of somebody else's," she hissed, not giving a tinker's damn what Papaw's will had decreed. Angrily, she yanked on another drawer, which was also stuck.

Liv winced. *Aww, shit.* "I'm sorry." She laid her hand on Kayla's back, feeling perspiration through the white T-shirt. "I didn't mean to sound so...callous. I'm just really tired." Her stomach rumbled on cue. "And hungry." *When I get hungry, I get mean as a junkyard dog. Remember this is her family, not fiction.*

"It's okay," Kayla answered softly, straightening and dropping her hands from the dresser. "Papaw let finding the missing history become an obsession. I don't want Marcy falling into that trap. The documents from the 1700s hint that my family's powers ran very strong during the mid and late 1600s. And I've already learned so many important lessons about controlling my ability from reading the histories. Who knows what information would be forever lost if we don't find those documents? It's important to my family and me. We just have to find it, okay?"

Liv nodded, not missing the hint of worry and desperation threading Kayla's voice. "We will," she assured with a new sense of purpose. Once Liv could attach a face to a problem, she latched onto it with a vengeance. It was why she had spent so much more time in Africa than she'd originally intended. The soft, chocolate brown eyes of the children she taught demanded her attention in a way she was powerless to ignore...at least until it seemed that Doug needed her more. *I wonder what that little bugger is doing now. Shit.*

Scratch that. I don't want to think about that. He's probably having the time of his life and hasn't given Kayla and me a second thought. He'd better be okay so I can wring his neck.

Kayla shrugged off her backpack, allowing it to hit the floor with a loud thump, sending a cloud of dust billowing gently around it. "Let's take a break," she suggested dejectedly as she dug into her pocket. *We both need a break. My eyes hurt, and she's tired. Even in the shadows, I can see dark circles under those pretty green eyes.*

This was the final room in this corridor, and so far they hadn't found one thing relevant to their search. Kayla fought the urge to explode on the spot. The history had to be here somewhere. Didn't it?

"Great idea," Liv moaned, closing her eyes as the previous night's lack of restful sleep came back to haunt her. Even through her closed eyelids, however, Liv could tell that the lighting in the room had changed. When she opened her eyes, she found that the room was bathed in a softer, more muted glow.

Kayla had shut off her flashlight and was busy lighting the candles that dotted the furniture around the room.

She must have refilled her lighter, Liv thought idly as she watched Kayla move, her thick, wine-colored hair taking on a nearly black tint in the candlelight. *God, how can someone so smart and funny be so beautiful, too?*

Kayla broke off the tip of a wick of another candle, cutting away some of the golden beeswax with a small Swiss Army knife. "Why don't you reach into the side pouch of my pack. I've got a couple of trail bars and some raisins, I think. Grab the water, too, okay?"

Liv nodded, wondering if she should turn off her flashlight too, now that the room was lit with several brightly burning candles. *This bad-boy must take a dozen batteries.* The candlelight gave the room a different, homier feeling. But Liv still shivered as she thought about spending significant time someplace without windows. *No way. I'd go mad; I know it.*

"There." Kayla gave a satisfied nod as she collapsed her knife's small but razor sharp blade and slid it into her pocket. Several long strides later, and she was back at the foot of the small four-poster bed. Her brows drew together in thought.

"Umm...these are really good," Liv mumbled, enjoying the tangy flavor of dried raspberry, not waiting for Kayla as she dug into one of the trail bars and took an enormous bite.

"Thanks. Granny makes 'em," Kayla replied absently. "I didn't know how long we'd be looking around in here, and I hate skipping meals." She yanked off the faded comforter and sheet and tossed them to the floor. Then she pulled off the bottom sheet and draped it over a two-cushioned, crushed velvet loveseat that sat kitty-corner to the bed. "Now we won't have to sit in a pile of dust and spider webs. C'mon." She motioned for Liv to join her as she sat down heavily, her mind already replaying the steps of their search. *Where are you? Are you really lost...or hidden?*

"Why Marcy?" Liv asked after a few moments of peaceful chewing, as much to fill the silence as to know the answer.

"Hmm?"

"Why Marcy as the guardian? She's just a kid."

"Mmm..." Kayla's face creased into a frown. "Usually the person in the family whose abilities run the strongest is appointed as guardian."

"And that would be you, right?"

Kayla took Liv's flashlight out of her hand and clicked it off. "Batteries," was all she said by way of an explanation. "That's kind of a hard question to answer. But to make a long story short—Marcy seems to have all the abilities that I do. She just doesn't recognize or use them."

"Like me?" Liv still found it nearly impossible to believe that she could have paranormal powers and be unaware of them.

Kayla nodded, looking over at Liv as though she wanted to say more, but stopping herself even as the words sat poised on her tongue.

Liv rolled her eyes as a wave of frustration passed over her. *Damn, how can I be falling in love with someone who doesn't talk?* She blinked. Twice. *Whoa. I can't be falling in love with her. Too soon.* Liv dismissed the ridiculous thought, but immediately faltered. *Isn't it?*

Then Kayla began again, pushing past her natural reluctance, completely unaware of the frantic thoughts whirling around in Liv's mind. "I...um...well, because of the telepathy thing, I didn't have a very easy time growing up. I trusted the wrong people with the information." She paused and swallowed around the sudden lump that had formed in her throat.

Liv's chest constricted. "And it made things pretty rough for you," she ventured, already guessing the answer and wishing she could turn back the hands of time, her heart reaching out to that little girl.

"Yeah, I guess you could say that." Kayla smiled weakly, sensing not pity but support coming from her new friend.

Anger, almost completely foreign in its intensity, welled up within Liv. She would have stood by Kayla no matter what. Always. *We should have met each other sooner, Kayla. There were so many times we both could have used a friend. We could have been there for each other.*

"My dad's abilities are on the very low end of the scale, and being an only child, he'd never seen someone grow up with my talents. He didn't raise me to hide what I had, thinking that in today's modern world people would be able to handle...me being different." Kayla stopped eating her trail bar. Her hunger had all but evaporated. "He was so wrong," she said flatly, having long ago gotten over the years of bitterness she felt toward her parents for not preparing her better, but not the sense of sadness over the lost years filled with rejection and confusion.

The Reddings had done the best they knew how. It wasn't until she was an adult herself that she realized that they had given her all they had to give. That acceptance, however, didn't stem the tide of anger she felt toward the world in general for the simple rejection she'd endured. And it didn't help that by the time she was fourteen years old, she was nearly six feet tall and already doing college-level homework; her burgeoning attraction to women only added to her feelings of confusion and isolation. "I guess my folks learned from their mistakes with me, and when Marcy started showing all the signs that I had, they did everything they could to hamper it, hide it, or make it seem so natural that she wouldn't call attention to it because she didn't even know it was happening. Paranormal abilities are like any other abilities, Liv. It's only when they're cultivated that they reach their maximum potential."

"You're worried that the missing history will contain information Marcy might need someday...to understand her own powers?" Liv ventured, starting to understand what was at stake with the search. "And you approve of this —" her hands gestured wildly, casting long moving shadows on the far wall, "deception?"

"No. But the choice wasn't up to me. And it was made out of love."

Liv sighed, not liking the idea that Marcy was basically being kept in the dark about her own nature. "How did your Papaw know about her?"

Kayla shrugged. "He just knew. The way she'll know who to appoint when the time is right. That's always been the way." Kayla's throat constricted with her next words. "His letter warned me that Marcy would be *very* powerful someday, and that she had to be prepared."

Liv's eyes widened. "Warned?" *Her powers might be dangerous? To herself or others?*

Kayla nodded, feeling a headache coming on. She didn't want to go into the long line of family members who had horribly abused their abilities, most ending in self-ruin. *No matter what, Marcy would never turn out that way, would she?* Even if they didn't find the history, Kayla vowed to keep that from happening.

Liv broke off a bit of her bar and offered it to her friend, easily sensing that this particular conversation was over. At least for now. "Eat a little, okay?" she directed in a soothing tone.

Kayla smiled and bent down, gently taking the offering from Liv's fingertips with her mouth, enjoying the immediate blush that shot up Liv's cheeks as her teeth softly raked across tasty fingertips.

Liv giggled nervously, her heart pounding a mile a minute. "One minute you're upset about a traumatic childhood and your sister's future, and the very next you're teasing me with your teeth and tongue." She shook her head, feeling the heat in her cheeks. "I don't get you."

"I never said I wasn't fucked up," Kayla protested dryly, drawing an outright laugh from Liv. "And you should talk. What you said to me about the dream. Jesus. And *now* you're blushing? Make up your mind, Liv. Are you a seductress or a Brownie?"

"Would you eat me either way?" *Oh, my God. I can't believe I said that.*

Kayla's jaw and trail bar dropped at the exact same second, both landing with a light thud.

"IT'S JUST ME, Marcy," Doug yelled loudly, the wind and rain pelting his back relentlessly.

Despite the vicious storm, hunger had driven the boy out in search of food. He insisted that Marcy lock the door behind him, but hadn't thought to bring along the room key. There was a small burger place about a quarter of a mile down the road from the motel and now he stood, armed with an incredibly soggy bag of cheeseburgers, waiting for Marcy to answer the door. He pounded again. "C'mon, Marse!"

Finally, the handle began to move in his hands and he backed up impatiently as the door swung open.

"What are you doing standing outside the door?" Marcy asked incredulously, her eyes running over his sodden form. "Why didn't you just knock?"

"I—" Doug stopped himself. *She just didn't hear me knocking. It's not her fault,* he told himself, trying to be mature about the fact that he'd be less wet if he were under water.

"Well, c'mon in, for God's sake," she drawled, giving his shirt a quick tug that nearly pulled the teenager off his feet. "Good thing I didn't bother drying my clothes, eh?" "Yeah, right, right. Did you get them?" Marcy questioned with all the patience of a strung-out addict.

Doug proudly held out the drenched bag. "I got 'em, we had enough money for five. But I had to skip the fries."

"Did you —"

"Remember extra pickles, no mustard, on two of them," the blond finished.

Marcy gave the sheet she was wearing a little tug up before roughly pulling Doug into a passionate kiss. "You're a prince, Doug," she said against his lips before yanking the bag out of his hands and greedily tearing at it, dumping its contents on the bed. She was oblivious to what her kiss and current state of undress had just done to Doug.

The teenager was starting to wonder if he was going to have to seek medical attention for his nearly continuous state of arousal. And did Marcy have to look so damn good in that sheet?

After taking a big bite of burger, not caring that they weren't hot anymore, Marcy mumbled, "These are sooo good." Her tongue snaked out and licked an errant drop of ketchup from the corner of her mouth.

Doug shifted uncomfortably and gave a long-suffering sigh, envying that ketchup in the worst way.

Suddenly Marcy stopped chewing. "Don't you want any?" She pointed at the sack she'd ripped apart like a ravenous beast.

I can do this. I can do this, he told himself as he moved over alongside Marcy, wondering whether he should sit down on the bed in his wet clothes. When Marcy scooted over to make a spot for him, she shifted her legs, and the sheet wrapped around her parted, exposing a long expanse of very naked thigh. *Have mercy!* Doug's brain began to short circuit. "I'll be back in a minute," he called over his shoulder as he bolted out of the door and into the night.

"What just happened?" a wide-eyed Marcy asked, as the younger Hazelwood disappeared and the door slammed shut.

A MUFFLED BOOM shook the house. It was the first time the storm had made its presence known since Liv and Kayla had begun their search.

"Great. I love storms. I'm especially happy this one is still raging," Liv muttered sarcastically as she blew out a puff of hot air, trying to dislodge a drop of sweat that hung precariously from the tip of her nose. As much as she disliked the dank rooms off the passageway, Kayla was right about their insulation. She'd been able to completely forget about the lightning, until now, which allowed her to focus on the search rather than her fears.

"Dammit all to hell!" Kayla seethed, slamming the door behind them as they left the very last room they could find to explore. After all these hours of searching, they'd come up empty handed. "It's not here." *It has to be.*

Liv studied her companion with a growing sense of unease. *She's starting to panic.*

As their exploration had progressed, Kayla's worry had mounted. She'd literally ripped apart the last few rooms they'd searched.

Liv laid a calming hand on Kayla's shoulder. "We should go back to the room where we ate the travel bars and break open that dresser. It's the only thing left we haven't checked."

Kayla nodded. "I know. I just hope I can remember the way back."

Liv cocked her head to the side, bringing up her flashlight and shining it directly into Kayla's eyes. Her voice was a low, menacing growl. "What do you mean *hope*?" *You'd better know the way out of here. I've been following you for hours assuming you knew what you were doing, Ms. Ghostbuster.*

Kayla's hands shot up to block the painfully bright light. "Stop it. Damn." She craned her head to the side, trying to look at Liv out of the corner of her eyes. "I know how to get us outta here. Relax and move the light, will ya?" The researcher pushed on Liv's arms until she lowered the beam. "I said I was concerned with finding my way back to that *particular* room, not out of the passageway completely. I'm not worried about that." *Damn. And I thought I had a temper.*

"I think the room is down this way," Liv pointed to a narrow corridor that veered off towards the left.

Two dark eyebrows edged upward. "I think you're right." *She's better at this than she realizes. We've been traveling around this maze for hours, and she knew which way we needed to go. She doesn't need my help at all.* "After you, Sherlock," Kayla teased, gesturing Liv forward.

Despite the circumstances of this search, Kayla found herself very much enjoying the time with Liv. She hadn't realized before tonight how much she'd missed pleasant company and easy companionship. How could she? She'd never really had them before. Even moving from country to country and going from job to job hadn't been able to maintain her interest and fill the void that was meant to be occupied by a flesh-and-blood person, a friend. More than a friend. A partner.

But tonight, she found herself unconsciously turning to Liv to remark on something interesting she'd seen in a drawer or on a table; anxiously awaiting Liv's insightful comments or youthful laugh, as though she'd been doing it all her life. They were inconsequential things, really, but it was still nice to share them with someone. Liv would stop whatever she was doing and join her to discuss the find as though she was *truly* interested.

Liv's curiosity and natural interest seemed to rival Kayla's own, and several times she'd found herself in the unusual role of storyteller, regaling Liv with several of her more fascinating adventures. It was natural in an easy sort of way that made Kayla question the direction her life had taken and the priority she'd placed on friendship and love.

Kayla tripped over her feet, landing face down in the middle of the hallway. *What did I just think?*

"Hey, are you okay?" Liv dropped to her knees, tucking a strand of pale hair behind her ear and scanning Kayla for visible injuries. "That had to hurt," she pointed out, wincing sympathetically.

"Yeah. I'm fine." Kayla swatted away Liv's seeking hands, trying to salvage as much dignity as was possible, considering she was sprawled out on her belly like a drunk.

"Let me help you."

"No."

Liv immediately backed away at the sharp tone. "I mean, no thanks." *Shit!* Kayla stood up, flinching as she bent her bruised left knee. She dusted herself off, shooting Liv an apologetic smile. "Sorry," she mumbled.

Liv nodded mutely, fully understanding Kayla's embarrassment but still finding it nearly impossible to stand idly by as Kayla struggled to her feet. She didn't miss her friend's faint groan as Kayla straightened.

Resuming their trek, Kayla moved down the hall with a pronounced limp, then turned to go down a different corridor. But Liv laid a gentle hand on her arm to stop her.

"It's this way." Liv shone her light farther down the hallway.

"But—"

"Trust me."

Kayla's mouth snapped shut. *Not a sidekick. Sometimes you just have to follow.* The unexpected words echoed faintly in her head. "Lead on."

"Here." Liv poked her head into the room that smelled faintly of smoke and beeswax.

"Wow. I'm impressed." Kayla walked past the blonde, relighting several of the candles.

Her eyes twinkled at the sincere compliment. "Don't be," Liv insisted with a small grin, proud of herself despite her protest to the contrary. "How are we going to get it open?" she asked, tilting her chin towards the dresser and setting her flashlight down on a table. She focused its beam on their target.

Kayla dropped her backpack on the floor in front of the short wooden dresser, glaring at it all the while. "I'm going to smash it to bits," she announced plainly.

Liv flinched. "Are you serious?"

"Very."

"Want some help?"

"Always."

"Isn't this the room that had the—"

"Umm. Hmm." Kayla agreed, already moving to a small closet where they'd discovered a pair of rotted, black leather boots and a rusty, pitted sword earlier that evening. She'd wanted to take the sword with her, but Liv had convinced her that it wouldn't be going anywhere and that there was no use traipsing around with something so awkward.

Kayla wrapped her hand around the hilt, whose tight leather bindings had crumbled away, her damp palm slipping a bit as it slid against the warm metal. Blade in hand, she stepped out of the closet to face Liv, silhouetted by the golden candlelight.

Liv's breathing froze as she took in the powerful sight before her. Her heart lurched, and a curious feeling of déjà vu prickled her senses. A vision of Kayla in a dripping wet cloak, holding a sword that morphed into a silver dagger flashed through her mind, as a wave of both security and sadness washed over her.

Without thought, Kayla released the blade, sending it clattering to the floor with a puff of dust. "What's wrong?" she breathed, wholly unnerved. The look on Liv's face when she'd faced her with the blade had been a frightening mix of affection, pain, and relief that rocked Kayla to her core.

"I...um..." Liv backed away a step. "I don't know." Confused eyes dropped from Kayla's. When she'd seen the sword earlier, she'd felt a gnawing in her guts that made her want to walk out of the room and never come back. But this...this was different. Seeing the blade tightly gripped in Kayla's hand had sent her mind reeling.

Kayla's back went ramrod straight. She turned bewildered eyes on Liv. "You're afraid of me, aren't you?" It was her worst fear, and the look in Liv's eyes mirrored it. *Who wouldn't be afraid of a freak?*

"No," Liv protested instantly. "I just...I..." she babbled, trying to think of a way to explain what she herself didn't understand. "I just felt strange for a moment there. It wasn't anything you did." She smiled weakly and began to walk towards Kayla, her voice soothing and calm. "I wasn't afraid you'd hurt me. I knew you were going for the sword. I think somehow I was just surprised to see you holding it."

The churning in Kayla's stomach eased a little with Liv's words. "Let's get out of here and go get some coffee. I can come back with an axe or hatchet or something tomorrow. Like you said before, nothing's going anywhere."

"No." Liv shook her head emphatically. *I'm sorry, I hurt you. Forgive me.* "We came to find the history, and we will. It's the only place left to look." *I know how important this is to you.*

Dark-red eyebrows lifted in question.

"I'm sure."

Kayla bent to retrieve the sword, but Liv beat her to it. "Let me," she said firmly as she grasped the sweat-slicked hilt, vaguely surprised by the long weapon's weight.

Before Kayla could utter a word of protest, Liv was standing in front of the dresser, her knees bent and legs placed shoulder width apart. She leaned back slightly as she swung the blade in a wide arc, shoulder muscles shifting under her soft T-shirt, the rusted blade gaining momentum with every inch. Then the sword was speeding toward the corner of the dresser top as Liv threw her back muscles into the swing. It struck with a thundering crack that echoed through the silence of the secret rooms and sent a shower of splinters skittering across the wooden floor. The corroded blade simply disintegrated in Liv's hand.

Kayla stood speechless, mouth open in wide-eyed astonishment. "Holy shit!" she finally exclaimed.

"Wow," was all Liv could think to say. She didn't think the time-dulled edge would do much more than gouge the old piece of furniture. Instead, in a single vicious stroke, the dresser had been reduced to a pile of planks and splinters. And the blade was now a chunky heap of steel shards and rust.

Shaking her head, Kayla stared down at the messy pile and laughed, "I guess it was more rickety than we thought. Still..." She flashed Liv a crooked grin as she sat down, flinching at the sharp pain that lanced through her bruised knee. She began digging through the rubble. "Remind me never to piss you off."

"Just remember that, Ghostbuster."

"Brat."

The tip of a pink tongue was Liv's response.

Kayla's attention was drawn back to her task when searching fingertips brushed against something cool and silky. With a tug, a remarkably well-preserved, scarlet silk bag partially emerged from chunks of wood. *Please. Please. Please. Just let this be it.*

Tossing what was left of the sword aside, Liv dropped to her knees alongside Kayla, tugging an errant lock of blonde hair behind her ear with an impatient hand, in a motion that Kayla already recognized as a nervous habit. With the back of her other hand, Liv pushed sweaty bangs out of excited green eyes. "Well, what is it? Please tell me we didn't search half the afternoon and evening only to find somebody's ancient Victoria's Secret stash."

Despite her pounding heart, Kayla let out a burst of laughter. Eager hands pulled the large sack free from the remains of the dresser. "It's a book, I think," Kayla said, hoping her words could make it true even as a slender rectangular shape became visible through the folds of the soft crimson material.

As she pulled the book from the cool silk bag, Liv scrambled over to retrieve the flashlight she'd set down earlier. "Well?" She shone the light onto the book's russet-colored, deeply tooled cover.

Long fingers traced a large picture that was carved into the leather. Kayla's touch glided over a massive oak tree, whose trunk was circled by a wicked looking, fang-bearing snake. Their eyes squinted, taking in the exquisite detail. Discreetly hidden in the tree's branches were all manner of weapons: swords, staffs, battle axes, lances, daggers, maces and bows.

"Knowledge is power?" Liv wondered aloud, marveling at the intricate work, and recognizing the scrolling pattern that adorned the book's edges as the one etched into Kayla's lighter.

"That's one interpretation," Kayla agreed, continuously impressed by Liv's intuition. Rubbing tired, stinging eyes, she slid a pair of dark-framed glasses out of a side pouch of her backpack and slipped them on. The researcher was so immersed in the book's cover that she forgot to be self-conscious about wearing them.

A small smile crossed Liv's lips. *I knew she'd look great in those.* It was on the tip of her tongue to say so, but she decided against drawing attention to the fact that this was the first time Kayla had worn them since they met.

Kayla adjusted the book so that both women had a good view of its cover. "The tree represents my family line, its many branches — knowledge gained through the ages. The snake that protects the tree is the Guardian. And the weapons are power and strength, and a willingness to fight for the tree."

"Fascinating." Liv spared a second to consider her family's legacies: varicose veins, shortness, an unnatural fondness for Scotch, and an unerring talent for getting into all kinds of trouble. "Is it a family crest?"

A dark head shook. "Nope. It only adorns the histories."

Liv smiled hopefully, her excitement making her appear to light up from within. "This is it, then?"

"Yeah," Kayla let out a long, slow breath as she pointed to the date and name carved neatly into the book's heavy binding.

Redding 1691

Kayla's eyes twinkled in the darkness. "This is it."

Chapter
Nine

Once Upon A Time

"THANK GOD, YOU'RE okay. I was worried about you," Marcy chastised seriously. "Where'd you go?" The dark-haired sixteen-year-old grabbed a towel and began vigorously drying Doug's short, waterlogged curls.

Doug felt like a spoiled puppy getting a bath, and gleefully leaned in to the touch. "I um...well, I remembered seeing a rack of movies at the check-in desk, and I thought I'd go check them out."

It had been either leave the room at that very moment or face the real possibility of spontaneous combustion. His tactical retreat proved to be exceptionally effective. After bolting from the room, he stood in the middle of the parking lot letting the wind and rain pelt him mercilessly. But for some reason, that did nothing to end his agony. One look at the greasy motel clerk, however, and the raging beast that was his teenage sex-drive had whined piteously in surrender and crawled back into its cage.

"We don't have any money to rent movies," Marcy reminded, giving Doug's head a final pat.

"True. But when I asked that slimy desk clerk how much they were, he got really pissed. He was still watching those stupid stock car races on the TV." Doug smiled mischievously. "Then I proceeded to ask his opinion about every movie, and what he thought of all the actors." The young man shrugged one shoulder. "Finally, he got so sick of me, he told me to just take a couple and get out," Doug finished triumphantly, kicking his wet sneakers into the corner of the room.

"Cool." Marcy moved over to the stack of movies on the bed nearest to the wall. "What did you pick out?" She scanned the titles. *Rambo, Platoon, Lawnmower Man.* She looked up in horror and complained loudly, "Douuuggg. Was there a twenty-bucket-of-blood minimum when you made your choices?" Then she looked at the last title and gray eyes narrowed.

"What?" Doug gulped nervously. *Damn. Damn. Damn.* But he

couldn't resist. He'd always wanted to see it. When it first came out, he'd asked Liv, who laughed for ten minutes straight and announced that *she* wasn't old enough for that movie and that he'd have to wait for *many, many* more years before seeing it.

"You got *Show Girls*?" She made a disgusted face. "That's...that's just so..."

"Interesting?"

"Possibly," she admitted as she popped open the box and slid the cassette into the dusty VCR below the television.

KAYLA SAT ON the sofa in the library in a clean pair of thin cotton shorts and a blindingly white T-shirt. Her damp, freshly washed hair hung loosely down her shoulders and back, and she was blissfully barefoot. A coffee table had been pushed in front of the low sofa and her left leg was resting atop it, an emergency icepack soothing her swollen knee.

She'd wanted to dig into the history right there in the hidden rooms, but Liv had talked her into waiting until they were back to the regular living area of the house—where it only felt like the fourth level of hell instead of the seventh. Again, she'd wanted to start reading the history, but Liv had insisted they both needed a shower, a change of clothes, and some food.

Kayla hated to admit it, but Liv was right. They had been covered in dust and cobwebs, the scent of rotting wood clinging to their clothes and hair.

Liv poked her head into the library with a flickering candle in each hand. "I was wondering where you ran off to. Wow." She spun in a circle. Kayla had lit ten large candles and placed them around the room. "I guess these two will just be overkill, huh?" Liv placed them on an end table alongside the couch that overlooked the sea. A flicker of light flashed across the room from a distant bolt of lightning, but there was no accompanying thunder. While it was still raining fiercely, the worst part of the storm had moved west, taking most of the lightning and thunder with it.

Kayla's mouth moved, but no sound came out as she gawked at Liv. "No, no, no, no, no!" she said, shaking her head frantically. "You are not wearing that." With a hasty swallow, she lowered her volume. "Please." The single word came out as a pleading croak that caused Liv to burst out laughing, pale eyebrows standing out in vivid relief as a blush worked up her neck, settling in fair hair.

Liv grinned broadly. "C'mon, Kayla. It's sweltering in here." After her shower she'd changed into a thin, pale pink, cotton nightgown. While it wasn't exactly revealing, it was sleeveless and ended mid-thigh, fully showing off several of Liv's more flattering attributes.

"No, it's not." And it wasn't. Kayla had opened a side window and allowed the much cooler breeze to blow past the light curtains, bringing down the room's temperature.

Pale brows furrowed as Liv walked around the sofa and sat down next to Kayla. The linguist's eyes slid shut and she exhaled delightedly, feeling an almost cool breeze brush against her skin and disheveled damp hair as a gust rattled the open window's screen. "Umm," she purred. "You're right. This feels wonderful." She looked at Kayla seriously. "Do you really want me to change clothes?"

Hell no. "Well, it's...um...just that um...you're *really* distracting in that." A slender eyebrow quirked playfully. "Jesus, you're like some fresh-faced teenage virgin in that." She swallowed again and dropped her eyes. "So pretty..." Kayla trailed off sheepishly.

Liv laughed and felt her cheeks grow warm again at the sweet compliment. "Well, I'm hardly a teenager and...ah...the other part is private. But, um, listen, Kayla, I think you know I'm attracted to you, right?"

Kayla nodded. *God, I hope so.*

"And you seem to feel the same about me, right?"

Duh. A second nod.

"I just wanted to tell you that I'm not trying to be a tease. I was hot, and this was the coolest thing that I packed. I didn't even think about how it would look to someone else." She absently fingered a thin strip of ivory ribbon that ran along the nightgown's V-shaped neckline. "If it makes you uncomfortable, give me a minute, and I'll go put on something else." Without waiting for an answer, Liv leaned forward to get up, but was held back by a firm hand on her shoulder.

"No. It's okay." Kayla's fingertips drifted across warm, soft skin for just a second, before pulling away. "I just lost my head for a minute. I don't mind. Really."

"Good," Liv smiled. "So, how much have you read? I know there was no way you could wait for me to finish my shower." Liv reached down to the coffee table and grabbed one of the sandwiches Kayla had prepared while she was getting cleaned up. *Nothing like showering in the dark in this creepy old house.* She shivered inwardly. *I should have asked Kayla to join me. Oh, yeah.*

At the mention of the history, Kayla's good mood seemed to evaporate. "I can't read any of it." She pointed an accusing finger at the text. "It's not in English."

Liv stifled a laugh with the back of her hand, trying not to choke on her food. *Is she actually pouting?*

"It makes no sense. Except during ancient times, the histories have always, *always* been transcribed in English."

Liv reached for the book, careful not to bump into Kayla's knee. Then she settled back into the cushion with the history in her lap and took another bite of sandwich. "Mmm...phis is gfud."

"It's just deviled ham and cheese."

"Mmm. Still..." Liv handed the last bit of her sandwich to Kayla, who tucked it neatly in her mouth. "Okay, let's see what we have here." The blonde wiped her fingers and mouth on a paper napkin, then carefully opened the book, the room's multiple candles providing more than enough light to read by.

"Well?"

Liv studied the stiff, yellowed paper. "It's Arabic."

"Dammit. That's what I thought." Kayla sighed dejectedly. "I'm sure you can't read—"

"Oh, but I can." Her eyes twinkled. "Read Arabic, that is."

An excited smile creased Kayla's face, then shifted into a full-fledged frown when the silence in the room lengthened. "You can read the history?" she clarified, wondering if she'd misheard Liv.

"Umm. Hmm..."

Kayla tilted her chin down as she lifted her eyebrows meaningfully. *Well?* "Aren't you curious to see what it says?" *I know you are.*

Liv did her best to keep a straight face knowing she was killing Kayla and enjoying making her friend wait in a sadistic but funny sort of way. "Whadda ya give me in exchange for reading it?"

Eyebrows rose even higher. "I have to give you something?" she asked incredulously.

Liv nodded slowly. "Umm. Hmm..." *I. Will. Not. Laugh.*

"But—" Then she caught the glint in teasing eyes. *Oh, I get it. This is a game of let's torture the...*she sighed mentally*...ghostbuster.* Kayla scooted closer to Liv until their bare thighs were pressed tightly together, and her lips curved into a roguish grin. "How about a kiss? I could give you that?" she offered quickly.

Round verdant eyes stared back at her. *Did she say kiss?* "Errr...Umm...well..."

Not waiting for an answer, Kayla slowly cupped Liv's cheeks with both hands, using her thumbs to gently stroke the warm, silky skin beneath her fingertips. *Her skin feels even softer than it looks.*

Nervous eyes darted wildly around the room, focusing on everything...anything, but Kayla. *She's going to kiss me? Yes! Well, what is she waiting for? Oh, shit, am I supposed to say something?* "I mean...umm...well...if you want...err...it'd be okay...well...you could..." Liv babbled foolishly, suddenly unable to string together a sentence to save her life.

Damn, she's adorable. A small grin twitched at the corners of Kayla's mouth as her steady, clear voice pulled Liv's eyes upward to meet hers. "Liv, you really need to be quiet. At least for a minute," she chided gently, her grin taking away any sting the softly spoken words may have held.

"Umm—" Liv stopped herself and took a deep breath. "Okay."

One look at the earnest, open face across from hers, and Kayla wasn't joking anymore. The researcher's grin broke into a full, heart-stopping smile, stretching her cheek muscles and showing off straight, white teeth.

Liv smiled back in pure reflex as time slowed down. The wind and hammering surf faded into the background, as the sound of her own relentlessly pounding pulse drowned out everything else. And then, in the tiny space before her next heartbeat, she was falling, deeper and deeper into a clear, intense gaze that tugged insistently at her soul and stole the breath from her chest. Liv tilted her head slightly as the palms resting against her cheeks slowly guided her forward, and her eyes fluttered shut.

Holding her breath, the younger woman leaned forward and lightly brushed her lips against slightly trembling ones that were unbelievably soft and yielding, and Kayla felt herself begin to melt as a soft sigh of pleasure escaped her throat. The same flood of overwhelming warmth and emotion she'd felt in the dream washed over her, only this was better—this was real.

Liv shifted sideways, threading her fingers into dark, damp tresses and drawing Kayla closer, answering the breathy sigh with one of her own as their lips met in flawless contact. Something faint and far off tickled the back of her mind, hanging just beyond her grasp. There were no words, only impressions and feelings mingling indistinguishably with her own. A rush of desire. A sense of completeness and peace. A tiny echo of fear. Then the vague images faded, leaving Liv alone with her thoughts, and the pressure against her lips disappeared. She couldn't tell if it had been seconds or minutes.

Both women pulled away, slightly shaken, not only by the intensity of the kiss itself, but by the flood of emotions accompanying it.

Kayla reluctantly opened her eyes, unable to stop a goofy grin from creasing her face when she was met by a sparking smile. "I know you felt that," she said softly, resting her forehead against Liv's. *It feels so nice to share this with someone.*

"I did."

"It wasn't something I was controlling," the researcher broke in, suddenly worried that Liv would think she was trying to manipulate her.

Liv pulled back and smiled reassuringly, giving Kayla's thigh a gentle squeeze. "I know that, silly." *Why would I even think that? I'd like to kick the shit out of whoever made you feel so insecure about your abilities.*

"Was what you were feeling...I mean, with the kiss...a good sort of thing?" Kayla was already fairly confident what the answer would be, but she wanted to hear Liv say it anyway. Even though it had only lasted for a few seconds, she'd clearly felt Liv's joy, arousal, and confusion when their thoughts began to merge.

Liv leaned closer again, pressing her forehead against Kayla's. Nodding, she moved Kayla's head along with hers as she scrunched up her nose in contemplation. "I felt...something...a lot of somethings. And the kiss was...mmm..." she hummed lightly in contentment. "The kiss was *perfect*."

An enormous smile split Kayla's face, and she drew in a deep breath before speaking.

"Almost."

The smile instantly disappeared, along with all the air in Kayla's lungs.

"It needed to be *longer*," Liv added quickly, not wanting to let the mild teasing go too far. Patiently, she waited for her words to register, and the bewildered look to leave Kayla's face before continuing. Liv's voice dropped an octave below normal, and her eyes visibly darkened when she whispered, "And much, much more...thorough."

Kayla closed her eyes and groaned her agreement as she slid the history off of Liv's lap with one hand, while pulling the other woman onto her lap with the other.

The new position gave Liv an unusual height advantage, and she smiled seductively, lacing her fingers behind Kayla's neck. "I like being the taller one for a change," she offered with a cheeky grin.

"I should have known you'd like being on top." Her eyes immediately widened as the implication of her words hit home. "I mean *taller*. Yeah. That's umm, that's what I meant to say."

Embarrassed, Liv chuckled, wondering exactly how much of what she thought and felt was an open book to Kayla. Then she surprised herself by deciding that at this very moment, she didn't really care. A small kernel of happiness exploded within her and she embraced it, deciding to enjoy it as much as humanly possible. "Well, since it appears I'm taking my payment for translating the history in installments, don't you think you ought to get right to it?" she prodded, not so subtly.

"You're absolutely right," Kayla said seriously. "Figuring out all those dots and squiggles is going to be a lot of hard work."

"Squiggles?" Liv laughed, knowing that after spending the past two years in several of Africa's Muslim-dominated countries, reading Arabic would pose no problem.

"Yup," Kayla reaffirmed with a slightly raised brow. "Squiggles." Then she tilted her head upward and placed a soft kiss on Liv's lower lip, and traced its edge with the tip of a pink tongue. "But I'm sure a cunning linguist, such as yourself, can handle it," the younger woman offered with a sexy smile.

A pale brow arched, but any hope Liv had of pursuing her thoughts was whisked away by the soft lips brushing tenderly against hers.

"Mmm...in fact, if this is going to be an extended contract, I think we should open things up for negotiations," Kayla laughed gently.

A hot, wet tongue danced along Liv's upper lip and, to her credit, she didn't pass out, although for a few seconds it was touch and go. She did, however, decide she was *more* than ready to continue negotiations.

"HURRY UP, MARCY. I wanna restart the film." *Women. What takes them so long in the bathroom?*

"Coming," the girl called back, shutting off the faucet and drying her hands on a dingy white towel. The young couple hadn't even made it through the movie's credits before Marcy asked Doug to stop the video so she could take a bathroom break. Now the teenager stood in front of the small bathroom mirror, the harsh fluorescent light making her look uncharacteristically pale.

What do I do? What do I do? What do I do? was her panicky mantra. She splashed some cool water on her face, lifting her head to see a part woman, part girl looking back at her. *I know what's going to happen if I go out there and sit on that bed with him. He'll touch me, or I'll touch him. Oh, God. I know what I want to happen. But am I ready? Is he?* The reflection in the mirror smiled at Marcy as she recalled the look on Doug's face when he came back with dinner. *He was ready yesterday. Still, it's a big step.*

"Marcy," a voice called softly from behind the bathroom door. "Are you okay? You're not sick, are you? That burger joint looked pretty trashy. Did your burger taste funny? Can I get you something?"

The bathroom door moved slightly and Marcy could picture Doug leaning against it, his mind racing, trying to think of something that would make her feel better, and her heart ached with the love she felt for him. "Coming, Dougie," she called quietly, knowing he'd hear her. With a quick flick of her wrist,

Marcy tossed the towel over the shower rod and clicked off the bathroom light.

When Doug saw the light go off through the crack of the door, he backed away, not wanting to look like a worrywart. It was on the tip of his tongue to correct her and demand to be called Doug, when he stopped his automatic response, realizing that when she said his nickname, just like with Liv, he felt content and happy and very...loved.

"Did ya miss me?" Marcy asked happily as Doug moved back over to the bed and awkwardly sat on its edge.

"I always do when we're apart," he said simply, unknowingly working his way even deeper into Marcy's heart.

She joined Doug on the bed, pulling his hand into hers, the video temporarily forgotten. A distant flash of light reminded her of the storm that still occasionally lit up the sky. "Do you think Kayla and Liv are okay on the island?"

"Liv hates storms. But I'm sure they're okay," he reassured, as much to convince himself as Marcy. "I think they're probably going nuts worrying about us. I'm surprised the police haven't barged in here already." Doug eyed the door warily, only really considering the possibility as he was saying the words. "I'm sure Liv has already called out the National Guard."

Marcy nodded gravely, certain her parents were driving towards them at this very moment. "I just hope they're still talking to each other. Kayla gets bored really easily, and then she gets grouchy. It's not a pretty sight. It's really best to avoid her at those times."

"Ha. You think Kayla gets grouchy?" Doug mocked. "You should see Liv when she's bored. She starts inventing chores to do. That house is probably cleaner now than it was when it was new. How annoying is that? Then add in the fact that they probably can't keep their minds off us, and they're cooped up together in that stuffy old house without a TV or radio even. I'll bet they're in pure hell."

HEAVEN. UNADULTERATED BLISS, were the only thoughts Liv's mind could manage for long moments. They were kissing deeply now, moaning their pleasure into each other's mouths, hot wet tongues sliding languidly together, mapping, tasting and exploring. *Oh, God. This feels too good to stop.* Their movements were slow, but their intensity was white-hot. Liv was rapidly approaching the point of no return and, despite her deepening feelings toward Kayla, she knew she should stop things before they went any further. She didn't want to sleep with Kayla knowing that in a few days she'd probably never see her again. She wanted a chance at a relationship—and that would require a conversation that consisted of more than "Oh, baby" and "God, yes!" Problem was...Liv's body had simply decided to ignore her cautious, overly meddlesome mind, and was responding with abandon.

"Olivia," Kayla rumbled softly, hearing the blonde moan loudly, passionately, at the sound of her name. "If—mmmm," she paused as one of Liv's hands worked its way underneath her T-shirt and a seeking tongue swirled around her own. *Fuck yes!* she mentally cheered. "Liv, if...we...I mean if I'm going to stop...maybe um..." *For Chrissakes, please move that hand a little higher.* "Maybe now would...would be a good time." *Or not,* she mentally pleaded.

Reluctantly, Liv pulled back, but not before giving Kayla's bottom lip a sharp nip, drawing an aroused whimper from the researcher. "I know. I know, you're right," Liv grumbled good-naturedly as she reclaimed her spot on the couch alongside her companion.

They were sitting so close together, their thighs were touching. But for some reason, Liv couldn't bear to put any more distance between them. Kayla simply had a seductive warmth that called to her in a way she'd never experienced. She couldn't ignore it or deny it, so why bother trying?

"Would you like to start reading now?" Kayla asked on an unsteady breath, already wishing she hadn't put a stop to their explorations.

Liv reached down and grabbed the book, very aware of Kayla's soft but ragged breathing. She nodded and replied, "Sure," all the while privately cursing her own lack of self-control. *Damn, I'm worse than Dougie.* She took a few seconds to allow the breeze from the window to cool overheated skin, promising herself that when the time was right, she'd talk to Kayla about what would...she winced...or what wouldn't happen between them once they got off the island.

Liv opened the large book, resting half on her right thigh and half on Kayla's left. After a moment of adjustment, both women propped their feet up on the coffee table so the book sat on an angle, allowing for maximum comfort. They were snuggled so closely together, a ray of light couldn't have slipped between them.

Kayla rubbed burning, tired eyes. "I'm sort of glad you're going to be doing the reading. My eyes are still stinging from all that dust."

Liv resisted the urge to look over and give the body part in question a thorough examination. *Not now. Not those gorgeous blue eyes. Not after kissing like that. I may be a glutton for punishment, but I'm not suicidal.* "Just close your eyes and listen, then."

"Liv," Kayla smiled wryly, "I don't think this is going to be much of a bedtime story. Most of the histories read about as well as a laundry list. Names, births, deaths, marriages — that kind of thing. Not much personal, and certainly nothing exciting." She shrugged one shoulder and nestled her head deeper into the back of the sofa. "Even though the discussions of our abilities can be very enlightening, they're usually pretty dry." Kayla's mind drifted to Papaw's disturbing letter. *Please let there be something in this book that will help guide Marcy. I'm not sure I know enough to do it on my own.*

The blonde crinkled her forehead, looking slightly troubled. "This —," she gave the book a little shake, "is about the people who lived here when this house was built, isn't it?"

The house answered for Kayla, letting out a long tortured groan that chased goose bumps up and down Liv's bare arms.

"It's just settling," Kayla assured softly. But she felt the sudden chill as well. She briefly considered getting her equipment and rechecking the house for paranormal activity, but decided against it. It could wait. After all, they weren't going anywhere until at least tomorrow night.

"I know," Liv answered, a little too quickly, the doubt in her voice obvious even to her own ears. A flash from the night sky lit up the room for the briefest of seconds before once again the women found themselves bathed in only candlelight. "I'm curious about the people in this book, what they were like, why they came here from —"

"England," Kayla finished for her friend. "And I'm curious, too. I just don't want you to be disappointed. It's not a novel."

"Fine," Liv groused playfully. "So we'll be bored."

But at least we'll be bored together, they thought in unison.

"Here we go," Liv began in a steady, clear voice that cut through the sound of the falling rain.

Cobb Island
January, 1691

It is nearing the time when I will lay this accounting to rest, having only decided to add this page at the last moment — not at all certain of my course of action. This is the family history for the Reddings of Cobb Island. I do not pretend to understand its full importance, for before I undertook this task, there simply was not time to explain everything to me. But I was assured by Bridget Redding, my master's sister, that generations to come will appreciate my efforts, and that I know enough. It is not for them, however, that I do this. It is for the people in this lifetime, both good and evil, whose words and deeds deserve to be remembered.

I have been tasked with placing the history out of harm's way. Out of her way; so that when the time is right, it will have survived to rejoin its grandparents, and kin far beyond that, on the tall bookshelves of this wretched, cursed place.

"Laundry list, my ass."

Kayla just smiled sheepishly and laid a warm palm on Liv's hand, closing her eyes and listening intently.

My true name is Afia, but when I was sold to my first master, a textile merchant, some twelve years ago, he renamed me Mary. Six years later, I was traded to Master Redding for two roan stallions. He was pleased with my Christian name and saw no reason to change it.

I have no family history of my own, for when I was stolen from the shores of my homeland and sold from an auction block like so much chattel, I was permanently separated from my kin. Before I close my eyes every night, I pray Allah will watch over them and keep them safe, knowing I cannot. I no longer speak the language of my homeland, a place the slavers simply call, Africa, although no single word could ever describe the breathtaking beauty of that land and its people.

I do not read or write English; to attempt to gain such knowledge is forbidden and carries a price of fifteen lashes. But like the other house slaves, I understand the spoken word very well. So I write this in Arabic, whose written letters I learned in the service of my first master, and which I practice in the black soil along the water's edge to this very day.

It may seem impossible that a mere house slave, such as myself, would know of the many private things contained in these pages. I assure you, it is not. The events not witnessed by my own eyes were described to me in such vivid, sometimes heart-wrenching detail, that they haunt my dreams; and I fear they always will. Beyond that...the walls of this very house, the trees, rocks, and bushes of Cobb Island have eyes. And but one pair belongs to me.

Cobb Island
September, 1690

THUNDERING HOOVES KICKED up a cloud of dark soil as Bridget Redding raced along the shoreline, her dark hair unrestrained, whipping wildly in the wind, the horse's lather mixing with the water's mist and dampening her buckskin trousers. She hadn't even stopped at the house before heading for the stable to exercise her favorite stallion, who she'd sorely regretted not taking with her. After three long months of exploring the mainland alone, she was called home by a sense of duty and unexplained curiosity.

"Whoa," Bridget ordered sharply, pulling back on the reins and slowing the spirited horse.

A wire thin black woman stood up from her task, placing a hand above her eyes to block the glare of the afternoon sun. "Mistress Bridget! When did you get back, child?"

Bridget stroked the large stallion's neck calmingly as the beast huffed and pranced, not at all happy with the interruption of their workout. "It's good to see you, Afia," she greeted warmly, smiling over the stallion's antics.

Dark eyes nervously scanned the shore, wondering if anyone had heard. "Don't call me that," Afia warned sternly. "You know what could happen if I don't use my Christian name."

Two dark, fiery red eyebrows rose, disappearing under a very wide, round-brimmed black hat. "Cyril is back, then, I take it?"

Afia pointed out to sea, where a large ship could barely be seen around the island's curve, several hundred yards from shore.

A long rowboat had been lowered into the water, and Bridget could see several slaves loading crates and trunks into the boat. "The insufferable prig has returned," she commented flatly, removing her hat and wiping the sweat from her forehead with her forearm.

Afia could only nod, echoing Bridget's sentiments completely. "I must go inside now. It would not be wise for me to be seen walking on the shore as though I've nothing to do." Before Bridget could object, she added, "I need to tell the others he's here." The African wiped her hands on her long skirt and regretfully dropped the rocks and shells she'd been collecting all afternoon.

Bridget frowned and dismounted the stallion, keeping a steady hand on the jiggling reins. "I'll accompany you back here tomorrow. You don't have to stay in the house every minute." But she knew her brother demanded that the house slaves be nearby to attend to him at a second's notice.

A tiny smile teased Afia's lips. "It is good to have you home,

Mistress Bridget. Come now, you should change into something respectable before Master Redding sees you." She shook her head ruefully. "Look at your skin. Soon you'll be as dark as I am. Master will have a fit."

"The sun is not my enemy, Afia." A teasing glint transformed the stoic face into a happy young woman's. "And I happen to think you have beautiful skin."

"Hush, child." Afia laughed. "You'll get me whipped for sure." She looked back to the ocean and the launch that was now halfway to shore. "I must go."

Bridget nodded and remounted, tugging her hat on as she kicked the horse into a full gallop towards the dock.

"STEER THE BOAT directly into the waves, fool!" Cyril commanded, cuffing one of the oarsmen harshly as the boat rocked dangerously to one side. "Are you trying to sink us?"

"No sir, Master," the boy immediately responded, continuing to row exactly as he had before.

"By God!" Cyril cursed angrily, his eyes taking in the sight before him. A woman clad in thin, russet-colored buckskin trousers and a matching shirt sat atop a dancing white horse, its hooves pounding loudly on the dock. A few more seconds and he could see the green-and-red designs that ran down the sleeves of her shirt and legs of her pants, and the hostile glint in eyes a few shades lighter than his own.

The boat clanked against the dock, and several slaves sent by Afia ran over and began unloading its cargo. "Move!" Cyril growled as he pushed aside the slaves and jumped onto the dock. "Still dressing like a savage, I see," he hissed as he strode over to his sister.

"Still dressing like a *French* royal footman, I see," Bridget shot back coolly, already looking bored with her brother.

Cyril's cheeks went scarlet. "No wonder no decent gentleman would have you and we've been shunned by the entire court," he answered angrily, preening his long-flowing black curls. He had stopped shaving his head and wearing a wig several years ago, his own hair easily passing for the fashion necessity. He was the very picture of English high fashion, from the billowing lace scarf tied around his neck to his long gold-and-black brocade jacket and gray hosiery, which admittedly came from France.

To his surprise, Bridget let out a hearty laugh. "How quickly you forget, brother. It was *I* who would have none of *them*." The smile slid from her face. "And our being shunned has more to do with your ridiculous investment schemes than my preference for a companion who wouldn't turn my stomach."

The older man simply sneered, his hand reflexively tightening on the hilt of his sword.

She scanned the open sea. "I take it you were successful. After three years, I was beginning to wonder if you'd ever return." She sighed internally. *One can always hope.*

"The island is finally ours." He puffed up his chest proudly; still not believing King James had originally awarded its possession to someone else after his faithful service. He found William and Mary far more palatable.

Cyril's poor business ventures had cast him to the fringe of the British aristocracy. But here he would surely make his fortune, no matter how godforsaken the land was, and return to England in triumph. "Henceforth, it shall be known as Redding Island."

Bridget rolled her eyes at her brother's ridiculous vanity.

"Cyril?" A gentle voice questioned from behind him.

Cyril turned, not bothering to extend his hand to help the small woman out of the boat, despite the fact that she held a sleeping child in her arms.

Bridget shifted angrily in the saddle, trying to see behind her brother and the milling slaves, causing the stallion to snort and stomp its front hooves.

When the elder Redding turned back to Bridget, he was holding the sleeping child, the toddler's clean white nightgown blowing gently in the breeze. "May I present my son," he squared his shoulders and lifted his chin, "Henry."

Bridget's jaw sagged slightly. "The child is your son?"

"Cyril?" The voice was a bit stronger now, but Bridget still couldn't see its owner, only a small caped figure.

Pulling a blanket around the toddler, he continued, "And my bride," as though it were an afterthought.

"To go with the son, I presume."

A woman wearing a thin navy cape appeared at Cyril's side. "May I present Faylinn Redding, formerly, Faylinn Cobb. This is Bridget." He hesitated briefly before continuing. "My sister."

A dark eyebrow lifted, and pale eyes that stood out in vivid relief against deeply tanned skin fixed on Cyril. *That was one way to get the island, Brother. Although outright purchase might have been the slightly easier path.*

Cyril smiled smugly.

Faylinn reached up and pulled back the hood of her cape, revealing a head of flowing red-gold hair and a creamy white complexion. She smiled shyly and approached Bridget, heedless of the high-strung horse. When she reached Bridget's side, she gently tugged on the tall woman's buckskin sleeve, green eyes briefly drifting over the Indian designs that adorned the leather. When Bridget bent down, Faylinn stood on tip-toe and placed a soft kiss on her lips. "Hello, Sister," she greeted quietly.

For a moment Bridget could say nothing, as she simply stared at Faylinn and willed her pounding pulse to slow. Then, with a small shake of her head, she seemed to come to her senses and slid off the horse, practically tearing the hat off her head. When booted feet hit the dock, she lowered her head and eyes in deference to her sister-in-law's position as mistress of the house. "Welcome to Cobb Island," she said warmly, completely ignoring her brother's impromptu name change.

Cyril stiffened. His sister had never shown him one-tenth the respect she now paid his wife.

Bridget lifted her eyes to meet Faylinn's, and held her gaze for several seconds before Cyril thrust the stirring child in his wife's face.

"One of the slaves will take you inside," he directed curtly over his shoulder, already moving back towards the boat to examine the pile of crates now sitting on the dock.

Having heard his command, a young man rushed to Faylinn's side. Mutely he pointed towards the house, and Faylinn began walking up the small path, cooing softly to the fussing child and sparing several backward glances at the mysterious beauty who dressed like the drawings she'd seen of the natives who lived in the American colonies.

Bridget watched Faylinn until she disappeared inside the gleaming white house. Then she turned on her brother. "She's just a child. You're old enough to be her father," she ground out, knowing that wasn't wholly true, but feeling an irrational surge of anger and jealously nonetheless.

Cyril laughed at his sister's sudden fit of temper. "Now, now, not everyone chooses to be an old maid. She's nearly nineteen. That's *more* than respectable," he dismissed.

"And that baby looks to be nearly three years old."

"Fine," Cyril huffed, not seeing any problem. The fifteen-year age difference mattered little to him. All that really mattered was that Faylinn had borne him a healthy son, as was her duty. "She was just sixteen when we wed, with her father's full permission of course. The Island was only part of her dowry," he bragged.

"Pig!" Bridget spat. *What decent family would allow you to wed their daughter?*

The Cobbs have spent the last ten years in Edinburgh, far from London's worst gossips, he answered, never having to actually speak the words. "Leave me now, Bridget." He flicked his wrist towards the woods as though he were dismissing a pet. "I've got work here."

Bridget ground her teeth together. "And have you no concern for the twin daughters you already have?"

"Ah, yes. How are Elizabeth and Judith?" he inquired absently, grabbing a crowbar from one of the slaves and beginning to pry open one the crates.

"They've waited three years for you to come home. You could have at least sent word that you'd remarried and had a child, for God's sake!"

He frowned, running his fingers over his thin mustache. "I'll see them later, when I'm finished here." Their mother, whom he had adored, had died in childbirth. And from that day forward, he could barely stand to look at them.

"You named your son after Father."

Cyril's hands stilled and he nodded slowly, daring her to question his right.

"Good choice," Bridget said flatly. Without another word, she mounted her horse and gave it a quick slap on the rump, sending them galloping into the surf and away from her loathsome brother.

Cobb Island
Present day

LIV PAUSED. "DO you know who you're descended from?" she asked Kayla, having become so totally absorbed in the story that she hadn't even noticed when the storm seemed to get a second wind and an occasional clap of thunder joined her voice.

Kayla thought for a moment, using her thumb to gently stroke the soft skin on Liv's wrist.

I don't think she even knows she's doing that, Liv thought contently.

"Judith Redding. She had a son out of wedlock in the early 1700s who kept the Redding name. Except for Judith, Cyril, and Elizabeth, the other names don't sound familiar. But then again, for some reason, references to my family during this time frame are really vague and almost totally limited to comments about the strength of their abilities."

"Bridget and Cyril's telepathy was different from yours." Her words were met with a lopsided smile from Kayla, "Ours, I mean. They could hear the actual *words*," Liv marveled, stretching her legs out flat while Kayla held the book.

"It's terrible that Cyril didn't even want to see his daughters after three years. But in a sad sort of way, I can understand why," Liv offered hesitantly, that part of the tale sticking out in her mind.

Kayla was surprised. She already found Cyril repulsive in the extreme, and hadn't even tried to understand his appalling behavior. "Why?"

Liv turned so that she was facing Kayla, seeing the interest written plainly on her face and wanting to share her past with Kayla, even the parts she wasn't particularly proud of. "When my folks were killed, I was nineteen years old and Dougie was only six. He's the spitting image of my father, you know. Right down to his curly hair." She grinned fondly, remembering how proud her father was of that simple fact. "Anyway, I was away at college when the accident happened. My dad hit a slick spot on the road and lost control of the car when they were on their way home from a local pizza parlor."

Kayla gently squeezed Liv's hand in empathy, understanding that no amount of time could make a tragedy like that completely painless to retell.

Liv smiled gratefully and dropped her eyes from Kayla's. "Aunt Ruth was living in Oregon at the time, and so Dougie had to wait at the Sheriff's Office until I could make the three hour drive to pick him up." She swallowed dryly as a surge of grief and guilt that she hadn't felt in years swelled within her, and her eyes filled with tears.

Kayla's heart twisted painfully in her chest, but she remained silent.

"When I first saw Dougie, he was sitting at the sheriff's desk. There were all kinds of candy sitting untouched on the desk in front of him. I guess they were trying to make him feel better." She chuckled humorlessly. "Anyway, the big chair practically swallowed him whole. He looked so afraid and...lost, I guess. He was still wearing the same sweatshirt he had on in the accident, and there were bloodstains on one of the sleeves. I found out later it was my mother's blood." Liv's eyes lifted to meet Kayla's steady, compassionate gaze. "Do you know what my first thoughts were? When I saw him sitting there all alone, waiting for me?"

Kayla shook her head, mentally bracing herself.

"I thought about how much he reminded me of my dad, and how much it hurt just to look at him. I wanted to run in the opposite direction and never stop." She hung her head in shame, feeling she deserved the aching tightness in her chest her admission had caused. "It should have been how grateful I was that he wasn't hurt, and how much I loved him. But it wasn't," she whispered in anguish, turning away. *I'm a horrible person. I wanted to leave him there all alone.*

Oh, Liv. Kayla closed her eyes at the raw pain and disgust in Liv's voice. "And then what did you do?"

"Huh?" Liv looked back at Kayla and wiped away her tears

with shaking fingers, having not really heard the question.

"After you thought about how much it hurt to look at Doug, what did you do?"

A puzzled look crossed Liv's face as she tried to remember, her initial reaction at seeing her brother having dominated her memories of that night for so many years. Pale brows drew together as she concentrated. "When, when he saw me in the doorway, he flew out of the chair and into my arms. We both sobbed until we were sick." She smiled sadly. "And then I took him home."

Kayla leaned forward and softly kissed Liv's tear stained cheeks. Then she moved up and tenderly kissed each eyelid. "You did everything right, Liv," she muttered as she pulled her new friend into a tight embrace. There was no awkwardness or hesitation — only comfort freely offered and accepted.

"Thanks," Liv said quietly, her nose buried in clean, sweet smelling hair that was still a little damp from Kayla's shower. "I'm sorry. I haven't thought about that in a long time."

"It's okay," Kayla reassured, loving the feel of the smaller woman in her arms, and pleased beyond reason that she seemed so comfortable there.

Liv was quiet for several moments, breathing in Kayla's scent and absorbing the strength that was from loving arms. "Do you think Dougie and Marcy are doing okay now?" she finally asked, feeling Kayla's body jerk with unexpected laughter.

"I think they're probably having a great time, not having to answer to anyone. I know if I were them I'd be —" Then she stopped, knowing that the relationship between Doug and Liv was really more like that of parent and child than brother and sister, and that sharing what she really thought they were likely to be doing was inappropriate. *Not that I like the idea any more than Liv.*

"Eww. Don't say anymore, okay? I'm trying not to think about that."

"Me, too," Kayla confirmed.

"But even though I've been *trying*, the thought has popped into my head a few times today. Actually, I'm glad for both of them that their first time will be with someone they love."

"Was it for you?" Kayla asked mischievously.

Liv's eyebrows shot skyward. "How did we get to talking about my sex life?" *Or current lack thereof.*

"I dunno." Kayla grinned broadly. "It seemed like a reasonable question at the time."

Liv cocked her head. "Do you really want to know?" She already knew she couldn't stand the thought of Kayla being touched by anyone else, so she decided to just pretend it had never happened. What could it hurt? It kept her from wanting to wring some unknown woman's, or man's, neck in a fit of juvenile jealously.

"Nah...you're so old, you've probably forgotten anyway," Kayla teased, glad to be past the moment of emotional turmoil. "Old? Now you sound like Dougie." Liv snorted indignantly and rose to her feet. "This old lady could use a beer for her parched throat before she reads anymore. Join me?"

"You bet."

The pair made their way into the kitchen with Kayla in the lead, carrying a large candle. A bolt of lightning lit up the kitchen and Liv jumped, reminded once again that this never-ending storm was still brewing.

Kayla set her candle down on the small kitchen table and opened the refrigerator, hoping that the beer would at least be cool, even though the power had been off for hours. When she opened the door, she let out a loud, vehement curse that scared the crap out of Liv. "Sorry," she muttered apologetically.

"Jesus, what's wrong?" Liv joined Kayla at the refrigerator.

"It's gone. All of it."

The women shared a knowing glance.

Liv turned her head skyward and shouted, "Enjoy your night, kiddies, 'cause tomorrow, I'm gonna kill you!"

Kayla shook her head. She was never this much trouble as a child. "Not if I see them first." She grabbed a Pepsi and handed it to Liv, then took one for herself. "C'mon, let's go find out what happened to my great-great-bastard Cyril. We've barely made a dent in the book."

Chapter
Ten

Second Glances

"IS THIS BETTER?" Doug set the flashlight on the table between the beds, shining its light straight onto the ceiling.

"Much."

The motel's power had gone out about thirty minutes into the movie, and with a quiet click, the TV picture went dark along with the rest of the room. The teens groaned simultaneously. If it weren't for bad luck, they'd have no luck at all.

Despite the late hour, neither wanted to go to sleep and end their evening. They'd waited months to see each other face-to-face again, and knew their foolish flight from the island was probably going to cut the rest of their trip short.

Doug, who wasn't even dry yet from his last trip outside, had sought out a candle from the desk clerk.

The man flatly refused to provide one, saying that if he gave out candles every time the goddamn power went out, some fool customer would have burned the place down years ago. He loved this motel. After all, what other job would pay him to sit on his butt and watch the races all day long?

Doug's brow had creased in frustration. He couldn't argue with that. But after the young man threatened to check back every ten minutes all night long, just in case he had changed his mind, the clerk relented and handed over an old flashlight he kept in a drawer below the cash register.

Now both teens sat in the semi-darkness with nothing to do other than think about what they *could* be doing. An awkwardness that they'd never experienced settled over them as each mind groped for a suitable suggestion. They had no money; they had no car; they couldn't stay outside; and it was the middle of the night.

"How about a drink?" Marcy offered bravely, remembering the beer she'd taken from the refrigerator when they'd left Cobb Island.

"I still can't believe you stole that," Doug kidded, placing another pillow behind his shoulders as he leaned against the headboard. "Our only prayer is that they don't notice that it's missing."

"I thought it was a case of soda. I didn't even realize it was beer until we'd already left the island," Marcy protested. "Would *you* have gone back to return it?"

Doug shook his head, wondering why things with Marcy always started out so simple, then went straight to hell. "No way, man."

"Do you think they'll believe it was an accident?" There was a hopeful quality to Marcy's voice that made Doug roll his eyes.

"Sure," he drawled. "We'll explain about accidentally taking the beer, right after we tell them how it was a marauding band of rednecks that kidnapped us from the island. But then we escaped and were forced to spend the night together in a sleazy motel because we couldn't remember Kayla's cell phone number and didn't want to disturb your parents by calling and asking for it," the boy snorted.

"But the part about the beer is true," Marcy whined, affecting a sad face.

Doug's gaze was unerringly drawn to Marcy's full, pouting lower lip. *She has such a pretty mouth. I wonder what it would feel like if that perfect lip began to caress —*

"Hello, Doug." Marcy waved her hand in front of Doug's face. "Are you still in there?"

"Huh?" Doug's eyes snapped up.

Marcy frowned. "Why is your mouth hanging open like that?"

Doug clamped his jaw shut and swallowed audibly, choking slightly on his own drool. "Well, are you gonna give me one of those beers or what?" he finally snapped moodily. *Ugghhhhh!*

Marcy got out of her bed and joined Doug on his. "Doug, now that I think about it, I don't think that's such a good idea."

"C'mon, Marse, we're already over our heads in shit. What's a couple more feet now?"

The girl laughed. "When you put it so eloquently, I do see your point." *Oh, well, in for a dime...* "The beer is in the bathroom." *Maybe a few beers will loosen him up a bit. He hasn't even tried to kiss me.* Marcy wasn't entirely sure how much beyond kissing she was comfortable with, but he could at least try to seduce her. What kind of boyfriend was he?

"I don't even want to know why you put it in there." Doug pushed himself off the bed and away from temptation personified. He was never going to make it 'til morning without begging her for sex. He just knew it. But the scariest part was, deep down he was getting the feeling that Marcy would say yes.

Marcy heard a sharp tearing sound as Doug tore open the

paper case. "Hey, Dougie, we can't buy any beer on our own. If we just take back all the cans, they'll know we didn't drink —"

Hisssss...the beverage dutifully sounded as Doug cracked open the can.

"...any," she finished lamely.

LIV AND KAYLA silently reclaimed their spots on the couch in the library, side-by-side, thighs pressing tightly together, both facing the picture window that looked out onto the black churning sea. Kayla settled the book between them again, this time wrapping her arm around Liv's shoulder and peering interestedly at the letters she couldn't understand.

A happy grin plastered itself onto Liv's face, and the blonde immediately gave in to the impulse to kiss Kayla on the cheek. She pointed to one of the many candles that surrounded them. "Can you bring that one just a little closer?"

Kayla wordlessly obeyed, moving the candle until Liv nodded.

"Thanks." Liv studied the page briefly. "It looks like more of Afia's narration. I think she's interspersed bits throughout the text. She's indented her portions so they're actually pretty easy to pick out." Liv flinched at the sound of more thunder, but paused for only a second before losing herself in the text.

Cobb Island
January, 1691

The day Master Redding and his wife came home to Cobb Island, I spent most of the afternoon pacifying, although in very different ways, Master's thirteen-year-old twin daughters Elizabeth and Judith. Or Night and Day, as the slaves call them. They are both dark-haired, beautiful girls, tall and slender, each with piercing gray eyes that remind me of the jungle cats that frightened me so as a child. They are like the snowflakes that dust the island in winter, and fascinate me beyond reason. At first sight, they appear exactly the same. But when you pay them more than a passing glance, see and not just look, you find that they are truly distinct.

Judith, the older by mere minutes, spent the afternoon weeping in her room, heartbroken that her father, who stood only a few feet outside the house, hadn't bothered to come in and greet them. She became so melancholy that even Elizabeth attempted to break her out of her mood. Judith is a stubborn but gentle soul, who tends toward poetry and drawing as ways to wile away the hours. Her undoing, I am convinced, will be the bond she shares with her sister.

For every ounce of warmth and kindness that is found in Judith, Elizabeth is lacking. She is selfish and spoilt and spends hour upon hour in this house's library, devouring page after page of the dusty old books as though her very salvation depends on it. There is a darkness about her that the slaves have come to fear. Their fear is not unwarranted.

They say when 'Night' was born, in a jealous fit, she tried to steal her newborn twin's soul. And that it was through force of will alone that Judith drew her first breath, long after the midwife had given up on her. Had you asked me on that sunny September afternoon when Master Redding arrived home, if this story was true, I would have merely laughed and called it fanciful, a tale imagined by restless slaves. But now, when I look into her eyes, a chill runs through my veins. I am certain the tale is true. Though, undoubtedly Judith will never forsake her because of it.

My real memories of that day, however—the ones I cling to after all that has been said and done—are of Mistress Bridget and Mistress Faylinn. For I believe, although neither of them knew it at the time, that it was that very night that they fell in love.

Liv looked up from the book. "Whoa. They fell in love? With each other?"

"I wouldn't think that would shock you, Liv," Kayla snorted.

"It doesn't *shock* me," she said playfully. "It just doesn't seem like a very good idea."

Kayla shifted her arm, snuggling a little closer to Liv. "Maybe they couldn't help themselves. Maybe their hearts decided for them." *Maybe she blinked her eyes, and it was right there in front of her.*

"How sweet." A delighted smiled broke out across Liv's face. "I would have never suspected you of being a softy," she laughed. *And maybe you're right.*

Cobb Island
September, 1690

"BUT, CYRIL—"

"I said no!" Cyril angrily slammed his fist down on the long, cherry dining table, rattling the elaborate place settings and causing the table's occupants to grab their glasses to avoid a watery mess.

Faylinn's stomach clenched as she nervously twisted the fabric of her dress. *Why is he being so unreasonable? Why is he always?* was her mind's immediate retort. "But—"

"No buts! Why do I keep a full stable of house slaves," he gestured widely with both hands, "if not to be able to eat my dinner in peace? I will not have the child anywhere near the table, or our bedchamber for that matter!" he roared.

"In Scotland—"

"We were in your father's home," he interrupted. "*I* am master of this one!"

Faylinn fought hard not to flinch as his voice boomed. It was enough that he had bought and paid for her future with the ease of any formal business transaction; she would not give him the satisfaction of seeing her fear. Her eyes drifted to Afia, who was holding the fitful toddler just outside the doorway of the candlelit dining room, cautiously awaiting the outcome of this argument. Faylinn briefly wondered whose plight was worse—the woman who shared Master Redding's bed, or the one who made it. She schooled herself in patience. "I asked Mary to bring the baby downstairs if she couldn't get him to sleep. He's been at sea for weeks and—"

"Enough!" Cyril jumped out of his seat, throwing his fork onto his dinner plate, which sat empty. Everyone was still awaiting Bridget's arrival. Unexpectedly, the tall man's hand shot out and wrapped around Faylinn's upper arm, roughly yanking her to her feet.

Judith looked away, her appetite gone.

Elizabeth, however, cocked her head slightly to the side, watching the interplay between her father and his wife with rapt fascination.

Faylinn had been as docile as a lamb all evening—agreeing with her father where appropriate, and serving him dutifully during the few moments when the slaves were out of the room attending to the meal. Even when he simply grew tired of the sound of her voice and rudely commanded that she shut up, Faylinn had said nothing, meekly complying with only an embarrassed blush. But now, when it came to the child, Elizabeth could see her new mother would not be so easily silenced.

"Do I need to remind you of your place within this household, dearest wife?" Cyril threatened coldly, pulling Faylinn toward him until she was leaning across the table, her already ample cleavage accentuated by her new position. "Allow me to refresh your memory. It is *beneath* me," he hissed quietly, his mustache so close that the prickly hairs tickled her lips. Then, with a deep exhalation, he pulled back slightly and visibly calmed. "I would hate to discipline you in front of the children," he added conversationally, gently stroking her cheek with the back of his hand in an unsettlingly tender gesture. "It would put such a damper on my homecoming celebration, don't you agree?"

Her eyes flashed for only a second before dropping to the table. "Of course. Forgive me, husband." The words grated at her soul. She pushed away her natural tendency toward anger, embracing a resigned sadness instead. Faylinn bowed her head, as much to escape Cyril's foul breath as to show her obedience. *The walls are closing in on me.* "I will leave you to enjoy your meal, and attend to Henry myself."

Cyril released his grip on her arm, smoothing a small bow that circled the puffed, ivory colored sleeve of Faylinn's dress with exaggerated care. "*You* will remain here." Straightening his own scarf, he reclaimed his seat. "The slaves will care for Henry." And with that, the subject was closed.

"I am ready for my dinner," he informed the young boy who stood poised at the entrance of the dining room, awaiting his master's command. As the boy hurried out of the room, Cyril heard the soft but sure footsteps of his sister. "Punctual as always," the elder Redding commented sarcastically, not bothering to look over his shoulder.

"I'm afraid I was delayed in the stables. It seems Apollo threw a shoe. My apologies, Brother." Bridget's gaze never wavered from Faylinn's as she descended the stairs that led directly into the far end of the room.

Faylinn felt as though the air had been sucked from her chest when piercing, sky-blue eyes captured hers. *My God!* Unconsciously, she leaned against the cool wood of the table's edge, bracing herself. *I can hardly believe that's the same woman from the dock this afternoon.* For a moment she lost herself in a sea of blue. *Breathe, Faylinn.*

"Well, it's about bloody—" Cyril paused when he noticed the look on his daughters' faces.

Judith's lips had curled into a small smile, while Elizabeth's mouth shaped an incredulous frown, but somehow they *both* looked astonished. Cyril turned around, his long ebony curls draping over one shoulder as he twisted. He expected to see an apparition. Instead, he was greeted with the sight of Bridget in a dress that their mother had purchased for her birthday, some five years earlier. At the time, Bridget had refused to wear it, thumbing her nose at English convention and fashion. Cyril's chest puffed up with pride. It was only fitting that she chose to wear it on *his* homecoming. Despite her appalling attire earlier, maybe time had mellowed the headstrong twenty-five-year-old, and she'd finally come to her senses. *Not likely*, he snorted inwardly.

Bridget swept past Cyril, the mid-length train of her gown swishing gently around long legs. She stopped to greet her nieces, removing her eyes from Faylinn's for the first time since entering the room. Bridget offered Elizabeth a short nod, not bothering to try to speak with the malevolent child, but vowing to talk with Cyril about the girl's abilities once they were alone.

Judith, however, despite being seated, received a playful pinch to the rump as Bridget passed. The girl clamped her hand over her mouth to stifle a giggle.

You needn't act as though you've never seen me in anything other than britches and buckskin, Bridget silently directed to her smiling niece.

The thick, blood-red mane that had blown wildly around Bridget's shoulders hours earlier had been tamed into a single, smoothly plaited braid running down the center of her back. Her dress was a shiny midnight blue, with brown and gold piping that ran the lengths of long, snug fitting sleeves. A gently scooping neckline showed off tan skin and broad shoulders; its fitted corset hugged a lean waistline. Hiding beneath the dark skirts was a bright gold underskirt that peeked out when Bridget held up her hem to walk.

She was simply stunning.

The youngster's giggles increased. *If the shoe fits, Auntie.*

All right, Judith, Bridget mentally conceded with a raised eyebrow and slightly crooked grin. *'Maybe it* has *been a while.'*

As Bridget slowly made her way around the enormous table, she took the time to appreciate her brother's wife. Faylinn was the epitome of youthful beauty and femininity. Her gown was the palest of blues, with three-quarter length ivory sleeves whose cuffs were decorated with small ribbons tied into bows. Red-gold hair was pulled up into a loose roll, with several free wisps curling softly around her cheeks.

Clear emerald eyes followed Bridget on her journey, drawing an unconscious smile from the taller woman.

A silent laugh. *Not so loud, Aunt Bridget. And yes, I agree. Faylinn does have startlingly beautiful eyes.*

Bridget stopped dead in her tracks as a chill passed through her. Turning slightly, she could only stare at Elizabeth. She hadn't directed her thoughts toward her. *How could she have known I was thinking about Faylinn? Only the stronger telepath can break in and hear without permission.*

The girl grinned wickedly, gray eyes dancing with devilment, knowing what she'd just revealed. *I've been practicing. And you're very lucky father doesn't know what you're thinking about his wife.* Privately, she thought her father a pompous buffoon. That, however, did not excuse Bridget's flagrant impudence. He was the head of household, and she his daughter. Surely, her stature as his direct descendant was more important than that of his sibling? But Bridget had never accorded her or her father their due, plainly preferring her unassuming sister.

Don't be absurd, Elizabeth. I...I was just admiring—

Auntie, I'd run you through if she were my bride. Elizabeth sniggered disgustedly, knowing that Bridget's admiration was not of the sisterly variety. Then she felt a sudden, almost painful void as Bridget's mind completely closed to her. Her hands flew to her ears as her Aunt's voice boomed in her head.

Never do that again, girl! You may think you're clever; but not everything can be learned from the yellowed pages of the family histories.

The projection was so loud that Judith's eyes snapped up, the words echoing in her own head, albeit not nearly so loudly. Cyril, whose own abilities were eclipsed by those of his sister and daughters, sat oblivious to their wordless conversation, wondering why Bridget and Elizabeth were exchanging murderous glances and Faylinn was still on her feet, gazing intently at his sister.

When Bridget finally reached Faylinn's side, she leaned down and placed a tender kiss on her sister-in-law's cheek. "Good evening, Faylinn."

Warm breath and soft lips caressed Faylinn's skin for the barest of seconds before they were gone. Faylinn felt weak in the knees. *God, what is wrong with me?* Bridget looked...felt like a different woman. On the dock this afternoon, the tall beauty had pulsed with a dark, feral energy that flickered only a hairsbreadth below the surface. Tonight, that energy seemed to be channeled into a bright, radiant elegance that commanded the room's attention with its presence alone. Faylinn found both personas utterly compelling, and undeniably attractive.

"Good evening, Bridget." Her eyes easily telegraphed awe. "You are simply divine," she muttered sincerely, just loud enough for everyone to hear. The words escaped quite without permission, causing Faylinn's jaw to drop in shock. *By God, girl, shut up! Have you gone mad?*

But Faylinn's mental slip was quickly smoothed over when Judith broke in and commented, "That dress is quite lovely." The girl had placed an almost imperceptible emphasis on the word dress, receiving a pathetically grateful look from Faylinn, who nodded her agreement.

"Yes, it is." The flustered young woman repeated the sentiment as she took her seat, hoping the heat in her cheeks didn't look as pronounced as it felt.

Cyril looked back and forth between Faylinn and Bridget quizzically before agreeing with his wife. "Quite."

"Master Redding?" The boy, who had gone to fetch dinner, reluctantly interrupted from just inside the doorway, nervously shifting from one foot to the other. He nearly fell when Afia gently nudged him aside so she could enter the room behind him.

Faylinn looked questioningly at Afia, who smiled and nodded, indicating that the toddler had finally gone to sleep. The young mother let out a shuddering breath.

Cyril stared at the boy's empty hands. Did no one obey him? Where was his damned dinner? "You had best explain yourself, boy."

"The ship that dropped off you and Mistress Redding on the Island this afternoon has returned. A launch is on its way to shore right at this very moment, Master."

For the first time all evening, Cyril smiled. "Excellent." The man practically jumped to his feet. "I have business to attend to then. Dinner can wait," he called over his shoulder as he strode out of the room.

"Welcome home, Father," Judith said brokenly as she bolted towards the stairs, distraught that the evening she'd intended to spend with her father was ruined.

Elizabeth felt her own eyes mist over, but stubbornly refused to let a single tear fall. He said it was business, after all. She'd see him later. Lifting her chin, she followed after her despondent twin, already thinking of ways to make her smile.

Both Faylinn and Bridget stood up to go after the girls, but Afia held up a forestalling hand.

"I'll go after them and bring supper to their rooms," the black woman assured. Dark eyes focused on Bridget. "Child, you know they'll only accept comfort from each other. That's the way of it with those two."

"I know." Bridget sighed in frustration. "Cyril is such a bastard," she said, then remembered she was in the company of his wife. "Faylinn, I'm sorr—"

Faylinn waved off her apology, agreeing completely, but politely keeping the uncharitable thought to herself.

Bridget tried not to grin as the sentiment flashed clearly in her mind.

Pale brows creased. "But I should go and try to talk with them." Although they were nearly young women themselves, she was their mother now.

"It won't do any good, Faylinn," Bridget admitted with a frown. "Judith will simply lock her door, and Elizabeth will undoubtedly be at her side when she does. They'll only come back down when they're ready. Nothing you or I could say or do would change that."

Afia patted Faylinn's back reassuringly, already liking this eager young woman. "You just relax, Mistress Faylinn. I'll see to the girls, and then check on Master Henry as well. Poor tyke was so exhausted when he finally went to sleep, I doubt I'll hear a peep out of him until morning."

"Thank you, Mary." Faylinn smiled gratefully. "But I'll be up to check on him later."

Afia bowed her head slightly. "As you wish, Mistress."

Bridget leaned back against the table as Afia disappeared up the stairs, leaving her alone with Faylinn for the first time. She tried to think of something to say, but found herself curiously tongue-tied around the pretty woman.

"Is your horse all right?" Faylinn finally asked, leaning against the table alongside Bridget but still facing the staircase, her mind split between her sleeping son and the beauty at her side.

"Apollo is fine. He only threw a shoe. He wasn't injured."

"He's young and spirited."

Dark eyebrows lifted. "You know about horses, then?"

"Oh my, yes," Faylinn assured quickly, immediately warming to the topic. "My family has always raised horses. Your stallion is beautiful, though still a bit wild by the looks of it."

Bridget smiled, clearly detecting the Scottish brogue that was mostly absent from Faylinn's speech, except, apparently, when the blonde got excited and spoke rapidly. "Would you like to see him? I was going to go out to the stables after dinner anyway."

Faylinn nodding eagerly, wanting to spend more time with what she considered the most intriguing thing about Cobb Island.

"Good. I'll meet you here in the dining room in an hour." Bridget's lips curved into a sheepish, lopsided grin. "I'm afraid it will take me at least that long to get out of this dress and into something better suited for the stables." She took a step towards the stairs, only to be stopped by a strong hand on her shoulder.

"Where...where are you going?"

Bridget looked puzzled. "To my room, to change clothes." Hadn't she just said that?

"I know. I mean *exactly* where. I want to look in on Henry, and I know his room is somewhere near yours. But I can't make heads nor tails of the layout of this house."

Bridget rolled her eyes. "Cyril spent months with architects back in London designing this ridiculous maze he calls a home. It took me days before I could navigate my way around." She bowed regally at the waist and offered her arm to Faylinn. "Would you allow me to escort you to your bedch—" she hesitated briefly, not wanting to mention the bedchamber she knew Faylinn would share with her brother. The mere thought mysteriously made her head pound and stirred an anger deep within her. "Allow me to escort you upstairs?"

"Yes, please." Faylinn curtsied playfully, then took Bridget's arm. But Bridget's reluctance to mention her and Cyril's bedchamber didn't go unnoticed; the thought of sharing a bed with her husband causing her own stomach to roil. Since her pregnancy, they hadn't slept in the same room. While this didn't stop Cyril from occasionally visiting her room, where she was not-so-pleasantly reminded of her wifely duties, it did afford her a measure of privacy that she'd come to not only expect, but crave. *But didn't he mention* our *bedchamber when he spoke with regard to Henry earlier tonight?* She cringed at the thought, hoping she'd somehow misunderstood.

Bridget felt a tremor run through Faylinn, and unconsciously moved a bit closer as they walked. "Is something wrong?" she inquired as they navigated the stairway that was lit by several softly glowing oil lamps.

Faylinn shook her head, not wanting to have her time with Bridget marred by ugly thoughts. "Tell me about the Colonies, Bridget. I've heard such stories."

Bridget didn't draw attention to Faylinn's obvious change of subjects. *She'll come to trust me, given time,* she assured herself as they turned onto the third floor.

Faylinn immediately began asking questions about Bridget's manner of dress that afternoon, as well as the curious drawings that decorated the leather, her animated voice breathing life into the quiet hallways.

My brother is a very lucky man, Bridget thought enviously. And if he ever does anything to harm this lovely creature, I shall kill him myself.

But Faylinn's excitement was contagious, and soon all thoughts of her brother vanished as the Bridget began regaling Faylinn with tales of her latest exploration of the mainland, the natives, and the wildlife she'd discovered along the way.

Chapter
Eleven

Intoxicating

Cobb Island
Present Day

"NO WONDER SHE was attracted to Bridget," Liv commented more to herself than Kayla as she looked up from the text. She could easily picture Kayla atop Bridget's dancing stallion or in a shimmering satin dress.

Kayla nodded, but her thoughts were centered on Faylinn and how Bridget must have found her irresistible, completely understanding how easy it was to get lost in a pair of soulful green eyes.

Liv lifted her feet from the edge of the coffee table, stretching them out, then shifting sideways a bit so Kayla could move the arm that had been wrapped tightly around her shoulders for the better part of two hours. She nearly jumped out of her skin when she was startled by a soft ringing sound. She craned her neck, looking through the shadows of the candlelit room. "What the—"

"It's my phone. I must have left it in here this morning." Kayla sprang to her feet and managed half a step before crashing to the floor. "Oww. Shit!" Not only had she forgotten about her injured knee, but her other leg had gone to sleep. She curled up on the floor, moaning as the millions of tiny pins and needles prickled one leg mercilessly, while the knee on her other leg throbbed.

Liv pushed the book off her lap and scrambled off the end of the sofa over to Kayla. "Are you okay?"

"I'm fine," Kayla said through clenched teeth. *God, why am I always wallowing on the floor like an idiot around her?*

The phone rang again but Liv didn't move, other than to offer Kayla her hand.

"Get the phone, Liv." Kayla pointed towards a small wooden table under the window she'd opened earlier. "It might be the kids."

Pale eyebrows rose. "Umm...okay, okay, I've got it." She made a dash for the phone, pushing aside the billowing curtains and fumbling briefly before figuring out which button was the on switch. "Hello," she answered quickly, tucking the phone under her chin and hurrying back over to Kayla to give her a hand up. With a slight tug, she encouraged Kayla to lean on her, giving the darker woman a sympathetic pat between the shoulder blades as she helped her friend back to the couch, where they both sat down.

"It's her. I-I-I can't believe I finally remembered the number. I was —" the female voice on the phone stopped mid-word and began to howl with laughter.

Liv grimaced and held the phone away from her ear when a second person's laughter joined the fray. "Who is this?" she demanded curtly. Kayla was hurting, and she wasn't in the mood to waste a single moment on some weirdo crank caller.

"Shh...shhh...Marse...which one answered it?" a muffled male voice whispered loudly. Then there was a loud clank as the phone fell on the floor and the receiver bounced on the carpet.

Was that Dougie's voice in the background? Liv pressed the phone back to her ear, her forehead deeply creased as she listened to the conversation on the other end of the line.

"It's not myyyy sister...and boy she shuuuuurr sounds pissed. You are de-eh-eh-eh-eh deaaaaaaad meat." Then the girl broke down into another fit of giggles.

"Marcy, is that you?" Liv asked angrily. *If they had the number, why didn't they call before now?*

"It depends on whether you're gonna make us go home from our vacation early," the teenager responded petulantly. "'Cause if you are, then this is *not* Marcy." Her voice suddenly became muffled, and Liv could tell she'd put her hand over the receiver. "Hey, Doug, don't call me Marcy anymore, 'kay?" the girl called loudly. "People are mad at Marcy, and I don't want to be her tonight. Call me Gigi; I've always liked that name. Yuck. Don't lie on the carpet. It's all gross."

"Ooooo, you're gonna be French?" Doug laughed from his spot on the floor between the beds. He had an empty beer can balanced on his forehead, and his arms stretched out at his sides as though he was walking a tight rope.

Liv closed her eyes and shook her head as she let out a small curse. "They're drunk," she informed Kayla who was already glaring at the phone. "Where are you guys?"

The girl stopped laughing long enough to answer. She surveyed the dimly lit motel room seriously before she responded, "Inside."

Liv blew out a frustrated breath. "Inside *where*, Marcy?"

Marcy's face creased into a frown. "Inside here, of course. Aren't you listening to me?"

Lord, give me patience. "Are you two okay? Do you have a place to spend the night?"

"Ohhhh, yeah." Marcy laughed lecherously. "The bed is reeeeeally soft and bouncy. See?"

Liv could hear the loud creaking of incredibly squeaky springs as Marcy tested the bed for a moment before remembering she was on the phone.

"Ewwww...but there are bugs. I don't like bugs. Oh! Oh! Did you know your brother is the best kisser ever?"

Liv smiled wryly as she listened to the girl's scattered ramblings. *She's so wasted.* "No, Marcy, I didn't know that. But I'll take your word for it. Are you at a motel? You need to focus and answer me, so we'll know where you two are."

Silence.

"Marcy, are you still there?"

"That's it!" Kayla's temper snapped, and she jerked the phone out of Liv's hands. "God dammit it, Marcy! You tell me where your ass is parked, right this very second!" she boomed, drawing a soft chuckle from Liv who was more than happy to relinquish the phone and let Kayla try her hand at wading through the confusion.

Whoa, she's sexy when she's mad. But Liv admonished Kayla with a reproachful look anyway. "Easy, Kayla, or she'll just hang up."

Kayla nodded grumpily. She hadn't thought of that. *And Mama wonders why I don't want children.*

"Marcy's not here right now," Marcy said in a fake French accent that sounded exactly like a drunk southerner trying to sound French. "This is Gigi. Bye." Then there was a thump, and a curse, and the boinging of bedsprings as Marcy let go of the phone directly over Doug's head and dove under the sheets to hide from her big sister.

"Marcy? Marcy?" Kayla looked at the cell phone receiver blankly, then at Liv. "Who the fuck is Gigi?"

Liv shrugged. "Ask for Dougie. I heard him snickering in the background earlier."

"Doug? Pick up the phone, Doug. I know you're there."

Doug sat up rubbing his forehead. The receiver had landed right on his perfectly balanced beer can. "This is Pierre. Doug is—"

"Don't screw with me, Doug," Kayla warned.

"Yes, ma'am," the boy replied instantly.

"Are you both okay? Other than being piss-ass drunk, I mean."

"We're not *that* drunk." Doug held his finger and thumb a tiny distance apart. "We only drank a little."

"You didn't drink the entire case, did you?"

"Nooo. There's a lot left.

"A lot?"

Doug burst out laughing. "Well, some."

"Do you know which motel you're in?" The boy seemed a little better off than her sister, but not much. They were going to have such a hangover tomorrow.

"I dunno." Doug scrunched his face up tightly. "It's by ummm...hamburgers...you know, the eating place. God, I wish I had some french fries."

"Get a phone number," Liv whispered to Kayla.

"He doesn't even know where they are, Liv. You expect him to know the phone number?"

"Tell him to look on the phone. The number is usually printed right there," Liv reminded.

Kayla nodded. "Doug, look on the phone and tell us the phone number."

"Okay...umm...it's too dark."

"Are your eyes open?" Kayla questioned dryly.

"I think so. Yeah...never mind, I found it. It's 9-1-1." There was a pause. "Why does that sound so familiar?"

Kayla's head sagged, and she wordlessly handed the phone back to a smirking Liv.

"Hi, Dougie. You guys call us in the morning, okay," Liv requested calmly. There was no reason to go apeshit now. They were both safe, and there was nothing she could do about the situation anyway. Tomorrow would just have to be soon enough.

"Is Kayla taking care of you?"

"What?" Liv hadn't been expecting that question.

"The storm. I know you hate storms. I'm sorry, Liv. I should be there with you. I really, really should," he admitted guiltily.

Liv could practically see him running a hand through his disheveled curls, his toe twisting its way into the carpet.

"Liv, sometimes somebody needs to take care of you, too."

Liv's heart lurched a bit at the sentiment and the sound of her brother's suddenly melancholy voice. How was she ever going to stay angry with Dougie long enough to kill him when he said stuff like that?

Liv turned to Kayla and smiled warmly, letting the affection she felt for her friend show plainly in her eyes. It was immediately reflected back at her in a brilliant smile.

"Yeah." Liv cleared her throat softly, surprised at its sudden tightness as she placed the icepack back on Kayla's knee. "We're taking good care of each other. You do the same for Marcy, all right?" She paused, then said it anyway. "Don't do something you'll regret later, Dougie. Neither one of you is thinking straight right now," she warned, hoping her brother wasn't too drunk to know what she meant. She only barely resisted the urge to yell, "No having sex!" The only thing that stopped her was the certain knowledge that it wouldn't do any good anyway.

"I'll be a perfect gentlemen," Dougie swore solemnly, his mind happily shifting to the lump under the bed sheet. Liv opened her mouth to say something else, but stopped when she heard a loud groan and several anguished murmurs in the background. "Uh Oh. No, Marcy, use the trash can..." Doug's voiced sounded desperate. "Don't...no...oh, gross!"

And then the line went dead.

"Ewww. In this heat that's not going to be pretty," Liv snorted disgustedly before turning the phone off and setting it on the coffee table alongside the history. "Well, at least we know they're someplace out of the storm. They'll be okay," she added firmly, feeling secure in that knowledge for the first time since that morning. Her relief was palpable.

"I guess that's something," Kayla acknowledged, closing her eyes and wincing a little as she felt steady hands adjust the emergency ice pack on her knee again.

Liv flashed her companion an empathic smile. "I'm sorry; I'm not trying to hurt you. I would never, ever, do that intentionally," she promised softly. On impulse, she lifted off the icepack and placed a soft kiss on the swollen knee.

Kayla jumped at the feeling of warm lips and hot breath on her icy skin.

Liv grinned against the flesh, then moved a few inches higher, soft hair dragging across Kayla's naked thigh as she deposited several more tender kisses.

Kayla moaned loudly, as a bolt of heat shot straight through her groin. She laughed weakly when Liv lifted her head and wiggled her eyebrows lasciviously. "You're mean, Liv."

Grinning from ear to ear, the blonde drew herself back up to Kayla's lips, where she whispered quietly, "No, I'm not. I'm really nice, I swear."

Kayla leaned forward just a fraction and brushed her lips against Liv's. Reveling in their warmth and softness, she drew a breathy sigh from her companion when they finally parted.

"Maybe I should have told your sister that *you're* the best kisser ever, too," Liv murmured dreamily, her eyes still closed.

Kayla laughed, loving the look on Liv's face and feeling a thrilling sense of satisfaction that it was directed towards her.

Finally.

Is this what falling in love feels like? Kayla shook her head in pure amazement. *I never knew.* A feeling of happiness welled within her, making her heart ache in a way she'd never experienced. A good way.

Liv sucked in a breath as an overwhelming surge of joy washed over her, tickling her consciousness for a split second before enveloping her. "That was you, wasn't it?" she asked, inhaling sharply and opening surprised eyes, her voice tinged with wonder and confusion.

White teeth glinted. "Yeah. If you're talking about a pretty great feeling, then I guess that was me."

Liv shifted her head to the side as she thought, absently stretching her neck and causing Kayla's gaze to roam along the smooth skin of her throat, then over soft red lips, finally landing on slightly glassy eyes.

"Liv, are you doing okay with this? I know it's sort of..." *Sort of what? Personal. Intense. Scary. Invasive.* "a lot to handle," was what she finally settled on, although it didn't seem to be nearly enough. *It will always be like this with me, Liv. And once you learn you have some measure of control over it, it will only get stronger as words blend in with the images and pictures start to form in your head. But the feelings...I can't explain the feelings. I've only ever felt those with you.*

"Yeah." Liv worried her lower lip as she contemplated how to put into words what was so sketchy in her own mind, but realized that if anyone would understand, it would be Kayla. "It's a little scary, feeling like someone is inside your head with you, and vice versa. And it sort of leaves me feeling, um...out of control, ya know?"

Kayla nodded and held her breath, waiting for the other shoe to drop as a knot formed in her stomach.

"But in a way, it feels good, too. It's different, but still natural." She ducked her head, wondering when she had become so inarticulate. "I'm probably not making any sense."

Kayla started to breathe again, her heart having skipped a beat. "No. You're making perfect sense. It's pretty much the way I feel, only I've had my whole life to get used to it."

Liv's glance flickered upward for the briefest of seconds before dropping to her lap. "It sort of makes me feel closer to you." *Please don't let that be a bad thing — something I'll miss when we leave this place and each other.* She swallowed hard. Just the thought of not seeing Kayla again caused her chest to tighten painfully. *No. I don't want that,* her mind whispered, as she felt the beginning of unexpected tears and turned away from her friend.

Kayla caught a glimpse of sadness in watery eyes before Liv turned away. But she didn't have time to wonder about its context before a jagged streak of lightning tore through the night sky, calling her attention outside. She closed tired eyes, deeply inhaling the fragrance of the salty ocean, wet wood, and a light floral shampoo that wasn't her own, and it brought an unconscious smile to her face.

Liv wiped her eyes with an angry hand, hoping Kayla wouldn't notice. But she felt gentle fingers grasp her chin, tilting her face up until she was forced to meet Kayla's worried frown.

"Hey," a gentle thumb brushed Liv's cheek, "what's wrong?"

Damn. "Nothing. I mean—" Liv stopped when she saw the look of hurt flash across Kayla's face at her obvious lie. "Can we talk about it tomorrow? I think I'm just a little strung out tonight... What with the kids—" A strong gust of howling wind caused the room's candles to flicker and the curtains to flap wildly. "And the storm." *C'mon, Kayla, not right now.* "Please?"

"Sure." Every fiber of Kayla's being was telling her to keep pushing, find out what had suddenly upset Liv. But Liv was asking her to wait. And so she would. "Are you ready for bed?"

Liv shook her head, mentally calculating the hours 'til dawn. "No. I'm sure it's still too hot upstairs." Another gust of cool wind blew a strand of pale hair across her face, and she sighed in relief as the breeze kissed her cheeks and throat. "This is the first time I've been comfortable since we got here. Can we stay in the library a little longer?"

Kayla brushed back Liv's errant lock, feeling a strong surge of protectiveness and sweet affection. Willing to say or do anything to make Liv happy, she agreed. "Of course. Whatever you want. Anything you want," she fumbled helplessly, until two fingers, pressed firmly against her lips, stopped her babbling.

"It's okay." Liv smiled fondly, feeling a pang of guilt. "I know I worried you for a second, but I'm really fine. Do you want me to read a little more? Have you heard anything yet that you think will help Marcy?"

Kayla shook her. "Not really. There was no guarantee I would. I just had to be sure."

"I know. But there's still a chance. We're not finished reading, right?" Her gaze flickered around the room. "I'll move some more candles over here. These are really starting to burn down."

"Let me—" Kayla leaned forward to get up.

"Stay put," Liv ordered.

Kayla blinked.

"Sorry," the older woman chuckled lightly. "I just want you to rest your knee." She gently patted the area above the body part in question. "It'll only take me a second."

"But—"

A fair eyebrow arched.

"Okay, I'll just sit here like a useless lump," Kayla grumbled, ignoring Liv's teasing grin.

When Liv stood, she briefly ran her fingertips along Kayla's tender scalp, then through long silky strands of dark-red hair. The researcher leaned into the loving touch and groaned contentedly. "Mmm...if I'd known all lumps were treated this nicely," she sighed happily, "I'd have become one a long, loooong time ago."

That comment earned Kayla's hair a playful tug as Liv laughed and moved away.

After a few moments of readjusting candlelight, the women wordlessly resumed their reading position, side-by-side on the sofa. Liv grabbed Kayla's hand and threaded their fingers together tightly before beginning again.

Cobb Island
January, 1691

Over the next two months, while the world around us began to die, transforming the island into a vision of burnt orange and gold and blood-red, Bridget and Faylinn blossomed. Every day, it seemed, they found an excuse to spend time together until, finally, they simply stopped making excuses at all.

Cobb Island
October, 1690

"FASTER." FAYLINN HEELED her mount to the sound of Bridget's raucous laughter. "Come on, girl, you can do it."

The women were engaged in a horse race of epic proportion, their furiously galloping animals kicking up scatterings of twigs and leaves as they flew up the sloping planes of a hill.

"It'll take more than that old nag to catch Apollo," Bridget taunted over her shoulder, despite the fact that she was barely two horse lengths in front of Faylinn.

"Nag?" the blonde panted incredulously, her eyes narrowing. This was one of the finest animals she'd ever had the privilege of riding.

One of Cyril's business associates, a captain in the Royal Navy, had gifted him with a muscular, sleek mare the color of midnight. The elder Redding detested horses, pronouncing them smelly, lowly creatures, whose care was far more troublesome than they were worth. When he told Judith that he'd be selling the horse immediately, Faylinn had waged an all out campaign to be allowed to keep the dark beauty — but all to no avail. It wasn't until Bridget subtly reminded Cyril that Virginia Governor Francis Nicolson's wife had taken to breeding horses as a ladies' hobby, that Cyril magnanimously gifted his bride with the animal. Satisfied that his actions would earn him bragging rights among his peers, he allowed his wife her tedious pastime.

Faylinn leaned forward in the saddle, her skirts and golden hair billowing out behind her as she moved several feet closer to Bridget. Apollo planted his hooves firmly on the grassy top of the hill. Snorting, the young stallion used powerful legs to propel himself over the edge and onto a suddenly barren plateau. But not before Faylinn and her mare hurtled past him, jumping over a large rock that stood between them and the women's appointed finish line.

"No!" Bridget howled piteously, but was unable to keep the smile off her face.

Faylinn threw her head back and laughed, the youthful, unrestrained joy in the voice tugging irresistibly at Bridget's heartstrings. "Oh, yes!" She wiped the sweat from her brow. It was an unusually warm autumn day, and both horses and women were drenched with perspiration.

Bridget merely shook her head. She certainly hadn't expected the surge of competition from her sister-in-law. "Well," Bridget slid off of Apollo's back, landing on the ground with a tired thud, her chest still heaving from the exertion of the race, "it appears, Faylinn, that I have lost our wager."

Faylinn took a moment to catch her breath, crooning soft words of praise to her horse as she moved to dismount the animal. Bridget wordlessly stepped forward and lifted her arms to help Faylinn down off the tall horse.

The younger woman's eyes twinkled gently as she slid from the saddle and into Bridget's waiting arms. "Thank you," she said softly, licking her lips and gazing up into Bridget's eyes.

Bridget swallowed hard, her throat suddenly dry. "You are more than welcome, Faylinn."

Several heartbeats ticked away where neither woman moved. Bridget's arms were loosely wrapped around Faylinn's trim waist and their eyes were locked, the sound of twin, thundering heartbeats drowning out the wind, the faint cries of the gulls, and the nearby surf.

Faylinn could feel the heat coming off of Bridget, could smell her skin and clean sweat on the late afternoon breeze. Her breathing quickened, and a flush rose to her cheeks as her body wildly responded to Bridget's closeness. She could have sworn that the brilliant blue eyes gazing so intently into hers had begun to darken, and that Bridget had ducked her head slightly as they were ever so slowly moving even closer together.

Apollo suddenly nudged Bridget hard on the shoulder with his nose, causing her to release Faylinn from their loose embrace and sending the tall woman stumbling sideways.

"Apollo," Faylinn admonished for Bridget, but it was clear she found the steed's actions more humorous than annoying. She stifled a giggle with the back of her hand.

Truth be told, a big part of Faylinn was grateful for the interruption. Something was happening between her and Bridget. Something exhilarating and terrifying, that she couldn't begin to explain or understand. Faylinn could feel it winding through her heart and soul, binding them together as sure and as strong as chains of solid iron. The young mother was anxious and mortally frightened at the same time.

Apollo whinnied loudly and nuzzled Faylinn's chest. She stroked his nose lovingly, watching Bridget narrow her eyes at the beast as she straightened.

"I see you've bewitched my horse."

One of Faylinn's eyebrows quirked playfully. "He's a perceptive boy."

Faylinn's own horse, not wanting to be left out of the action, clomped over to her mistress and demanded the same attention Apollo was receiving. Faylinn laughed at the mare's antics. "No need to be jealous." She set out to scratching the sensitive spot behind the horse's ear.

Like me, Bridget thought bluntly. She took off her hat and smacked it across Apollo's rump. But there was no malice in the action, and Apollo merely snorted. "Unruly beast."

The white stallion stomped one of his hooves and swung his head over to Bridget, who couldn't resist giving him a gentle pat. "Well, now," Faylinn said, intentionally riveting her gaze to the piece of horseflesh she was scratching, "I do believe it's time for me to collect on my wager." She didn't even bother to hide her smirk.

Bridget's eyes swept over Faylinn, and she began to chuckle. "I suppose you're right. After all, my word is my bond. However, I refuse to comply with our agreement with you in your current...indelicate condition." Bridget made a face.

Faylinn's head snapped sideways and her jaw dropped. "Indelicate condition?" She focused on Bridget's soaked linen shirt. "Why—"

Before Faylinn could say another word, Bridget swept her off her feet and settled Faylinn in her arms as she began stomping across the small plateau, the smell of the sea growing stronger with every step.

"What...what are you doing?" Faylinn screeched, though she

couldn't find it in her heart to try to wiggle out of her current position.

Bridget worked her way down the far side of the plateau, easily navigating the cragged slope that lead to the ocean. "You did say you expected me to fulfill my end of the wager, did you not?"

"But—"

"No buts," Bridget announced firmly, a wide smile stretching her tanned cheeks. "Except this one." She hoisted Faylinn over her shoulder like a large sack of flour and gave her bottom a stinging swat.

Faylinn yelped, then burst out laughing. "Bridget."

"Hello, Afia," Bridget announced cordially, just as her boots began to splash through the edge of the surf.

Afia shook her head. "Hello, Mistress Bridget." The wiry slave was sitting on a large flat rock, her bare feet dangling in the water as she sorted through a mass of seaweed that would be added to that evening's soup. She had seen the women on the plateau, and watched in delight as Bridget carried Faylinn down to the ocean. On rare occasions, just like this, the women played like happy children. It brought a smile to Afia's face when she caught a glimpse of them away from the house, with young Master Henry napping and Master Cyril far from their thoughts.

"Afia?" Faylinn squeaked, wriggling wildly to try and see who else was witnessing this most pleasant humiliation. Then Faylinn's eyes widened and the words *current indelicate condition* repeated themselves in her mind. *I'm not that sweaty.* "Oh, no you don't Bridget. You wouldn't dare."

Bridget merely laughed.

"I'm not taking a bath in the sea."

Bridget stomped deeper into the water, the small waves now at her knees. "I beg to differ," was all she said before launching Faylinn off her shoulder and directly into the ocean.

The young woman let out a surprised yell before hitting the water with a gigantic splash.

Afia looked down at the green weeds in her hands, her body shaking with silent laughter.

When Faylinn surfaced, she blew out a mouthful of salty seawater and glared at Bridget, who managed to look mildly innocent, considering the circumstances. And though she would now have to take a bath to wash away the salt and the muck when she returned home, she did feel much cooler. "Very funny. I don't think I'll be making this particular wager again."

"It won't matter, because you won't be winning again," Bridget boasted, only partially certain she was right.

Faylinn stood. She was drenched from head to toe, her

dripping, reddish-gold locks taking on a dark tint from the water, her sodden skirts clinging to her legs as she stumbled towards shore.

"Let's get on with this then," Bridget said haughtily, earning a scolding look from Afia, though the older woman knew Bridget was merely playing with Faylinn.

Bridget joined Afia on a rock and waited for Faylinn to trudge her way over.

Faylinn stopped in front of both women and put her hands on her hips. "Well?"

"You shall have your payment, never fear." Bridget reached out with both hands and blew out a slightly embarrassed breath. "Lift."

Faylinn lifted her right foot and set it on Bridget's lap. The red-haired woman pulled off Faylinn's boot, dumping out a pool of seawater with exaggerated slowness. Without further prompting, Bridget slowly slid her hands up Faylinn's calf.

The younger woman gasped at the unexpected touch and Afia looked away, somehow feeling she was suddenly witnessing something private between the two.

"Ticklish?" Bridget's fingers began to dance over Faylinn's skin.

"No. And get on with it, Bridget," Faylinn laughed.

Bridget shrugged. She lifted Faylinn's small foot and brought it to her lips, kissing it gently. She looked up at Faylinn, who was watching her with suddenly serious eyes. "And to the victor..." she paused and kissed it again for good measure, "rightly goes the spoils."

Cobb Island
January 1691

Until my dying day, I know that I shall remember the blaze that would ignite like so much tinder when their gazes would lock, for I am positive I shall never see its like again.

They were physically affectionate, as sisters might be. But even the most curious of observers would have been forced to attest to the simple truth that their touches never went beyond what propriety dictated. As I write this today, I am certain that Mistress Bridget was fully aware of the nature of her feelings for her brother's wife. I am equally certain that Mistress Faylinn was awash in a sea of confusion. But it mattered little that their bodies had not followed the course their hearts had already chosen. That they were in love was plain to see, to anyone who bothered to look. And for reasons I do not pretend to understand, Master Redding chose not to look. Or, maybe it was simply that his quest for endless spoils blinded him to all else.

His business associates, several officers in His Majesty's Royal Navy, made frequent stops to the island, which was destined to become a stopover for the slaves on the way to market on the mainland. Bridget argued bitterly with her brother over his choice of business ventures, and vehemently refused to take part in them. But his position as head of household, assured both by his birth order and gender, meant that the Redding estate was his to control, and his alone. Mistress Bridget had little choice but to stand by and watch as he invested their family resources in Evil's own trade.

One wretched day, words between the siblings actually led to blows, with Master Redding taking a beating the likes of which he would neither forget nor forgive. Although, at the time, I privately wondered if it was the lurid, purple bruise across Mistress Faylinn's cheek, and the announcement that he would be expecting several more sons sometime soon, that truly motivated Mistress Bridget's rage. Had several slaves not pulled her from her brother, there is no doubt that she would have murdered him where he stood. Praise Allah there were no blades near.

Cyril exacted his revenge on his sister by concocting a cruel plan while she and Faylinn were out riding one afternoon. Faylinn had told him she would be back in an hour, and when she returned one hour and fifteen minutes later, Cyril pronounced her inexcusably tardy and in need of a lesson. He marched out to the barn with three strong slaves in tow. Master commanded two of the slaves hold Bridget, and the third to secure Mistress Faylinn. Then, before their wide eyes, and to the sound of Faylinn's screams, Cyril slit her gentle mare's throat with his long sword, before calmly walking back into the house to wash his hands.

Faylinn would never be late again.

To say that during these months Bridget's relationship with Elizabeth deteriorated even further would be a ridiculous understatement. Where the girl's father was oblivious to the tender feelings that had developed between her new mother and aunt, she was not.

I believe Elizabeth has always dwelled in the darkest part of the human spirit, feeling most comfortable in its gloomy, putrid confines, her only lifeline found in her lighter, loving twin. But when Judith turned a blind eye to Faylinn and Bridget's obvious connection, Elizabeth took it as a personal betrayal. She willfully turned away from what little light Day could provide her, embracing the darkness deep within herself with both hands. She strove to increase her knowledge of her abilities — a mystical family power that the slaves only whisper about, but I know for a fact to be real — without guidance or restraint.

Only Allah knows the true price the inhabitants of Cobb Island paid for allowing Elizabeth to stew in her own malevolence, her very soul festering with hatred.

Chapter
Twelve

Merging Minds

Cobb Island
November, 1690

"BE REASONABLE, CYRIL," Bridget implored, but couldn't keep a slender eyebrow from arching in a challenging manner. "As Henry's mother, she has the right to know what's happening to her own child. The boy is already as cunning as a fox and is showing signs of his abilities years before even Judith and Elizabeth did."

Bridget wondered whether Cyril was aware of how powerful his children actually were. Both Judith and Elizabeth had a wide range of paranormal abilities that went far beyond telepathy, the predominant family ability for the past several centuries. She had every reason to believe Henry would share the dynamic powers his half-sisters possessed. "Only the other day, Faylinn told me she was thinking of a tune that she hadn't heard since her own childhood, when, out of the blue, Henry began to hum the tune in time with her thoughts. She fears something is terribly wrong with the child, or that she's simply going mad. Every moment you don't tell her, *especially* now that she's inquired, is nothing more than a lie.

"Are you listening to me, Cyril? We have had this conversation before, and I refuse to be a party to your lies or cause Faylinn undue distress in any case. She cannot be kept in the dark about our abilities forever."

The man turned away from his ledger, finally giving his sister the courtesy of his undivided attention. Cyril's face creased into an obnoxious smirk as he began twirling his long quill. "Why does this concern you so, Sister?" His fingers stilled. "I shall instruct Henry on his abilities when the time is right." Cyril chuckled inwardly and set down the quill. It was a rare occasion indeed that Bridget came to him seeking anything. He was already taking great pleasure in her frustration.

Leaning forward, Bridget placed both fists on the desktop and looked her brother dead in the eye. "You've already done a monstrous job with your daughters. Judith fears her powers. And Elizabeth shows no discretion whatsoever when it comes to using her abilities. Am I to believe things will be different with Henry? And Faylinn—"

"Is my wife!" Cyril suddenly boomed, feeding off his sister's tense energy.

"Don't you think I know that!" Bridget's face turned an ugly shade of purple and her hand twitched, longing to feel the cool hilt of her blade or Cyril's glass jaw. "I am reminded every waking moment that she is regarded as your *possession*, a brood mare," the redhead spat.

"Sister, are you jealous that it's my bed that she shares and not yours?" he hazarded in the midst of an unusual moment of insightfulness.

Yes! her mind screamed. "I...well...I...I..." The younger woman was momentarily flustered, the question having caught her completely off guard. *Have my feelings for Faylinn become so obvious that I cannot conceal them from this pompous fool?* She cursed her own lack of discretion and control, desperately wanting to tell Faylinn about her family's abilities herself—gently—so the young woman wouldn't be frightened, or worse, repulsed.

He grew tired of waiting for Bridget to answer. Not that it mattered. She was no threat to him in that arena. "Why are you wasting my time this morning, Bridget? I've ten men arriving this afternoon to transact business." He shooed her away with one hand, a gesture she'd detested since childhood. Bridget ground her teeth together. "This discussion is not finished, Brother."

His attention shifted back to his calculations, and he turned his back on Bridget. "You will tell Faylinn nothing," he forbade in a tight, condescending voice. "You know as well as I do that until Elizabeth attains the age of sixteen and is ready to fulfill her role as Guardian, I, as her father, act as de facto Guardian, making decisions of this nature on her behalf."

Family protocol concerning revealing the abilities or the contents of the histories was inviolate. It was the Guardian alone that decided who should and should not be told.

Bridget's temper flared. "How dare you abuse your position as caretaker! It is within your power to grant this request, but you refuse me out of spite? At the expense of your own wife and son?" Then she hit her brother where she knew it would hurt most, his purse. "I wonder if your business associates know what manner of pig they're dealing with, Brother?" Her gaze flickered to Cyril's sword, which was propped up against the wall behind his desk. She was pushing him, she knew, hoping he would reach for the weapon and give her another excuse to thrash him.

"Cyril, have these businessmen, who are no doubt as disreputable as yourself, heard how your poor business sense led your former partners to ruin?" Bridget laughed cruelly, noting her brother's now rigid posture. "It was truly amazing how quickly the news of your deplorable actions spread through the whole of court. And then, as they always do for us, the rumors of strange happenings began."

Cyril's pulse was racing, perspiration gathering at his collar. "You keep your trap shut! I will *not* allow gossip and rank speculation to affect my new business venture." The slender man slammed his ledger closed and stood nose-to-nose with his sister, his chest heaving. "I have come half way around God's earth to begin anew and escape the cursed rumors that have surrounded our family for generations. Here we start fresh, with a clean slate. Do not presume to ruin that because of some misguided proclivity toward absolute honesty. I will not allow it!"

A soft knock at the library door interrupted the siblings. They both stopped talking but their eyes remained locked, neither breaking their challenging gazes to look at the door.

After a few more seconds, the door slowly opened. A golden-haired head poked in and looked around, not sure what to expect after hearing yelling and then dead silence. "There you are," Faylinn said, as she moved into the room. She smiled warmly at Bridget, although her words were directed to her husband. "I've been looking for you." She stopped. Her gaze flickered from Bridget to Cyril and back again. A pale brow twitched in question. "Am I interrupting something?"

"Yes."

"No," Cyril responded, overriding his sister.

Faylinn's eyes widened slightly, and she took in the siblings' poses. The tension in the room was palpable, and she unconsciously sucked in a breath, holding it.

Cyril finally dropped his eyes from Bridget's and took a small step backwards. "Do come in, Faylinn." He gestured for the young woman to come all the way into the room, ignoring Bridget's slight growl.

Hesitantly, Faylinn began to move towards Bridget, but when she stepped past Cyril, who had moved out from behind his desk, he suddenly grabbed her, pulling her into a rough embrace and crushing his lips against hers, his tongue demanding entrance. Completely caught off guard by her husband's repulsive actions, Faylinn pawed at his chest as she tried to pull away, only to be held firm. Several seconds later, when Cyril was certain he'd made his point, he released her, their lips making a loud smacking sound as they separated.

When her husband's arms suddenly fell away, Faylinn stumbled, until Bridget's strong hands captured her, steadying her. "I was hoping you would come by for a morning kiss," Cyril announced smugly, retreating behind the large desk and out of Bridget's immediate reach. "I'm certain Bridget doesn't mind a simple show of affection and devotion between loving spouses. Isn't that right, Sister?" he taunted.

For the moment, Bridget did her best to control the wild surge of pure rage coursing through her. *He is going to die today*, she promised bitterly. *And it will be by my hand.* Blue eyes darkened by fury and worry met frightened, tear filled ones, as she carefully searched the pretty young woman's face for signs of injury. Adrenaline was making her hands shake, but with effort, she managed to gently cup soft cheeks, drawing her thumb across Faylinn's bruised lips. It came back smeared with a light coating of glistening, dark blood.

"I'm all right, Bridget," Faylinn whispered softly, completely tuning out Cyril's revolting chuckles. "Don't." She knew Bridget was on the edge of a murderous rage. Anger was pouring off the darker woman in crashing waves, and her furiously pounding pulse matched Faylinn's own. "Please. I am all right."

Bridget shook her head slowly and dropped her hands from Faylinn's face. Then she reached down and took two smaller hands in her own, bringing them up and placing a tender kiss on each palm, the intimacy of the act drawing a soft gasp from Faylinn. "No, dearest."

The blonde's face broke into a dazzling smile at the new endearment.

"You are most certainly *not* all right." Bridget smiled gently down at her friend. "But you soon will be," she promised softly.

Then, in a lightning move that was so quick Faylinn barely saw it, Bridget lifted her heel and drew a short, double-edged, steel blade from her boot. Before Cyril even had a chance to wipe the egotistical smile off his face, she was upon him, slamming his head against the expensive desk with vicious force.

Millions of tiny stars invaded his vision as his head swam. When he was finally able to see straight, he realized that he was being pinned to his desk by Bridget's bone-handled knife, which had been stabbed through his lace scarf and the lapel of his jacket. One of her hands remained threaded tightly in his luxurious black curls, tilting his chin up so that he was forced to meet her eyes.

He thought he heard Bridget speaking, but the ringing in his ears prevented him from understanding the words. "Un...unhand...me," he panted weakly, wishing he could reach his sword, craving her blood on his hands. "Godless savage," he spat stupidly, despite his fear, causing both Faylinn and Bridget to wonder whether he truly did have a death wish.

"Answer me, Brother! Or are your meager faculties so easily addled? Does it make you feel important to control those around you with an iron hand?" When there was no immediate response, Bridget slapped him soundly with the back of her hand, her knuckles rapping loudly against his teeth and nose.

Once.

Twice.

Three times.

Her own skin breaking.

Four times she struck, until both his nose and mouth were bleeding profusely. She raised her hand again for a fifth blow. "Bridget, stop!" Faylinn begged, tugging hard on the sleeve of the older woman's rough-spun cotton shirt. She dug her heels into the Persian rug that partially covered the hardwood floor.

"Enough!" This time her voice was firm and it snapped Bridget out of her single-minded task.

"By God, why?" Bridget turned wild, confused eyes on Faylinn. "Why?" she demanded as she let go of Cyril, his head thumping back to the desk. Bridget wrapped her hands around Faylinn's biceps and pulled her close. "He is a vile beast who will never be capable of anything more than hurting you. Why should I stop?" she repeated with the bewilderment of a child. *How can you want me to?*

Faylinn laid her palms on Bridget's chest, her fingers resting solidly against the soft, exposed skin just below Bridget's throat, where the top two buttons of her shirt were undone. Firming her resolve, she gingerly steered the livid woman away from Cyril. When she spoke, her voice was confident and compelling, drawing Bridget in with every word and making her believe. "You should stop because he is not nearly worth it," she said honestly. "And because you are not a murderer." Faylinn was very conscious of the hot skin beneath her fingertips and the pounding heart that began to slow with her calming touch and voice. "And because he is my son's father. And despite his many shortcomings, he is the only father Henry has." *And only God knows how much I regret that bitter truth.*

"And because you are in love with him?" Bridget choked out, somehow speaking past the lump in her throat. *Please...anything but that. I am certain I shan't survive hearing that.*

Faylinn shook her head. "You know that I'm not, and never have been," she answered in a hushed tone, her heart aching for her lost youth and horrid marriage, and for how she felt about Bridget, which made no sense. Deep in her soul, she knew the connection between them was utterly right, and wondered how that could be true and still be a mortal sin.

A flash of movement caught Faylinn's eye, and she noticed that Cyril had freed himself from the desk and had a bloodstained handkerchief pressed tightly against his dripping nose.

Awkwardly, he held out Bridget's blade, ready to ward off any further attack. "You are a raving lunatic," he sputtered to his sister, having recovered some of his bravado now that the knife was in his own hand. He wiped away an errant drop of blood that trailed through his thin mustache and over his chin.

Bridget closed her eyes tightly, vowing that somehow she would rescue Faylinn from this existence. That whatever it took, they would leave this place forever. Together. She opened her eyes slowly, allowing some of her dark energy to bleed away. "Faylinn just saved your life, Brother. I would say that warrants at least a smidgen of gratitude, wouldn't you?"

Cyril just sneered as the color began to return to pallid cheeks. He folded the blood-soaked handkerchief in half and began dabbing his lip, already concocting the lie that would adequately explain his swollen mouth and nose to his business associates that afternoon.

Bridget took a step towards her brother, causing him to point the tip of the blade in her direction. Heedless of his aggressive posture, she walked right up to him and yanked her knife from his hands. Then she drew him to her by the scruff of his neck. "Harm her again, Cyril, and you won't hear her begging for your miserable life," Bridget's jaw muscles twitched as she paused for effect, "because you'll *already* be dead." The tall woman tightened the grip on his collar until her knuckles stood out in vivid relief against his crimson and black jacket. "Have I made myself abundantly clear?" She gave him a stiff shake for good measure.

Cyril opened his mouth to hastily agree, but no sound came out. He tried again, but the most he could muster was a squeak as his face began to take on a bluish hue. Bulging, beseeching eyes sought out Faylinn, who stood silently alongside Bridget, pointedly *not* coming to his aid. *Red-haired bitch!* he seethed inwardly, as Bridget released her grip and he drew in a gasping, shuddering breath.

Bridget pushed him away in disgust, gently grasping Faylinn's hand and leading her out of the room.

Cyril's loud, but notably raspy voice interrupted their departures. "I am entertaining business associates this afternoon, Faylinn. Wear the dress I bought you in Paris. The green one. You will be expected to make at least a brief appearance," he ordered, effectively ignoring everything that had just taken place and settling back into his role as master of the house with practiced ease. He was the head of household because it was his birthright. A violent fit by his sister couldn't change that. Besides, she had only gained the upper hand because of a cowardly surprise attack. He would be more vigilant in the future, and that wouldn't happen again.

Faylinn considered her next words carefully, trying to put Henry's needs above her own. "I promised Henry I'd take him to feed the ducks this afternoon before it got too cold. He's been asking for you." *He doesn't understand what a filthy swine his father is...yet.* "That's why I came looking for you in the first place, to see if you'd join us."

An annoyed look flitted across Cyril's face as he discarded his soiled handkerchief in the small trash bin that stood alongside his desk. "The slaves can take him," he answered without thought. "You will be otherwise engaged."

"Brother, I am still inclined to slap you senseless, although I admit, it would be a bit redundant."

Despite the recent violence and the fact that the anxiety in the room was still taut, Faylinn stifled an impertinent giggle. "Were I you," Bridget continued, "I would be wise enough not to press my luck."

"Faylinn," Cyril warned in a low voice. It was one thing to deal with his unmanageable sister. But he refused to have his wife disobey him.

Bridget took a step forward but was held firmly in place by Faylinn, who didn't want things to escalate out of control again. "I'll be ready, Husband," she conceded graciously, earning a compassionate but frustrated look from Bridget.

Cyril straightened, having won, at least in his own mind, this battle of the wills. Then he sat down at his desk and began poring over his numbers once more, occasionally wiping away a trickle from his still bleeding nose with a clean cloth.

Cobb Island
January, 1691

I pause here, at the risk of confusion, because it was at this point in her accounting to me, that Mistress Bridget stopped to gather her thoughts and then, unexpectedly, proceeded in another direction entirely. I fear that the events that took place soon after her argument with her brother fractured her very soul. During their retelling, her mood was somber, and her eyes, usually brighter than the summer sky, were dull and weary. It was more than I expected.

I watched silently, not presuming to prod along such a personal tale, as Bridget's gaze drifted to the elongated shadows that painted the stable walls. With a deep, resigned sigh she explained that she didn't have much more time, and it was necessary to break the chronology of her telling so that the truly pertinent information might be conveyed. It was then that she made what she called her most important contribution to history.

In my unrepentant heart, however, Allah knows I do not believe that to be true. And that is why, even after Mistress Bridget conveyed that which she considered her sacred duty, this story...their story...continues.

Cobb Island
Present Day

"GOD, KAYLA. CYRIL was a real — "

"Asshole? Misogynistic pig? Butt nugget?"

Liv laughed. "That wasn't *exactly* what I was going to say, but it does convey the general idea. Yeah. He, um, basically seems like a clueless control freak. I'm not sure whether he knew his sister was in love with his wife and just didn't care, or whether he was too ignorant to conceive of the fact that that kind of love was even possible."

Kayla let out what could only be described as a frustrated grunt. "Faylinn was only a few years older than Marcy, and she was completely trapped." Somehow, the researcher found herself in the nonsensical position of wanting to solve Faylinn's predicament, despite the fact that the woman had been dead for hundreds of years.

"Mmm," Liv agreed, smiling affectionately at the look of utter concentration on Kayla's face, as the wheels in that brilliant mind began turning even faster. Liv's hand drifted to the crinkled skin around brilliant blue eyes and with a gentle motion, she smoothed away the worry lines. *I am. I'm sitting here falling in love with her. I'm letting it happen. Hell, I'm loving the fact that it's happening.* She sighed softly, trying to remember what they were talking about. "I think in those days, being nineteen meant something different than it does today. And at least she wasn't alone. She had Bridget, who obviously loved her. And unless Afia went crazy with some sort of serious creative license, Faylinn had to know that." *For some reason,*

I really hope she did.

"Can we read a bit more?" Kayla asked softly, pushing aside her thoughts of Faylinn's problems and feeling a little guilty that she was sitting snuggled up to Liv while the linguist was doing all the work. "This upcoming part sounds like it may be what we're looking for."

"Of course. But only because you asked so sweetly," Liv teased, giving Kayla a little peck on the cheek before starting again. She read on for another half an hour, pale brows drawing together in puzzlement, before she finally stopped, completing the only passages in the history that appeared to be written completely from Bridget's point of view. "Is this—" The blonde paused and let out a frustrated breath. "Kayla, I'm sorry. Maybe my Arabic isn't as good as I thought it was. This isn't making much sense. It's all jumbled."

"It makes perfect sense." Kayla shook her head, a loud boom of thunder interrupting her next words. Liv's body jerked at the earsplitting sound, and Kayla carefully pushed the book off their legs, pulling her friend closer. *I wouldn't let anything hurt you. Ever.*

"It's okay," Liv whispered. "Go on."

"It makes perfect sense," Kayla resumed, hoping to get Liv to focus on her voice and not the howling wind. *This fucking storm isn't going to move on. It's gonna have to burn itself out right over us.* "You're just hearing it out of context. God, this is more than any of the other texts have contained. Bridget's telepathy was truly incredible. Not only could she directly project her thoughts into someone else's head, but she could read theirs nearly word for word." Animated eyes glinted excitedly. *I can't wait to study this alongside some of the other histories.*

Liv still looked confused so Kayla reined in her excitement in order to do a little backtracking. "She's describing several techniques used to help you control your telepathy, and open or close your mind to other telepaths. But she's sort of picking up where other histories have left off, and then adding to them. Without the other texts it makes no sense. With them, it creates a knowledge bridge. It's the missing piece to much of what comes before and after."

Liv grinned at her companion's nearly giddy speech, Kayla's eager expression making her look very much like a child on Christmas morning. "This is what you were hoping for, then?" she laughed, glad for the break in what was turning out to be a very intense story.

"No, Liv. This is beyond what I was hoping for," she clarified with a smile. "In less than ten pages, Bridget has answered a couple of questions I've had since I was a child."

"But will this help Marcy?"

Kayla's expression suddenly sobered. "I...I don't know. I'm not even certain how powerful Marcy's abilities are. I..." A brief hesitation, born of habit. *It's okay, you know you can trust her.* "I know they include telepathy and levitation. When she was a little girl I thought I had a pretty good bead on them. But—" Bridget shrugged as she moved the melted ice pack off her knee and lifted her feet off of the table, setting them on the ground with a slight grimace. "After what Papaw said, I'm not so sure anymore. If he knew something, I wish the old man would have had the courtesy to mention it while he was alive." Her voice was bitter. "I've been tied up in knots over this ever since I got that letter."

Liv's hand moved to Kayla's belly where she gave it a light rub, acknowledging the nervousness and anxiety Kayla must have felt. *That's it, Kayla. Relax.* "I'm sorry about that. I'm sure he didn't mean to...wait. Did you just say levitation?" Liv's eyes widened. "That can't be possible. Wait." She stopped Kayla again, clamping her hand over Kayla's smiling mouth. "I don't know why I keep saying that. Of course it's possible, or you wouldn't be talking about it."

Kayla let out a surprised chuckle through Liv's fingers, tempted to lick her palm. "It's okay. It's pretty wild, I know."

"Levitation, huh? Well, for both the kids' sake I hope Marcy doesn't figure out about that little power tonight."

A lopsided grin eased across Kayla's face. "Good point. I wouldn't want her giving Doug a heart attack."

"Oh, God." Liv covered her eyes with her hands and chuckled ruefully. "And I'm sure it would. Well, unless Marcy has already told him about all—" she waved a hand in the air, "this. The histories, your family's abilities, the house and spell."

"I don't think she has. That was something we were going to talk about this week. But nothing is really stopping her, other than knowing it's a big step, and in my family it's one that we take very, very seriously."

"Mmm...I can see that. But you told me within just a couple of days of us meeting," she reminded. *And I think that meant a whole lot more than I realized at the time.*

"It felt right." Kayla tried to shrug it off as no big deal, but Liv wasn't buying.

"Thanks." Liv smiled warmly, letting how she felt about Kayla show in her eyes. "A lot of things feel right when we're together, don't they?"

Kayla smiled reflectively—her gaze locking with Liv's. And as it always seemed to do, the world fell away. "Yes. They do."

Liv finally dropped her eyes, feeling very much like a lovesick adolescent. She shifted so that she was facing Kayla; drawing up one knee, she wrapped an arm around it. "Why would you need to use some sort of special mental technique for the telepathy?" Her free hand drifted upward and began idly twisting a lock of wine-colored hair, enjoying the silky-soft texture of the strands. "I know I'm not doing anything special when all of a sudden I...I...get these feelings and images from you."

"Ahh...but you only think that because you haven't got a clue."

Blonde eyebrows shot up indignantly.

Oops. Kayla immediately raised a forestalling hand. "I'm sorry," she apologized sheepishly, but couldn't help the few chuckles that managed to trickle out. *Ohh...I'll bet that look makes Dougie pee himself.* "That didn't come out right at all."

One arching eyebrow dropped, but the other remained in Liv's hairline. "Explain yourself, Ghostbuster." Liv would have put her hands on her hips for effect, but her current position made it impractical.

Another bolt of lightning struck the island, causing the house to shake and Liv to nearly crawl out of her skin. Even Kayla jumped.

"Whoa. You okay?" Kayla asked worriedly, gently pushing away Liv, who was now stuck to her like glue, in an attempt to see her face.

But Liv refused to be dislodged. "No," she replied shakily, her breathing nearly out of control as she tucked her face into Kayla's T-shirt. "Isn't this damn storm ever going to end?"

"Soon," Kayla promised, wrapping both arms around Liv and resting her chin atop Liv's head. "Let me tell you about the telepathy." Then Kayla stopped, her mind temporarily derailed as she remembered something she'd been meaning to ask her companion. "Liv, how come you've never asked me to demonstrate my ability? Anyone who's ever known about it has made that request in the first five minutes. You've pretty much ignored it." *Does it bother you to talk about it?*

"Un huh." A pale head shook. "Not ignored. I've been curious." She shrugged, her face still pressed tightly against Kayla's shirt. "I figured you'd tell me more—show me—when you felt comfortable." *If you ever felt comfortable enough.* "It's not like you're a trick pony or something."

"Ha. You're the first person to think that," Kayla snapped, the words sounding sharp to Liv's ears. She was silent for a moment, allowing the unexpected surge of bitterness to run its course.

Liv felt soft lips graze her temple, causing her eyes to flutter shut in pure reflex. "Am I really?" she questioned seriously, her voice soft and worried. Liv turned her head slightly so she could gaze out the window and down to the sea beyond.

Kayla nodded. "Really." Her voice was a little hoarse, and she hoped it didn't sound like it bothered her as much as it did. "Except for my family, of course." Then she made a conscious effort to brighten her mood, which for some unknown reason, and despite her efforts to the contrary, was rapidly heading south. "For some strange reason, your decision *not* to ask me has got me itching to show you what I can do. I'd also like to try out a couple of the things Bridget mentioned in the history. Interested?"

"Absolutely." Liv pulled back just enough to see Kayla's face, a wide smile showing off bright white teeth. *Anything to make you not sound so sad.*

"Okay, I'm not as strong as Bridget, so don't go expecting me to do the things we read about," Kayla warned semi-seriously. "But, well, occasionally I do see words. It's just not consistent." She reached up and drew a slender, teasing finger along Liv's jaw bone, around a dainty pink ear, finally trailing it down her friend's tender throat before letting it rest on her collarbone. "But with you—" Kayla leaned in a little. *Mmm...How can she always smell so good?* "All bets are off. I'm hoping that just maybe, I'll be able to go farther into your thoughts than I have with anyone before. Really get deep inside you," Kayla purred in a low sexy voice.

Liv sucked in a breath. *God, how bad do I want her? Bad. Very, very bad. Oh, man, and she knows it, too.*

Kayla smirked and wriggled her eyebrows, amazed at how much fun playing with Liv truly was, and how quickly her mood could change. *This is what I've been missing.* She let out a slightly surprised breath. *Of course it is,* her mind whispered back.

Liv shook her head and laughed at herself, marveling at the effect of Kayla's voice and eyes. *She doesn't even have to touch me to turn me inside out.* "Okay. What do I have to do?" She slowly tilted round, innocent eyes up to meet Kayla's. "You might have to be very specific and talk slowly, seeing as how I don't have a clue."

Kayla groaned dramatically. "Jeez. I said I was sorry. All I meant was that you're clearing your mind and opening it to me when you're sensing my thoughts, you just don't realize you're doing it. You're unconsciously making it easier for us to enter each other's thoughts." She could see Liv's skepticism, and the researcher picked up the gauntlet, her expression filled with mischief. "When the telepathic connection between us feels the strongest for you, what have we been doing?"

Liv thought about it for a moment, a faint smile crossing her lips. She was starting to like where this was heading. "Kissing," came the expected response.

"Mmm...hmm...it's the same for me," Kayla rumbled in a sexy voice that threatened to turn her companion into jelly. "And when we're kissing, what are you thinking about?"

Pale lashes batted playfully. "You mean *besides* Julia Roberts?"

"Funny." Kayla's eyes narrowed. "You aren't —"

"Don't even ask," Liv warned, smacking Kayla's thigh. But her voice was teasing. "Let's see, what was I thinking about? I think of you and what we're doing." *And all the other things I'd love to be doing to you.* A blush began working its way up Liv's neck, causing Kayla's smirk to grow even larger. "And well, um, mostly I'm not thinking of anything specific at all. I guess I just kinda let my mind go blank and enjoy what's happening."

Kayla nodded, feeling a quiet sense of satisfaction at Liv's blush, which she found beyond adorable, and the nonverbal confirmation of what she herself had been thinking and feeling. "Believe it or not, in a roundabout way, that's what Bridget was talking about in the history. It's about opening your mind and letting things happen. But without focus, you can only go so far. Shall I demonstrate?" Her eyes twinkled knowingly.

"That...was a very stupid question," Liv answered wryly, licking her lips in anticipation as she sat up a little straighter. She felt a twinge of excitement.

"Okay." Kayla's heartbeat began to pick up as she stared into the darkening jade eyes across from hers. She'd never announced a kiss before, and suddenly she felt a little nervous about it. *I might as well make this count. Everything I feel, but I'm still too chicken to say. No holding back.*

Liv smiled gently, easily picking up on her friend's anxiety.

Kayla's response was a grin of her own. Then she simply started to melt. *Jesus, what you do to me, Liv.* "Don't do anything special. Just relax, and in a minute I'll tell you to think of something specific. Then I'll try to read your thoughts." With a slight bob of the head, Liv told her that she understood.

Liv's eyelids slid shut when Kayla tilted her head slightly to the side and slowly moved forward. She expected to feel soft, full lips brushing gently against hers. Instead, a hot tongue suddenly plunged deeply into her mouth, rocking her backwards and throwing her off balance with its demanding, aggressive force. A strong hand splayed across her lower back, holding her firmly in place then guiding her closer, despite the overwhelming momentum pushing her in the opposite direction. *Oh, God!* Her mind screamed its approval as the hungry kiss delved deeper: wanting, needing, giving and taking all at the same time. It was the culmination of hour after hour of thick sexual tension and blossoming love. It was wholly unexpected, passion unrestrained.

Liv didn't have a chance to think or even breathe, her mouth reflexively responding with its own assault, devouring, tasting, conquering. She felt Kayla shift back a bit, reducing the contact of their lips and bodies by just a hairsbreadth. She would have none of it. Small hands roamed frantically, then found their purchase in thick, dark hair the color of sweet red wine. She tugged Kayla tighter against her and crushed their mouths together once again to taste soft, wet lips. Her reward was a low, rumbling groan that was torn from Kayla's chest and immediately swallowed in the blistering heat of the moment. The sound alone caused Liv's abdomen to clench tightly, making her grateful for the strong hand at her back. It was the only thing keeping her upright.

Kayla let her mind completely empty itself of anything and everything other than Liv, which was exceedingly simple, considering it was difficult to tell where one woman ended and the other began. She mentally projected outward, trying desperately to piece together bits of newly acquired knowledge with her own natural instinct, which was relentlessly driving her forward. She extended her senses. Projecting further. Diving deeper. Feeling Liv's hammering heartbeat and ragged breaths and the hot coursing blood pulsing wildly through both their veins. Kayla gasped into the mouth attached to hers, her body shuddering with arousal as she pushed beyond her mental boundaries, dropping them as she went.

Blending.

Joining.

A warm rush of desire spread from Liv's belly to her groin, enveloping her, wrenching a deep guttural moan from her throat. The pure sensuality of Kayla's lips and tongue dancing intimately, deeply, against hers flushed through her, and she felt the almost staggering urge to draw Kayla closer still.

Merging.

And then Liv sensed it, recognizing almost immediately that it had been there from nearly the very beginning, but in the midst of sensory overload, she hadn't taken time to notice. It was more than a physical or emotional presence. In her current state, Liv could only define it as...spiritual. The vague, slightly dislocated sense she'd encountered before was noticeably absent, replaced by the solid, tangible feeling that Kayla was right there alongside her, in her own mind. Or maybe she was in Kayla's. There was no beginning or ending, they simply flowed together. With a sudden clarity, she realized that what she was feeling was the total sum of both of their thoughts and emotions, desires and needs. It was intense and profound, and nearly painful in its pleasure.

It was completeness.

Kayla willed her mind to focus, knowing it was next to impossible but grasping for it just the same. Her eyes rolled back beneath closed lids as Liv's desire intertwined with her own, forming an intoxicating brew that threatened to overwhelm her. Never. Never had she shared her mind like this, or had another's open so completely to her. Without reservation or boundaries. Without hesitation or doubt. Apart from the spectacular physical sensations they were creating and sharing with each other, the combined emotional intensity of the moment was rich and satisfying, and only made her want more. But one by one, Kayla untangled her senses from Liv's, trying to gain enough control to speak, a good part of her simply wanting to let herself drown, feeling Liv pulling her in deeper and deeper.

Kayla finally pulled her lips from Liv's, immediately attaching them to her tender throat, sucking on the pounding pulse point and settling Liv against her, giving her hands freedom to roam over the thin cotton nightgown. *Now or never*, she thought, fully aware that she was slipping into a sexual haze from which she wanted no reprieve. "Liv...think somethin'. Oh, God," she muttered against the salty skin of Liv's neck as hands slid beneath her T-shirt and bra, cupping aching breasts. A moan of pure pleasure tickled her ears, and for another brief moment she lost herself in the firestorm of sensation. Then insistent hands were helping her out of the shirt altogether, and her own nimble fingers began working on the small ivory-colored buttons on Liv's nightgown.

The blonde thought she heard something, but decided she must be mistaken. Liv had completely forgotten what the purpose of this little exercise had been to begin with. She could think of several incredibly important uses for Kayla's mouth, and none of them included talking.

"Liv?" Kayla whispered again, bringing her mouth back up to Liv's and kissing her tenderly...slowly.

We're not stopping, again? Tell me we're not stopping, came Liv's frantic mental plea. A resounding "No!" sounded in her mind, but she wasn't sure if it was her own thought or Kayla's. At that moment, however, it simply didn't matter.

Kayla's kisses slowed and took on a more loving, emotional edge. The change in intensity caught Liv's attention and she answered with a breathy sigh, her fingers finding the hooks of Kayla's bra as a strong breeze blew out more of the room's candles, sending the women deeper into the shadows. The gust caressed sensitized skin; her gown was opened wider, pushed off her shoulders to expose her completely to the night air and Kayla's purposeful, coaxing touch. "Hmm?" she finally answered, recalling Kayla's question. "God, yes!" she cried harshly, throwing her head back when warm lips surrounded her nipple, suckling gently.

"Never mind. Later," Kayla murmured in a barely audible

voice against the soft pale skin, losing herself completely.

A sudden shift and Liv felt herself lifted slightly, then her shoulders were hitting the couch and Kayla's body was covering hers. "Mmm...you read my mind," were the last words spoken for a long time.

Chapter Thirteen

A Test of Faith

LIV RE-LIT SEVERAL candles in the room, knowing that dawn was soon approaching but wanting the additional light for reading, anyway. She settled onto the sofa, her gaze wandering briefly to the doorway, through which she expected to see Kayla hobbling any moment.

The storm had finally stopped raging, allowing more windows to be opened and a temperate breeze to fill the room. Liv took a deep breath of fresh, moist air, letting it out slowly. She was comfortable, cool, and sated. *I could get used to this feeling*, her mind supplied happily.

They had made love with a soul-searing passion that took her breath away just remembering it. It had gone beyond her most intense prior experiences—and then some—taking intimacy to a level she didn't even know existed. Kayla had treated her with a tender reverence that left her feeling utterly worshipped and caused her heart to ache with happiness. Liv's thoughts were interrupted by the soft footsteps of her lover.

Her eyes twinkled at the sight of Kayla in yet another clean white T-shirt and pair of shorts. "Hi...mmm...these are really good but they'd be so much better with a cold glass of milk," Liv mumbled, taking another large mouthful of chocolate chip cookie and humming contentedly. "We gotta get off this island tomorrow and back to modern refrigeration, or my stomach will be in big trouble."

Kayla perched on the arm of the sofa, towel drying her freshly shampooed hair for the second time in as many hours. She regarded her companion fondly, pleased to see that Liv's appetite seemed to be making a reappearance. "Did ya save any for me?" she teased, gesturing toward the tall stack of cookies Liv had piled on a paper plate and set next to the history on the library's coffee table.

A pale brow lifted and the tip of a pink tongue poked out

impudently. "I *was* going to share. But now..."

Kayla moved closer to Liv, tilting her head slightly and leaning forward. Liv swallowed hastily, her eyes fluttering closed as she prepared for another heart-stopping kiss. When Kayla was a hairsbreadth away, her breath caressing Liv's mouth, she shifted quickly, snatching Liv's cookie out of her hand with sharp teeth.

Liv's eyes flew open and she stared at her empty hand dumbly, then pinned a very smug looking researcher with outraged eyes. Her fingertips were still tingling from Kayla's wet lips. "You ate my cookie?" she shouted in disbelief, turning her hand over as if she still expected to see the tasty treat hiding somewhere in between her fingers.

A sexy smirk stole over Kayla's face as she opened her mouth...

"Don't."

"But—"

Liv shook her head. "Just don't."

Round eyes peered at Liv, trying their best to convey complete innocence. "I was just going to apologize for taking your cookie," Kayla lied sweetly.

The linguist just snorted.

"Here." Kayla retrieved a cookie from the stack and brought it to Liv's lips, lifting her brows in entreaty. "You can have this one."

Liv remained unmoved.

"C'mon," Kayla tempted. "You know you want it."

Liv's eyes narrowed. *Yummm...chocolate.* The rich, tantalizing scent wafted up to her nostrils, making her mouth water in anticipation. But even as her lips twitched, she refused to move towards it. "You're going to yank it away from me when I try to take a bite, aren't you?" she asked knowingly.

"Would I—"

"Yes," Liv said flatly.

Kayla chuckled softly, bringing her other hand up and resting it against Liv's warm cheek. "You are so beautiful," she whispered, her heart welling with affection as she admired how the candlelight bathed Liv's skin in a muted, golden glow. "I missed you."

A dazzling smiled lit Liv's face as she tried to push down an impending blush. "We've only been apart for fifteen minutes, Kayla. I just shower faster than you do." Her hand wandered into thick, wet hair that felt cool and silky to the touch. Liv idly considered how much she'd enjoyed shampooing it. She'd never washed another person's hair before. Well, except for the time when Dougie was eight years old and got gum in his. And despite her best efforts, he'd ended up with a very short haircut that summer.

With a gentle tug, Liv pulled Kayla closer and softly kissed her lips, taking her time, and removing any hint of chocolate with a thorough tongue. "And I missed you, too," she admitted quietly when they finally broke apart, drawing a broad smile from Kayla.

For long seconds the women said nothing, enjoying their closeness, and reveling in the peace and comfort that each other's company brought.

Kayla leaned over for the history, letting out a quiet groan.

"Your knee?"

"Yeah." She let out a tense breath. "It's pretty sore, but I think I'll live."

"Do you have another one of those emergency ice-packs?" Kayla shook her head. "I'll have to wait until tomorrow." She pointed to the closed book, wishing she had taken the time to learn something besides English. Despite her high IQ Kayla just didn't have a knack for languages. She'd tried to learn German in college, but her natural impatience wouldn't allow her to get past the basics. "Can we do some more?"

"Of course."

"If you're too tired, then—"

"No, I'm ready," Liv assured, surprised that Kayla had managed to sit quietly for the past few moments without asking. She knew the younger woman was anxious to find out more, and had almost offered herself, but was loath to break the moment.

Cobb Island
November, 1690

A COLD RAIN HAD soaked the island and the late-autumn temperature had plummeted. Not wanting to be out slogging through the mud, or near Cyril or any of the other iniquitous slave traders, Bridget had holed up in the stable, happily soaking in the smell of sweet hay and horse flesh.

She ran a brush down Apollo's gleaming coat, working by rote as her mind rapidly conjured, then disregarded, plans to get Faylinn and Henry away from her brother. "I know she loves me, boy," she informed the stallion, patting his sleek muscular neck with a loving hand, her breath sending puffs of fog into the early evening air as she spoke. "Even if she doesn't know it herself yet. I'm sure of it. I can feel it."

Bridget rubbed the horse's nose affectionately as he nuzzled her chest. The young stallion snorted with pleasure when her hand began to move in a firm scratching motion between his eyes. "Hedonist," she laughed. "But it is time for me to go inside. You'll have to wait until tomorrow for me to spoil you again."

With a loud creak, the stable door swung open and Afia dashed inside, her breath coming in short gasps, a panicky look distorting her normally cheerful features.

"What is it, Afia?" Bridget turned sideways to don the heavy black cape that she'd draped over one of the stall walls. She shook it out, then with a twist settled it around broad shoulders.

"It's Master Henry! He's...he's..."

"Slow down, woman. Here." Bridget guided the older woman to a bale of hay and sat her down. She wasn't sure whether Afia's teeth were chattering because she was cold, or just plain jittery. "Now, what about Henry?"

"He's ga...gone. He should have been back hours ago, but I've looked everywhere and I can't find him."

Bridget scowled, her heart speeding up at Afia's obvious distress. "What do you mean *gone*? He can't be gone." With a snap, she fastened the clasp, securing the cape around her neck. "I saw Faylinn bring him to you myself."

The black woman's gaze dropped from Bridget's and rooted itself firmly on her feet. She shook her head quickly. "I had Master Henry all ready for our trip to the duck pond when Master Redding stopped us on the way out the door. He told me to see to dinner for his guests and said the two new slaves could take the boy to the pond."

Bridget's brow creased as she tossed Apollo's brush into a shallow bin just outside the large stall. "Jasper and William?"

The black woman nodded.

"Cyril purchased them only last month. He left Henry in the care of almost complete strangers?" she asked incredulously. Cyril was a pig. Of that she was certain. But she couldn't imagine him being so careless with his son, whom he so plainly valued, if not loved.

"Yes, child. By Allah, I swear that I tried to explain to Master Redding that Henry would be happier with someone he knew, but he simply took the boy out of my arms and handed him to Jasper, who just happened to be passing by."

Bridget scratched her jaw and began pacing, her dark cape billowing out behind her and her boots scattering bits of hay and kicking up an occasional puff of dust. "God, they should have been back from the pond hours ago." Her nose twitched as she sniffed the cold air. "It's nearly freezing out." She stopped her restless motion and stood in front of Afia. "Have you checked the pond?"

"Of course. It was the first place I looked after I scoured the house. I've been back twice, and there is no sign of the child or Jasper and William." She hugged her wool shawl tighter around her wiry body.

"Damn!" Bridget cursed fiercely as she began saddling her mount. "Have you told Faylinn?"

"No, Miss." Tears began to well in worried dark eyes. "Master Redding took a rowboat out to his business partner's ship to pick up a few supplies. He left Mistress Faylinn entertaining a group of officers from His Majesty's Navy in the dining room." Afia swallowed nervously and laid a cool hand on Bridget's shoulder. "I thought you would want to be there when I told her, child. I would have come for you sooner, but I was looking for Master Henry."

Bridget nodded, knowing Afia had long since recognized her feelings for Faylinn. There was no reason for pretense around her. Anxiety caused Bridget's fingers to fumble with the bridle as she quickly prepared Apollo. "Bloody hell!" She tore the unfastened saddle from the animal's back, deciding it would just be easier to ride bareback. "As much as I'd like to avoid it until the boy is found, we must inform Faylinn."

Bridget pushed open the stable door and marched out into the cold evening air with Afia hot on her heels, struggling to keep pace with her long, smooth strides. Bridget's eyes turned skyward as her gait continued to eat up ground. "It will be full dark soon. We'll need lanterns." She tightened her cape around her shoulders. "And a blanket for when we find the lad."

Afia let out a shaky breath. The island was a harsh, unforgiving place, but everything would be all right. Mistress Bridget would see to it.

An owl bellowed from an old tree beyond the garden. His call, the rhythmic thump of footsteps, and the light rustling of dead leaves were the only sounds that fractured the tense silence as the women made their way back to the house.

FAYLINN STOOD IN the green, long-sleeved gown that showed off her creamy white shoulders and slender neck. Her golden hair was worn in a loose, becoming braid. She was surrounded by a group of full-time naval officers/part-time businessmen, who wore their full dress uniforms and wigs, each buckle and sword sparkling in the candlelight, their black leather boots gleaming. One particular young officer never left Faylinn's side. He seemed a cut above the rest in both manners and demeanor, and she wondered why such a sweet, if tiresome, young man kept such wretched company; and whether it was the nature of their business that lured in the scourge of the earth, or the other way around.

"Oh, look." Out of the corner of her eye, Faylinn spied Bridget, who was standing quietly in the doorway of the dining room. She said a little prayer of thanks, grateful for any excuse to remove herself from the presence of Cyril's loathsome business partners. Their over-inflated egos and generally repugnant natures were matched only by her husband's. "If you'll excuse me," she said politely. "It appears that I'm needed elsewhere." *Thank God.* With a gracious bow of her head, she lifted her skirts slightly and headed toward the far entrance of the room, and Bridget. A relieved smile split her face.

As she approached Bridget, Faylinn noticed that Afia was standing at her side, slightly behind her. The blonde's smile faded when she observed the lines of tension that creased the skin around two sets of eyes. Both women were flushed and breathing heavily, as though they had just rushed in out of the cold evening air. A knot formed in Faylinn's belly. "What's wrong?" she asked immediately. She looked to Afia, who wouldn't meet her eyes, then Bridget. "Is it Henry?"

"Faylinn, my dear, sit down." Bridget pulled over a chair and gestured toward the cushion. "Please."

"No." She pushed the chair away angrily. "What's the matter? You're frightening me."

She closed her eyes. Even though there was no time to waste, Bridget found herself dreading the words she knew she had to say. "Faylinn, I'm afraid Henry is missing."

Round verdant eyes widened further. "What do you mean miss...missing?" Her voice was thick with disbelief and growing fear.

"Cyril removed the boy from Mary's care and instructed two of the new slaves to take him out this afternoon. They haven't returned yet."

Faylinn sucked in a breath and her face went ashen. "Oh, God. Oh, God," she muttered. "We've got to find him!" Desperately, she pleaded with Bridget. "He can't still be outside! It's too cold."

Bridget pulled the trembling woman into her arms, tucking the fair head under her chin, and running a calming hand down her back. "Shh...shh...I'm going this very minute. I will find him," she soothed, as the men gathered around them, having picked up on the young woman's distress from all the way across the room.

One of the men motioned for a slave boy, who was standing quietly in the shadows with a bottle of wine in his hands, to come forward. "Boy!" he barked, clapping his hands together. "Don't just stand there. Go fetch Mrs. Redding some brandy."

The boy complied, walking to the long dining room table on suddenly wobbly legs and grabbing a bottle. His hands were shaking so badly that he soaked the linen tablecloth as he tried to fill the crystal glass.

An eyebrow quirked as Bridget watched the nervous slave.

Licking dry lips, the boy wordlessly handed Faylinn the glass and all but scrambled away.

Before he could disappear completely, however, Bridget entrusted the younger woman to Afia's care and followed him out of the room. Directly behind Bridget came the officer who was so clearly taken with Faylinn. He hadn't missed the young slave's curious behavior, either. That boy wasn't upset because of Henry's disappearance. He knew something.

"Michael," Bridget rumbled low in her throat, causing the boy to stop mid-step.

He turned around, his lip twitching nervously. "Yes, Mistress Bridget?" His voice was barely audible.

Bridget walked up to the boy and grasped his shoulders tightly, looking down at him with icy, intense eyes. "Do you know what happened to Henry?"

"*No,*" the boy blurted out, fearing he'd soil himself. The slaves were all talking about what she'd done to Master Redding that very afternoon. He was right to fear her.

Don't lie to me, Michael. We have to find him, she projected directly into the boy's thoughts.

Michael paled, his coal black eyes widening larger than Bridget thought humanly possible. She maintained her stare until the boy's jaw began to quiver.

Answer me! We don't have time to waste.

Were it not for Bridget's strong grip, the frightened slave would have crumpled to the floor.

The British officer stood several paces behind the powerful woman who clearly was unaware of his presence. He was totally mesmerized by the scene before him. Unable to see Bridget's face, he wondered what manner of browbeating it would take to cause a Black boy to appear as white as a ghost.

Michael tried not to think of Jasper and William's plan to escape from the island on a raft they'd built and hidden under the dock, but in a few short seconds, Bridget had all the information she needed.

You knew they were taking Henry, but said nothing? she boomed silently. *Is he to be ransomed?*

Then, before he even realized he was doing it, he began responding to her questions in his mind. *I...I don't know,* the boy thought wildly, his heart racing a mile a minute when he heard Bridget's acknowledging grunt to his words. Sweat poured off his face and neck. *I don't think so. They had talked about leaving this afternoon. They were always talking. I did...I didn't know what to believe. I don't think they meant for...for Master Henry to be with them. I was there when Master Redding handed over the child. Jasper said they were too busy working on the dock to take him to the pond, but Master Redding slapped him in the face and told him to shut his insolent mouth or he'd remove his tongue.*

Bridget let go of the frightened boy's arms, having been able to understand enough of his mental ramblings to get an excellent idea of what had happened. She turned around, only to run right into the perplexed naval officer. Bridget didn't bother trying to explain, nor did she offer excuses to the slack-jawed man, instead, she pushed past him and sped back toward the dining room.

Bridget's mind spun out several different scenarios. Either the slaves would have killed Henry outright, or simply left him somewhere near the dock. If there was to be no demand for ransom, it wouldn't make sense for them to take a burdensome child along to the mainland in their bid for freedom.

"I'M GOING TO search the duck pond," Faylinn announced determinedly, tearing a lit oil lamp from the wall to use in her search.

"Of course," an older man replied, sending one of the men to fetch Cyril from the ship anchored off shore. "My men and I will gladly help you search."

At that moment, Faylinn would take assistance from any source she could. The blonde woman nodded her thanks. "Come then. Let me lead the way. It's but a few moments walk south."

"Wait," Bridget called, striding into the room, stopping directly in front of Faylinn. "The child's not there. He'll be somewhere on the other side of the island near the dock that is under construction. I'll need the men to come with me so we can search the area thoroughly."

"How do you know he'll be there?" Faylinn asked anxiously, tangling her fingers in Bridget's long, ebony cape.

"I...I..." Bridget fumbled momentary as she swung her gaze up from Faylinn's to see the waiting eyes of ten men. *Damn! But I've no time to waste.* "Michael, the young slave told me."

"He did nothing of the sort." The officer who had been in the hallway with Bridget and Michael inserted himself between Faylinn and Bridget, literally prying the younger woman's hands off Bridget's cape. "She's lying," he accused self-righteously. He looked at Bridget with disgust; he'd seen the tall woman comforting Faylinn when she told her the news of Henry. He had heard of her kind preying on sweet young women, but thought them restricted to the slums of London and other wretched places. He would not stand idly by and allow such a creature to lie to a woman of such obvious quality. "I was there. The boy said nothing."

Faylinn looked confused. Her mind was already reeling.

"Bridget?" she questioned bewilderedly.

"I have never, nor would I ever, lie to you, dearest. You know that," she reminded gently but urgently.

"But that dock is across the island. There is no way Henry could have wandered that far through the dense forest."

Bridget shifted impatiently, knowing every moment they wasted here reduced their chances of finding Henry alive. The temperature was continuing to drop and the moon was already lighting the sky. "Faylinn, believe me, I beg you. I don't have time to explain everything now."

"She's lying. The boy never said a word. I swear it, as an officer of the Crown," the man vowed solemnly, his eyes flashing in challenge.

Bridget's mouth curled into a sneer; she wanted to bury her knife in the bastard's heart. Why was he doing this?

Faylinn's head warred with her heart in a struggle so fierce she felt light-headed. *Bridget wouldn't lie to me, would she? Of course not*, came her heart's immediate reply. *She must just have misunderstood. Yes, that has to be it.* Faylinn desperately wanted to believe her sister-in-law, and yet, she could not conceive of a single reason why her son would be over two miles away. "He has to be near the pond," she finally said. "Mary must have simply passed him by. The woods are so thick there, it would be easy to miss a sleeping child, especially in the waning light."

"By God, Faylinn! Listen to me! I need the men to come—"

"She's made her decision," the man said coolly, looking back towards his superior for confirmation. Receiving it in the form of a crisp nod, he continued. "We shall follow Mrs. Redding to the pond." Turning towards Faylinn, he bowed slightly. "We are honored to be at your service."

The hurt in Bridget's eyes caused a stabbing sensation in Faylinn's own heart. *No. No. No. She wouldn't lie to me.* The young mother opened her mouth to change her mind, but before she could speak, Bridget turned on her heel and dashed from the room. *Oh, God, what have I done?* Faylinn agonized briefly, as her stomach threatened to rebel and Bridget's furious boot steps grew more and more distant.

BRIDGET EXPLODED OUT of the stable atop a racing Apollo, her fingers tangled tightly in his coarse, white mane. Muscular legs were bent at the knee and pressed firmly against the steed's sides, compensating for the lack of a saddle. She leaned forward over her mount's muscular shoulders, her cape flying straight out behind her, her scarlet hair gleaming in the moonlight as they rounded a small hill and made for the rugged beach. It was a longer route than cutting across the island; but with only the moonlight to guide her, she knew this was her safest choice. It would be faster in the long run because she could ride Apollo at the very edge of the surf, avoiding most of the larger rocks and branches.

The salty spray stung eyes gone violet in the moonlight as Apollo splashed through the shallow water, having to turn inland several times when the beach simply disappeared or the water began to deepen. After minutes that felt more like hours, Bridget finally saw the half-completed dock in the distance.

She extended her senses, calling to Henry in her mind, only to be greeted by a thunderous silence. "C'mon, lad," she mumbled as she slid off the panting horse's back, landing in ankle-deep, cold water.

"Henry!" she called, her gaze flickering on and below the dock. "Henry!" Her search began in earnest and she literally left no stone unturned, moving every branch, poking through every wiry bush, even peering into pitch black tree hollows that appeared about the right size. The possibilities of where a two-and-a-half-year-old could be hiding were nearly endless. Her mind kept up a constant stream of calls, seeking, searching her consciousness for any sense of the boy. Still she heard, felt, nothing. After more than two hours of endless hunting and yelling, her voice began to grow hoarse and self-doubt began to cloud her mind.

What if she was wrong? What if Faylinn needed her help, far across the island? She had read Michael's thoughts clearly but that didn't guarantee that the boy was correct. *Oh, damn! I frightened him. I confused him and pushed too hard. What if...what if...*

The mental ramblings stopped abruptly, and she tilted her head to the side. An animal? No. She squinted into the darkness, taking in the rich scent of wet leaves and sand and the salty surf. "Henry," she called out again. But this time she was greeted with a faint whimper. *Yes!*

She moved towards the barely audible sound, trying not to stumble over the thick underbrush. "Henry? Where are you, lad?" The whimpers grew louder until, just off to her right, she spied a huddled mass under a tall tree, blending in almost perfectly with the shadows.

"Thank God!" Bridget dropped to her knees, running her hands over the toddler, flinching at the icy feel of the boy's clothing and skin. "By all that is holy, is there no end to your mischief?" she joked weakly, her eyes brimming with tears. "Did you have to play in the water, too?" He was soaked to the bone.

As gently as she could, Bridget scooped him up, carrying him out into the moonlight where she could see his face. He was unconscious but still murmuring and crying quietly, as though in the throes of a nightmare. His skin was frigid and held a bluish tinge. Thick, dark hair was matted with dirt, and leaves clung damply to his forehead. Bridget pulled the boy close and tucked her cape around his shivering form, whistling for Apollo.

She took several long strides then leaped onto the horse's back, managing not to jostle the boy any more than necessary. With a stiff kick, she set Apollo in motion, his hooves pounding through the surf once again.

The trip home seemed even longer than the trip out, and she cursed the house's position on the outermost corner of the island. The child began to fuss in her arms and she pulled him a bit closer, still feeling the remains of the unnatural chill of his skin through his clothes. A nervous dread welled within her and she urged Apollo faster.

She didn't stable the stallion. Rather, she flung one leg over his head and dropped off his back, right in front of the house, leaving him to his own devices until later. As Bridget passed through the doorway, she could hear yelling and correctly guessed that Cyril had finally shown up. Then she heard more muffled voices and cursing as she ran into the dining room with Henry still tucked neatly inside her cape. The boy hadn't as much as made a peep over the last few moments. Their shared body heat seemed to help bring up his temperature, though it was still far below normal.

The first person she saw was Faylinn, who, by her dress and the rosy color to her cheeks, had obviously just returned to the house herself. She was arguing with Cyril and trying to wrench free from the grasp he had on one of her arms. Several slaves were furiously pouring oil into lanterns, and most of the naval officers that Bridget remembered from earlier were in the room, preparing to go back out into the cold once the lanterns were ready.

Bridget didn't even get a chance to call out before Faylinn turned around and they locked eyes. The smaller woman rushed forward, crying out when she saw that Bridget held Henry in her arms.

"I'm sorry, I'm so sorry," she whispered fiercely, kissing Bridget hard on the cheek and immediately taking the filthy toddler and wrapping him tightly in her arms, oblivious to the wet leaves and grime staining her dress and cloak.

"It's all right," Bridget said gently, although she was still feeling the sting of Faylinn's lack of faith. "I told you I would find him. I'm only sorry it took me so long."

Faylinn shook her head frantically. "I should have believed you; you would never lie. I just...I—" The words came out in an endless stream until she stopped abruptly, seeming to notice the boy wasn't just sleeping. "Henry?" she searched his face, then felt his forehead. "Sweet mother of God! He's freezing!"

Judith and Elizabeth stood mutely alongside their father, who seemed to be in shock. The girls stared nervously at their brother's limp form.

"We need to get him out of these wet clothes and into a warm bed," Faylinn said in a calm assertive voice that was very different from that of the nearly distraught woman that Bridget had left only a few hours ago. The determined mother began heading toward the stairs, but not without a backward glance at Bridget. Tired eyes glistened with unshed tears, easily telegraphing profound relief, thanks, and devotion. She wanted to voice her feelings, but her throat felt as though it was in a vice.

"It's quite all right, Faylinn," Bridget assured, with what she hoped was a comforting smile. "Go now, and get Henry out of those clothes. I'll track down what medicines we have that may help the lad."

Faylinn nodded and pulled her son's face next to her own cheek, cooing softly to him as she moved up the stairs. Afia and Judith soon followed, wanting to do anything they could to help.

Bridget dropped down on a chair and placed her palms over her eyes. It spread dirt across her cheeks, but she didn't care. She was already filthy and exhausted, her heart aching for Faylinn and her son, who she knew was not nearly out of danger.

Bridget's world was suddenly tilted on its side when a heavy blow exploded against her jaw. She fell off the chair and retreated backwards across the floor trying to gather her bearings. Her tongue snaked out, and she tasted the sharp metallic flavor of blood.

Cyril had hit her with the hilt of his sword and now stood over her, gray eyes blazing. "You helped them, didn't you? You helped those savage slaves escape and steal my son!"

"Brother, what in the devil are you raving about?" She was truly astonished. Had she not just found Henry and returned him home?

"Admit it. You want me destroyed," he spat. "I know how you feel about the slave trade. You've made no secret of your disgust and loathing for me and my business."

The eyes in the room all turned to Bridget, as several of Cyril's partners stepped behind the raging man in a show of support. They needed this island, and it was his. That made them all his new best friends.

"You're mad," Bridget accused, rubbing her jaw and rising to her knees.

"How then? Henry was supposed to be at the duck pond. Not miles away."

"I know how." The young officer who had accused Bridget of lying earlier that evening stormed into the room with Michael in tow. The boy was squirming and crying, and was obviously frightened out of his wits.

The officer pointed an accusing finger at Bridget, who merely sneered in his direction, her sharp, bloodstained canines glistening in soft candlelight. "The woman is a witch!"

Chapter
Fourteen

Accusations

Cobb Island
Present Day

LIV PAUSED WHEN Kayla made a soft hissing noise and closed her eyes at the word witch. The blonde winced, surprised at the sudden turn of events, though she could see that Kayla wasn't. "I don't think he means that in the you're-a-little-grumpy-today way, does he?"

"No. I don't think so." Kayla smiled weakly at her friend's attempt to lighten the mood. "Umm...throughout history the Reddings have been accused of witchcraft and sorcery. Even during feudal times, when it was common for people to die in the very house where they were born, rumors of black magic kept my family moving around England, Scotland, Ireland, and Wales."

Kayla grasped Liv's hand and brought it to her lips, staring into compassionate eyes full of affection and empathy. *Do you know I'm falling in love with you, Liv?* Kayla swallowed hard as a sudden surge of raw emotion tore through her.

The redhead cleared her throat awkwardly. "The stories of persecution have been kept alive in the histories. My parents didn't want to frighten me, so they kept them from me, which only made things worse because it forced me to learn the hard way how people might react to my ability. I didn't start reading the CD-ROM version of the histories for myself until a few years ago." *After what already seemed like a lifetime of disappointment.* "The accusation was actually a rather common one."

The note of sadness in Kayla's voice didn't escape Liv. *God, no wonder she's so sensitive about being different.* "No one would accuse you of witchcraft nowadays, but their rejection and ignorance still hurts," Liv said softly, instantly regretting that she had stated the obvious when Kayla's eyes turned glassy. She suddenly felt extremely protective of the woman beside her. "Kayla?"

"Hmm?" Kayla's gaze was firmly trained out the window.

"Kayla?" she repeated until the other woman reluctantly turned to face her. "Those people, whoever they were, who didn't accept you for who and what you are, were just...just...just dumbshits." She paused for a moment, allowing her words to take hold in Kayla's brain. "I, on the other hand, am not a dumbshit. I would never make that mistake. I'd be missing out on way too much," she whispered earnestly, relieved to see the beginnings of a small, lopsided grin shaping Kayla's lips. She felt Kayla's grip on her hand tighten and saw the younger woman's throat working as she swallowed.

"Thanks," Kayla finally said, knowing that didn't begin to express how much Liv's acceptance meant to her, but trusting that Liv would understand nonetheless.

"You don't have to thank me, sweetheart. Trust me." She placed a soft kiss on Kayla's cheek, then wiped it away with a gentle swipe of her thumb. "It's purely selfish on my part."

Kayla's grin broadened at the use of the new endearment and she hugged Liv tightly, releasing her only after her friend squealed with laughter, confessing that she couldn't breathe.

When Kayla didn't say anything else, but looked much more relaxed, Liv took that as her cue to continue.

Cobb Island
November, 1690

BRIDGET PHYSICALLY RECOILED at the word witch, hearing several gasps around the room as the men shifted nervously.

"Shut up, whelp," Bridget spat at the young officer. "You don't know what you're saying."

The soldier puffed up his chest indignantly. "The slave has turned on you, witch. Rightfully, he does not want *his* soul rotting in hell."

Cyril looked back and forth between the man and his sister, clearly confused.

"Sir." The officer turned toward Cyril, who was still clutching his sword, his blade pointed towards Bridget. "The slave has admitted that which I witnessed with my own eyes. Your sister used some form of magic on him to find out about the runaways' plans. She wormed her way into this boy's very mind." For emphasis, he shook the slave, who looked ready to pass out from fright.

"Sister, you had best explain yourself." Cyril felt sick. He would not let Bridget ruin everything. He could not. This had to stop now, before the entire family was tainted by these wild allegations.

Bridget rose to her feet, wiping away a trickle of blood from a small cut on her jaw with the back of her hand. "Don't be ridiculous, Cyril. You *know* I'm no witch."

At her slight inflection of the word know, Cyril went pale. "Search her room for evidence," he commanded finally, enjoying the look of astonishment on her face. "I'll tolerate no servants of Satan in this household." Once she was discredited, nothing she could say would matter.

"Of course, Sir." The young officer snapped to attention, despite the fact that Cyril didn't appear anywhere in his chain of command. He took a step forward, then paused, unsure of where to start looking in the massive house.

Cyril flicked his wrist towards Elizabeth, who had been silently watching the scene in quiet satisfaction. It was about time her father grew a spine and dealt with his arrogant sister.

"Take Officer Richards to Bridget's room, Daughter. And be quick about it. Wait." He held up his hand to stop the officer. "Don't forget to gather any evidence that leads you to believe Bridget was in collusion with the runaway slaves."

A round of approving hums sounded in the room and Cyril squared his shoulders, basking in his business partners' support and admiration. In their eyes, he'd just cemented that he was not a man to be trifled with, even by his own kin. It was the kind of respect he'd always sought and never been able to achieve...until now.

"Yes, Father." Elizabeth smiled sweetly at her aunt, arching an amused eyebrow before leading the eager young man upstairs.

"You bastard!" Bridget spat, lunging toward her brother just as several soldiers moved in between them. "I had nothing to do with Jasper and William's escape. And I'm no more a witch than you are."

The soldiers had meant to physically restrain Bridget, but stopped several feet from the woman. She was covered in mud, and blood was slowly dripping down her jaw, splattering one drop at a time onto the wooden floor. Her dark-red hair was windblown and tangled, her wild eyes glinting with rage. They could easily believe this woman was a witch.

"Then you have nothing to fear," Cyril stated unequivocally, his voice hard and full of hatred.

Bridget turned icy blue eyes to the men now surrounding her. "Do not presume to lay a single finger on me," she warned gravely, her voice quivering with barely suppressed fury. Her stare and the deep, growling timbre of her words caused several men to draw their swords and take a step backwards. *I won't forget this, Brother!* she boomed in his head.

So help me, Bridget, he silently replied, his internal voice shaking with anger, *if Officer Richards finds one shred of evidence that links you to Jasper and William's escape, I'll see you hanged as a conspirator in Henry's kidnapping. I will not allow your pious notions of right and wrong to affect this family's future prosperity. By helping those savages, you've gone too far.*

Brother, does your obsession with business cloud your mind to all else? My ability only came to light when I was trying to save your son. Even now, you are more concerned with your profit margin than his wellbeing.

Cyril's hard gaze began to falter as his thoughts briefly drifted to the toddler upstairs.

Officer Richards came barreling into the room, breathless from taking the stairs two at a time, his sword rattling in its scabbard as he jumped off the last step. He had removed his jacket and was clutching the wadded material to his chest. Several seconds later, Elizabeth was at his side. They both stood silently in front of Cyril as the room collectively held its breath.

"Well, fool? What's the delay?" Bridget hissed. "I've nothing to hide. What did you discover that was so interesting you find it necessary to cradle it against your chest as though it were a wee babe?"

The man's face colored and he pointedly addressed Cyril, ignoring Bridget's remarks. "I found nothing that leads me to believe your sister conspired with the escaped slaves."

Bridget smirked at her brother, who was already thinking of ways he could escape this vile situation gracefully. Cyril's shoulders slumped a bit. He was so sure she'd helped those savages escape.

"I did, however, find ample evidence of witchcraft." The young man lifted his jaw — vindicated.

"What?" Bridget and Cyril shouted in unison, both clearly taken aback.

The officer carefully opened his jacket, revealing a pile of handcrafted charms and amulets. Beneath these were several short candles. The soldier withdrew one, and held it up, making certain everyone in the room saw his find. "These candles were sitting atop a chest of drawers and arranged in the shape of a pentagram," he announced in a clear loud voice. Then he pulled a soiled handkerchief from the pile. It was stiff with dried blood, and appeared a reddish-brown in the glowing lamplight. "This was sitting in the evil design's center."

"That's mine!" Cyril snatched the cloth out of the soldier's hands, immediately recognizing it as the one he'd used to wipe his bloodied nose after Bridget's cowardly attack, earlier that very day. He turned disbelieving gray eyes on his sister. "You kept something soiled with my blood? For some manner of magic?" The disgust in his voice was clear, even as it was tinged with fright.

"It is obvious, Sir, that your sister was attempting to cast a spell using the devil's own tools," the man finished triumphantly. Once he had all the facts, there could be no mistaking what he had seen between Bridget and the slave.

Bridget was in shock. Save the handkerchief, which Cyril had discarded as rubbish, she'd never seen these items before. She opened her mouth to protest but before she could speak, the senior officer in the room, an older white-haired man with an enormous belly that hung over his belt, stepped forward.

"I arrest you in the name of the Crown for crimes against man and nature." He jerked his chin toward Bridget. "Take her into custody to await judgment."

Cyril stood by silently, as several men tackled Bridget and a violent scuffle ensued. It took nearly five minutes for one of the men to finally knock the powerful woman unconscious. They continued to rain blows upon her still form until the senior officer called them off, ordering her bound and gagged.

Elizabeth's lips curved into a small, cruel smile.

Mainland, Virginia
Present Day

"LORD, HAVE MERCY," Doug whined into the pillow he had crushed against his face. *How can I be so thirsty after drinking so much? It doesn't make any sense.* He lay quietly for a moment, trying to listen, and wondering at what point he'd ended up buck-ass naked. A constant pitter patter was filling the otherwise quiet room. *It's still raining?* Reluctantly, the teenager pushed the pillow off his face and pried open one sea-green, very bloodshot eye.

Gingerly, he opened the other. "Marcy?" he said in a hushed voice, closing his eyes at the first rays of sunlight that streamed between the curtains and into the dingy room. Pushing the pillow farther aside, he glanced from wall to wall, seeing no sign of his girlfriend. Then he realized that it shouldn't be sunny and raining at the same time. *Shower?* He lifted his head and cocked it slightly to the side, listening as intently as his pounding head would allow. *Yup. Well, at least she's up and moving.*

He moved his leg and the warm sheets brushed against the sensitive skin on his upper thighs, drawing his attention back to his nakedness. He closed his eyes again, searching his mind, replaying the events of the night before.

Marcy had gotten sick. Yeah, that was sort of unforgettable. But he'd tried to help the pretty teen the best he could, which really consisted of nothing more than whispering words of sympathy and running a cool washcloth over her pale face. When her stomach had finally expelled the last of the beer, she'd pulled out the toothbrush that she always carried around in her purse and disappeared into the bathroom. A long time later, so long that Doug had actually fallen asleep, she curled up next to him on the bed and thanked him for taking such good care of her, waking him with her soft words. Gentle fingers roamed across his face and scalp, as Marcy let tendrils of dark-blonde hair curl around her probing digits. Rolling over, he looked deeply into her eyes before leaning in to softly kiss her lips.

Doug groaned just thinking about it, shifting in the bed as his body began to remember as well. The kissing had been... He groaned a little louder, covering his face with the soft pillow to muffle the tortured sounds. It had been the most intense thing he'd experienced in all his sixteen years. With a will power he didn't know he had, he'd backed off once, asking Marcy if she wanted to continue, if she was sure, as Liv's words about doing something that they'd both regret rang out annoyingly in his head. But Marcy was insistent, and it wasn't like he needed any real persuading. Neither one of them had wanted to stop there. So they didn't.

Sheets and towels fell away as hands and mouths roamed over naked skin. A moment's fumbling with a condom that had taken up permanent, but hopeful, residence in his wallet; and they were making love.

He hadn't known what to expect, exactly. Sure, the guys had talked about it, boasting about this and that. But Doug was smart enough to realize that most of what they were saying was a combination of wishful thinking and outright lies.

All he knew was that *he* had not been disappointed. Marcy had been sweet and luscious and loving, and he shivered remembering her skin sliding against his. But how would she feel about him this morning? The morning after. He suddenly frowned. Doug hadn't meant to break the land speed record for sex, but he couldn't help himself. He'd wanted her since forever, and just the *thought* of actually being with her caused things to be nearly over before they began. She was friggin' gorgeous. And she was touching him everywhere, and he was doing the same thing to her. It was all too much, and his senses had simply gone into overload.

Doug's brow furrowed and his frown deepened. Marcy hadn't complained or laughed in his face, but she hadn't screamed his name in ecstasy, either. And she didn't writhe around moaning, like he'd seen in the movies. *I must have been doing something wrong. Or not doing something. Shit. Who can I ask about this? Nobody, that's who.* He gave a fleeting thought to asking Liv. Then he nearly coughed up a lung. Nope. That would be way uncool, not to mention totally disgusting. He shook his head to clear the repulsive thought from his mind.

"Stamina," he mumbled to himself, figuring that was the biggest problem. None of the guys had ever mentioned that. *Useless bastards.*

Doug's frown turned sad and his heart rate began to pick up as he let his insecurities have free rein. *She probably didn't enjoy it at all. Maybe she was bored. I'll bet she's in there thinking of ways to dump my pathetic ass.* Doug's bleary-eyed gaze drifted to the bathroom door. *Apologize. That's what I need to do. Girls like sensitive men like those wusses on the soaps. I could fall on my knees and profess my undying love. It's not like it's a lie. I love her more than anything. Maybe I can convince her to give me another chance.* He threw his pillow against the wall and sat up forcefully, immediately regretting the quick movement as his stomach roiled. He wrapped his arms around his middle. "Fuck!" His grimace quickly shifted into a pout. "I'll improve with practice, Marcy. I just know it."

A wet head poked its way out of the bathroom. "Who are you talking to?" Gray eyes surveyed the room, half-expecting to see Kayla or Liv with Doug.

"Oh...Hi, Marcy." *At least she's still talking to me.* "Mornin'."

"Good morning. Dougie, I—" The girl stopped mid-sentence as her eyes locked on his face. "Hey," she prompted in a gentle voice, "are you okay?" In three steps she was out of the bathroom and at his side, her thumbs brushing across his cheeks. She searched his face worriedly, waiting for an answer, noticing that his eyes refused to meet hers. "What's wrong?" She felt a pang of worry. *Uh Oh.* Was he regretting what had happened?

"You're just in a towel." *Brilliant, asswipe. State the obvious, why don't you?*

"I was drying off when I heard you talking to someone. Why? Is that a problem?" she asked incredulously, a little hurt creeping into her voice. "It didn't seem to bother you yesterday. Or last night, for that matter."

A disheveled, pale head shook, and Doug cringed at the mention of the night before. "Do um...do you remember last night?"

"Of course." Her eyes widened with realization. "Why?" She licked her lips, suddenly nervous. "Don't you?"

"Um...sure. I remember everything. I wasn't that drunk." Doug shifted so he could search Marcy's face, his embarrassment evident. "You um...well, you just didn't say much after, and I...well—" *Christ! Why can't I talk without bumbling like an idiot? Isn't it obvious that she just doesn't want to hurt my feelings?*

Oh. Marcy tried not to look as guilty as she suddenly felt. "I fell asleep really quickly after we—you know—didn't I?"

Doug just nodded.

"It was the booze, Dougie," she offered contritely, taking one of Doug's hands in hers. "You know I've never drunk like that before."

"Was it really horrible?" Doug suddenly blurted out of nowhere, only able to concentrate on one thing and confusing Marcy.

Her brows drew together. "Well, it started out fun, but now I feel like crap, I'll have to admit." Marcy scrunched up her nose in disgust. "All I know is that I'm never doing that again. I've learned my lesson."

"Never?" Doug squeaked, his heart sinking. *Oh, shit. Never? As in not ever again? Ever? No more?*

Marcy thought about that for a moment. "Well, I guess that's not totally realistic. Maybe I'll try again in a few years. Just on special occasions, mind you."

"I didn't think—" the boy swallowed hastily and lowered his gaze. "Was it really that terrible, Marse?"

"Hell yes," she chuckled ruefully. "But at least I don't feel like I'm gonna throw up anymore."

"Oh, God," Doug moaned. *It just keeps getting worse and worse.* The teenager jumped to his feet, taking the sheet with him and clutching it around his waist. He felt dizzy. "I'm so sorry, Marcy. I...I'll never ever touch you again. Shit. Shit. Shit," he berated himself ruthlessly. "I promise. I—"

"What?" the girl asked, obviously startled by Doug's prattling. "What in God's name are you talking about?"

"I know last night wasn't what you wanted." Doug's free hand began to flail around as he spoke, a gesture he'd picked up from Liv. "We never should have done it. God, but when you started touching me, I just, I just—" *Short-circuited.*

"Hang on just a minute. And quit freakin' out for a second, will ya?" Marcy rose to her feet, grabbing his wildly gesturing arm. "Doug, I have no idea what you're talking about."

"The sex, of course. What else?"

"Oh."

"Yeah. Oh." He squared his shoulders ready to admit his apparent deficiency out loud. "I blew it big time, I know."

A relieved but tentative smile curled Marcy's lips as she finally caught a clue as to what was happening. "I was talking about the beer, not about making love with you, Dougie."

He pulled away from the girl's grasp and began to pace around the bed. "We don't have to do it again," he said firmly, hating that idea more than words could express. "And I won't pressure you. I... What did you say?"

"Jesus, you're neurotic." Marcy shook her head as she rolled her eyes. Doug was nothing, if not predictable. *If I had been thinking straight last night, I would have done something to head this off, she thought grumpily.* "While I was in the shower, you were out here thinking all kinds of crazy, stupid things, right?"

Doug's eyes widened a bit. "Well, I uhh...no," he immediately denied, pretending Marcy didn't know him as well as she obviously did.

Marcy crossed her arms across her chest and waited, as a dark eyebrow arched.

Doug visibly flinched. *Fine. I won't take the coward's way out. I'll just ask.* "Was it everything you wanted it to be, Marcy?" he finally questioned softly, plopping back down on the bed and dejectedly sprawling across it, wishing he had some aspirin and was somewhere else.

Oh, boy. Ask me something easy, why don't you? "Umm," she hesitated, not wanting to lie, but wanting to make sure Doug didn't misunderstand what she was saying. "That's kind of a toughie, Doug."

"No, it isn't. A yes or no will do nicely."

Marcy made a face. "Okay, then the answer is yes and no." She joined him back on the bed, rolling onto her belly and tucking a pillow under her chest as she propped herself up on her elbows.

"You were disappointed." It wasn't a question.

A drop of water rolled down her throat and onto the bed. "Not by you."

"You're lying."

Marcy blew out a frustrated breath. Doug was the kind who always made her work for things. Lucky for him, he was totally worth it. "Look, I would have preferred that we had been someplace a little more romantic than this flea trap." She rolled over on her back and began to study the ceiling, noting the dingy brown smoke stains directly above the bed. "And I would have preferred that we were both completely sober. But it felt right at the time," she added honestly. "So, I'm not sorry it happened."

Doug thought about what she'd said, pretty much agreeing with her, but still not feeling much better. "But what about me?"

"What about you?"

"Did I...make you feel good?" He felt himself blushing, but

was unable to stop it.

A small nod came without hesitation. "You sure did."

Doug waited expectantly. "And?" he finally prompted.

Marcy shrugged. "And what?"

"Jesus fucking Christ!" he exploded, finally tired of beating around the bush. "Did you have an orgasm or not."

"Hey!" Marcy yelled back indignantly, her hackles rising at his tone of voice. "Don't you think that's a little personal?"

"Personal?" he asked flabbergasted. "After what we did, why is that personal? I wanna know."

"Don't get all huffy with me, Dougie. Fine, then. The answer is no."

Doug's anger suddenly melted away. "Aww...crap," was the only thing he could think to say. He shifted to his side, facing the wall.

Gray eyes softened at the sight of the teen's slumped shoulders. "It's not like that's the end of the world."

"It's not, huh? Call me crazy, but I was hoping you'd enjoy yourself, too."

"I did enjoy myself." *God, do people actually talk about this with each other? That can't be right.* "Well, it's not like we've had any practice or anything," she reminded him sensibly.

"That's true," he admitted reluctantly. But for some reason, Doug was determined to stew in misery for as long as possible. He sighed and rubbed his face. "Practice could only help, right?"

She nodded. Marcy opened her mouth to say something, then held her tongue for just a second to decide whether she should. Since they were already talking about it... "And I've sort of discussed this general subject with my girlfriends and they said it might take a little time to...you know...work on things so that, well, we both enjoy ourselves to the fullest extent possible." *Oh, great job, Marse. Like that made sense.*

Doug turned back over and stared at Marcy with wide eyes. "You mean you've actually talked to girls who admit that their boyfriends couldn't...that they didn't—"

"Well, it's not like it's a character flaw or anything." She smacked him with a pillow, drawing a reluctant laugh from the boy. "Women are ruthless; we talk about everything, Dougie. And sometimes we're even honest with our friends," she drawled wryly.

"I know. I know. But I bet their boyfriends still wouldn't like it." Doug suddenly felt worlds better. If girls were talking about it, then it couldn't just be him. And Marcy sounded prepared to work on things, which meant he would get another chance. Hopefully, lots more chances. Yeah. He could live with that. "How long do you figure we can hide here and work on things before our sisters root us out?" He smiled, and reflexively, Marcy smiled back, snuggling closer.

"They're probably asleep. I think it's *way* too early to call them now, don't you?" Marcy could feel Doug's relief so keenly that it was almost as though she was feeling it herself.

Doug's grin broadened. "Absolutely."

Chapter
Fifteen

Justice In All Its Glory

Cobb Island
Present Day

"DON'T BE MEAN."

"It's not mean," Kayla insisted, even as she was unable to keep a devilish smile from her face.

Two pale brows rose in disbelief, but Liv grinned right along with her companion. "Of course it is. Otherwise, you wouldn't bother doing it."

"You know you want me to," Kayla taunted in a sultry voice, her eyes sparkling beneath thick, dark lashes.

"You're bad."

"Of course."

Liv bit her lower lip and chuckled. "Okay."

"Ha. You're easy."

"Clearly."

Kayla pressed a button on her cell phone and retrieved the number of the motel Marcy and Doug were staying in. It was the crack of dawn, but she decided a little wake up call was in order. Especially, after the kids' drinking escapade.

Grinning wickedly, Kayla gathered several sheets that were draped over pieces of furniture to keep the dust off. With her free hand, she grabbed the history and tucked it, and the sheets, under her arm. Grasping Liv's hand, she led the blonde out onto the porch. The morning sun was barely beginning to peek over the horizon, dimming the blanket of twinkling stars above and painting the sky with shades of crimson, violet and finally, gold.

Shocked eyes surveyed the land.

"Jesus!" Kayla splashed through shallow puddles as she crossed the wooden porch, leaning over a side railing to get a better view of the island. Absently, she tossed the sheets onto the wet porch swing, letting out a slight groan as her knee twisted to the side.

Liv's jaw sagged as she stood speechless.

"Jesus."

"You already said that," Liv finally muttered, spinning in a circle as she took in the damage.

Nearly a third of the trees had been downed, strewn in a tangled mass all along the shore. Most had simply snapped in half from the force of the wind, but several had actually been uprooted. There was another sizeable group that had been reduced to charred, smoldering splinters by the numerous lightning strikes. The fresh, salty air brought with it just the lightest hint of smoke and the pungent fragrance of wet, burnt wood.

"Jes —"

"And you wondered why I don't like storms?" Liv interrupted.

Kalya shook her head. "Not anymore."

Liv joined Kayla along the railing, the phone forgotten for the time being as they focused on the sea. Kayla wrapped her arm around Liv's waist; pulling her close, several strands of fair hair brushed against her shoulder. "Were they ever this bad in Africa?"

Liv nodded. "Oh, yeah. But most of the damage was done by flooding, not lightning." She briefly closed her eyes, trying to block out visions of entire villages that were there, then simply weren't, all in a matter of moments.

Kayla could feel Liv's mood beginning to grow dark. She turned to face the shorter woman and, cupping her cheeks in her hands, placed a tender kiss on soft, pink lips. "Are you tired?"

"Mmmm," Liv hummed into the kiss, continually amazed at the depth of emotion and eroticism that could be conveyed in such a simple, nearly platonic gesture. "A little," she admitted. "I never was very good about staying up all night. I'll probably crash later today." She took a deep breath of the cool air. *God, it's good to be out of the house.*

The confines of its walls seemed dark and heavy, oppressive even. Liv tried to shake off the feeling, considering that it might be nothing more than lingering fear over the storm. But then, why was "misery" the first word that came to mind when she thought of the house, despite the fact that she and Kayla were obviously safe? The deeper she delved into the history, the worse the place seemed. The thought of a spell protecting the ancient home only made it seem haunted in her mind. She couldn't leave this island soon enough. But the water was still churning heavily, and she knew it would be hours before it would be safe enough for the kids to make the two mile trip to the island. She sighed, training her eyes on the ocean and concentrating on the fresh feeling of the outdoors.

Kayla gestured towards the porch swing and adjusted the layers of sheets across the seat and back to protect them from the wet wood. She sat down with a barely audible groan, making the swing creak loudly under her weight. Liv immediately joined her and, for a few moments, they continued to watch the sunrise in perfect silence, allowing a profound sense of peace and togetherness to envelop them. Finally, when she heard the faint beeping as Kayla began to dial her cell phone, Liv's attention was drawn to Kayla's lap.

The redhead grinned and brought the phone to her ear, listening to it ring. On the fourth ring, she began to scowl. On the eighth ring, she was ready to hang up. Kayla was about to push the off button when she heard a faint voice.

"'Lo."

"Doug?"

Kayla heard the rustling of sheets. Her eyes narrowed. Was that a moan in the background? "Doug, is that you?"

"I—" A shuddering breath. "I'llcallyoubacklater. Bye." Then the line went dead. Kayla simply stared at the phone.

"Well?" Liv asked, snuggling a little closer and still enjoying the much cooler morning air. "What'd he say?"

"He hung up on me!" Kayla continued to stare evilly at the phone as a dark blush worked its way up her neck and onto her face.

"What?"

"I think they um..." Kayla's flush deepened. "They were busy, and Doug said they'd call back later."

"Busy? At sunrise? What in the hell—" Liv's own blush made a startling appearance. She covered her ears with her hands. "No. No. No. I didn't need to know that," she whined pitifully, shaking her head as if trying to remove the thought.

"God, neither did I." Kayla made a face. "I will not go crazy and rant. I will not," she chanted, not quite under her breath.

Liv sighed. "If you won't, I won't. Let's finish the history. It only looks like there are a few sections to go." She glanced up at the sky. "It'll be nice not to read by candlelight. I just couldn't stand it in that stuffy house any longer."

Kayla nodded and wordlessly passed over the book, her eyes roaming over the reddish highlights in Liv's hair that were accentuated by the rising sun. She smiled gently, but her face quickly melted into a more stoic facade as she thought about the story that was unfolding. Kayla had a bad feeling about the history's outcome, but didn't feel the need to share that with Liv. She'd been wrong plenty of times before, and she could hear the empathy in Liv's voice as she read the tale.

"Huh." Liv traced over the ink stained paper with the tip of her finger as her eyes took in the neat lines. "Her handwriting looks bolder in natural light." She turned to Kayla, who had her arm wrapped around her shoulders and her eyes closed. An involuntary smile shaped Liv's lips. *God, she's drop dead gorgeous.* "Are you ready?"

A short nod and small smile were Liv's answer as Afia's words were carried away on the light morning breeze.

Cobb Island
January, 1691

It was four days before I saw Mistress Bridget again. And when my eyes first lay upon her, the very breath was sucked from my lungs. She had not been washed since her search for Master Henry or the brutalities that were inflicted upon her that very same night. Allah knows she was a sight. Her appearance and the strength she showed despite it, compel me to take time to detail it, even now.

Her cheeks were sunken, and I wondered if she'd been given any food or water during her captivity. She had one black eye that was still nearly swollen shut, and several jagged cuts adorning her forehead and chin. The wounds had not been stitched, and one look told me they would scar her lovely face. Another long cut began at her collarbone and disappeared beneath the stained, white, man's rough spun cotton shirt she still wore. The wound appeared to be infected, and red streaks shot out from it in several directions, marring her lightly tanned skin. Her hair was a loose and tangled mess, streaked with dried mud and blood.

Mistress Bridget's clothing reeked of rancid wood, urine, and death. It was a smell I remembered all too well. With shocking certainty, I knew that she had been housed in the slave hull, in the bowels of the ship anchored off Cobb Island. My heart ached for the child, knowing she'd been kept in that horrid, squalid place, even as her experience could never match mine, when the hull of my ship had been crammed with living and dying bodies on my never-ending journey across the great sea.

It seems that Master Cyril couldn't stand the putrid stench of the ship's underbelly when he'd gone to see his sister, and he'd requested that the prisoner be kept in the house, or perhaps the stable on the island. Mistress Bridget was manacled with heavy irons that circled her ankles and wrists, and Master had had a rather easy time convincing the senior officer that there was really no need for her to be held aboard ship while she awaited trial. Truth be told, the naval officers were relieved by this request. None of them wanted to be anywhere near the fearsome witch who had fought them with the Devil's own strength. Now, in shifts, they would simply stand guard outside her door.

Mistress Bridget was led into a spare room; she couldn't be trusted in her own room, for fear she'd use some unknown device to ply her witchcraft. Her feet shuffled along in short, abbreviated steps that contrasted sharply with her normally purposeful stride. Even in those small steps, it was apparent that she was favoring one side. At the time, I wondered if it was her leg or ribs that had been injured. I soon found out that it was both. Before the guard shut the door, Mistress Bridget sneered at him, flashing white, straight teeth in a chilling, feral grin. The young man nearly soiled himself on the spot. It was the first time that I had smiled in four days. I had no way of knowing at the time, that it would be the last for many days to come. It was also then that I realized that although her body appeared broken, Mistress Bridget's spirit clearly was not.

Cobb Island
November, 1690

"HOW IS SHE?" were the first words out of Bridget's mouth when the room's door clicked shut. "And the lad, how is he?" she questioned eagerly.

Afia's eyes remained on the cloth she was dipping into a basin of warm water. Now that she was in the house, Cyril had ordered that his sister be made more presentable. Witch or not, she was still a Redding; and she would face her judgment in as dignified a manner as possible.

"Afia?"

A deep sigh. "Not well, child." The black woman wrung out the thin cloth. "The boy's fever has only gotten worse; it has been over two days since we were able to awaken him to feed him or give him water." The skin around Afia's eyes crinkled deeply with worry. "Now he only sleeps."

Bridget sucked in a breath, her eyes taking on a slightly dazed quality. "Damn!" she hissed. She'd heard nothing about Henry's condition deteriorating. "And his mother?" she asked a bit shakily.

Afia picked up a bar of soap, absently wondering how Mistress Bridget was supposed to wash while manacled. "Mistress Faylinn hasn't left his side since you found him. She is beyond the point of exhaustion, and she continues to ask about you." Afia left out that Faylinn had gone into an all out fury when she found out what had happened to Bridget, smashing every piece of furniture the room held, save the bed where Henry lay unconscious.

Bridget said firmly, "I must go to her."

Afia finally turned to face Bridget, her chocolate brown eyes warm and soft. "You cannot, child. Your brother forbade it."

Bridget squeezed her eyes shut in frustration. "Dammit, Afia. She needs me. And maybe I can help the lad. The natives on the mainland showed me—"

A heart-wrenching wail filled the house, immediately followed by a slightly higher pitched keening that seemed to drown out every other noise.

The island went deathly still.

Afia and Bridget stopped breathing, and just as abruptly as the keening began, it was replaced by a sobbing the likes of which neither woman had heard before. Afia simply dropped the wet cloth and rushed out of the room, leaving Bridget to stare blankly at the closed door, a solitary tear streaking down her cheek. The tall woman's heart twisted painfully in her chest as a wave of nausea swept over her. She tried to raise her hands to cover her ears and block out the horrific cries, but her chains had been securely fastened to the heavy chair in which she sat. The lone tear splashed silently onto her thigh, landing atop a crusted stain of dark, crimson blood.

The sound had been Faylinn and could only mean one thing.

Young Henry was dead.

Cobb Island
Present Day

LIV PAUSED IN her reading, swallowing convulsively as she looked up from the yellowed page.

"Let's stop," Kayla said gently, her voice breaking a bit as she reached for the history. "I've already found what I was looking for. We don't need to continue."

"No." Liv sniffed and looked up at Kayla with glistening eyes. She smiled weakly. "I'm just being silly, I know. I mean, they're dead. It doesn't really matter now how they got that way."

Kayla frowned. "It's not silly, Liv. He was just a baby. It's right that you should feel sad for him and his family." Long slender hands reached up and tucked back an errant wisp of golden hair that fluttered in the morning breeze.

Verdant eyes welled again, and this time a couple of tears managed to escape, only to be swept away by gentle lips as Kayla claimed them.

Kayla's arms circled Liv, squeezing her with a firm, steady pressure. "Let's —"

"No. I don't want to stop. I want to know what happened."

Kayla deposited another soft kiss on the soft skin just below Liv's ear, the warm breath tickling Liv's throat and sending a small shiver down her spine. "Okay. If that's what you want, let's keep going."

Liv nodded, and the women settled back into what had become their reading position and began again.

Cobb Island
January, 1691

The day that Master Henry died, his father went a little mad. Master Cyril charged into the room where Mistress Bridget was being held, and beat the poor child into a stupor while she sat restrained to the chair. I believe the only thing that stopped him from murdering her right then was the sure knowledge of what was to follow.

Master Cyril insisted that his sister be tried that very moment for witchcraft, Henry's murder, and conspiracy involving the slaves' escape. When it became clear that no amount of torture would convince her to confess these crimes, Bridget was bound, gagged, and placed in the corner of the room to watch the thirty-minute proceeding.

The trial was a farce from beginning to end, with Officer Richards, Elizabeth, Cyril, and the young slave Michael being the only persons permitted to testify. The Master's business partners acted as judge and jury.

Elizabeth informed her sister of what was to happen only moments before it was to begin. Mistress Judith went into such a state, demanding that she be allowed to make a statement on her aunt's behalf, that Cyril locked the nearly hysterical child in her room until the trial was over and she could regain her senses.

As Bridget sat in the parlor, her trial going on almost in spite of her presence, her gaze continuously traveled to the door. My heart ached from the realization that it was Faylinn she was waiting to see. At Master Cyril's direction, Mistress Faylinn, who remained in the room with Henry's body, remained oblivious to the entire proceeding.

The look on Bridget's face when the child finally

realized she would truly face her judgment alone was a sickening combination of hurt, bewilderment, and anger. To my everlasting shame, I confess here, as I have in my prayers to Allah, that it was only my own fear that kept me from rushing upstairs and informing Faylinn of these abominable proceedings myself. I know in my heart now, as I did then, that the young woman would have done everything and anything in her power to help Mistress Bridget.

It surprised no one that Mistress Bridget was found guilty of all charges. Her judge, being a senior officer of the Royal Navy, felt it well within his rights to impose her sentence immediately — as military law governed in the colonies. For Mistress Bridget, justice would be swift and severe. Her brother, as the injured party, along with the Crown, was consulted on the proper punishment for her crimes.

I know at several times in the pages of this history I have spoken of things I shall remember in my dreams. The judge's voice echoed in the parlor while slave, soldier, and family alike looked on with a mixture of fascination and disgust.

Cyril's eyes locked on his sister's, and for a moment, the room went deathly still. The sound of my own breathing was thunderous, and I had to force myself to relax for fear I would faint. I half-expected something to happen between them, although neither sibling said a word. After a moment where neither one would break their gaze, Cyril walked over to the judge and spoke quietly in his ear. His exact words remain a mystery. But the judge nodded and rose to his feet, sucking in his belly as Bridget pinned him with an intense stare that literally caused a sweat to break out across the fat man's brow.

His words are forever scalded on my soul. They chill me even now, as I put pen to paper.

"Bridget Katherine Redding, having been found guilty of crimes against man and God, which include conspiracy, murder and unspeakable acts of witchcraft...you are hereby sentenced to death. As punishment for your crimes, and in the name of their Majesties King William and Queen Mary, I direct that you be burned at the stake until you are dead, and your ashes scattered in the sea without benefit of Christian burial. Your sentence to be carried out immediately.

May God have mercy on your wretched soul."

Chapter
Sixteen

Realizations of the Soul

Cobb Island
November, 1690

"TAKE HER TO the stables. I won't have her vile presence infecting my home for another second." Cyril motioned for several of the officers to remove his sister from his sight.

"I'll show them where to go, Father," Elizabeth said helpfully, smiling at her aunt's obvious pain as she was unceremoniously yanked to her feet by her hair.

Cyril nodded, stroking his thin mustache with fingers still shaking with anxiety from the day's events. "Of course, my dear. Excellent idea." A slight frown flittered across his face before disappearing completely. "Then see to Judith. It seems your sister is distraught at the thought of her aunt being a witch." He focused dark gray eyes on Bridget and spoke in the arrogant tone that had grated on her nerves her entire life. "I'm off to speak with my wife to inform her that her presence is required at tonight's...festivities."

His words caused a small growl to erupt from Bridget as she was jerked towards the door. She stumbled, but two pairs of strong hands kept her upright. Bridget tried to project a warning into her brother's mind, but her own thoughts were such a jumbled mess, she wasn't quite certain whether she was coming or going. How many times had she been hit on the head? Her brows contracted as she tried to concentrate. After a while, she simply lost track.

Elizabeth glowed under her father's meager praise. "Father—" Her mouth shut with an audible click when Cyril walked past her as though she wasn't even speaking to him, ignoring her completely. The girl's back stiffened and her lip quivered for just a split second before twisting into a slight sneer, but she said nothing, donning a heavy cape as she quietly escorted Bridget and her guards to the stables. She purposely left Bridget's cloak hanging on a hook by the door, chuckling to herself as her aunt was pummeled by the cold autumn rain that had been drenching the island in misery all afternoon. The girl took the long way to the stables, navigating the puddles carefully so she wouldn't soil the hem of her dress.

Bridget was roughly pushed down on the coarse wooden surface of an empty half-barrel, then securely chained to one of the stable's support posts. She hissed under her breath as the manacles were tightened further, digging into tender, raw flesh.

"I won't be but a moment," Elizabeth assured the two officers who were waiting at the door. "I'd like a word with my aunt before her execution." She let a brief flash of sadness creep into her expression before smiling sweetly and batting her eyelashes at the men, both of whom perked up under the attentive stare of the pretty young girl.

Bridget's execution had been scheduled for midnight. Elizabeth's mouth shaped a wry grin as she turned away from the door, kicking aside stray wisps of fragrant hay as she walked. *The witching hour — how wonderfully appropriate.*

Bridget faintly heard Elizabeth's words and wondered, fleetingly, whether the girl had said them or merely thought them.

As soon as the stable's door creaked closed, Elizabeth roughly pulled the gag from Bridget's mouth, causing the woman to cough and choke. Dropping the filthy rag, she strode across the stable, her back to Bridget, stopping only when she reached Apollo's stall. "He's a beautiful beast, really," Elizabeth offered conversationally, watching the stallion prance and stomp, puffs of steam escaping his nostrils. The steed snorted and danced nervously, seemingly disturbed by her very presence. "I'll see that he's well cared for..."

Bridget didn't know what to say. Her forehead wrinkled in confusion, as thoughts that had been ephemeral only moments ago seemed to come into focus. The icy rain had awakened her senses and chased away the thick fog she'd been wandering through since her last beating. Elizabeth's behavior confused her to no end. At times the girl was almost contrite, then, a second later, she seemed to revel in Bridget's torment, goading her with cruel words and crueler deeds. "Thank you," she finally offered hoarsely, licking cracked, dry lips.

Elizabeth scowled when the young stallion backed away, refusing to allow her to pet him. She felt an icy rage grab hold of her heart and tug at the darkness within. Momentarily pushing it down, she turned and studied Bridget, taking in the almost imperceptible slump of her shoulders, her slightly sagging head, with grim but determined satisfaction. "Oh, I don't think you'll be thanking me, Auntie." Elizabeth could barely contain her excitement. "Not after what I'm about to tell you."

"Why are you here, girl? It is most certainly *not* to say goodbye," Bridget said acidly, not wanting to waste these precious hours in the company of her spiteful, malicious niece. "Or, are you merely here to gloat?"

Elizabeth tipped her head back and let out a shrill laugh that caused Bridget to wince and wonder at the girl's sanity. "I suppose you're right, Auntie; I am mainly here to gloat. But I must admit, I am rather proud of myself. Opportunity beckoned and...well...I'm sure you can figure out the rest. But there was something I wanted you to know before you were reduced to a smoking pile of ashes." Elizabeth approached Bridget. Bending at the waist, she placed her palms on her aunt's knees and leaned forward until they were nose-to-nose.

Bridget blinked, feeling as though she was looking at a much younger, far more disturbing version of herself. The obvious familial resemblance caused Elizabeth's actions to cut even deeper.

The girl smiled. "You. Don't. Exist."

Bridget jerked her head away, annoyed at her niece's close proximity, but held captive by her shackles. With a violent thrust, she yanked her legs forward, sending a bolt of pain through her lower back. But she was held firm. "What?" She had to grind out the word.

"You heard me." Elizabeth straightened, making a conscious effort not to stamp her foot and appear like a peevish child, although her efforts were very nearly undone by the expression on her face alone. She took a calming breath and began again. "You don't exist. Just like Henry won't. It will be as though you were never born." The slim teen paused a moment, letting all the hate and resentment she felt for Bridget show clearly in angry gray eyes. "Consider it a token of my affection," she muttered as she placed an entirely cold kiss on Bridget's cheek, her own stomach roiling at the smell of Bridget's unwashed clothes and infected wounds.

"Be gone, brat. You make no sense."

Elizabeth stiffened, more than a little disappointed. She was so hoping her aunt would figure out what she was saying on her own. *It would have been so much more delicious to see realization dawn across that battered face.* The girl sighed dramatically. *I should have told her before her last beating. She really did seem much more coherent then.*

A long streak of golden light shot across the floor then disappeared, drawing Elizabeth's attention to the fact that the rain had momentarily stopped, and that late afternoon sun was trying to peek under the stable door. She knocked one fist against her aunt's forehead as though it were a piece of wood. "Think. You have no heirs. Where is the only place your memory would live on, once this day is through?"

I pray God, in Faylinn's heart. A shudder of pain lanced through Bridget as her utter failure regarding her beloved hit home. *...Months ago,* she anguished. *I should have spirited that bright young thing away from this horrid island and my despicable brother the moment I laid eyes on her.* Tears welled in bloodshot eyes, blurring Bridget's already cloudy vision as the accumulation of the events of the past week came crashing down on her. Her own kin were orchestrating her execution and, despite her best efforts, Henry was dead. And Faylinn, whom she loved above all others, had failed to believe in her when it mattered most. Confused green eyes haunted her dreams and tormented Bridget's waking moments. She felt like she was drowning.

Elizabeth cocked her head slightly to the side. "Have you figured it out then, clever?"

Bridget just shook her head from side to side as her defenses began to bottom out and she felt herself sink deeper into misery. Her breathing hitched as a sob threatened to escape and unexpected tears stung her eyes. "Where is Faylinn?" she muttered, trying desperately to maintain at least a shred of dignity and not break down in front of Elizabeth. *I cannot...I...I cannot fall apart now.*

The girl frowned. How was she supposed to torment her aunt if Bridget was too consumed with her own misery to pay attention? Elizabeth threw back slim shoulders and stated proudly, "I am the histories' Guardian." She intentionally pretended she hadn't heard Bridget's question about Faylinn and forged ahead with her own agenda. "And as far as future generations will ever know, our family consists of Father, Judith, my *true* mother, and myself. *No one* else." The harsh inflection of her voice emphasized her last words.

Bridget looked up at her niece in pure disbelief, her mouth opening slightly, but no words coming forth.

Elizabeth's eyes lit with glee and she clapped her hands together, grinning like a Cheshire cat. "I'm so glad you decided to pay attention, Bridget," she said excitedly.

"You...you can't do that," the older woman sputtered.

Elizabeth's smile broadened. This was the reaction she'd been hoping for. "Ahh, but who would stop me? Certainly not you." She spun around in a circle, her arms clasping her skirts as they billowed.

Bridget wondered briefly if the girl would actually take flight. But as quickly as the euphoria came, it was replaced by Elizabeth's usual somber mask. Drawing nearer to her aunt, she whispered, "In the end, who was the more powerful one, Bridget? You or I?"

Bridget's face reddened with fury. *Was that what this was about? By God! She would desecrate the histories out of jealousy and spite?* "It is a sacred duty to properly and accurately maintain the histories. You know this, Elizabeth! They exist separate and apart from us, to guide the future and chronicle the past."

The dark-haired girl looked completely unmoved and simply crossed her arms over her chest as if bored, awaiting a more convincing argument.

Bridget's fists clenched, causing the manacles to dig deeply into her wrists. "I have been documenting the family's powers in a journal for years. Its contents must be properly recorded. It is an *obligation* to pass on the knowledge." Bridget cursed her fool brother and his incompetence when it came to instilling the true importance of the histories in his daughter.

"Oh," Elizabeth bit her bottom lip, "your journal, I'm afraid, has been...misplaced..." she smirked, then added, "permanently."

"Bitch!" Bridget seethed, closing her eyes at the grating sound of her niece's laughter that somehow seemed to shift into a cackle. "And what of your brother?" she tried again. "You would deny him his place in history?"

"My *half* brother was the son of that sniveling slut my father married for no other reason than to obtain this island. She is a *business* arrangement." Elizabeth's thoughts veered toward her stepmother. "She is not nearly good enough for him, and still she dares to think she can replace my mother," she ranted, pacing back and forth in front of Bridget like a caged animal.

A challenging sneer twisted Bridget's face. "It seems, my dear, that you've developed a rather *unnatural* obsession with your father."

Smack!

Smack!

Bridget's head snapped backwards with the force of the second blow. "Do not pretend to lecture me on what is natural, you perverted whore!" Elizabeth virtually screamed, her eyes flashing dangerously as her slender frame shook with unsuppressed rage. "My father may have chosen not to act on what you arrogantly parade before his very eyes, but where he failed, I did not." Elizabeth suddenly sobered. "Judith will never forgive me," she said softly as she licked her lips, her face easily conveying true pain at that notion. "But I did what I had to do...for all of us," she finished somberly as if she had merely done her duty and nothing more.

Bridget spat a mouthful of blood onto the straw near her feet. She didn't bother denying her niece's implied accusation concerning her and Faylinn. That she and Faylinn hadn't slept together didn't really matter. She was in love with her, just the same. But she tried not to dwell on thoughts of her brother's wife.

These thoughts were private, and she'd just as soon not share them with this girl-turned-monster.

"Oh, sweet Aunt." Elizabeth smile was full sympathy. "You may have your last, fleeting thoughts of Faylinn *only* because I must see to Judith and I *choose* not to share them."

Elizabeth turned on her heel, satisfied that she'd made her point. As she began to move towards the door, Bridget's ragged voice caught her attention.

"Ask Mary to come here with a change of clothes and wash basin, won't you? Wait. Never mind." *I wouldn't want my stench to offend Cyril or those bastards he calls partners, now would I,* she thought sarcastically.

Elizabeth had her refusal poised on the tip of her tongue when Bridget's thought made itself plainly heard in her mind. "I'll send Mary in," she said happily. Tilting her head towards Bridget, she wrinkled her nose and made a show of sniffing the cold afternoon air. "You do stink."

Bridget's lip twitched but she managed to nod silently, trying to look annoyed and keeping her mind as blank as possible until Elizabeth left the room.

"FAYLINN! FAYLINN, OPEN this door before I break it down!" Cyril demanded, pounding on the heavy wooden slab, causing it to shake on its hinges.

Somewhere deep in the back of Faylinn's mind, Cyril's insistent pounding registered, but she simply ignored it, not caring whether he broke the door in or not. *You can burn this monstrosity of a house to the ground, for all I care, Husband,* her mind cried spitefully, but she lacked the will to say the words out loud.

After a few more seconds of furious banging, Cyril apparently gave up, and the house went utterly still.

The sun had set hours ago, but Faylinn hadn't bothered lighting a lamp. Why should she? There was nothing to see. In the shadows of the room, she was alone in her misery and self-hatred. The room's quiet, empty darkness matched the aching hollowness in her heart perfectly.

It was her fault. All of it. Her lack of faith in Bridget had delayed Henry's rescue and cost her son his life. She had cost her son his life. *What kind of mother lets her own fears and doubts override what is best for her child? I didn't deserve him or Bridget, and now they're both being taken away from me, one at a time,* she thought miserably. *Oh God. They both loved me, and I repaid them with stupidity and betrayal.*

Glistening eyes were riveted on the small pale child lying in a pool of sheets and disheveled woolen blankets. *His hair reminds me of yours, Bridget — so soft and shiny.* Rising from her chair, Faylinn sat on the edge of the bed beside Henry, brushing her fingertips through soft, curly locks no longer sweaty from fever. Her glance dropped to his still chest, where she stared with morbid fascination, part of her still expecting to see its gentle rise and fall as she always did when she sneaked into his bedroom to check on him each night.

"I'm so sorry, Henry. Pu-please forgive me," she pleaded brokenly, her knuckles grazing his downy-soft cheek, its unnatural coolness causing her heart to twist painfully in her chest.

With a groan, Faylinn dropped her hand and moved to the window as a strong gust rattled the glass in its frame and a soft rain began to pelt the house again. She leaned her forehead against cold glass that was slick with moisture. *He's dead because of me. Her life is in danger because of me.*

Guilt and unrelenting anguish sent her guts churning. Dropping to her knees, she emptied the meager contents of her stomach into a chamber pot alongside the bed until dry heaves racked her body, and an acrid taste burned her throat. With a shuddering breath, she pushed the pot away and scrambled back to the wall. Pressing her shoulders against the cool wooden surface, she drew her knees to her chest, wrapping her arms around them, and burying her face. Grief and loss overwhelmed her and she let them, embracing the pain with the sure knowledge that that was all she had left.

Oh, Bridget, I am so...so very sorry. Had I not questioned you, none of this would have happened. You hold my very soul. How could I fail to believe in you, trust you, when you have always shown me only the greatest dedication and affection? She closed her eyes and tilted her head skyward, hot tears spilling down her cheeks as she thought of the woman who was charming, and strong. Who, like a force of nature, simply swept her off her feet, leaving her breathless and confused.

But this time, Faylinn refused to back away from her feelings, accepting her loss as the punishment for her own lack of faith. Admitting to herself, for the first time, what her heart had been whispering all along: she didn't just care for Bridget as a friend and companion; she loved her with a completeness and devotion that was nearly frightening in its intensity. At times, it all but robbed her of rational thought.

The older woman's bold, lusty laugh, riveting pale eyes, and gentle touch had filled her dreams and ignited her passions from the very start. Suddenly not fearing the eternal damnation that was the subject of so many sermons of her youth, she craved Bridget's touch as one lover craves another. Tear-filled eyes turned to the small bed in the center of the dark room. For a long terrifying moment, she truly considered her life and future: a future without her son and, very likely, Bridget; a life without hope or love or peace or even faith. Anguished eyes widened as waves of unbearable sorrow washed over her, making her heart lurch. She wondered darkly why it still bothered to beat at all. *Why should I fear hell?* She snorted bitterly, paying no heed to the silent tears scalding her cheeks and neck. *I'm already in hell.*

Faylinn's chest heaved as her body convulsed with helpless sobs, shattering the silence. Her spirit ached desperately to find its way to the only place where she knew she would receive comfort and forgiveness — Bridget's arms. The thought that Bridget probably couldn't stand the sight of her only added to her misery.

Long moments passed before Faylinn's cries quieted and her pounding pulse slowed, allowing reason and grim determination to begin to replace fear and grief. *I've got to talk to Cyril and help her. I can do no more for my baby, and she needs me now. I failed Henry. I've already failed her once. I'll die myself before I do it again.*

Sniffing, Faylinn grasped the windowsill and shakily pulled herself to her feet, wiping her tears and lips with the back of her hands. Throwing open the window, she drew in a deep lungful of tangy, salty air and the scent of wet leaves, the night's breeze scattering long, fair hair around her shoulders. The relief was immediate, as the gut-wrenching nausea she'd been plagued with for days slowly began to ease. Her body greedily absorbed the freshness as the foulness of death and illness was whisked away. *God, how many days have I been in this room?* During Henry's illness, she'd simply lost track of everything.

A loud clank below Henry's window drew Faylinn's gaze to several soldiers who were working by lantern light, loading a small cart with wood, hay, shovels, coils of rope, and...Faylinn squinted, trying to peer through the ever-increasing raindrops...a tree trunk? The men appeared to be doing their best to keep things dry, though they were failing miserably. With a shake of her head, she closed the window, readily dismissing the slave trader's nasty business as none of her concern.

Moving back to Henry's bed, the young mother bent down and placed a long, loving kiss on her son's cheek, wiping it away with a gentle thumb out of pure habit. "You were truly my heart," she said in a hushed voice as she nestled the boy's stuffed doll tightly against his shoulder and wrapped his limp arm around the bedraggled little beast. Faylinn lingered there, not nearly ready to say goodbye.

So she didn't.

Unshed tears glistened on pale lashes as she pulled the sheet up over his head. A solid lump formed in Faylinn's throat and she swallowed painfully, gathering her courage. "I love you, Henry," she whispered softly, before disappearing into the dimly lit corridors of the house.

Chapter
Seventeen

A Heart's Leap

Cobb Island
Present Day

LIV ABSENTLY CHEWED the inside of her cheek as she strolled onto the porch carrying two tall glasses of lemonade, minus ice, her thoughts centering on the section of the history she'd just completed. They had stopped reading, even though they were very close to the end, to take a break.

Afia's words were affecting both women, and Liv finally admitted that she'd had enough for a while, even though her natural curiosity was nudging her forward towards completion. Kayla seemed to be brooding angrily about the tragic events, while Liv found herself experiencing a mixture of empathy and outright frustration. *God, I feel as though I know those women. I hate what's happening to them.* She sighed quietly, pushing the history out of her mind for the time being.

The sight of Kayla leaning forward slightly, forearms on the porch railing, staring intently out over the sun-drenched waves, stopped Liv dead in her tracks. Her eyes fairly glowed with appreciation and affection, as she happily indulged in a long, leisurely look at the lanky woman, realizing, not for the first time, how much of their time together had been spent in darkness. *Which is so not fair.* She shook her head as she admired how the sun's bright rays brought out rich, burnished highlights in dark-crimson hair.

Kayla shifted restlessly from one foot to the other, every twitch causing lean calf and thigh muscles to stand out in vivid relief against tanned skin. A small smile that was on the verge of being an outright leer plucked at Liv's lips, but a pensive look soon replaced it as she began to wonder whether Kayla's body language might indicate more than simple impatience or boredom. *What's going on behind those baby blues? I could always just come out and ask her. I think she'd be a lot more receptive to my questions now that we're...hmm...now that we're what? Friends?* She chided herself gently, knowing her feelings ran deeper.

This being-in-love thing was different, she decided. Different from how she'd felt with other women. Things that were truly frightening, like telepathy and spells, were somehow made manageable, while everyday emotions like insecurity, or affection, or lust, easily spun out of control. The feelings were curious and compelling, and she found herself more than willing to simply let them envelop her. It was time.

Liv chuckled to herself as she willed her feet to start moving again, thinking how she'd gone half way around the world looking for something that would make her feel...complete. Whole. How ironic that she found what she'd been looking for practically in her own back yard — right here in Virginia.

"Penny for your thoughts," the linguist prompted as she sidled up to the railing and passed a glass to Kayla. The younger woman's pale eyes were firmly trained on the surf; her cell phone dangled loosely from her fingertips.

Kayla shrugged as she took a satisfying drink, then set her glass on the wide railing. "They're free for the asking, Liv," she finally offered, following the shorter woman's expectant gaze to her hands. "I um...just got a call."

"I see that," Liv murmured, squeezing herself between Kayla and the railing, smiling when long arms immediately wrapped around her waist. "Was it the kids?" She knew the answer before the words left her mouth. When her lover hesitated for several seconds, Liv felt an unexpected sinking sensation in the pit of her stomach.

A dark head shook. "No." Kayla frowned as though she were puzzling over her exact words. "It was...a friend, I guess."

"You guess?" A pale brow arched sharply. Liv wrapped her own arms around Kayla's trim waist, an unfamiliar surge of jealousy surprising her. "What kind of friend?" she asked carefully, knowing full well it was none of her business but asking anyway.

Kayla shrugged again, preferring not to talk about the phone call at all. *Couldn't I just tell you later?* Liv's gaze pinned her. *Guess not.* "The old kind."

"Uh huh." Liv nodded speculatively, her eyes turning to slits. "Old as in, 'I've fallen and I can't get up' old, or old as in you've known them for a long time, old?"

Kayla grinned and her eyes twinkled softly. *She's jealous? There is no way that should make me feel as good as it does.* "Old as in we've known each other for quite a while."

Hmm...no gender yet. Brat. "Did you meet in school? Study

partners? Or..." Liv unclasped her hands from Kayla's back and laid a flat palm against the sun-warmed fabric of her T-shirt, feeling the strong heartbeat beneath her fingertips, "a sorority sister perhaps?" she continued innocently, tracing a small pattern across Kayla's chest, not daring to look up.

Kayla burst out laughing. "I was never in a sorority."

"Kayla," Liv finally whined as she slapped Kayla's shaking belly, which only made it convulse more. Liv glanced up at Kayla from behind long pale lashes, poking her bottom lip out for added effect, and trying not to laugh herself. "Puuleeeez, tell me. You know damn well, I'm dyin'."

Kayla grinned broadly. "My friend's name is —" a slender eyebrow danced playfully, "Pat."

"Liar," Liv accused flatly, hands now on hips.

"Robin?"

Liv glared.

"Glen?"

"Kayla." This time her voice was a low growl, but she couldn't stop her smile. Kayla didn't seem too upset, so whatever it was couldn't have been that bad, right?

"Okay," Kayla relented, chuckling at her friend. "It was about work. But her name really is Glen."

"Sure it —" Liv's words were interrupted by the ringing of Kayla's phone.

Kayla jumped at the sound of the ringing, fumbling the phone. After a few seconds of bobbling, the small machine was deftly snatched out of the air by Liv, who refused to relinquish it.

"Hello, this is Kayla's phone speaking. Kayla is unavailable at the moment, but how can I help you? Ouch!" the shorter woman squawked as Kayla gave her a sharp pinch on the rump.

There was a long silence before the voice hesitantly asked, "Is that you, Liv?"

"Dougie?" Liv's gaze immediately swung out over the water. While it wasn't as placid as when they'd arrived on the island, the crashing waves from the day before had been replaced by much calmer seas. "Are you okay? Where are you?"

Kayla bent down and pressed her head alongside Liv's so she could listen, placing a gentle kiss on a soft cheek while she was in the neighborhood. Liv nuzzled closer to Kayla and tilted her head to the side so she could return the kiss, happily noting they were both grinning at each other like love-struck teenagers.

Doug cleared his throat. "We're, um, good. I mean fine." Another long pause.

Liv sighed at the awkwardness between them. "It's gonna be okay, Dougie. Don't worry, okay?"

This earned a disbelieving stare from Kayla, whose eyebrows disappeared behind windblown bangs. Liv cringed, knowing Kayla wouldn't appreciate what she was doing but continuing to reassure her brother nonetheless.

"Really," she promised softly, smiling at the audible sigh of relief from Doug. "We'll work it all out, so you and Marcy can both relax a little."

A relieved chuckle. "Thanks, Sis. We're getting ready to leave for the island in a little bit. We docked by the boat rental shop and the guy who works there said we should be able to take the boat out after lunch."

"Are you sure it's safe?" Kayla interrupted in a no-nonsense voice.

"Yeah, the guy wouldn't risk his precious — Kayla?" Doug squeaked. He felt much safer talking with Liv. It had taken Marcy an hour of begging to get him to make the phone call, and he had nearly cried with relief when it was his sister that answered.

"Oh yeah." *That's right, punk. You're not off the hook yet with me.*

The boy gulped and Kayla's grin broadened. "You guys feel like shit, right?" she asked knowingly.

"Umm...yeah," Doug admitted, the remnants of the previous night's drinking escapade still very fresh in his mind, despite the fact that Marcy had considerably brightened his morning.

"Well, that's too bad," the tall woman snapped. "'Cause you and Marcy and I are going to have a little chat when you finally get back to the island. Is that understood?"

"Yes, ma'am," the teen replied obediently.

"Be careful coming back," Liv chimed in, sensing this conversation was about to be over.

"Okay. Bye."

Liv pushed the phone back into Kayla's hands after Doug hung up. "That wasn't nice, Kayla."

Kayla's jaw clenched and her back stiffened. "What in the hell do you think you were doing? Of course it wasn't nice. It wasn't meant to be nice. How could you forgive them so quickly? They haven't even explained themselves, *or* apologized for worrying us sick."

"I know." Liv exhaled very slowly, trying not to respond to Kayla's obvious anger. "And I haven't completely forgiven them. But one of us needs to stay calm," she reminded reasonably, instinctively knowing that Kayla would have trouble reining in her temper. "It's not like it's the end of the world, and the most important thing is that they're safe."

"Bu-but..." The younger woman began to stammer uncharacteristically. "Of course I'm glad they're safe. Don't you think I know that's the most important thing?" Her voice was rising. "But you still shouldn't have included them both in your little pep talk. You had no right. I'm damned mad at Marcy, and she should know it."

Liv visibly flinched at Kayla's words, feeling well and truly chastised, and hating the fact that Kayla was right about this. She was about to apologize when Kayla started again.

"Fine!" Kayla groused as she stomped across the porch, sending a spray of water up around her calves as she splashed through the shallow puddles. She yelped inwardly at the pain the action caused her swollen knee. "You can deal with things your way, and I'll deal with them mine," was all she could think to say as she sat down heavily on the porch swing, pushing the chair into motion and deliberately not stopping its swinging when Liv stood in front of it, obviously waiting to sit down.

Liv's own anger bubbled to the surface and she turned to leave, not knowing exactly where she was going. She spun around, but before she could even take a step, she heard the swing stop and Kayla's soft voice.

"Don't go."

Liv spun back and opened her mouth to...

"I'm sorry."

The blonde threw her hands up as the air drained out of her lungs and her anger began to melt away. "What?" she finally asked in confusion, letting her hands drop to her sides and plopping onto the sheet-covered swing beside Kayla.

"I shouldn't have yelled."

"You're right. You shouldn't have," Liv said stubbornly, but she grasped Kayla's hand and kissed her knuckles, trying to take the sting out of her words. "I don't like to be yelled at," she added quietly.

Kayla nodded, still not looking at Liv. Her stomach was in knots over these few cross words. "Then I'll try not to do it again."

"I shouldn't have included Marcy in what I said to Doug; I'm sorry, too." After a long silence she finally added, "Are we finished being mad?"

"I um...I think so."

"Good," Liv muttered as she pulled Kayla into a warm embrace, feeling the other woman's pounding heart against her own chest. "It's okay," she whispered, squeezing Kayla a little tighter. "Do you want to finish the history now? 'Cause when the kids get here, I want to jump on the boat and get the hell off this island." A pale head tilted in entreaty. "Is that okay with you?"

"Yeah," Kayla agreed after a deep exhalation. "That's more than okay with me. There are some decent hotels in Jacksonville, about thirty miles away. We could get a couple of rooms there tonight?"

Liv's smile turned wistful. "I wish it was me who will be sharing your room tonight."

With a gentle hand Kayla guided Liv's lips to hers, kissing her softly but deeply and tasting the sweet tang of lemonade. "I'd love to be sharing a whole lot more than the room with you, Liv," Kayla mumbled against the soft lips, drawing a groan from the linguist.

Kayla pulled back and pressed her forehead against Liv's. "Maybe the kids will want to go to a movie or something tonight."

Liv nodded and smiled hopefully. "Maybe we can find them a double feature."

Cobb Island
January, 1691

Bundling myself against the miserable rain, I brought Mistress Bridget a pair of soft doeskin pants, a leather shirt lined with rabbit fur, and her cloak, knowing she would be cold and praying to Allah that I would be able to offer her at least the smallest measure of comfort. I also brought bathing and medical supplies to tend to her numerous wounds, but the child stubbornly refused them, insisting that we had no time to waste.

She explained what Mistress Elizabeth intended to do as Guardian, and what that meant. And only through the power of my own faith was I able to stifle the urge to run out of the stables and turn the malevolent brat over my knee. But as much as it would ease my own guilt, for I, as much as the next inhabitant of Cobb Island, had had a hand in raising the child, I cannot say that Mistress Elizabeth was oblivious to the consequences of her actions. The girl knew what she was doing every step of the way, although an important facet of her motivation was unknown to me at the time.

Mistress Bridget tasked me with remembering her words and recording them, telling me of the events contained in this history from her own perspective, and painting a picture so vivid that I sat spellbound for hour upon hour. She spoke in low tones with a steady voice, and I opened my mind and soul to her words, knowing their importance simply by the way in which they were spoken.

Bridget also asked that I speak to Mistress Faylinn, for even though Henry could not impart his own knowledge concerning the family's abilities, he and his mother were Reddings, just the same. And their place in history would be assured, despite Elizabeth's evil intent. It is because of Elizabeth, and what she would do if she ever found it, that this particular history will not be kept in the library, but secreted away, hidden deep within the walls of the house on Cobb Island.

Though her request was not without personal risk, I could no more deny her than deny my own breath. The rest of what you are about to read is that which I witnessed with my own eyes, or heard with my own ears, for what I learned specifically from Mistress Faylinn, that only she could have known, has already been incorporated into the pages of this text.

Within the infinite loop of beginnings and endings, I am unable to reconcile the events of that cold November. I only know what I saw and heard, and what I believe in my very soul to be true. That these events are inconsistent, is but another layer of mystery in an existence fraught with uncertainty but characterized by hope.

Cobb Island
November, 1690

AFIA AND BRIDGET became silent when they heard voices outside the stable door.

Tears filled dark eyes, and Afia's lower lip began to tremble. In the midst of Bridget's tale of love and magic, she'd nearly forgotten what was to take place this night.

"Shh...fear not, old friend," Bridget soothed in a gentle manner so at odds with her normally fiery personality. "It simply must be time. Do you understand all that I've told you?" Bridget's steady voice held no fear, calming the slave who was fighting back a sudden wave of nausea.

"I...I think so, child." The wiry woman wiped her face with shaking hands. "Your history will be safe. By Allah's name, I swear it."

Bridget nodded, satisfied that she had done all she could to preserve a sense of duty to family that she feared would die with her. "Thank you, Afia. You deserve a better fate than that of a slave. That I did nothing to change that is to my everlasting discredit."

"Hush, girl," the dark-skinned woman scolded. "That was not your doing, and we both know it."

The stable door flew open and three soldiers marched in. Afia stood tall, blocking the men's view of Bridget. "Master Cyril ordered her cleaned and dressed. You'll have to remove the shackles so I can finish dressing her. Her clothes can't be fastened over the chains."

Bridget smiled to herself and shook her head at the absurdity of Afia standing vigil, protecting her virtue from the prying eyes of the naval officers.

"All right," one of the men said, nervously picking up a coiled rope that lay alongside the stable wall. "But step away." The men fashioned two nooses at the end of two long lengths of rope. They slipped each noose around Bridget's throat and then held the ropes taut — pulling in opposite directions.

Exactly the way you break a colt, Bridget thought to herself, as the third man tossed the keys to the shackles to Afia, his sword drawn and pointed at both women.

Once Bridget was dressed, one of the soldiers tied her hands in front of her body, but, to her surprise, for the first time in days she wasn't shackled. The man saw the question in her eyes and simply commented, "The fire would ruin the locks, I'll warrant. Up with you, witch," he ordered once her wrists were secure. When Bridget didn't move, each officer gave his rope a sharp tug, causing her to gasp and choke.

Afia opened her mouth to protest but Bridget silenced her with a look of warning.

"It's nearly midnight, and we've got to make it across the island," the youngest of the men said firmly, hoping his hands weren't shaking. Surely, God would protect those who sent a witch to hell, wouldn't He? He worried his bottom lip nervously. "Cyril asked that the execution take place as far from the house as possible, so that no evil ashes be allowed to soil his home."

"The north cliffs, then?" Bridget snorted, knowing it was the highest and most distant point on the island. The rocky ledge was over forty feet high; the cliff's bottom, a mass of jagged, sea-washed rocks and crashing waves. She suspected her brother's penchant for drama had him imagining himself scattering her remains into the sea from its rugged edge.

He nodded. "We've a cart and mule ready outside. Your family, and the rest of the slaves, are already on their way to the cliff to witness your execution."

A rough burlap bag was shoved over Bridget's head, and her world went black.

SHEETS OF RAIN were making it difficult to see, as a violent storm erupted around them sending bolts of lightning streaking across the night sky. A small group of people stood safely back from the cliff's edge, clustered around a tall wooden post that had been set into the muddy ground.

Bridget, whose head was still encased in the darkness of the sack, sat motionless in the cart as a whirlwind of activity spun around her. She had tried to make her escape on the way to the cliffs, only to be recaptured in the tangled woods and beaten into submission. She cursed her injuries, knowing that if she were healthy, these sad excuses for men would never have been able to subdue her. Afia heard the angrily muttered phrases but remained silent, unable to think of any words that would comfort Bridget now.

The pounding in Bridget's head was nearly intolerable, and for the first time she began to crave the peace that death would surely bring. She told Afia as much, as hot tears spilled over the slave's cheeks, mixing with the cold rain. Unable to hold back any longer, the dark-skinned woman reached back to wrap a comforting arm around Bridget.

Spotting the movement, a zealous guard slashed his sword down against the cart wall between them. The loud, dull thud of the blade against the sodden wood caused Afia to flinch, her heart skipping a beat. Black eyes bore into the soldier's as she slowly withdrew her hand.

Bridget could hear Cyril and Elizabeth's voices along with those of some of the soldiers and slaves. She listened quietly as Elizabeth explained that Judith had refused to attend the execution, locking herself in her bedroom.

"Is she here?" the tall woman asked brokenly, tilting her head to the side, listening intently for just one voice.

Dark eyes scanned the drenched crowd then turned downward. Afia's silence was Bridget's answer.

The senior officer, who had acted as Bridget's judge, marched up to Cyril, his mind more on the storm and his ship than the execution. "Cyril," he began, "even the mostly dry wood from the barn won't burn in this storm. We're barely able to keep our torches lit, no matter how we try to cover them. Why not simply run the witch through and be done with it?" he suggested impatiently.

"That murdering witch deserves no such mercy!" Cyril spat.

The officer shifted angrily, adjusting his sword belt beneath his cloak. "Cyril, we must leave for the mainland tonight if we're to moor the ship in a harbor safe from the worst of the storm."

"My family shall have its justice. This storm be damned! It is nothing—" A clap of thunder boomed loudly, drowning out the rest of his words.

"And your wife?" The plump man scanned the slaves and

soldiers, his eyes lingering briefly on Elizabeth before moving on. "She didn't feel the need to be present at the execution of her son's murderer?"

Cyril blanched, but smoothly explained that she was too distraught over Henry's death to attend.

The officer nodded, his gaze drifting to Bridget and the ropes already around her neck. "Hanging then? It's a more than acceptable method of execution."

Cyril pulled his cloak more closely around his body as flashes of lightning bathed the ground in silver and reflected brightly off the pools of standing water, illuminating the macabre execution scene. "Very well," the eldest Redding grudgingly conceded.

"Father," Elizabeth interrupted, pointing to Bridget who was coughing and pawing weakly at the soaked bag covering her head. "If she chokes to death on wet burlap, there won't be any need for an execution."

Cyril jutted his chin towards a nearby soldier. "You, there, remove that and pull her from the cart. Make sure her back is to the cliff's edge," he directed, smiling internally at how the soldier immediately obeyed him. Yes, he'd only needed a catalyst to earn his business partners' respect. This was it. He would forevermore be considered a man to be reckoned with. He could see the fear and awe in their eyes, and savored it like a fine wine.

Bridget was pulled from the cart and sent head first into a deep mud puddle, then hauled to her feet. When she emerged she squared her shoulders, standing proudly. She'd stopped shivering long ago. Now she was just numb. The ends of the long ropes around her neck were uncoiled and tied to the post from where she was to have been burned. Now they would simply loop the rope over the top post and hoist her up by the throat as her means of punishment.

The sack was ripped from Bridget's head just as she heard the furious pounding of hooves and the sounds of splashing water and mud. She jerked her head from side to side, willing the one eye that wasn't completely swollen shut to adjust to the faint light of the torches and the nearly constant white flashes from the lightning.

Apollo, in all his glory, reared and danced, while Faylinn, her dark cloak whirling in the wind, maintained her seat atop the stomping beast. Every set of eyes turned towards them as the young woman kicked the horse into motion and he galloped right up to Bridget.

Elizabeth sucked in a breath. This was a Faylinn she had yet to see.

Faylinn slid smoothly off the stallion, her boots splashing loudly when they hit the ground. Panting, she simply let go of the reins, sending Apollo galloping freely away as the lightning worked the young steed into a near frenzy.

Small hands pushed back a rain soaked hood revealing a mass of wet gold hair. "By God!" A tortured moan was torn from her throat as eyes darkened with anguish and fury widened. "What have they done to you?" she asked as she gaped helplessly at Bridget's bruised and bloodied face, flashes of light from the sky illuminating every cut and bruise in vivid, sickening detail.

"Faylinn." Cyril moved over to his wife, desperately hoping to keep things from spiraling out of control. "I'm glad you came to your senses and decided to attend the execution of Henry's murderer," he announced smugly, in a voice loud enough for his partners to hear as they looked on with interest. Even Elizabeth shifted nervously as she sensed impending disaster.

Cyril was promptly ignored by his wife as Faylinn shrugged out of his grasp and focused entirely on Bridget.

"I am so, so sorry," the young woman said softly, her heart pounding so furiously she was certain it would beat out of her chest. "I...I...I've been looking for you. I just spoke with Judith." Disbelieving eyes darted wildly to the men and their flickering torches, and the pile of planks and straw around the wooden post. *They're going to burn her alive?* Then, when the sky grew bright again, she noticed the nooses around Bridget's neck. *Or hang her? God!* Faylinn's eyes slid shut, and she groaned as if in pain. "I didn't know, please believe me," she begged, trying not to dissolve into tears.

"You came," Bridget whispered, her voice catching on the words as the pelting rain streaked the blood and mud that covered her skin and clothes. "I...I...was beginning to give up hope. I thought...I thought maybe you believed..." Bridget's jaw worked silently as she tried in vain to continue.

Faylinn lowered her head in shame before lifting her gaze to meet Bridget's head on. The insecurity and pain in Bridget's voice shredded her heart and tore at her very spirit. "Never." The young woman's tone brokered no disagreement, and Bridget felt her doubts about Faylinn's love melt away like ice in the springtime. "I would never believe such monstrous lies. I will not forsake you," she said hoarsely. The word "again" was added in the barest of whispers.

Murmurs could barely be heard above the rain and waves as the slaves and soldiers alike sucked in shocked breaths at Faylinn's words, and began to talk among themselves.

"Faylinn." Cyril laid a hand on his wife's shoulder, still clinging to the hope he could somehow manage to save face.

"Bastard!" Faylinn seethed, knocking away Cyril's hand. "Get your filthy hands off of me!" The man stiffened at the words, and Faylinn immediately saw her error. *I cannot directly challenge him. Not here in front of these men.* "Cyril, I'm begging you," Faylinn tried again, but this time her voice was calm and pleading, meant for his ears only. "Think, Husband. It was Bridget who tried to save Henry. If she'd had a part in the slave's escape, she would have come with me to the wrong part of the island instead of looking for Henry and actually finding the boy. There was never any plan for ransom, it was *you* who gave Henry to the slaves."

Cyril's brows drew together in confusion, so Faylinn pressed on. "Stop this madness before it's too late. She is your *sister* for God's sake. This will be an error you can never undo."

Cyril stared at his wife as if looking at her for the first time. "Why do you defend her, after all that has happened, against me, your own husband? The woman, she—" He paused, then his jaw simply dropped. "You're in love with her?" he whispered incredulously. He had seen a doe-eyed look of devotion in Faylinn's eyes many times when she looked at his sister, but he thought it nothing more than a schoolgirl crush. His sister was undeniably a beautiful, if wild, creature. But now...now he saw things clearly; and it stung as though he'd been slapped in the face. "What has that unnatural witch done to you?" he whispered harshly, his lips so close to Faylinn's ear that she could feel his hot breath tickling her wind-burnt cheek.

He would never relent. She knew that now. Faylinn could see the challenge and fury growing in his eyes as she pulled away from him again. Her gaze was icy cold as her eyes pinned him, and they stared at each other for several charged seconds, the hatred between them growing as the heavens opened up and the rain turned to hail. "She has made me feel more with a single glance than you in all your fumblings have accomplished in over three years."

Cyril paled at the words, knowing he was not the only one that heard them. He turned away from his wife to see several soldiers uncomfortably looking away, refusing to meet his glance, and others still whose gazes were filled with pity. A few snickers from the slaves in the background caused him to lose control completely, and he whirled around to face his sister. "Hang the witch!" he shouted, as he glared at Bridget with undisguised loathing.

Faylinn turned on her heels and flew to Bridget, nearly knocking over the already unsteady woman with her zeal. The younger woman crushed her lips against Bridget's in unrestrained passion, pressing a small dagger in her love's hands. "I love you," she whispered fiercely against Bridget's mouth as she kissed her thoroughly, smiling through the kisses when she heard her words echoed. "Please live," she whispered again as Cyril tore her away from Bridget, and the tall woman tucked the dagger underneath her cloak, out of view.

Bridget staggered back, touching her lips with trembling fingers, not believing what had just happened. When she found her legs she took a menacing step towards Cyril, her eyes hard as diamonds, her body reinvigorated by hope. Her reason to live had just risked her future to save her. From Bridget, Faylinn would get no less than her very soul.

"The witch has enchanted my wife!" Cyril cried, dragging a kicking and fighting Faylinn away from Bridget as quickly as he could manage. "Destroy the demon before she claims your souls as well!"

Several soldiers drew their swords at Cyril's words. This seemed to spur the other men who were standing in stunned silence, shocked by what they had just seen. In a matter of seconds, all ten soldiers were gingerly approaching Bridget, blades drawn, hearts in their throats, as they feared for their immortal spirits. They fanned out and began stalking Bridget as they would a rabid beast. Each time one of them moved to pick up one of the ropes binding her, she would step forward, scaring the man off.

The hail shifted back to rain and Bridget tilted her head back, opening her mouth to the icy liquid. She let out a loud feral laugh, sending chills down the men's spines and causing several of them to step backwards in terror. She knew she couldn't defeat all of them, but she would die fighting, taking as many of them with her as she could. Faylinn would not see her hanged.

Bridget tightened the grip on her blade, preparing to take out the closest man, when she saw something that caused the blood to drain from her face. Cyril had Faylinn firmly in his grasp, his sword at her throat. Brother's and sister's eyes locked, and in her heart, Bridget was certain that Cyril would do it. He would slit his own wife's throat, all the while righteously claiming he was saving her soul from damnation.

The men were only a few feet from Bridget, her back to the cliff. Her breathing came in short pants as adrenaline coursed through her veins; pale eyes gone silver quickly studied the endless darkness that lay beyond the cliff's edge, then they swung back to Faylinn, whose own eyes widened. The smaller woman's struggles redoubled as she sensed what Bridget was about to do.

Faylinn shook her head wildly, heedless of the blade at her throat. Then she stopped abruptly, viciously stomping Cyril's foot with the heel of her boot, causing the man to release the hand he had clamped over her mouth, though his sword held firm. "No, Bridget! *Noo!*" she cried out, confusing the men who had heard no more words pass between them.

For the women, the moment was timeless. There were no more words. None were required; everything that needed to be said had finally been spoken. Bridget would not be executed, nor would she cause Faylinn's death. She had no choice. After one last glance into panicked green eyes, Bridget hurled herself over the edge of the cliff, disappearing into the rain and wind and blackness, Faylinn's screams still ringing in her ears as she plunged to her destiny.

All eyes darted to the wooden post as the long ropes snaked out after Bridget, every man and woman holding their breath, waiting for the inevitable. A few seconds more and the ropes reached their limit, going taut for a brief instant before abruptly going slack and falling limply to the muddy ground.

Faylinn fell to her knees sobbing as the men sheathed their blades, too stunned to even speak. Suicide was the last thing they had expected from Bridget Redding.

Afia closed her eyes and tilted her head skyward, saying a prayer to the background of the rolling thunder and Faylinn's soul-shattering cries.

Cobb Island
January, 1691

The men from His Majesty's Royal Navy left the island without even going back to the house, promising to return shortly after Christmas when another shipment of slaves was due to arrive. None of Cyril's business partners directly mentioned Faylinn's behavior, but their looks of pity and disgust were undisguised. The respect that he had worked so hard to gain had been destroyed. Master Cyril's humiliation and devastation was complete. To say that he was angry would be akin to calling Mistress Elizabeth a mischievous child.

Not two hours after his sister's death, Cyril ordered his wife locked away in one of the rooms hidden deep within the walls of this house, far out of his sight. I knew of these secret places, for I was here when the house was built, and part of my duties include changing the bedding regularly and storing fresh water so the rooms are ready for use at a moment's notice. When the house was built, I simply thought Master Cyril mad or eccentric or both. Now, however, I believe Master's primary motivation was fear of being hunted for his family's unnatural abilities. On an island, there is no good place to hide.

Carrying a glowing lamp, I followed along silently as

Cyril led Faylinn to what was to be her jail cell for an indefinite period of time. The young woman neither cried nor fought her internment. She simply walked into the dark room and didn't look back. Her apathy tore at my heart more than tears ever could have; for deep down inside, I truly believed her soul had died along with Bridget that very night.

After I turned down the bed and lit a small candle, I was ordered to leave the room and not to return under any circumstances — not to bring food or water, or remove the chamber pot. His words chilled me to the bone, and I knew long before he finished speaking that I would not, could not, obey him. Even passively, I would not assist Master Cyril in doing to Faylinn's body what had already been done to her heart. I had had enough of death. But more than that, I had a promise to keep to Mistress Bridget.

That next evening, while Cyril was more occupied with his brandy than anything else, I snuck into the secret room with bread and cheese hidden in the folds of my skirt. If Faylinn was surprised to see me, she didn't show it, remaining mute as I explained that with which I had been tasked by Bridget. By the end of my short tale, her cheeks glistened with tears. She even managed a weak laugh when I repeated a humorous phrase that Bridget had used just the day before.

Then something happened that I shall never forget. Mistress Faylinn dried eyes that suddenly possessed a measure of wisdom far too ancient for someone barely a woman herself. Squaring her shoulders, she gently cleared her throat, launching into the story of young Henry's life. She told the tale with a mother's pride that caused me to long for my own children, now grown and so very far away.

Next, she spoke of Bridget with a lover's intensity, and I found myself riveted to her every word, her voice painting a tapestry so brilliant it stole the very breath from my chest. I smiled at her sweet words, stretching muscles that I'd had no reason to use in recent memory.

Despite all that had transpired, it was obvious that a fire still burned brightly within Faylinn. And in a moment of blinding clarity, I saw something about the young woman that I doubted she even knew about herself: she was a survivor.

Our time together was interrupted by the sound of

boot steps echoing in the silent hallways. To my shame, I flew into a panic, knowing that Cyril would not hesitate to have me beaten, or worse, for my disobedience. Mistress Faylinn remained eerily calm, shuffling me into her closet after extracting a promise that I wouldn't emerge no matter what I heard. I agreed with a bob of my head as the closet door shut tightly behind me.

Reluctantly, in the pages that follow, I have attempted to record only that which I heard and nothing more, for I am mindful that my own desires may have colored my perception of what happened that night. The narrative is as free from bias as my memory will permit, allowing future generations to judge for themselves exactly what took place. In my heart, I know the truth, and that is enough.

I had assumed the horrors of the last few days were over, ending with Bridget's plunge over the cliff and into the night.

I was wrong.

Cobb Island
November, 1690

AFIA PRESSED HER ear to the door, though, she reflected grimly, it really wasn't necessary. Cyril's slurred words and Faylinn's emphatic ones were more than loud enough to burn their way into her brain.

"My son is dead," Cyril gabbled, his sword clanking loudly against the chest of drawers that sat alongside the canopy bed.

"How nice of you to finally notice," Faylinn shot back coldly, walking away from the closet.

Cyril laughed without a hint of humor as he drew his blade, the sound of ripping fabric mixing with his words. "No longer resigned to your fate, I see. What a pity. I rather preferred you with your mouth closed."

"You're drunk."

"How nice of *you* to finally notice. Now come here," he commanded, his voice dripping with anger.

"Why should I come anywhere near you?" Faylinn moved again, her shoes making a soft clicking sound on the hardwood floor. "Get away from me!"

Get out of this room, Mistress Faylinn! Afia thought frantically. The slave's hand moved to the door handle, when suddenly something slammed against the wood, then dropped limply to the floor. Afia gasped, clutching her chest as she tried to remain quiet. The initial boom had nearly given the dark-skinned woman a heart attack.

"What in the devil do you think you're doing?" Faylinn's voice held a note of surprise and disgust, and Afia felt her own breathing quicken in response.

Cyril responded with an arrogant snort.

"Why—" Faylinn swallowed loudly, "why are you taking off your boots and jacket? Surely you don't intend to sleep here tonight?"

The sound of what Afia assumed was Cyril's second boot hitting the door sent her scurrying to the back of the closet. She closed her eyes, already guessing what Cyril wanted, and debating whether to break her promise to Faylinn. *Allah protect her*, she prayed silently.

"Shut your mouth, bitch!"

Afia heard the rapid, heavy thudding sounds of Cyril's stocking feet as he marched across the room. Then a body was slammed into the closet door with such vicious force that the walls shook.

Faylinn began gasping for breath, and in Afia's mind's eye she could clearly see Cyril's meaty hand around Faylinn's slender neck as he squeezed the air from her throat. The older woman wondered if her pounding pulse would give her away as a cold sweat broke out across her back and face, drenching her blouse. There was a slight shifting of the body against the door. Their voices were quieter now, but they were so close that it didn't matter; she could hear every word.

"I will have a male heir." Cyril slurred harshly. This time it was Faylinn's turn to laugh. What began as a light chuckle, soon turned to near hysteria. Afia's eyes widened at the unexpected sound.

The faint golden light coming from under the closet door faded in and out as Faylinn and Cyril's feet shuffled on the floor in front of the door. The wooden slab shook again as Faylinn tried to push Cyril's body from hers.

"I will die before I sleep with you, you murdering pig! I would sooner lay with Lucifer himself. You can go straight to—" Her words cut off as her head was slammed back.

"I thought I told you to shut up!" Cyril roared so loudly that Afia flinched, her hands flying to cover her ears.

The pressure on the door eased, and there was another shifting of light as Faylinn and Cyril began to struggle.

"Did you fight my sister like this, slut? Did she enjoy it?" Cyril grunted against Faylinn's neck, causing the young woman to hiss in pure revulsion at his proximity.

"Get...get off me," Faylinn ground out, her voice shaking.

The bodies swung further from the closet, taking the struggle to another part of the room where Afia heard the ripping of material and curses as furniture was knocked over and blows were exchanged. She wiped a sweaty palm against her skirt, then lifted a shaking hand to the door handle once again. She had to do something.

Grasping the cool knob, she had just begun to twist when she heard another door fly open and bang against the wall. The room went as quiet as a grave for several agonizingly long seconds, and Afia held her breath, wondering what had happened.

"Oh my God!" A loud sob escaped Faylinn's chest and the sounds of struggles intensified, becoming more violent and frenzied. Afia told herself to get out of the closet; but an icy fear gripped her, leaving her hand frozen on the knob, her breath coming in short pants.

"Die, bitch!" Cyril screamed frantically, his voice unnaturally high.

The wiry slave jumped at the sound of his sword swishing through the air, striking at the furniture and occasionally the walls and floor.

Faylinn howled, "Nooo!" And two heartbeats later, a blade clattered noisily to the ground, followed by a tortured groan and the dull thump of a body crumpling to the floor.

There was a slight pause before rapid footsteps skittered across the room and Faylinn's sobs began again, only this time they were muffled.

Afia clasped her hands together, praising Allah for his mercy. Soft, broken murmurs and the sound of more crying drew the slave's ear back to the door, but she couldn't make out any words. Soon even the murmurs disappeared, and Afia heard footsteps, then nothing more.

The slave finally gathered the courage to escape from her self-imposed confinement. Cautiously, she opened the door, its creaking ratcheting her own fear up another several notches as she peered around it, looking out into the quiet room, not at all certain what she'd find waiting for her.

Several pieces of furniture were strewn across the floor or tipped over, while the bed's canopy hung in tatters. In the center of the floor, Cyril lay face up in a pool of dark blood, a knife, buried to the hilt, protruding from his still chest. His gray eyes were open, staring lifelessly at the ceiling and glinting dully in the muted glow of the candlelight. His sword lay several feet from his outstretched hand.

Faylinn was nowhere in sight.

Afia approached Cyril warily, poking him with the toe of her shoe, half-expecting him to jump up and frighten her like an apparition from a child's story. She exhaled shakily when a closer look at the man's face left no doubt that he had passed over. Afia bent and examined the silver knife sticking out of her owner's chest; it was his own, though she didn't recall him wearing it as of late.

"Mistress Faylinn?" the small woman called out, peeking into the black hallway. She was greeted by a cold silence. Afia swallowed reflexively, wide eyes scanning the room again, her mind replaying every word, every terrible sound.

"Mistress Bridget?" she whispered incredulously. But there was no one left to answer her question.

Cobb Island
January, 1691

I sat on the bed in the secret room staring at Cyril's stiffening body, trying my best to dredge up an ounce of pity for the vile man, and failing utterly. My first thoughts were to hide his body in the closet. I threw his boots and blade into the tiny, dark room, and began to drag the big man across the floor. I was nearly finished, when something made me stop and reconsider my actions. Shaking my head, I admitted to myself that Master Cyril's daughters should not have to endure never knowing whether their father was dead or alive.

I left the secret room with every intention of finding Mistress Faylinn and trying to concoct a story to cover how Cyril died, so that neither she nor a slave would be blamed for his death. But the young woman had simply vanished. And while I didn't know it at the time, I would never lay eyes upon Mistress Faylinn again.

Hours later, just before dawn, I set a hastily formulated plan into action by removing the blade from Cyril's chest, stitching shut his wound, and changing his clothes to remove any traces of blood. I poured a little more brandy down his throat and sprinkled his clothes with the liquor for good measure, trying my best to recreate the condition he was in when I left him in the library the night before, despite the fact that I'd just spent an hour cleaning him. Then, with the help of two strong slaves—who were more than willing to oblige me—and a well-tied noose, I hung him from the rafters in his bedroom and hoped all would believe it was a drunken suicide.

When the scene was complete, I sent the cook, who I found lighting the stove in the kitchen for the morning meal, to ask Cyril what he wanted for breakfast. The oblivious woman agreed readily, thinking it wise to appease our volatile Master.

Her screams woke the entire house.

I watched from the doorway as Mistress Elizabeth ran into her father's room to find him hanging by the neck, his limp body twisting ever so slightly as the beams straining under his weight let out an occasional creaking groan. She stared at the body for several long moments, lips quivering and silent tears streaking her cheeks. I took this opportunity to slip away, knowing that if she tried to invade my thoughts, I would be powerless to stop her from finding out the truth.

As I knew she would, Mistress Elizabeth questioned the poor cook until the woman was in tears, but as she knew nothing, she had nothing to share. Elizabeth never even inquired about Faylinn, spending that entire next day locked away in Judith's bedroom with the new head of the Redding clan.

The day after that, seven slaves went missing, presumably leaving the island on one of the several rowboats that Master Cyril kept chained to the dock. Among these men was the slave foreman whose job it was to prevent escapes. I, myself, contemplated my own opportunity at freedom. But my genuine affection for Judith prevented my leaving.

Slave or no, other than her sister and a few distant cousins, I am the closest thing to family she has. I have no reason to fear being resold, for I am certain when Cyril's business partners return to the island, arrangements will be made to send Elizabeth and Judith back to England, and I will surely follow.

In the days after Cyril's death, when no amount of searching could produce Faylinn, Elizabeth began to speculate that her stepmother had simply flung herself off the cliff after Bridget. To Judith and my distaste, Elizabeth seems rather fond of the gruesome notion. But Judith accepted the idea and let the matter drop, though I suspect the real reason is because she believes her sister is somehow responsible for their stepmother's mysterious disappearance.

Bridget once warned me that Judith would never be free of Elizabeth's influence, though her words were spoken without rancor. For as Bridget and Faylinn needed one another for balance and completion, so do Judith and Elizabeth. What I found out that New Years' Eve morning shouldn't have shocked me. But it did.

Cobb Island
December, 1690

AFIA, JUDITH, AND Elizabeth sat together around the breakfast table eating hot porridge and drinking sweetened tea as the winter snow continued to fall, blanketing Cobb Island in a thick cover of pristine white. They were the island's only remaining inhabitants, every single slave having escaped to the mainland on one of Cyril's rowboats or on the homemade rafts they had fashioned openly.

There was no conversation between the sisters. Something was wrong, and no amount of prodding by Afia could get Judith or Elizabeth to explain themselves. To the woman's surprise, it was Elizabeth who snapped first.

"Would you like to read together today, Sister?" Elizabeth asked hopefully, sorely missing the afternoons she and her sister would spend engrossed in a collection of novels that had belonged to their mother.

Judith refused to answer, slowly taking another mouthful of porridge, her eyes never leaving her bowl.

"Judith, did you hear me?" Elizabeth ground out, her patience with her sister having long since dwindled to nothing. "By God! Is there no forgiveness for me!" the girl finally shouted, rising to her feet and throwing her napkin across the table at her sister.

Judith flew to her feet as well, knocking her chair over in the process and throwing her own napkin back at her twin. "Why should I forgive you? You didn't have to do it!"

"I did it for you. And it cannot be undone, nor am I sorry. You were in danger."

"Stop saying that!" Judith covered her ears as if to drown out Elizabeth's words. "Don't ever say that to me again!" she cried. "What you did was for yourself and no one else."

"My enjoyment was my own," Elizabeth admitted without shame. "But that doesn't change the fact that it had to be done."

"No, no, no!" Judith burst into tears and fled the room, leaving her distraught sister behind.

Elizabeth fell back into her chair with a loud thud. Wrapping her arms around herself, she began to sway back and forth. "She's never going to forgive me. She's never going to forgive me," the girl chanted quietly, her eyes screwed tightly shut.

"Can you blame her?" Afia finally inserted, her own temper flaring as she thought of Elizabeth's horrid treatment of her aunt and how Judith plainly adored Bridget.

Gray eyes swung toward the black woman and widened slightly. In her anger and misery, Elizabeth had completely forgotten the woman was even in the room. "You don't understand," she complained softly, her usual arrogance and cockiness replaced by genuine anguish. "Someone would have found out."

"You're right, child. I don't understand. How did you do it?" Afia had wondered about this from the very start. "When your father asked you to take the soldier upstairs to search Bridget's room, you left immediately with the wretched little man. You had no time to place the evidence of witchcraft in Bridget's room. I know Bridget was no witch."

Elizabeth continued to rock, ignoring Afia's question and allowing the words to roll over her.

"You led them to *your* room, didn't you?" The black woman looked at Elizabeth with growing apprehension. "You're the witch," she accused in a startled whisper.

Elizabeth chuckled softly, her eyebrow quirking. "Slave, you're not nearly as clever as you think." The tall girl stood up and wiped her eyes, staring longingly at the staircase where Judith had disappeared. "It was not my room that I took Officer Richards to that night." Gray eyes pinned Afia. "It was Judith's."

Elizabeth shook her head at Afia's gasp, sensing her disbelief. "They wanted blood and would have searched the entire house to find evidence that Bridget conspired with the escaped slaves or that she practiced sorcery." Tears welled in beseeching eyes. Someone had to believe her. "It would have been Judith tied to the stake if they'd gone into her room, knowing it was hers."

Afia looked away, trying to process what she'd just learned. "And the night of Bridget's execution?" she asked weakly.

Elizabeth sighed. There was no reason to hold back anything now. "I told Judith that father refused to free Bridget, even after knowing the truth. She locked herself in her room, wailing and chanting, and calling up that blasted storm."

"Oh, Allah!" Afia groaned, finally understanding the depths of Judith's pain, guilt, and power.

"That's right, pray to your heathen god, slave," Elizabeth laughed sadly. "There is, most assuredly, a fearsome witch on Cobb Island." The girl began making her way towards the stairs and her sister, though her steps appeared weary. She spoke without looking back at the dumbfounded slave. "It's just not me."

Cobb Island
January, 1691

What I learned that morning both sickened and enlightened me. Judith and Elizabeth are far more alike than I ever suspected. Each, though in vastly unequal proportions, possesses a measure of darkness and light. From that day forward, I never thought of them as Night and Day again, for that was much too simple a characterization for these complex young women. It did neither one justice.

The rift between sisters carries on as of the writing of this final page. But in the end, I am certain that neither will wholly abandon the other. They simply cannot. Though at times, I believe they both wish it were possible.

I told Judith about Elizabeth's plans as Guardian, and of the secret history Bridget asked me to prepare. I explained that the book would be hidden in the house, but left it at that, glad when she didn't inquire further. The reasons for this disclosure are mine alone, but it is enough to say that I trust the child and wanted her to know that her brother would have his rightful place in the annals of the Redding family. She did not disappoint me. I had only hoped for Judith's understanding and agreement. What I received was much more.

For her beloved aunt, and for generations to come, Judith made three vows, all of which I am certain she will keep. First, she promised that Cobb Island would forever remain a part of the Redding family estate. I do not pretend to understand the legalities of ownership, but if it is possible to achieve it, it will be done.

Second, she will do all in her power to make certain that Elizabeth does not produce another history, recording—or failing to record—the true events of this terrible time. It is her belief that a gap in texts will spurn future generations to search for the missing history that I will secret away. She is also determined that Elizabeth not be rewarded for her horrific actions.

Finally, although I argued vehemently against it—for its basis surely springs from the darkest part of the human spirit—Judith informed me that she intends to protect the house, and thus the history, with a spell. She admitted that her powers as a witch are wild and unreliable. But Judith is convinced that she was meant to exploit these powers for the greater good. And what she cannot accomplish now, she has a lifetime to achieve.

The thought of what powers Judith may realize as an adult makes me shudder in amazement. She and her sister, although for different reasons, will both be forces to be reckoned with.

I expect Cyril's partners to return to the island any day now. If they hope to know exactly what happened to Master Cyril, then they are bound for disappointment, as no living soul on this island, myself included, can explain the true happenings of that fateful night. They will simply have to live with the story they will be told. But as you have no doubt already gathered, I entertain my own notion of those events.

It is my fondest hope that as I pen these words, Bridget and Faylinn are alive and well somewhere on the mainland, having secured one of the rowboats for themselves. I can offer no rational explanation as to how Bridget could have possibly survived her jump off the cliff. All I do know is that two halves of one whole are simply not meant to exist apart.

Call my belief the fanciful hopes of an old woman, if you will. You would not be mistaken. But things that are meant to be...have a way of happening. They exist on a plane all their own; and somehow, just sometimes, they manage to defy the laws of man and nature alike.

Love is one of those things.

Afia, Recorder of the Redding Family History, January, 1691.

Chapter
Eighteen

Two Halves of One Whole

Cobb Island
Present Day

LIV SLOWLY CLOSED the leather bound book, running a reverent hand over the tooled cover. "Wow," she finally breathed, unable to think of anything else to say. "You were totally right, Kayla."

"Huh?" Kayla dragged herself out of her own deep thoughts to respond to her lover.

With a quick smack of her hand against her forearm, Liv murdered her millionth mosquito. "I said, you were right. That was dry as hell." Her tone was wry, and she hoped to lighten the somewhat somber mood that had settled over them.

Kayla dissolved into surprised laughter, immediately responding to Liv. She slid her arm around Liv's waist, squeezing tightly. "Okay, okay. But didn't you already give me a bad time about that, darlin'?" the tall woman drawled.

Liv smiled wistfully as the gentle lilt of Kayla's voice caressed her eardrums. She'd missed hearing a sweet southern accent during her travels in Africa.

"Yeah. I guess I did." Her fingers innocently drifted to Kayla's ribs where they began a merciless tickling campaign. "I wouldn't want to go around repeating myself, right?"

"Riiiight," Kayla squealed as Liv found a particularly sensitive spot beneath the soft cotton fabric of her T-shirt. But when the questing fingers finally threatened her bladder control, Kayla grabbed them, giving each digit a sloppy kiss before relocating them to a more manageable spot on her lap.

Two sets of eyes trained themselves on the sun-kissed, rolling waves of the ocean as a silent peace stole over them, each woman once again lost in her own thoughts. After several quiet moments where the sound of the water, the wind whistling through the trees, and buzzing insects were all they heard, it was Kayla who spoke first. "What do you think happened?" She didn't need to be more specific, for Liv to know what she meant.

Liv exhaled slowly, thinking hard about what she really thought and how, deep in her soul, she could believe something so improbable with utter conviction. "It would make the most sense to assume that Faylinn tried to escape the hidden room while she and Cyril fought, and that was why Afia heard a door open," she began with an almost clinical air. "Afia never actually said she heard anyone other than Cyril and Faylinn in the room. Then somehow, Faylinn got hold of Cyril's dagger, killing him, and later, herself."

Kayla frowned at the thought, knowing it was the most logical explanation but hating it nonetheless.

"But that's not what I think happened." Liv shrugged a little. "I wanna believe they made it."

Kayla nodded in thought. "So do I. But do you actually believe it," the red-haired woman laid a warm palm on the skin directly above Liv's heart, "in here?"

Liv sucked in a breath at the unexpected touch. Placing her hand atop of Kayla's, she absently began to stroke the soft skin on the back of Kayla's hand. "Yeah." She smiled gently. "I guess I do." Liv turned to face her friend, biting her lower lip. "Does that make me nuts?" she asked, curious about how Kayla's analytical mind might have interpreted things differently from her own.

Kayla's brows furrowed briefly before she shook her head and smiled broadly. The hand on Liv's chest began a gentle rubbing motion. "Nah. I don't think it makes you nuts. It makes you a hopeless romantic at heart." Kayla lightly pinched the spot on Liv's chest above the organ in question.

Liv grabbed the tweaking fingers and flattened Kayla's palm against her chest. "Just like you," she marveled in a surprised voice, catching a glimpse of something she had yet to see in the quiet woman.

Kayla tried to frown, but failed completely. Instead, pale eyes twinkled and she let out a long-suffering sigh. "Just don't tell anybody, 'kay?"

Liv laughed and leaned forward for a kiss, taking a deep breath of her lover's indefinable scent. "I won't." The blonde brushed her lips lightly against the full red ones that were so tantalizingly close. Pulling back slightly, she asked, "Is this little bit of information something that your friends would be surprised to hear about?"

Kayla chuckled. "You have no idea." The smile abruptly slid from her face when Liv's comment reminded her of the phone call she'd gotten earlier. "Umm...Liv...we should really talk about that phone call before the kids get here."

"Okay," Liv said slowly, feeling her guts immediately knot up with tension.

Kayla closed her eyes as she absorbed a wave of sensation that was coming from Liv. She frowned. "Hey." Her hand dropped to Liv's belly. "What's wrong?"

"Nothing," Liv covered quickly. "Nothing's wrong." *Fuck! I'm sitting here trying to lie to a mind reader. You know she can feel it, just like you're feeling her nervousness and concern.*

"Nothin', huh? I don't—" Kayla's words were interrupted by the faint hum of an engine.

"Looks like they made it." Liv eased her way out of Kayla's embrace, causing the porch swing to protest with a loud creak. Jumping to her feet, she stalked her way over to the railing, glad of the reprieve. "We should go help them, Kayla. I don't think that charred dock will hold their weight." Leaning over, she waved at the teenagers who were nearly to the shore.

"Liv."

"C'mon, let's go." Liv took two quick steps, stopping abruptly when she realized that Kayla hadn't moved.

"We weren't finished talking," the researcher chided firmly, crossing her arms over her chest and stretching out her legs in front of her, wincing slightly at the soreness still present in her knee.

Liv nodded as she padded back to Kayla, stopping right in front of her. She sighed to herself. "I know. But I have a feeling I'm not going to like what you're about to say, and I'm trying to avoid it." Liv put her hands on her hips and cocked her head slightly to the side. "You're not making it very easy, Ghostbuster."

Kayla smiled weakly. "That's the whole idea. And even *I* don't like what I have to tell you, not to mention the fact that my sister is going to wish me dead."

Liv took a deep breath, shoving down her uneasiness. "Okay, what is it?"

"I have to cut short our vacation." Kayla's gaze suddenly dropped to the deck's wooden slats. "It's business, Liv. I really don't want to go so soon," she finished in a rush.

"I see." The words were colored with disappointment, despite Liv's attempt to sound neutral.

"Come with me?" Kayla blurted out, her eyes darting upward to pin Liv's. She wasn't certain she'd have the nerve to ask, until the words were already out of her mouth.

Sea-green eyes widened. "Wha-what?"

"Liiiivvvvv." Doug called from the shoreline. But the teen's words were completely ignored.

"Will you?" Kayla's heart was pounding so loudly she barely

heard her own voice. *Say yes, dammit!*

Liv hesitated for several excruciatingly long seconds that made Kayla realize just how much she was counting on Liv's answer. She began on a slightly shaky breath, "Kayla—"

"Please," Kayla interrupted as she stood up, stuffing her hands in the pockets of her well-worn denim shorts to keep herself from grabbing Liv and kissing her senseless until she agreed.

Liv ran a nervous hand through her hair as she tore her eyes away from Kayla's. "I can't just pick up and go to...to..." Her hands flailed as she waited for Kayla to fill in the blank.

"Edinburgh."

"Right. To Edinburgh with you." Liv looked back up and was immediately swallowed whole in a pleading gaze. "Oh, God, Kayla, don't look at me that way," she begged. "You don't understand."

"I understand that you're the partner I *haven't* been looking for because I didn't even know I needed one until I met you," Kayla corrected gently, and with a deep breath decided to go for broke. "I'm tired of working alone...being alone. You're a natural researcher, Liv. I could see that when we were hunting for the missing history." She licked her lips nervously. "It's not like your education would be wasted or anything. Your skills as a translator would come in handy all the time." Kayla took Liv's smaller hands in hers, absorbing their warmth and squeezing them tightly. "Give it a chance," she urged, watching Liv's face intently, searching desperately for any sign that Liv wanted this as much as she did. "We'd be a great team. Give *us* a chance to be together."

For a moment Liv stood speechless, the sound of the sea and the wind blocked out by the rhythmic thumping of her pulse. Her heart had already agreed with Kayla when her head reminded her differently. "Look, Kayla, I'm....well...I do want us to stay friends." She paused, trying to ignore the immediate look of hurt that leapt across Kayla's face. Looking away, she tugged a strand of gently blowing pale hair behind her ear. "I really...I mean I think I...lo...lo...like you...but..." Liv winced internally as her words spilled out in a jumbled mess. *Oh God, that sounded so bad. I didn't mean for that to come out like "kiss off."*

Kayla felt the blood draining from her face as she worked her jaw silently. "You *like* me?" she finally managed to repeat, an emotionless mask dropping over features that only seconds before were both vulnerable and hopeful. "I understand," she replied automatically, feeling a stab of pain at her horrendous miscalculation. *How could I have been so wrong about this? Sweet Jesus, I'm in love with her...and she likes me. Argh! Fuck!*

Liv regarded Kayla seriously. "No." She shook her head adamantly. "I don't think you do understand, Kayla. I—"

"There you two are." Doug panted as he climbed the last stair, pushing sweaty bangs off his forehead with one hand. "I thought I saw you heading off the porch. What are you guys...ahhh...err —" Doug's mouth clicked shut as his footsteps ground to a halt.

Kayla and Liv's gazes were still locked and their hands tightly gripped together when Marcy joined her boyfriend on the top step. "Oh boy," the teenage girl said awkwardly, as she glanced at the women then back at a nervously shifting Doug. "We are so interrupting something," she breathed gravely. *Good Lord, if the looks they're exchanging get any more intense, they'll both spontaneously combust.*

Doug's curly head bobbed vigorously in agreement.

Liv's mind raced, knowing she'd just given Kayla a very wrong impression, but wanting more than a few seconds to explain herself. "Can we talk about this later? Please," she pleaded with growing agitation. The look on Kayla's face was scaring her.

Kayla clenched her jaw and gave Liv a curt nod. "That's fine, Liv. Don't worry about it, I guess there's nothing to talk about. I was arrogant to presume...assume... Well, anyway..." Her voice trailed off as she dropped her friend's hands, taking a large step backwards when Liv tried desperately to recapture her hands. "No hard feelings, okay?" Try as she might, Kayla couldn't keep the hurt and sarcasm out of her last statement.

The researcher pushed down the ache that had developed in her chest.

Stupid! Stupid! Stupid! Kayla's internal voice screamed. "This was just a fling," she remarked to herself in a strained voice that everyone still managed to hear. Then she leveled a cool glare right at Liv. "Just sex, right?" *Wait a second, Liv...give me a moment to move my heart out of the way of your stomping feet.*

Liv caught the subtle twitch of muscles that indicated Kayla was about to bolt. Kayla turned, but before she could take a step, two hands roughly grabbed her T-shirt, spinning her around to meet raging green eyes.

"How can you even *think* such a thing?" Liv said, an angry flush already coloring her cheeks and neck. "You know it was more than that! It *is* more than that!"

"And just how would I know, Liv?" Kayla lashed back sharply. "You just wanna be buddies, right? Christ, I've used that, 'I still want us to be friends' line, myself. I know what it means!"

"That's *not* what I meant!" Liv pounded her fist against the wooden railing, scattering water droplets across the porch and acquiring several splinters in the process. "I was trying to say that I'm in love with you, you idiot! It just came out all wrong!"

Doug and Marcy's jaws hit the floor simultaneously. Marcy

turned to Doug and silently mouthed the words "love and sex" as though she were asking a question. Doug shrugged and shook shaggy blonde curls, raising his palms to acknowledge his own confusion and mimicking Marcy's shocked look.

Kayla's eyes widened to an almost comical degree, and she took a step closer to Liv. "You...you..." Her throat was suddenly dry. "What did you say?" she asked softly, begging any god listening that she'd heard right.

For some inexplicable reason, Doug chose that very inopportune moment to interrupt. "Listen, guys, we...Oooff!" He blew out an explosive breath when Marcy elbowed him in the gut.

Liv's head snapped up, her glare causing her brother to take an unconscious step backwards and teeter precariously on the edge of the porch. She'd completely forgotten the kids were there. "You listen to me, young man!" His frustrated sister marched across the porch and poked Doug in the chest with an irritated finger, forcing him a step lower. "Now is *not* a good time for you to be interrupting me. Your ass is grass as it is."

"But you said—" Doug swallowed hastily, wisely deciding to stop while he was still alive. "Never mind."

Liv crossed her arms in front of her chest; her eyes were now even with his. "I. Changed. My. Mind," she enunciated slowly. A sharply raised eyebrow and tapping foot dared him to complain. She pointed a slender finger toward the door, arm fully outstretched. "You get your butt into this creepy, godforsaken house, and get our bags," she ordered, watching intently as Doug began nodding furiously. "They're all packed and waiting in the living room. I want you back out here in *one* minute. Understood?"

"Yeah, sure, Liv." The boy was still nodding. "No, no...problem. I understand."

In the blink of an eye, he was tearing into the house as fast as his feet would carry him.

Marcy was reluctant to leave, but felt compelled when Doug began wildly signaling from just inside the door for her to join him. "You need to do *something*, Kayla," the girl whispered urgently to her sister as she passed by her on the way inside the house.

Once the teens were out of sight, Liv focused on her lover. "That was a horrible thing to say, Kayla." Tears threatened to spill over. "And you couldn't be more wrong," she whispered brokenly, suddenly sounding more hurt than mad.

Kayla's eyes slid closed at the look of pain and confusion on Liv's face. Liv was trying valiantly not to burst into tears, and her sniffles caused a pang deep in Kayla's chest. *Okay, now would be a good time for divine intervention and assistance. I don't know what the hell I'm doing here.*

The shorter woman squared her shoulders and consciously allowed her anger to bleed back into her voice. "That's some kind of ego you have, Ghostbuster, expecting me to uproot my life on a whim." Liv began nervously picking at a splinter with blunt fingernails.

Kayla winced at the ice in Liv's words, feeling more socially retarded than ever. "It's not a whim," she asserted defensively.

Liv flicked the tiny shavings of wood she'd scratched from the railing over its edge, watching as they were picked up by the fragrant summer breeze. Turning unseeing eyes out towards the horizon, she wrapped her arms around herself. "I came back to the States for Dougie. I have responsibilities, Kayla. I just can't pick up and leave him again."

Kayla nodded, her own misery mixing with Liv's until she wasn't sure who was feeling or thinking what. "Of course." She rubbed her temples, feeling the beginnings of a killer headache as emotions, words, and images that were not her own bombarded her senses. There was nothing concrete to grab hold of, nothing she could use to help herself or Liv. They were a tangled mass, confused and raw.

Her mind is racing, Kayla realized. With an effort that left her covered in a fine sheen of perspiration, she painstakingly separated Liv's thoughts from her own, slowly tuning them out one by one. "I'm...I only...I'm an asshole," she admitted freely, after nearly a full minute where she was too distracted to speak. "And I'm sorry. When you said that thing about us staying *friends*, I thought—"

"That I was just out for easy sex. A fling?" Liv finished angrily, wiping a tear from the corner of her eye, hoping Kayla didn't notice her shaking hand.

Liv didn't have the ability to block out Kayla's thoughts and feelings, and when they combined with her own, a strong wave of frustration, anger, and fear washed over her, settling heavily in her chest and in her stomach, making her want to throw up.

Kayla lifted her hands, then let them fall to her sides helplessly. "I'm sorry. I was embarrassed and angry. It was a stupid thing to say."

Liv's glance flicked up to the other woman's face, not ready to let go of her anger. "If that's what you really think of me, Kayla," she said, doing her best to control her roiling stomach and effectively ignoring Kayla's attempt to explain herself, "we *don't* have anything to talk about."

Kayla's back stiffened, and she swallowed a few times. *She's not accepting my apology? Fine!* "I guess you're right," came the stubborn, but slightly raspy reply.

There was a loud creak, and two sets of eyes reflecting equal parts hurt and anger swung toward the doorway to find Marcy and Doug waiting sheepishly with their bags piled haphazardly at their feet.

"Oh, man," Doug groaned pathetically. The tension between Kayla and Liv was making his brain want to explode. They were interrupting something big. Again.

"How long were you eavesdropping?" Kayla demanded, pale eyes snapping as she scrambled to collect her scattered emotions. *How many times does Liv expect me to apologize?*

"We weren't eavesdropping," Marcy answered sharply, her frustration at Kayla and Liv's pigheadedness showing clearly in her expression.

"We need a few more moments...in private," Kayla ground out impatiently.

"No, we don't," Liv corrected coolly, breaking into the conversation but then refusing to meet Kayla's intense stare. But not looking at her friend didn't keep her from sensing the other woman's edginess and frustration, or from knowing the exact heartbeat when Kayla's mind cried, "Enough," and her urge to bolt won out and she took off down the porch stairs.

Liv looked at Marcy helplessly, a fist tightening around her heart.

"I'll go," the girl immediately responded, running after her sister, who had made it a surprisingly long distance in what seemed like only a few seconds, despite the fact that she was limping.

MARCY CAUGHT UP to Kayla quickly, her footsteps crunching loudly as she made her way over the masses of fallen branches that littered the island's floor after the fierce storm. When Marcy reached Kayla's side, she stopped her, pulling her into an unexpected, heartfelt hug. With only a second's hesitation, Kayla returned the tender embrace. When they broke apart, they started down the shoreline, Marcy's rapidly moving hands and Kayla's rigid stance easily telegraphing the seriousness of their conversation.

"DAMN, SHE'S GORGEOUS," Doug commented honestly, shielding his eyes from the late afternoon sun with a cupped hand as he watched the Redding sisters disappear between a tiny break in the twisted, low-hanging branches that formed a wall around the island's edge.

Doug's gaze dropped, and he studied his sneakers. "I can't

think straight around her sometimes. It's not Marcy's fault." The boy sighed, absently scratching a fresh mosquito bite. "It's like my body goes into hyper-drive while my brain is still stuck in park."

Despite herself, a small smile crossed Liv's lips at Doug's apt description.

"Do you have any idea how worried we've been about you two?" she finally asked, her voice laced with remnants of fear but devoid of the burning anger she'd turned on him only moments before.

"I...um...I think so." Doug wrapped his arm around Liv's shoulder, guiding her over to the porch swing and allowing her to sit down first before dropping down next to her. "How did you handle the storm?" he inquired worriedly.

"It sucked. How was the motel?"

Doug blushed to the roots of his hair.

Liv closed her eyes briefly. "Dougie." Her tone was slightly reprimanding, but resigned.

"We were safe, I swear it."

Liv let out a long breath. "That's not the only consideration, and you know it." She paused, wondering just who Doug needed her to be—his mother, or his sister. Deciding they both wanted to know the same thing, she continued. "Are you guys okay?"

Doug patted her knee, hoping she and Kayla hadn't been arguing the entire time they were gone. "We're okay, Liv." A deep breath. "And I was wrong to make you worry. I'll try my best not to do it again. That was a stupid, immature stunt, and I'm very, very sorry."

Liv's eyebrows shot skyward. "Holy shit, Dougie. Have you been practicing that?"

"Umm...only if it worked," he admitted hesitantly, innocently peeking at his sister from underneath fair lashes, looking very much like a scolded puppy seeking a reprieve.

Liv rolled her eyes and simply gave up trying to be mad. The truth was, she'd forgiven Doug the day before. It was Kayla that she was truly angry with. But then Kayla's confused eyes and multiple apologies came flooding back, and even that anger began to fade away.

"I'll say it again if you want," Doug prodded.

A light chuckle. "Yes, you butthead, it worked. But don't ever do that to me again, Dougie. I mean that," she said sternly. "You won't get off so easy next time."

Doug smiled and crossed his heart. With his free hand he laced his fingers through his sister's. "What happened with Kayla?"

Green eyes gazed seriously at their twins. "We had a misunderstanding. How much did you hear?"

Doug winced. "Waaay more than I should have."

It was Liv's turn to blush. "Does it bother you?"

Doug grinned engagingly. "Nah. I don't see how you could resist her. She's almost as pretty as Marcy." *And the sparks you two were giving off...Damn! I couldn't tell whether you wanted to kiss her or kill her.*

A little laugh escaped Liv's throat as she shook her head at her brother. "You're such a pervert, Dougie. Are you in heat twenty-four hours a day?"

"You already know the answer to that question. And I'm right, aren't I?" he pressed, wiggling fair eyebrows.

"Yeah," Liv conceded grumpily. "Most of the time she's pretty irresistible."

"So what happened?" he repeated, straightening the crumpled sheet that covered the still damp porch swing.

"She asked me to come to Edinburgh with her and help her with her research." Liv considered what had happened next, deciding she really didn't understand herself. "And well, things sort of went downhill from there."

Doug's forehead creased. "Research? She finally told you what her job is, huh?" *I was gonna ask Marcy about that, too.*

Liv nodded, still not believing there really was such a job. "It seems Kayla is a ghostbuster."

"No way!" Doug jumped to his feet, passing into one of the new shadows created by the slanting sun. "For real? That is so totally cool."

Liv's lips twitched. "Yeah." She shrugged one shoulder. "I guess it is sort of cool."

"So, when are you leaving, and can I go somewhere with you guys during Christmas break, and does she have any pictures of actual ghosts?" he asked in an eager rush.

Liv made a face. "I told her I couldn't go. And, I overreacted."

"What?" Doug crowed, shaking the swing. "Why wouldn't you go? It's not like you have another job yet." He sat back down.

Liv's blinked. "Bu...bu...I thought—" She paused. "You mean you wouldn't mind if I took off again?"

"Let me guess. All my whining and complaining finally got to you, so you thought you'd just ignore anything that came your way so you could baby-sit me?" Doug wasn't sure whether to feel shitty or flattered or both.

"Awww, Dougie, it's not like that." Liv bumped shoulders with her brother.

"Do you want to go?"

"I want to be with you." Without hesitation.

"But you *need* to be with her."

Liv's jaw sagged, and she looked at Doug with narrowed eyes.
"Who are you, and what have you done with my baby
brother?"

Doug smirked. "It's not so tough to figure out. It's the same
with Marcy and me." He affected a look of mock indignation. "Stop
looking at me like I'm an alien. Jeez. I thought girls were supposed
to be in tune with this kind of crap."

"Okay," Liv laughed. "I'm starting to believe it's you again."

"Listen, Sis, to be totally honest, when I came on this trip, I
was thinking of asking you if I could come to D.C. and live with
you again."

Liv held her tongue. Doug didn't need to know she'd figured
that out the very first day.

"But I've talked to Marcy about it, and I've decided I'm going
to stick it out with Aunt Ruth for another year." He shrugged self-
deprecatingly. "I'm doing really well in school, and if I play my
cards right I should be able to get an academic scholarship to
college."

A broad smile split Liv's cheeks. "Mom and Dad would be so
proud of you, Dougie. I'm so proud of you," she added warmly, her
eyes twinkling. "Even though sometimes I think you're doing your
best to make me prematurely gray."

Doug nodded, feeling a warm flush cover his face. "I know."
He squirmed as Liv ruffled his hair. "Quit it, Liv!" He slapped her
hands away, clearing his throat and shooting her an annoyed look
that still managed to be full of affection. "Anyway, changing
schools might mess up my grades. So I'm going to stay right where
I am."

Liv chewed the inside of her cheek. It wasn't what she wanted,
but this was Doug, after all. "Maybe I could move—"

"Are you nuts? There is no way you're moving back."

"But—"

"Call more. Get on the damn computer every once in a while
and say hi. That's all it'll take to make me happy."

Liv studied her brother's face for a long time. "You really mean
that." It wasn't a question.

He cocked his head to the side and smiled charmingly. "I just
said it, didn't I?" His face grew serious. "You said you loved her. Is
that true?"

Liv nodded miserably, she hadn't meant to blurt it out like
that. "That still doesn't mean she can just snap her fingers and
expect me to drop everything and run off to Edinburgh with her,"
she said resentfully, even as her heart was urging her to do exactly
that.

Doug's eyes danced with mischief as he took in his sister's

obstinate demeanor. *Oh, yes it does. You're as whipped as I am.* "Of course it doesn't," he lied smoothly. "But it's at least worth thinking about, right?" The young man grinned again. It was about time that his sister found someone to love. "So which one of you owes the other some chocolate?"

Liv scratched her jaw, replaying the argument with Kayla in her mind. Each of them had hurt the other's feelings, and allowed their original conversation to get so sidetracked it wasn't even recognizable. She sighed. "That's a good question."

NEARLY THREE HOURS had passed, and Marcy and Kayla still hadn't returned to the house. Liv worried her lower lip, figuring they had less than an hour of daylight left before they'd be forced to spend another night on the island. Boating to the mainland in the dark wasn't an option, but neither was staying.

The island, with its gnarled ancient trees, inky black soil, and overgrown vines that insidiously wove themselves across every conceivable surface, held a note of foreboding that hadn't disappeared with the rain and lightning. Liv felt an anxious uncertainty that was only intensified by Kayla's absence. Her pulse increased in response. No. She wouldn't stay here another night.

"I'm going to find them," she announced over her shoulder, trotting down the porch steps and making her way along the steep, winding path that led to the shore.

"Not without me, you're not," Doug called, racing to her side as they both moved in and out of the uneven shadows painting the muddy, branch-strewn soil.

"I think they went in here." Liv pointed to a slender opening in the foliage that lead them away from the clean, salty smell of the sea, and further into the darkness beneath the island's massive trees. She examined the ground. "It looks sort of like a trail...almost."

Doug's eyes flicked from the trees to the forest floor. The rustling of branches and leaves, as some unknown critter skittered beneath the undergrowth in front of them, caught his attention. He really didn't appreciate the outdoors, and wondered wistfully why they didn't go on vacation to Disneyland, like everybody else in the known world. "Liv, maybe it's not such a good idea for us—" Doug's words were cut off when he turned a blind corner and ran directly into Marcy. "There you are," he said, grasping the girl's shoulders, noting the slightly dazed look in steel gray eyes. "Are you okay, Marse?"

She nodded quickly, but Doug wasn't convinced.

"Where's Kayla?" Liv asked, looking over Marcy's shoulder.

Oh God. They must have had a talk about her psychic abilities. She looks shell-shocked.

Marcy gave Doug a reassuring pat and addressed his sister. She exhaled very slowly. Kayla had explained some things she'd always wondered about. And a few new things that she still couldn't believe. "Keep going straight about another fifty yards, and you'll hit a small meadow. She's there."

Liv looked at Marcy in question, moving closer and giving her shoulder a sympathetic squeeze. Being a teenager was hard enough without adding the extraordinary to the mix.

"She said she'd only be a minute or two behind me," Marcy explained, reaching out and taking Doug's offered hand. Her face turned serious, making her look much older than her sixteen years. "She's still pretty upset, Liv."

Liv swallowed, ducking her head and acknowledging her role in that. "Did umm...did you guys have a nice talk?" She drew her eyes up to meet Marcy's gaze, watching as it dawned on Marcy that Liv knew at least part of what she and Kayla had discussed.

Marcy gave Liv a tiny, slightly unsettled smile. "Yeah, I...well, we had a very *interesting* talk."

Doug crinkled his nose, confusion coloring his fair features. But despite his immediate worry for Marcy, he decided now wasn't the time to press. He'd get the details later.

"You kids go on to the boat." Liv gestured back toward the house and dock which, although hidden by the trees, wasn't very far away. "We won't be long."

Doug hesitated, not wanting to leave his sister, but Marcy began tugging him along in the opposite direction. "Are you sure, Liv?" he questioned, even as Marcy gave his arm another firm yank, causing his sneakers to slide across wet leaves.

Liv shook her head as she focused on her feet, trying not to stumble over the moss-covered rocks and slick, twisting vines. "No. But I'm doing it anyway," she answered dryly, slowly making her way deeper into the woods. After several moments, she began to wonder if she'd somehow missed Kayla. *Marcy said to keep going straight.* She spun in a circle, taking in her surroundings with a frown, noting that the path seemed to disappear a few feet behind her. *Could I have somehow gotten turned around?*

Several tentative steps further, and Liv found herself pushing through what appeared to be a solid wall of ivy. She poked her head through the bruised, wet leaves. Moving forward, Liv emerged into the small clearing that Marcy had described. She immediately spotted a familiar form perched on a large stump in front of a pond, head tilted skyward, observing the first streaks of crimson and violet that streaked the evening sky.

Liv made no attempts to hide her presence, and by her next step, Kayla's slightly wary gaze had settled firmly on her face. She approached Kayla in silence, pausing several feet directly in front of the seated woman, not sure how welcome her close presence would be. From the very start, the usual physical boundaries that separated relative strangers hadn't seemed to apply to them. A subtle ache formed in Liv's chest as she considered that a few harsh words in a relationship so new might change that.

When Liv was nearly close enough to touch, Kayla took a deep breath then held out her arms with a childlike uncertainty that caused Liv's heart to lurch. In utter relief, she surged forward, allowing those long, strong arms to wrap tightly around her and pull her so close she could feel Kayla's pounding heartbeat and warm, unsteady breaths against her chest. She laid her cheek atop Kayla's head, stroking her fingers through silky tresses, greedily absorbing the heat and raw affection pouring off the darker woman. And with her very next breath, Olivia Hazelwood made a decision that would forever alter her life's path. She tightened her hold on Kayla and decided that she wasn't letting go.

Ever.

Kayla mumbled a heartfelt, "I'm sorry," into the slightly damp fabric of Liv's shirt, hearing Liv's softly uttered, but slightly wordier apology at the exact same time. *Well*, Kayla gave Liv another long squeeze, *at least she accepted it this time. Maybe I still have a chance.*

Soft lips kissed Kayla's head before the pressure eased, and she felt Liv pull away. She turned her head up to speak and was immediately swallowed in a pair of soulful eyes, whose penetrating gaze affected her so deeply she felt her knees go weak, even while sitting down.

Liv lifted her palms to Kayla's face, lightly running her thumbs over well-chiseled cheekbones. "The argument was my fault, Kayla. I knew I'd given you the wrong idea, and then I overreacted when you got angry. I'm so sorry I hurt your feelings," she whispered sincerely, her eyes conveying more than her words ever could.

"I'm sorry I let things get so out of hand," Kayla immediately countered, shifting nervously on the stump and closing her eyes. "I couldn't think straight." She touched her temples as if rubbing away a headache. "Your thoughts were mixing with mine. And we were both upset and...well, I...I should be able to control my ability better than that, but—" *But my mind was all over the damn place*, she thought disgustedly.

"It's really okay." A palm grasped Kayla's chin, lifting it upward and forcing eye contact as Liv tenderly brushed dark-red bangs out of Kayla's eyes with her other hand. "I know exactly what you mean."

Of its own accord, Kayla's hand lifted and threaded itself in soft pale hair, rolling the strands between its fingers. Eyes still locked, Kayla's other hand began to roam, finding a spot on the small of Liv's back and drawing the smaller woman closer. Their lips met in a surprisingly passionate kiss that immediately set Liv's blood aflame before it shifted into one that was slow and deep and achingly tender.

Liv moaned in pleasure, relishing every second and savoring Kayla's mouth as though it might be her last opportunity. Her lips stopped cold as realization hit her squarely in the gut. That's exactly how Kayla was kissing her, too.

Liv used the hands still on Kayla's cheeks to break the kiss, pushing away slightly and studying Kayla's face with an unnerving intensity. "Are you kissing me goodbye, Kayla?" she asked, doing her best to keep her voice even, despite the fact that her stomach had twisted into a solid knot.

Kayla suddenly rose to her feet, a look of pain marring her features for only the briefest of seconds before vanishing. "Not permanently," she hoped aloud. "Not unless you want me to." Her heart stopped beating as she waited.

"God, no!" Liv's hands moved to Kayla's shoulders, giving Kayla a shake for emphasis. "That's not what I want at all."

Kayla's breathing hitched before she exhaled explosively, her relief so profound she actually felt light-headed. "Then it won't be goodbye," she vowed, the crinkle between her brows disappearing along with her tension. "I'll come back to the States as soon as I can, and we can arrange to see each other and—"

Liv shook her head. "That won't be possible."

Kayla blinked several times in rapid succession. "Bu...but...you just said—" She was silenced by two fingers pressing tenderly but firmly against her lips.

"No more misunderstandings." Liv smiled wryly, gently removing her fingers. "My heart just can't take it today." Slender fingers laced themselves together behind Kayla's neck, not nearly ready to give up the delicious contact. Rising up on tiptoes, Liv brought herself nose-to-nose with the tall woman. "It won't be possible, because I'll *already* be with you." She paused, letting her words sink in. "Assuming your offer for a partner in crime is still good," she teased, the look on Kayla's face answering for her.

Liv's eyes slid shut at the warm explosion of undiluted happiness that flooded her senses as Kayla literally swept her off her feet, pulling her into a crushing embrace.

"I'll take that as a yes." Liv laughed delightedly when she was finally deposited back on the forest floor, her face becoming the blissful recipient of dozens of wet kisses.

Kayla let out a small grunt when she set Liv back on the ground.

"That hurt your knee, didn't it?" Liv scolded gently after an exasperated chuckle.

A kiss on the tip of the nose. "My knee is, well, you're right." Another kiss, this time on the chin. "That hurt like hell, and I won't be doing it again anytime soon." Kayla's lips brushed the corner of Liv's mouth but disappeared before Liv could move to increase the contact, earning Kayla a frustrated whine.

"And you can take it as a yes, or anyway you like, Liv," Kayla mumbled, nuzzling the baby-soft skin on Liv's throat and showering it with kisses more playful than arousing. She laughed as Liv began to squirm under her tickling lips. "As long as you don't take it back." She stopped her kisses so Liv could catch her breath, and offered her a lopsided grin with just a trace of worry. "You won't do that, right?"

Liv shook her head adamantly. "I won't. I talked with Dougie, and he doesn't want to come to D.C. with me for at least another year...when he starts college. And seeing as how I'm currently unemployed—" *And so in love with you, I'd follow you anywhere.*

"You're hired," Kayla drawled, her eyes gleaming brightly in the rapidly fading light.

Liv cocked her head in question. "Just like that?"

"Just like that." A dazzling smile lit up Kayla's face. "It's one of the perks of being self-employed." She sobered, trying in vain to dampen the rampant enthusiasm that was spreading an enormous and undeniably goofy grin across her face. "You do believe it's a real job, doncha?" she teased. "I mean, you'll get a salary and your own room when we travel." *When we have a room, that is*, she mused, deciding she'd let Liv discover the joys of research for herself.

Liv frowned, pretty sure she wasn't pleased with that last bit of information. She put her hands on her hips, playfully glaring at her new partner. "Don't think I'm gonna be sleeping alone in some spooky, haunted house, Ghostbuster. Been there, done that... And except for an admittedly exceptional dream," she smirked, then laughed when a light blush turned the tips of Kayla's ears pink, "I didn't like it."

A trickle of laughter escaped Kayla. "Well then, I guess I'll be forced to spend as much time as possible with you, and do everything in my power to insure your continued supply of erotic dream fodder," she purred, letting her voice take on a sensuous edge that rumbled down Liv's spine.

Liv's eyes darkened slightly, and her throat went dry. "See that you do," she croaked blithely, the soft hooting of an owl drawing her gaze upward.

Kayla's eyes tracked hers. "Don't worry. It's only about a half an hour trip to the mainland. Even after sunset, we'll still be able to travel for a while before it's actually dark." She smiled reassuringly. *I am definitely going to have to get her over her dislike of the dark.* Her mind was already spinning out pleasant nighttime activities when she added, "We'll be fine."

Both women began making their way out of the clearing, doing their best to avoid the larger puddles. When they passed the clearing's halfway point, Liv stopped and asked, "What happened with Marcy? I know you told her something. After all that reading, are you any closer to being able to help her?"

Kayla nodded, swatting away a buzzing dragonfly that seemed particularly fond of her. "I told her as much as I thought she could handle, leaving out Papaw's warning completely." She shifted her weight to her good leg, whose muscles felt tired and strained from overcompensating. "It seems this has been a big weekend for us all. She had some questions of her own."

"She's starting to figure out her abilities?"

Kayla nodded. "It looks that way. They weren't going to stay hidden forever. It was only a matter time." A small sigh escaped her throat. "After this trip to Edinburgh I'm gonna come back and spend a little time with her, see if we can't reconnect a bit. Besides, it'll give us a chance to study the history in greater detail. But even if it doesn't end up helping me, Marcy's gonna be okay." This said in a voice lacking the uncertainty and dread that had, up until then, always managed to spill into Kayla's words when discussing Marcy's abilities. "We'll work through whatever we have to— together."

Liv quietly considered her partner's words as Kayla reached up and tucked a strand of gently blowing pale hair behind her ear. The smaller woman wrapped her arm around Kayla's waist as they turned to regard the sunset that was too magnificent to ignore. But as lovely as it was, her attention was drawn downward, to the meadow and pond...to the island itself. It was changing again, she realized. Damp air mixed with cooler evening temperatures had formed a layer of mist that was slowly but steadily creeping between the trees and into the meadow. Liv grinned in wonder, a bit surprised that she didn't find it spooky or haunting. Instead, it was beautiful, containing a mystical, ethereal quality that called to her. *Like Brigadoon*, she mused silently.

As they stood, pressed tightly together, Kayla's thoughts drifted to the neatly written passages and the woman whose voice had brought people, centuries-dead, back to life. After everything, she didn't really believe the true lesson in the history would ever be found in the pages describing techniques for telepathic control.

Kayla imagined Liv could come up with something beautiful — moving prose about love lost and opportunity squandered — suspecting that anyone so enchanted by the written word probably had literary tendencies themselves. But she was a scientist, not a poet. Even so, to her logical mind, the carefully scribed events held undeniable meaning. Kayla smiled at her final conclusion. All the love in the world wasn't worth squat without the courage to reach out and grab it and make it your own. It wasn't quite poetry, but it still worked.

Long arms shifted Liv in front of her, and with a gentle hand against Liv's cheek, she garnered the shorter woman's undivided attention. Kayla's heart warmed when the face opposite hers broke into a brilliant smile. Taking a deep breath, she closed her eyes, focusing her thoughts and projecting outward with all her might. Before she could open her eyes, hands had found purchase in her hair and soft lips covered her own.

"I love you, too," Liv whispered fiercely, an errant tear streaking her cheek.

More kisses were followed by more sweet words until, reluctantly, the women separated and crossed the final feet to the meadow's edge, with Liv leading the way.

Something strange tickled Kayla's senses, causing her feet to slow then finally stop. A chill raced up and down her spine, making her nape hairs stand on end, and goose bumps break out across her limbs. Her curious gaze darted from tree to tree trying to catch a glimpse of...something...

"You okay back there?" Liv asked over her shoulder as she tried to find the spot where she had pushed through the vines earlier.

"Yeah." Kayla's brow creased, and her voice was distracted. "I just thought I heard something." Shaking her head, she took a couple more steps and drew even with Liv, finding the opening they were looking for after a few seconds of prodding. Kayla held open a cluster of vines so Liv could pass through the thick wall of flora.

Liv dropped a quick kiss on Kayla's cheek as she moved past her. "Must have been a deer. They come out to feed at sunset, right?"

Puzzled, Kayla glanced back at the meadow one final time before turning and focusing forward. "Right. Ready?"

"To go with you?" Liv grasped Kayla's hand, threading their fingers together. "Always."

Epilogue

TWO HIDDEN FORMS, one tall with flaming hair, the other shorter and fair, emerged from a blanket of rising mist at the far end of the clearing, watching silently as Kayla and Liv disappeared into the forest.

"She felt us."

A blonde head nodded. "I know." An indulgent shrug. "But she had more important things to attend to."

A sardonic eyebrow twitched knowingly. "So do we."

The fair head shook again, but this time with laughter. A larger hand tightly wrapped itself around a smaller one as the figures traveled across the meadow, stopping to share a kiss in the dying rays of the summer sun before vanishing into the murky shadows of Cobb Island.

Don't miss the sequel to Cobb Island:

Echoes from the Mist

In this sequel to Cobb Island, paranormal researchers Kayla Redding and Olivia Hazelwood begin their professional and personal partnership as they tackle their first case together in the world's most haunted city - Edinburgh, Scotland. While in Edinburgh, the women visit the Cobb family ancestral home. The Cobb family historian takes the women on a journey back through time to 17th Century Colonial Virginia. He weaves the tale of Faylinn Cobb, explaining what happened to her and her family after her sister-in-law, Bridget Redding, was branded a witch.

ISBN 978-1-932300-68-8

FORTHCOMING TITLES

published by
Quest Books

IM
by Rick R. Reed

A gay thriller with supernatural overtones, *IM* is the story of a serial killer using a gay hook-up website to prey on young gay men on Chicago's north side. The website's easy and relatively anonymous nature is perfect for a killer.

When the first murder comes to light, the first detective on the scene is Ed Comparetto, one of the police force's only openly gay detectives. He interviews the young man who discovered the body, Timothy Bright, and continues his investigation as the body count begins to rise. But, Comparetto hits a snag when he is abruptly fired from the police force. The cause? Falsifying evidence. It turns out that Timothy Bright has been dead for more than two years, murdered in much the same way as the first victim Ed investigated.

The case becomes a driving force for Comparetto, who finds more and more evidence to support that the person he first spoke to about the murders is really dead. Is he a ghost? Or, is something even more inexplicable and chilling going on? As the murder spree escalates and Comparetto realizes Bright is the culprit, he begins to fear for his own sanity...and his own life. Can Ed race against time and his own doubts to stop the killings before he and his new lover become victims?

Available May 2007

Tears Don't Become Me
by Sharon G. Clark

GW (Georgia Wilhelmina) Diamond, Private Investigator, dealt in missing children cases—only. It didn't alter her own traumatic childhood experience, but she could try to keep other children from the same horrors. She'd left her past and her name behind her. Or so she thought. This case was putting her in contact with people she had managed to keep a distant and barely civil relationship with for fifteen years. Now the buried past was returning to haunt her. When Sheriff Matthews of Elk Grove, Missouri, asked her to take a case involving a teenaged runaway girl, she believed it would be no different from any other. Until Matthews explained she had to take a cop as partner or no deal. A cop who just happened to be the missing girl's aunt.

Erin Dunbar, received the call concerning her niece from an old partner, Frank Matthews. It should have been from her sister, but their estrangement, compounded by her having moved to Detroit, kept that from happening. Now she would have to work with a PI. One had nearly killed her and Frank years ago; she expected this one would be no different. Matters were only made worse by discovering it was a "she" PI—a Looney-tune one who gave new and literal meaning to: "Hands Off." For the sake of her niece, Erin would put up with just about anything, until...GW seemed to be strangely affected by this case and Erin, to her chagrin and amazement, was strangely affected by her.

If Erin could solve GW's past, give her hope, could they have a hope of finding her niece?

Available May 2007

OTHER QUEST PUBLICATIONS

Gabrielle Goldsby	Wall of Silence	1-932300-01-5
Gabrielle Goldsby	Never Wake	978-1-932300-61-1
Trish Kocialski	The Visitors	1-932300-27-9
Lori L. Lake	Gun Shy	978-1-932300-56-7
Lori L. Lake	Have Gun We'll Travel	1-932300-33-3
Lori L. Lake	Under the Gun	978-1-932300-57-4
Helen M. Macpherson	Colder Than Ice	1-932300-29-5
Meghan O'Brien	The Three	978-1-932300-51-2
C. Paradee	Deep Cover	1-932300-23-6
John F. Parker	Come Clean	978-1-932300-43-7
Radclyffe	In Pursuit of Justice	978-1-932300-69-7
Talaran	Vendetta	978-1-932300-70-3

VISIT US ONLINE AT
www.regalcrest.biz

At the Regal Crest Website You'll Find

- The latest news about forthcoming titles and new releases

- Our complete backlist of romance, mystery, thriller and adventure titles

- Information about your favorite authors

- Current bestsellers

- Media tearsheets to print and take with you when you shop

Regal Crest titles are available from all progressive booksellers and online at StarCrossed Productions, (www.scp-inc.biz), or at www.amazon.com, www.bamm.com, www.barnesandnoble.com, and many others.

Printed in the United States
96117LV00002B/470/A